Phantom and Rook

WHEN AN IMMORTAL FALLS IN LOVE WITH A WITCH

AELINA ISAACS

Contents

Dedication

To those who hide in their hoodies, under their hats, and on the
sidelines. You are loved, and you belong.
Those who desperately want to be seen just as much as they
want to hide.

Before Reading

This is an adult fantasy novel with queer characters who swear, smoke, get tattoos and pester each other with inappropriate comments.

There is mention of a past suicide attempt, reference to a previous prolonged physical and mental abuse situation, and alcoholism. Several of the characters live with mental illness and it is discussed several times.

There are a few graphic sexual scenes towards the end because this is undoubtedly a slow burn with lots of pining.

If you like to listen to music and read, I do have a playlist for this book. You can find it by visiting linktr.ee/aelinaisaacs

Lastly, this is a feel good book with a happy ending, but perhaps not in the way you'd expect.

Enjoy,
Aelina

Watch Your Language

The 'Old Common' used in the book is based on the Hebrew language, and some meanings have been adjusted to fit the story. They are listed here in the order they appear.

Etz Hayim - Great Tree.
Mayim - Water.
Leva - Heart.
Rasha - Wicked person who commits grievous acts.
Ahuvi - Love.
Khawbar - An internal spirit inside shedim that awakens only when bonding to another soul.

Who Goes There?

I n addition to the usual elves, dragons and centaurs, there are a few homebrew magickal races in this world. Here are the basics and their rarity in regards to Levena's population.

Golem: An undead race that can vary widely in appearance but is characterized by the lack of a beating heart, common form is similar to Humans.

Qieren: A humanoid race characterized by their colorful skin tone, at least one set of horns on their head, and a prehensile tail. Common.

Draconian: Dragons in their humanoid forms, characterized by their vertical pupils. It is uncommon for most Draconians to live in highly populated areas.

Katan: A short statured, humanoid race ranging up to four feet in height, with slightly pointed ears. For every fifty male births a female is born, making this race slightly uncommon.

Krakeni: A semi-aquatic race with eight to eighteen tentacles, able to dwell on land for short periods of time with misting. Common.

Tannin: A shifter race with draconian characteristics and lack of a full dragon form. Their shifted form is humanoid in appearance with iridescent scales, a full snout, tail and leather-type wings. Common.

Malakim: A celestial race of angelic origins, characterized by their feather-type wings, their influence over the shedim race and passive magickal ability to sense good. Uncommon.

Shedim: A celestial race of demonic origins, characterized by three different wing types, their influence over the malakim race and passive magickal ability to sense evil. Uncommon.

Behema: A general term for animalistic shifter races, defined by their ability to shift at will regardless of the lunar cycle. Most behema choose to live in their shifted form which can range from mostly humanoid to complete animal. Common.

Dybbuk: A type of malicious spirit that feeds on a soul while possessing their body with such ability they often go unnoticed. When the soul has been devoured the Dybbuk must move to a new host body, living or dead with a trapped soul. It is considered 'contagious' as it can efficiently invade a body.

Selth: A humanoid race characterized by a star shaped array of prehensile tentacles protecting their mouth and lack of pupil, possessing completely black eyes. Uncommon.

Gadol: A humanoid race that is born in the same form as Humans but grow exponentially after puberty, reaching heights up to thirty feet tall.

Where Are We?

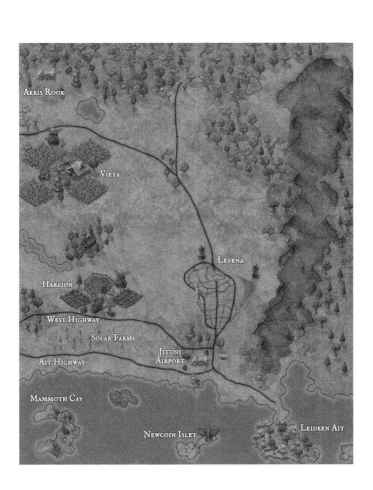

AERIS ROOK

VIETA

HARLION

LEVENA

WEST HIGHWAY

SOLAR FARMS

JITUNI
AIRPORT

AIT HIGHWAY

MAMMOTH CAY

NEWCOIN ISLET

LEIDEEN AIT

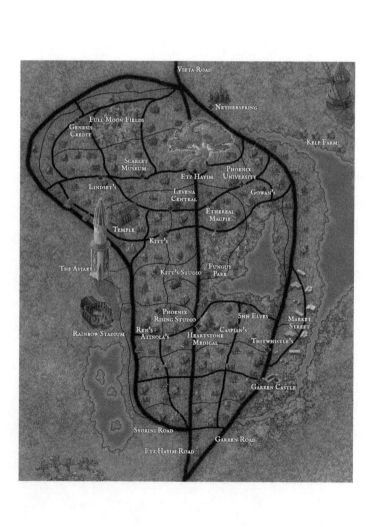

Prologue

There is a certain beauty in being the first and last of your kind, but no one can argue it's *fucking* boring.

Long ago, I promised I would help out those souls once, *only* once. However, it became rather euphoric. After the fire, I started leaving behind riddles followed by food for them to enjoy and returned again and again. A blip in time to look forward to, which in my cursed life is hard to come by. Food became bits of technology for them to puzzle over, then trinkets and other things people seem to love.

Naturally, setting up a cottage on the outskirts of Levena came many decades later, and I found myself calling the once small fishing village *home* for the short bursts of free will I'm allowed. It's not like I have anything else better to do.

Of course, no one knows who puts on the perennial 'Game' that's blessed the now sprawling city for centuries. They've tried to catch me a few times, but I only postponed it and discreetly left the same warning note each time in the pockets of unsuspecting fellows.

Try to catch me, and the Game will end.

I'm proud of what Levena has become, and I say with all modesty that it *absolutely* has to do with me. The modernization of the world hit my favorite place first and hardest, nourished by strong minds, full bellies and giving hearts. That's what I've always loved about Levena, no matter how grand it became, the people never changed.

They're absolutely wonderful.

But, there's one being in particular that caught my eye the last time I visited, which regretfully was ages ago, but it's not like I can help it. He was going through quite a time, and I hope he found the gift I left behind especially for him. I *do* have duties such as ushering titans to where they belong and keeping the balance of the universe, or so I'm told, but my work has never kept me away from home for so *long*.

I'm bored again, and this time, my entire attention is dedicated to this blissful interruption of my cursed existence, and it will be an event to remember.

The Game is almost upon Levena and I am filled with a giddiness that has nothing to do with my grandest scheme yet. No, I am most interested in reconnecting with the man whose heart beats eerily similar to my own, which should be impossible.

Because I'm the only one like me.

And maybe, just *maybe*, he'll remember me.

Friday

My Heart

Arlo

Levena

Present Day

C harms and Death are my specialties, which are practically useless against a dedicated best friend.

"Why don't you just live with me? It's fine, and honestly, I'd rather have your cooking than Lindsey's." Kitt relays her thinly veiled, and *misplaced*, concern.

"How about no." I glare at the haughty projection floating over my phone on the kitchen counter. Waves of near black hair partially curtain my face, flowing from under my beanie, but Kitt catches my animosity all the same. "Speaking of, have you called her yet?"

"Deflecting, Lo, deflecting." Kitt muses, shaking out violet and electric blue tresses interrupted by two black horns curling from her forehead.

I continue working on my illustration and attempt to convince the *qieren*, and myself, that this *is* a good thing. "Listen, I'm a big boy, I *can* do this. I'm going to talk to Dusan." My last few words verge towards high pitched. It's Kitt's turn to give me a look, knocking my tone up another notch. "Serious! *Serious*, it's fuckin' time I get out of here, become a functioning member of society or whatever it is they call it. I'm better."

Kitt throws her leather clad arms up in exasperation, but her painted red lips curve upwards. "Alright, if you say so. Just," her teasing smile falters and *there* it is, what I've been waiting for the moment I brought this up.

"Don't push yourself, it's okay to have a roommate or something, that still counts as doing it on your own. Being alone does not equal–"

"Hey, I gotta go Kitty, Market is going to be flooded soon and my hands are still a mess," I say, more clipped than usual. "Misfits night still on?"

"Fuckin' better be, oh, *don't* forget the oranges." She warns, then the projection cuts out from my paint splattered phone.

I sigh, bracing my dark hands awash with color on the counter's edge. I allow my head to hang for a moment, recharging myself for the chaos of the festival. I expected her to be hesitant in her nonchalant, Kitt way, but I'm so *fucking* tired of people waiting for me to break apart again.

I suppose a small part of me hoped she'd have a little more faith in me than the others, but apparently none of them think I can live without being coddled. Caspian is a whole other matter, he'll be fretting over me worse than a mother bird. Kitt gets a free pass because ... well, because she does.

One of the many drawbacks of living in the place you grew up in is everyone knows what you've done, perhaps even better than you do. I resolve to give Kitt a bear hug when I see her, then lift my head and take in the kitchen, reminding myself what I'll be leaving behind. If I can muster the courage, that is.

A chorus of children playing echoes in the halls outside of my Kitchen nestled into the rear of Garren Castle. The sprawling, fading green grounds behind the estate are in full view through the floor to ceiling windows lining the southern wall of my nook which is used for everything but cooking. Fruit trees, kaleidoscope colored flowers, pirate ships and wizard towers litter the lawn out back.

Numerous kids run between the vibrant play structures built over the years by those who left this place behind. Back in my time, there was only one treehouse. Then, Caspian learned the joys of pyrotechnics and blew it to smithereens. Three grew in its place.

The shadow of a smile escapes me as I recall Dusan's face on the last summer day of my youth, the first time I ever saw the draconic Headmaster truly surprised, and perhaps proud.

I straighten my spine, hands leaving the marble counter island as my gaze drifts to the greenery lining the sides of the windows. Ivy crawls along the inside of the old stone walls, yellow and purple flowers bloom alongside bright green leaves that blanket most of this place. Plants live in nearly every inch of vertical space of the castle, ready to absorb hexes, along with protective sigils and charms created by none other than myself.

The wide, double doors of oak opposite me are shut, something that doesn't occur too often. I don't mind when the kids keep me company, begging for stories as they watch me concoct my latest batch of charmed potions, balms, trinkets and a dozen other magicked items that sell faster than I can create them. When the doors *are* shut, the kids know today's not a good day to visit.

But whenever I reopen them, they find me within minutes.

A smile breaks through at that and I absently pace the room, stroking the dragon tattoo on my wrist. Gold and green ink shimmers to life as the beast takes flight, swooping up to my elbow with a wave of warmth and comfort before it settles on the inside of my arm once more. Its thin tail curves around to meet an unmoving planet, forming an abstract symbol that reminds me to keep moving beyond the pause.

The grandfather clock situated beside the doorway chimes six times and I jump out of my skin at the first, slinging paint everywhere. I had lost myself to nostalgia and forgot to wash my hands, now I'm late. I scrub my hands in the industrial sized, steel sink overlooking the windows, gathering courage. Market Street is near impossible to navigate in the evening any time of the year, but the festival leading up to the Game makes it pure hell.

I decide with 90% certainty I'll be fine as I dry off, but I make a visit to the spice rack just to be safe. I dig through jars filled with herbs, crushed crystals and vague body parts that are recognizable only by my questionable script on the label. Nothing is in its place and I sigh. I *just* fucking organized this yesterday, must be Kleo and Felix were in here again.

I finally find the empty, pocket sized glass jars on the bottom shelf, instead of the middle where they're supposed to be. By the time I fill one with black tourmaline, lavender and a few other random things that call to me from the wood and iron rack, my heart's racing a mile a minute. Black threatens the edges of my vision and I steady myself.

Kitt's advice swims in my mind. *You don't have to push yourself so hard.*

I shake my head and take my knitted duster from its home on the coat tree beside the spices, then slip it on over my loose tank top and drop the jar into an inner pocket, one of many. I fish out the talisman hiding against my chest, then hold it in a moment of reverence and utter my usual incantation in attempts to stave off any negative energy that might want to latch onto my growing pool of anxiety.

In my hurry, I nearly forget the canvas. I retrieve it from the counter, accidentally smudging the colors in the corner, but at this point if the painting makes it to its owner in one piece, I'll be happy. I perform a series of conjurations using one hand, then exhale heavily onto the painting. My magick infused breath dries the last tacky bits of paint and imbues the spell needed for his mural. I gaze upon the work I spent my day and part of last night on; I wanted to give Gleason a goodbye present before he left, but procrastination got the better of me.

Art born of pressure and intensity comes out the best, I think. Honest, raw and true.

The moment my fingers wrap around the door handle inlaid with golden leaves, my companion who's been otherwise resting contentedly in the corner wakes with an unimpressed yawn. I glare at Bosko as his moon-like eyes blink open and fixate on me, one pupil dilating before the other.

"We're *really* doing this?" He asks in a whisper of annoyance only I can hear.

"Do you not see me walking out the door? Let's go, Dusan is waiting, and we still gotta go to the Market." I lower my right shoulder when his wide golden wings spread, but the old barn owl lands on his usual place instead, nestled into the slouchiness of my sage green beanie. He burrows down, talons gently taking hold of the wool expertly knit by Gowan.

I roll my eyes. "*Really?*"

"Don't forget your phone." Bosko reminds me before dozing back off again.

"Fuckin' bird." I mutter with a half smile, darting back across the room to find my phone and pocket it into my jeans. When I open the doors, the sounds of Garren Castle erupt into a waterfall that crashes over my slightly pointed ears. A gaggle of children run down the hall to my left and out the back door to my right. They stop in their tracks upon seeing my face.

A second passes, long enough for me to think, *'oh shit.'*

In the next, they're climbing me like a tree, poking at Bosko and pulling on my hair. One kid latches onto my back, Kleo wraps around my front as she buries her face into my neck, must be Felix on my back. A child sits on each of my purple Converse and I glare at each dirty face with mock fury.

But they know better. Squeals erupt as the monster that is Arlo Rook rough houses with them the entire way to the Headmaster's office, much to Bosko's chagrin. The old man takes off the moment we're captured; but I know he'll find me in Dusan's office, he won't leave me alone for that nerve wracking talk. I hold the painting out to my side to keep it safe, but the rest of my limbs are occupied with fending off small kids of all races.

Wide halls filled with plants, professors, children and stones older than I am lead the way to the Headmaster's office which rests in the front of the castle. Giant windows cut through stone in the shape of arches allow me to catch a glance at the vivacious New Town waiting at the bottom of the hill, cast in a dazzling array of magickal lights. Garren Castle is situated in Old Town, the original site of Levena.

"Alright, alright, *really* now, I've got to go. And shouldn't you all be collecting wild flowers for the Scarlet Illusionist, no?" I raise a brow, setting down the last child before me, rebellious eleven year old Kleo who *usually* never stops smiling.

But now she's *pissed*.

"That's just a *story*! We all know it's you and Miss Garren that does it!" Kleo stomps her foot, bouncing the twists hanging around her face. The others around her murmur in agreement. Felix doesn't look so sure, but the rest of their group follow

Kleo's word no matter what. Felix's the only one stops to ask questions, but it's not like Kleo has any ill intention. The pair remind me a lot of Kitt and me at that age. Perhaps that's why they occupy the soft spot in my heart.

Dusan's door cracks open, and I'm the only one who notices, but the Headmaster doesn't intrude on my teaching moment as I kneel before the kids. I set down my canvas against the wall behind me, then wash my gaze over them all for a tenuous moment. Intense chandelier light brightens all their faces, highlighting the glimmer in their curious eyes.

I'll miss teaching them.

"You don't believe in the Scarlet Illusionist?" I ask with warm sincerity, extending my hand to Kleo's. Paint lingers in the crevices of my nails and I inwardly curse myself. I only washed away half my mess.

"Well!" Kleo starts, glancing at Felix who naturally keeps close to her side. They both inch towards me and Kleo slides her dark hand into mine. The rest of the children flank out behind the two. I make sure to give each one my attention, not just Kleo and Felix.

"How could one person do all that, in one night? And for so long?" A small, unsure voice brings my attention back to the pair. I'm surprised to find it belongs to Felix, who hardly speaks unless he deems it important. When the boy does speak, all listen with intent.

I find the silver pendant on my neck, what could be considered to some quite plain, but it's my most prized possession. A palm sized locket in the shape of a compass, adorned with script initials for the cardinal points. I've never been able to open it, and after it zapped Kitt when she tried, I didn't bother to try again, or feel the need to. Most things I *need* figured out, plans made and details known, but this necklace ....

The children's pupils dilate farther than before, if possible, and Kleo reaches out for the compass. I hold up a finger and raise a brow, stopping her curious fingers.

"Listening?" I ask, and all nod in unison. "A long, *long* time ago, I solved the Game, and this was my prize, along with my very first paint set. At the time, I had never even *thought* about painting, but look at me now."

A few murmurs of disbelief bubble throughout the group.

"And the necklace? What's special about that?" An orc teen in the back asks, head tilted with the start of tusks poking past their lips. A few of the other older kids have joined in, hanging back behind the younger ones.

"Well ... don't tell anyone," I lower my tone conspiratorially, although it's no big secret. I gesture for them all to come closer. I take Felix's small, freckled hand and guide it to my locket. "This is *magick*, and I won it."

Felix gasps when his fingers enclose around the locket, his hand too small to entirely wrap around it. "My heart, it's ... *happy*."

Excitement festers in his comrades but I silence them with a soft look. "You'll all get a turn."

And they do, one by one I allow the children to take hold of the necklace that has been my calm through every rocky moment in my life. Well, *almost* every moment.

After the last child, a faun who has marked a few trees out back with their horns, takes their turn, I tuck the necklace back under my shirt and stand with tired knees.

"There's not much mystery left in the world, and the Scarlet Illusionist is one of those legends best left at just that, a legend. Out of all places, they've chosen to bless our town for centuries, and all they ask is to remain a secret."

"A real person ..." Kleo's eyes go wild, as if she's *just* realized something. She turns to face her friends, essentially dismissing me as she barks out orders. "We must collect as many wildflowers as we can. This year will be the largest offering yet! The Scarlet Illusionist will know our names and gratitude!"

It's all I can do to stifle a laugh. She's so fucking cute and bull headed, a true leader. Felix however, tugs on my sleeve. I bend down and he whispers into my ear, "Have you ever met them?"

I smile, patting his hand on my arm. "No, but I'd be honored if I ever did." I don't tell him that I glimpsed them once, or thought I did.

Felix nods, blushing furiously. "Um, Mister Arlo, Kleo and I might have—"

I hold up a hand, saving him from the confession. "I know, and I *also* know you won't do it again, hm? In case of emergency it's always best to know right where things are. Can I trust you to talk sense into that one?"

I gesture to Kleo and his rounded ears turn red as we watch his elven friend stir up the others. "Y–yeah. I can do that, Mister Arlo. Um, thanks, for letting me touch your necklace. I could ... *feel* how important it is to you."

That gets my attention and I sense Dusan's gaze on us through the crack in her door.

"Is that so? Think you might be magickal like me?" I ask softly. Felix's round, brown eyes brighten so much they rival the sun, and he stands straighter. He nods a few times, mop of hazel hair bouncing as he does. "Let's say tomorrow just you and I have tea together, hm? Say, two o'clock?"

"Really!" He blurts out, then swiftly covers his mouth, but not without catching Kleo's attention. Felix gives me a searching look for help.

"What's up?" Kleo bounds over.

Must be he wants to keep this to himself, which is surprising.

"Telling this one to keep you in line, don't think I didn't notice you were messing around in my Kitchen." I raise a stern brow at Kleo but she only sticks her tongue out at me. I chuckle, snapping my fingers which gives her tongue the tiniest of electrical snaps. She yelps in protest and I rustle both her and Felix's hair, then give my goodbyes to the others and pick up my canvas from its resting place.

The draconian, untouched by time, swings the door open as I approach. Dusan Garren is full of warmth and pride as I enter her office for perhaps the five thousandth time. "Seems you've re-inspired our most skeptical of the bunch. Sure *you're* not the famed Illusionist?" Dusan intones from behind me as she shuts the door.

I make way for my usual chair at the mahogany desk that's probably just as old as Dusan is. I favor the right seat as opposed to the left and lean my painting up against the chair's leg. Dunno why, but my ass always seems to land in the same spot no matter where I go, same as my right leg always slides into socks, pants or shoes first.

Dusan slides into her high back chair, then straightens the cuffs of her crisp black and white suit as she leans back, vertical pupils fixated on me. I've only ever seen her break this form once, and it was fucking glorious. At least, Kitt and I thought so. Caspian, not so much.

Even in humanoid form, Dusan Garren carries all the grace and wisdom you would expect from an ancient Gold Dragon. Her narrow eyes shine the same bright yellow they always have. Her silver hair is cut in pixie fashion, highlighting the array of jewelry hanging from her ears and the cut of her wide jaw. Dusan created this orphanage back in 'the olden days', when the water side city was nothing more than a fishing village and dirt roads.

Some dragons hoard treasure, but this one hordes orphans, and she protects them just as fiercely as any hunk of gold or shiny gem. Don't get me wrong, Dusan is eternally polished and accessorized with gold or crystals, but raising children is what gives this woman life. It's hard to feel sad about aging out of the system with a guardian like her.

Nevertheless, loneliness eats at my heart from time to time.

"Like I've got the time to make riddles and give out gifts, I only told her the truth." I scoff and wave a hand, allowing a sly grin to appear. Bosko nonchalantly returns, giving me some dignity by landing on my shoulder. "What do you think of Felix?" I ask in a significantly less teasing tone.

"I've been wondering about him for some time, haven't you?" Dusan counters, resting her chin on knitted fingers as her elbows perch on the desk.

"I've noticed an aura around him a couple times, but I wanted to give him space, see what he did with it on his own." I shrug, leaning back in my chair with a sigh. "Still a bit young yet I think, but I'll talk to him tomorrow."

"You were already causing trouble at his age." Dusan points out.

I wrinkle my nose. "I have magickal blood, that's no surprise. He's human though, the Witching Hour doesn't typically start til' his race is closer to eighteen. He's seven years early."

"Almost six, don't forget." Dusan echoes the sentiment Felix has been holding onto lately. He's almost twelve. "Perhaps he'll be a force to be reckoned with." Dusan remarks, half turning in her chair to stare out the wall of windows to my left, at the city.

The thought curls a tendril of worry in my heart. I can't imagine soft Felix possessing so much power with no one to guide him. I floundered for so long on my own, and the shit I've gone through because of the witch's heart inside my chest will turn any sane person mad.

"I hope not." I murmur, choosing to focus on the ancient tomes lining her impressive bookshelf at my right instead of the bright city. Magick is a blessing, and a curse. It doesn't run as freely as it used to, not the wild, raw side of it that can be commanded by witches like myself, and now Felix. My hands curl into fists at the thought of Leon cutting us down to nothing.

Molecules of energetic magick enchant our everyday lives, powering technology and running in the blood of magickal creatures, but it's tame, civilized and limited. Even those who have magick lineage in their veins can't *command* it without a witch's heart, as opposed to the days when *everyone* could wield it with a mere whisper. Magickal beings benefit from immortality or whatever boons their race naturally offers, but unless they're a witch, that's all they can do.

Passive possession, or so the scholars say.

Witches aren't rare but definitely uncommon after Leon's 'Taking.'

In Old Town, I'm one of just over a dozen registered witches, mandated by law to make ourselves known to the government. What our specialty is, our magick signature, and fingerprints. All in case one of us wants to turn super villain and burn the place down, which hasn't happened before, on purpose, that is. Crime doesn't usually live in Levena, but when it does, I'm one of the people they call. Either for ferrying the dead or taking care of the perpetrators.

"What's on your mind, Arlo?" Dusan asks, breaking me from my train of thought.

"Just ..." I bow my head for a moment, removing my beanie to run a hand through my wild waves of *almost* black, when the light hits it a soft, barely there brown is visible. Like my soul, Kitt teased once, but I don't think she's wrong. Bosko's talons dig into my shoulder, but otherwise he keeps steady despite my anxious movements. The pinpricks of pain center me.

"Wondering why magick chooses us the way it does. Why Felix and not Kleo, or one of the others. He's too ... *good* for it."

Dusan blinks, slowly. "Do you think your magick is a curse?"

My eyes flick up to hers which are ever patient, my fingers stop their yanking through my hair. "It can be."

"Curious." She murmurs, rising slowly to pace the length of her study, rubbing her wide chin in contemplation. I wait for her lecture on self-worth, but instead she leans against the length of her desk closest to me and nudges my sneaker with the toe of her pointed boot. "Did you have something you needed to tell me?"

I chuckle at the sentence that has drawn many confessions out of Kitt, Cas and me, always said with the same gentle tone. "Yeah, I'm going to start looking for a place. I want to live on my own." I roll back my shoulders and replace my beanie, not breaking my stare into her sunshine eyes that are filled with only kindness.

The most subtle of laugh lines curve upwards. She nods once. "Do you feel happy about this decision?"

I blink but don't backtrack, not now. "Y—yeah. *Yes*. I want to try again ... I want to start my life. I'm ready."

That causes her smile to falter slightly, but she doesn't jump into the discussion I thought she would. Instead, Dusan says, "If you say you're ready, then I believe you. If you change your mind and want to come back home, your room will always be waiting for you, as will I."

Well, *fucking* hell.

Tears prick my eyes and I inhale a strangled bit of air, then stand and wrap Dusan into a bone crushing hug. Well, to anyone else it would be bone crushing, but the draconian's marrow is of steel. As the years have passed, I've had to hunch over more and more to hug the Headmaster. She's not afraid to show affection to any of her charges, but her iron will is just as strong as her love.

"Thank you, Dusan. For everything."

"Of course Arlo, but if you think you'll be free and clear without visiting you're sorely mistaken, and it won't be just me that comes after your hide. The kids will miss you," Dusan says softly into my broad shoulder. She only comes up to my chest now, as most the people around here do.

I nod, then slowly pull away and hold the Headmaster by the shoulders. "I know, but I have to do this." I remind her, and myself, through a choked voice. "I need to take control of my life."

"As you should, my dear, but live by your terms, not what's expected of you." She remarks softly, then kisses my cheek. A clock matching the one in the Kitchen chimes seven times from behind Dusan's desk, reminding me the night is young and I have more people to see.

I don't startle this time.

We say our goodbyes and before I step out of her office, canvas in hand, Dusan calls to me from her seat at the desk. "Have fun tonight, eh? The Scarlet Illusionist's biggest believer has to partake in the festivities as well."

The wicked, heated grin that overtakes my face is unfamiliar, but I allow it. "As Kleo says, they will know my name and gratitude. Hell, maybe I'll play this year."

Dusan Garren laughs, a throaty and wild sound that follows me out into the night.

Hey, Witch!

Thatch

"As you can see, everythin's in working order, buildin' has been standing longer than I have, but you'll have that in Old Town. Contracts were just renewed with the kingdom, shipments come once a month and the staff are great, though the mural out front will have to be fixed up. Oh, the latest one I hired, he'll need some trainin', but he's a good one, I promise."

I follow behind the shopkeeper that doesn't remember me, but that bothers me not. I'll visit his mother's grave tomorrow, not that she would remember me either. Guilt eats away at my insides. I wish I could've seen Mrs. Thitwhistle off to the next world. She was the epitome of hospitality, and her son takes after her gentle side. The old man was a down right bastard, but he left when Gleason was just a babe, and it seems the boy turned out more than alright.

I trace along bookshelves, caressing the engraved detailing hidden in the wood. I find no tacky dust there, same as the last time I visited. The town, no, *city*, has changed infinitely in the last eighty years, but Thitwhistle's hasn't changed a bit. Most of Old Town is the same as it's ever been but especially here.

"It's perfect," I say, smiling down at the half *katan*.

Pride lifts Gleason's chin high. He re-ties his mousy hair back, and we leave the expansive back end of the shop behind, where aisles upon aisles of books sleep.

We enter the open and spacious cafe section. The barista counters and refrigerated display cases are centered on a raised, half moon plaza that dominates the head of the cafe. The once white tiles of the dias are painted cobalt and spattered with star dust clouded constellations. Vibrant colors of the night flow beneath our feet, extending into a river that swirls around the raised area and spreads out to blanket the rest of the wood floor in starry clouds.

The lapis astronomy theme accented by gold continues throughout the shop, much different from the earthy tones Mrs. Thitwhistle used, but I think it's a rather nice touch. The lofty ceiling of the entire place is filled with golden galaxies and meteors, milky ways and dying planets. More paint detailing shows up in random places, the artist's touch reaches every subtle inch of the room.

A line of planets along the edge of a table, shooting stars over top of a curving window frame, explosive golden bursts of light that make my heart ache.

Curtains drape alongside each of the unique round windows facing the street, which are quite a few. The heavy, royal blue fabrics are embroidered in simple gold along the edges and match the upholstered lounge chairs and couches nestled by the fireplaces. Dual hearths rest on the east and west sides of the room, accompanied by chess boards, small tables, and the furniture which the college kids are currently taking advantage of. Enormous groups congregate around both roaring fires, laughter rolls through the gossip and small talk thickens the warm atmosphere.

Thitwhistle's feels like someone's grand study open to the public rather than a bookstore, complete with coffee beans and scones, and I've never felt more at home. The crowd is equal parts magickal beings and humans, young, old and everything in between. There are a few older folks tucked into a corner, eyes crinkling and steam curling around mugs which hide their smiles. A set of half shifted werewolf pups tug on their mother's sleeve, begging for the 'Monster Hot Cocoa' complete with candy and whip cream on top. She rolls her eyes with a smile, in humanoid form, then orders three of the drinks and half a dozen donuts for the bus ride to Full Moons Field.

"Scone?" Gleason asks from my side, patiently watching me take in the scene with a sly smile on his slightly creased face. Half *katan* don't live as long as their magickal parents usually do but a couple hundred years all the same.

I reach down and take it from him, then bring the pastry to my nose and inhale deeply. Mocha and walnut. I glance down at Gleason with a wicked smile, despite myself. "You *do* remember me."

Gleason flushes, then tucks a strand of escaped hair behind his softly pointed ear. "Indeed, but I must admit, I thought ya' were just a childhood fever dream at first, but that's not true, is it?"

That's how most people describe their memories of me, the blurred edges of a dream that fades the harder they try to remember. It doesn't hurt when old friends, acquaintances at best really, forget me. I've long gotten used to the feeling of perpetually being alone, but my heart aches in an unfamiliar way.

"*Ai*, I apologize I wasn't here to see your mother off, truly. She was a wonderful woman, and to be honest, the thought of owning this place ..." I inhale sharply and a moment of worry creases Gleason's thick brows. "It would be an honor. May I ask, why are you selling?"

Gleason glances at the trio of baristas flitting behind the counter and throughout the patrons, then gestures for me to follow him. I do, and he leads me out front, to my surprise. Bells ring when the door, paned with colored patchwork glass, opens. The nightlife of the Old Town meets my ears the moment he opens it, but Gleason abruptly stops in the doorway. I halt in time so I don't step on his heel and his wide eyes catch my attention.

Gleason presses a hand to his chest and takes one small step at a time, staring reverently at the front of the store. "That kid," he whispers breathily, and it's not until I've joined his side again that I find what he's looking at.

The once crumbling storefront has been restored to beyond its former glory. The faded mural which held a portrait of Mrs. Thitwhistle hauling two armfuls of books over her broad shoulders has been painted over. A mural of the solar system, with the unique bookstore itself as the center of the universe, stretches from one end of the storefront to the other. The family sigil of the Thitwhistle's hides in the stardust of a galaxy, along with the words, '*Knowledge is Life.*'

Standing tall in the center of the tremendous round, two storey building is the paned door we came through, flanked by the mishmash of round windows on either side. The same gold and blue color palette from inside the bookstore inspires the mural and trim. The paint *shimmers* underneath the lamplights lining the street, smooth against the cobbed surface. Underneath a window, I notice a decent sized canvas that matches the mural.

I kneel before it and brush a thumb over the artist's signature done in white, indecipherable, but my heart skips all the same. I take the canvas and offer it to Gleason, but he's caressing the miniature bookstore floating on a cloud of stardust. His fingers settle on the family sigil, then he clears his throat, glancing sideways at me.

"Shit like this makes me want to stay." Gleason huffs out a laugh, then gently takes the canvas from me and studies it. "Kid down the street, he's the one who's done all the artwork on the inside over the past few years, and now this. Always when I'm not looking, won't take any money for it. 'He's bored' he says. Agh, fuck, sorry." Gleason wipes his wide nose with his flannel sleeve, sniffling.

"Don't fret, tears bother me none. Good for the soul, I say." I pat his shoulder and he nods. The streets have begun to thicken, patrons move past us to enter the bookstore, waving to Gleason as they do.

He nods to them, rallying himself once we're alone again. "I want to see the world. Took me so fuckin' long to even think about it. 'What would mama say?' you know? She always said this place was enough, and it is, but ... I want *more*. I want to go on adventures, Mr. Phantom, that's why I want to sell. Silly, isn't it? Leave this behind for some fantasy, at my age."

I stare *directly* into his eyes. "Doing what you love isn't silly. I admire you, Gleason, and I think you should do it. And I'm not just saying that because I want your bookstore, but because I think your mama *would* want you to. As long as you don't forget to visit, of course. I can hear her saying it now."

I gesture dramatically before us and he chuckles, eyes brightening. "You're a devil, Mr. Phantom. Alright, let's sign some paperwork."

"Wonderful."

Gleason wipes his eyes and I brush the dust off my earthy joggers, then straighten my hoodie. Casual, low key as always. "Oh, I almost forgot to show you upstairs, that comes with the place too," Gleason says over his shoulder.

"A studio, right?"

"Oh, well, after mama passed, I split it up into apartments. Keeping up with the times, enough college kids keep them full usually. They'll both be empty, if you wanted to keep one for yourself and rent the other, not sure if you have prior arrangements."

I think about the flooded cottage waiting for me by the lake side. Even after I fix it up, I'll be secluded. I don't want to hide away this go around, I want to enjoy the time I have here *with* the people. "What a splendid idea."

I am a lone rock in the chaotic river that is Market Street. My heart swells with each inhalation of spices and bump of the elbow. The harmonious notes from saxophones, clarinets and guitars ride the wind and a soft breeze lifts the tussle of curls poking out from beneath my hood. I ever so slowly turn in place, attempting to absorb the heart of Old Town one smidgen at a time. Garren Castle is a sentinel in the distance. Another old friend I need to visit is there, but not tonight.

If she doesn't remember me, that will hurt infinitely more than Gleason's blurred memory. She will, she always does, after a little reminding.

I bury my hands in my pockets and begin my descent into madness. The wide berth of Market Street diverges from the pleasant Garren Road which houses the relics of the olden days, such as the Castle itself, along with cozy cottages and vital businesses of old.

The entirety of Market Street is swallowed by gorgeous vendor stalls decorated in vibrant oranges and reds. Trolley lines are the only interruption in the crowd. Musicians linger on the street sides, which eventually double back on Garren Road but not before taking a *long* walk downhill.

Not much has changed on this flat paved street. The same brick residential buildings that have been here for a century or two hide behind the endless, rainbow array of merchant stalls. All the brick has been freshened up, canary yellows and apple reds, ocean blues and rosy pinks. Stall locations are kept in the family, corresponding to the residences behind them, and rarely move once a spot is claimed. Only the vendors change over time. Or, that's how it used to be.

What they sell has changed drastically over the years, that's for sure. Where food and raw materials used to reign are now finished crafts, fine jewelry and specialty materials for trade work, along with the basics like fresh food. At the distant end of the street are the stalls intended for witches. The vendors there are some of my favorites. I take out my notepad and pencil, jotting down a few things that are noticeably different this time around, from phones to clothing and slang I've picked up thus far.

I don't miss the oversized posters plastered on building sides, all dedicated to the Scarlet Illusionist. The sight of the vigilante hidden under a masquerade mask in the shape of a leaf and layers of ruby fabric always makes me chuckle. I've yet to find out who coined that term or who decided I *wear* red. The only visible physical features of the Illusionist are the eyes. Which of course are the wrong color, a bright green that rivals the first born leaves of spring. I put away my notepad and continue down the street.

Wreaths of butter yellow sunflowers, burnt orange and red leaves, violet asters and earthy sage hang around iron wrought lamp posts. The fifteen foot tall sentinels are simultaneously powered on by the local leeries, warming the night by way of stored solar power that sparks to life like an honest fire. That was an up and coming technology last time I visited and it seems they've gotten the hang of it.

Red and orange silk flies in triangular banners from one side of the street to the other, criss-crossing back and forth down the entire path. One symbol marks them, an infinity sign. I chuckle upon seeing it, but my amusement dies swiftly.

The civilians of Levena seem to top themselves year after year with festivities, especially in the downtown, but here the decorations scream hominess and welcome, the beautiful hand-crafted quality is apparent in every detail. I try to reconcile who I truly am with what they think of me, and although I love the praise, it feels ... too much. All I do is hide, that's all. Is that *worth* celebrating?

I become truly lost for the first time, neck craned and eyes wandering fenced in rooftops. I'm curious as to what one group of people in particular is doing, situated on a widow's peak and whooping loudly. Sparks are flaring, is that *fire*?

And that's when I crashed into him, or he crashed into *me*, rather.

Paper bags launch into the air. Glass jars loaded with herbs and paint rain down around me. My ass plummets towards the

ground. I brace myself and throw my arms back, slamming my
eyes closed, but ....

I don't make an impact with the stone.

Instead, I find a thick arm around my waist and a strong pair
of eyes that can't decide if they want to be green or brown.

Air whooshes out of me and time stops as I stare deep into
them, right down to his soul, one that *clearly* does not remember me but calls to my heart all the same.

It stings more than I thought it would.

I briefly give the rather pissed off barn owl circling above us
a moment of attention, then I study his face once more. He's
changed *immensely* since the last time we met. Dimples and
laugh lines have been replaced by hard set creases of worry and
irritation. By the stars, I didn't even need to look for him. Once
again, we're pulled together.

Not that I would need a second confirmation, but the dark
splash of a birthmark along the right side of his severely angled
jaw is present, flaring the same bright gold as the first time we
met. His cheeks are soft, flushed and partially hidden beneath
waves of soft black falling from beneath a knitted beanie. He's
hiding. He blinks once, black lashes sweep across his cheeks and
catch the lamplight.

And just like that, time marches on.

I shakily recompose myself and take hold of his thick bicep
veiled in a loosely knitted rainbow duster that extends to his
wrists. Underneath is an incredibly loose black tank top, revealing miles of deep brown skin. I pull myself to standing and we
separate by inches, but it takes another moment for his hard
stare to leave me. During the seconds when the world stopped,
his eyes never strayed from me.

Searching.

I pray for the first time in a long time. Even though I know *they* don't care about me, I pray that they allow him to remember me. Just once.

But instead, he remembers the mess we created, now currently being trampled on by the crowd around us. "Er, watch where you're going, y'know?" He mutters in a rusty baritone, like he meant to come off as pissed but instead its quiet annoyance.

I lock away my weeping heart and kneel down to help him, gathering glass jars full of paint that definitely should've broken, and pads of paper that are now covered in footprints. I frown at the dirty prints, I don't remember the people here being so careless. I hand them to him, my fingers brush against his which are stained with blue paint and I receive a buzzing sensation in my fingertips.

His eyes flick between our hands and the paper, as if I've tainted his things. His irises are a rich brown now, deep and near black, the hazel green magick gone from them. We both stand and stare at the other.

"I apologize, I'm ... new to Levena, got a bit turned around. I didn't mean to—"

The warm, syrupy voice I've pulled on, one that melts even the iciest of hearts, is reduced to a *screech* when explosions rock the night. Shamelessly, I yelp and take hold of the bewildered man's sides, clinging to his duster. The yarn is soft beneath my panicked grip. He's a full two heads taller than I am, my face presses against the bottom of his sternum. His hands hover at my sides, but don't touch.

"Are we under attack? Why? Where?"

The incredibly heated and firm body pressed against me shakes, and after a moment I realize it's with *laughter*. I look up, finding amusement written across his face. A hint of plum paint plays at his upturned lips, oh my, that suits him. "Newcomer I guess so, it's just the fireworks."

He doesn't put hands on me, but one lifts.

I step back, preparing for him to push me away; I am a stranger to him after all.

But he only points up.

The stars are exploding.

I watch in pure awe as red and orange streak into the sea of twilight overhead, the scent of black powder and magick burns out my nostrils. With each *boom*, my heart rattles out of its cage with eye watering joy. I've seen many things since this rock started turning, but none so beautiful as this. Green intermingles with the Scarlet Illusionist's color theme, and I sigh.

Speaking of beautiful, I glance back at the witch, only to find empty space. His first name is there, right *there* on the tip of my tongue, but not his last. He didn't have one before, but I'm sure he does now. I can't yell out his name, he doesn't remember me.

I'm a stranger. A *stranger*.

He sticks out in the crowd, nearly the same height as the few treants and centaurs milling about, and that damned barn owl is perched *on* his head, nestled into his slouchy beanie.

I call out to him the only way I know how, waving ridiculously. "Hey, witch!"

He stops, as do others in the crowd. Curious eyes bore into him and I. He pulls the front of his hat down, but not far enough to hide the daggers he glares at me over his shoulder.

Whoops.

Well, I've already caused a scene. I sprint through the crowd which seamlessly parts for me as more onlookers become interested in our ordeal, or rather, the presence of a witch. Witches weren't infamous the last time I was here, so why are they making a big deal about him? Or maybe it's me acting a fool. That's probably it.

By the time I reach him, he still hasn't moved a muscle, not even to tilt his head towards me more. I breathlessly reach his side and pull back my hood. His jaw flickers and his eyes dart up to my hair. I'm betting it's a mess. "Let's go out sometime, I owe you that much for making a mess of your things."

He balks and the slightest bit of green swims to life in his eyes. A mischievous smile takes hold, but then he shakes his head, and the smile away. "Can't, but thanks. Enjoy the festival."

I open my lips but the owl chirps, a bizarre noise, and cracks open a yellow eye to glower at me. The man rolls his eyes at the bird, then glances back at me with a renewed emerald glow ringed around his irises. He makes to leave, but I wring my hands and blurt out ridiculousness first.

"I'd enjoy it much more with a local to show me around. I'm not ... *looking* for anything, just a friend." I manage to squeak out.

Oh dear stars, am I *blushing*?

All I earn for my awkwardness is a seconds-long sly grin, then the back of his head as he walks away from me. Again. I become a stone in the river, allowing the crowd to part around me. I wonder when the last time was that I experienced embarrassment.

Have I ever been truly embarrassed?

Well, I certainly have now.

Qualms of Queers

Arlo

Kitt is less than impressed with me, of course.

I forgot the fucking oranges.

"Look, all I'm saying is that a date wouldn't be the worst thing in the world. When's the last time you had a good fuck?" She wiggles her brows from behind the bar, causing Lindsey to choke on her drink beside me. "Or *got* fucked, either way."

Lindsey straight up spits her drink out at that one.

Caspian sputters from the opposite side of the blonde between us.

"Dear *Gods*, your mouth is going to be the death of you." I mutter, taking a swig of my own whiskey. I'm going to need a few more of these.

"That's what she said when I was ... *making up*, a few hours ago." Kitt winks at her elven companion, flushing Lindsey's fair cheeks to a deep red.

"Kitty!" Lindsey slaps Kitt's tattooed arm, brown eyes wide with feign shock. These two are voyeurs at best, but Lindsey likes to pretend she has a moral compass.

"You guys are on again then, yeah?" Quentin rolls his eyes at my left. The moment I look over, he pointedly avoids my casual glance. I look past him, down the bar to take in the rowdy crowd. On the other side of Quentin is the usually quiet one of our group, Gowan. She smiles at me, waving a moss covered hand as Lindsey and Kitt argue about the logistics of their relationship.

The Ethereal Magpie is stuffed to the brim, typical of a festival night. Our old haunt is a secret tucked between Old and New Town, the crowd and atmosphere a pleasant combination of the two. Only those in a select crowd are able to enter this place, thanks to enchanted cards I made for the owner years ago. Even so, the dance floor is an ocean of limbs and dim lights, and all the stools at the bar are occupied.

All the usual patrons are allowed up to eight guests on a card during festival week, and it seems most people have taken advantage. Our group takes up quite a bit of space, but at least a couple dozen other patrons fill the other high backed, velvet green stools, each face unfamiliar. I watch a group of mermaids splash about in the generously sized freshwater pool at the head of the gathering space, situated beneath an elevated loft which houses the disc jockey. A few sirens join their mer companions, their glowing and beautiful complexion a contrast to the sharp fangs, fins and claws the mermaids have.

Beneath the tank is a tunnel intersection stretching three ways. East to Water Street, west to Syorini lake, and south to the river. The aquatic population petitioned for accessible, direct routes a few decades ago and it's one of the better things to happen to Levena. Situated on the loft over the water, a set of complex turntables are manned by a *krakeni*.

Their many tentacled limbs are dressed in leather, their face is hidden by a sleek black mask. *Krakeni* don't need to stay in the water like the mermaids and sirens, but occasionally need a dip or to be misted. On cue, one of the various tentacles not busy with setting the beat presses a button and water falls into a massive cloud over the *krakeni* and crowd below, special effects but with a purpose. Luckily, we're out of the splash zone over here. I don't care to get wet right now.

My skin itches with a sense of *wrong*. I look around the room again, finding nothing immediately out of the ordinary.

"Don't listen to her, well, not that part, but she's right. And it sounds like he really did just want a tour. Why'd you turn him away?" Lindsey leans forward on the bar, blonde hair falling onto the slick countertop. I open my mouth to answer her but catch Cas watching expectantly, so I shrug and look away, procrastinating.

Everything in this place is crisp, modern and clean. That's to be expected in an establishment run by a *shedim,* especially when they're the most powerful demon in the north. The bar is carved from an intricate black marble, a nice complement to the simple gilded embellishments, soft golden globe lamps overhead, and the forest green furniture. A wall of liquor rests behind the bar and plants hang down from overhead, growing upside down from their place in the vegetation filled ceiling.

An ivy teases my neck and I catch eyes with a werewolf at the end of the bar. He grins at me, all fangs and a thick beard that screams hipster. I can't say much. I don't care for growing facial hair, but I'm dressed the part otherwise.

"Listen, just because *you* two are horn dogs doesn't mean everyone else is, eh?" Caspian chides, grinning at me. He knows very well *that* isn't the problem. I cross my arms and lean back, quite tired of this. I ignore the werewolf giving off fuck me vibes and my fingers tingle with the need to zap Kitt in the ass.

"Correct me if I'm wrong, but don't we have a housing crisis to solve?" Gowan muses and my shoulders relax a little, the docile dandelion fae is ever the mediator in our group. I peek at Cas to gauge his reaction.

Her, Quentin, Lindsey and Gowan are the newest to the group, but the rest of us grew up together as orphans, for a few years, that is. Even after Kitt and Caspian left, we didn't stop talking. Caspian and I had a fling for a hot minute, or *two*, but it burned out, to put it nicely.

Kitt latched onto Lindsey shortly before I left, and Lindsey's human friend Quentin followed not long after. I met Gowan in the local studio Doc referred me to, and seamlessly integrated her into our weekly Misfit night.

Well, there's only been two consecutive weeks out of this past year so far.

Before that, it was weekly.

"What's this? Lolo's moving out?" Caspian teases, amber eyes hazy and wide. They always seem to be hazy these days, but that would have to mean he's piss poor drunk every time we see each other. Since that isn't likely, I file it away as parental exhaustion. He's dressed in jeans and a sweater Gowan made him last yule, complete with his usual five o'clock shadow.

I glance at Kitt who shrugs. "Figured he'd be bothering you the whole night if I told him earlier, no better time than now while you're here."

Well, shit. Thanks, Kitt, *making* me deal with my own problems.

"It's really not a big deal, I'm just looking for my own place, that's all." I allow, rubbing the back of my head and avoiding

Gowan's inquisitive stare. I haven't wanted to tell the rest of them my *other* impending news, not just yet, not until I know more. "And no, I don't want to crash on your couch, but thanks, Cas."

Caspian folds his muscled arms, pouting. "It *is* a big deal, to me."

I take that as my cue and hop off the stool, stretching my arms overhead. "Gotta take a piss."

I slip through bodies and fend off requests to dance from a *tannin* I know and a faun I don't. I bypass the bathrooms completely to slip out the back door. I step out onto a deck that faces New Town. All bright lights, noise and sky scraping buildings. The *Etz Hayim* in the distance is a silhouette against the neon night, its great branches caress the clouds and block out the near full moons.

Most of the benches are occupied by intimate lovers or those looking to sate their vices, like myself. I find an empty seat at the edge of the deck and heave down with a groan. I kick my feet up, resting them on the iron railing keeping me from a nasty fall. I inhale an autumn breeze, crisp and tainted with the scent of a distant bonfire. The chatter out here is low, a soft bubble compared to the frenzy inside.

I reach inside my duster and retrieve my pouch from one of the endless pockets. I prepare a pipe, then light it with a small flame brought forth from a snap of my fingers. I close my eyes, soaking my lungs in the earthy smoke. The man from the Market comes to mind immediately, his wide eyes the color of a summer day absorbing the fireworks as if they were heaven on earth.

I choke on the smoke and try again.

The thing is, I truly contemplated his offer, which in the past is something I'd *never* do. Sex with strangers is off the table for me, and love ... love nearly killed me twice, and I'm not about to break myself open again. I give myself props for even *thinking* about it, then chastise myself for being such a coward. Lindsey's probably right, he most likely wanted someone to show him around. If that ended in a quick fuck, would that have been a bad thing?

Yes.

I don't think like this about people. And I know enough about myself to know that even a one night stand would crack its way into my heart and feelings would spill out onto the floor like they did before. I take another deep hit, but his features swirl to life in my mind's eye and there's nothing I can do to stop the heat that follows.

He was classically handsome, splattered with galaxies of freckles which *did* things to me. His body was soft against mine for the precious seconds I held onto him. When our hands brushed, magick *sang* in my veins. I didn't know it could do that and I sincerely thought I was having a heart attack.

And don't even get me started on his *hair*. It was ... beautiful. I wanted to brush the curls away from his face and lose my fingers in the vibrant copper.

I haven't been with anyone since Cas, and only a few guys before him, and like a freight train it hits me that I haven't had sex in *years*. I was fumbling and dumb then, no wonder why .... Well, there's no doubt I'm not the greatest lay now, either. I frown, wondering why that man was interested in me at all. I give off a general 'fuck off vibe' as Lindsey would say, so most people don't approach me unless they want something.

Everyone always wants something.

Need a bit of magick?

A shoulder to cry on?

Life advice?

Lips to try out?

Arlo's there, until he's not.

I close my eyes and bring the pipe to my lips again. When I exhale, a soft weight takes up space on the bench beside me. I look over to find Quentin smiling at me, one dimple warily showing. He nods to the pipe in my hand. "Can I?"

I appraise this elegant man dressed in black slacks and a fancy collared shirt with one too many buttons undone, then chuckle halfheartedly and hand it to him. "Didn't know that you partook." I wait for him to start coughing, assuming he's trying to show off, but instead he exhales a series of rings. He watches them flow with satisfaction curling his thin smile. For some reason, Elochian comes to mind.

"Impressive," I say eventually.

Big emerald eyes blink rapidly, as if he forgot I was there, and he hands me back the pipe hurriedly. His leather shoe bounces and he chuckles. "Not such a square, as Kitt would say."

"Ah, nothing wrong with it if you were." I grin and we smoke the herbs down to nothing.

A comfortable silence rests between us as the world turns, oblivious to the qualms of queers hopelessly in love with their best friends. Quentin is like me in that sense, doesn't talk very much, but otherwise we're from two different worlds. He came from a well off family, is an established member of Levena and teaches elementary kids during the day, while a few evenings a week he teaches physics at Scarlet University.

When I came back, he didn't ask questions, and it was like he'd always been there.

"Um, I saw the other day in the paper that Thitwhistle's has a couple apartments for rent. I'm looking for a place too. Lindsey is great, but Kitt's been over a lot, and ... you know." He blushes furiously.

I chuckle, nodding. "Yeah, I think so."

"If you wanted, we could … talk to Gleason together?" Quentin lifts a shoulder, eyes on *Etz Hayim* in the distance. It's Kitt's dream to live in those fancy apartments, not mine, and I don't picture Quentin wanting to live in the tree's lofts either.

The idea of living with a roommate is unpleasant and defeats what I'm trying to achieve, but if someone I knew was in the place next door, that wouldn't be so bad. I hate to admit it, but going from a constantly full castle to pure nothingness is probably not the greatest idea, and it'll placate Cas and Kitt. Thitwhistle's is quiet, small. Perfect, really.

I give him a pleasant smile. "Sure, that would be great, thanks Quen."

"Yeah, of course." He grins wide, stars in his eyes.

We sit together, watching the festivities spill through the nightlife in the city beyond. Yeah, this is good. I like the bookstore, and Quentin. Gleason is a good man, I imagine he'd be a fair landlord. I wonder what he thought of the mural.

I was too scared shitless to stick around, thinking he would be pissed. I was going for modern, but paying homage to his family and Gleason's love for astronomy. At the very least, it should give him some good business. Not that he has a problem with that.

"Arlo," Quentin says, pulling me from my thoughts. "They're waiting on us."

I nod, then rise and offer my hand to him. "Well, we can't have that now, can we?"

Quentin pulls himself up eagerly, lingering in my loose grip for a thick moment. The dim lights out here cast shadows on his petite jaw and highlight the sharpness of his nose. His jet black hair is short on the sides with a thick length tousled on top. The hint of a tattoo peeks out from underneath his dress shirt, one I've never noticed before and can't discern fully.

"Arlo, I wanted to say good luck, too. I know I'm not supposed to know, but ... I'm on the board of directors at Scarlet. In my opinion, I think you'll get it." He smiles nervously up at me.

Heat washes over my neck and I let go of his hand. Of course, I didn't even think of that. "Oh, thank you. I ... I just–"

Quentin's warm smile holds as he eases my worry. "I won't tell the others, some things are meant for just ourselves, you know?" He takes hold of the familiar crystal necklace at his throat, one I gave him for an occasion I don't remember.

I nod and anxious air leaves my chest. I readjust my beanie and sheepishly grin. "Thanks, Q. I owe you one."

"Don't mention it. What are friends for?"

The rest of Friday night passes in a karaoke and laughter filled blur. I didn't sing, but it was fun watching the others. Caspian has the best voice out of all of us and I always love hearing him. After smoking with Quentin on the balcony, I had eased up on the drinks, unlike the others. Only the mind softening effects of my herbs are present as I take the last misfit home.

Caspian.

He's been silent since we dropped Lindsey, Kitt, and Quentin off a few blocks away. Gowan had diverged from us, walking home in the opposite direction back at the bar. Bosko has found his perch atop my head, awake but silent as Caspian rolls on beside me.

As we near his house nestled between Kitt's and Old Town, Caspian abruptly stops and I prepare myself for tears. Caspian's quite the emotional drunk, and we haven't really had it out since I came home from the hospital, nor have things gone back to normal. While things between Kitt and I aren't *normal*, per say, she doesn't act like I'm going to implode at any moment.

I know she thinks it, but she hides her thoughts well.

I knew keeping Cas out of the loop would piss him off, but I'm tired of him looking out for me. He's got it good, and I don't need him feeling responsible for me. And ... yeah, I'm still a little mad at him. The logical part of me knows there's no reason to be, but still.

Instead of tears, I find a murderous scowl hiding under his raked back locks of brunette accompanied by burning gold eyes. He's handsome, but even more so when he's pissed off. Maybe that's why I poke at him so much. Caspian crosses his arms and I throw my own up, exasperated already. "Well, let's hear it."

"Hear *what*?" He arches a brow, tapping his toned bicep with trapped fingers.

"You're pissed I left you out of things."

"Obviously." Caspian rolls his eyes, then looks away. His wide shoulders loosen and when he focuses on me again, true hurt cuts through his drunken anger. "You did it because of me, didn't you?"

I step back, hands up between us. I did not expect this turn. My magick flares up, twice as pissed since I restrained it once already at the Market. It burns through my veins, hot and dangerous. "Oh, *fuck* off, Caspian. How could you even think—"

"From where I'm sitting, it's pretty fuckin' plain don't you think?" He grits out. "It's time we hash this out."

"You're so fucking selfish to think for even a *second* that was about you." I spit out, because even now I can't admit the truth.

I'd been spiraling for years, but watching my best friend marry someone else was the nail in my coffin, literally. Not so much that he fell in love with Tobias, but that I was alone.

"My problems are mine, you had *nothing* to do with it, and you know something? I think I would've done it even if you *hadn't* left me." I gasp, admitting a truth I haven't dared to uncover yet, but there it is, abysmal and grotesque.

My magick dies, as does the bodily green glow escaping through the loose knitwork in my duster, veins and arteries fading to their normal hue.

Caspian's face crumbles and his knuckles blanch as he takes hold of the arms of his wheelchair. I kneel beside him, offering my hand in the space between us. He stares at my fingers warily, chest heaving like my own.

"How can I not worry about you when you say shit like that? You've been keeping me out of things, you treat me differently than you do the others." Caspian whispers, truly hurt.

I sigh. "I don't know, I'm just ... tired of everyone *worrying,* waiting for me to fail. What's the point in trying to ... *live* if no one thinks you can do it? You can't keep smothering me, Caspian, and you have to stop taking blame for what *I* did. I'm serious, I'm my own person."

"Oh, Arlo." Instead of taking my hand, Caspian leans over and presses his forehead to mine, a move we've done since we were kids. No matter how pissed we were at the other, our heads pressing together meant *we* were okay.

We hold the other underneath the night sky waning into the threat of dawn. Caspian cries into my shoulder and I watch the fading stars, wondering when it will be my turn to cry. I haven't in years, but not for lack of trying. Starting at the attic wall and waiting for them to roll is my favorite way to pass the late nights.

I walk Caspian the rest of the way home with a half smile, listening to him vow not to be such an overbearing jackass. We come to a stop at the end of his driveway and I overlook his suburbian paradise. The yellow cottage with white shutters is one I don't frequent often, only for special occasions or late nights to tuck Caspian in. There's a garden at the right with a few old trees shading it, complete with a swing for the kids and a patio for grilling and eating, a place I've yet to enjoy.

"Could you help me in?" Caspian asks and I raise a brow, earning a defensive glare from my old friend. He doesn't ask for help, often. A trait we share. "Listen, the old man will be a lot less pissed at me if you're there."

"I'm the culprit, remember?" I yawn, taking hold of the wheelchair's handlebars and pushing Caspian along the smooth, stone path. Better to get it over with than argue, and I feel bad for fighting with him. "It's my fault you're out late."

"Psh, Misfits night is sacred, nothing comes between that."

"Sick kid?" I retort, and Caspian shrugs.

"Well, that's life or death now, come on, Lolo."

I chuckle, winding around the ramp and onto the front porch, dodging the hanging baskets full of iridescent moonflowers soaking up the silver and golden rays of the near full moons. With practiced silence I open the door and immediately find Tobias on the other side. The *malakim* kindly smiles at me with disheveled pink hair and askew reading glasses. A fussing child rests in each of his tired arms and his wings are spelled away, like they always are.

I've never seen his wings.

"Oh no, did we wake the angels?" I coo, taking hold of both adolescent terrors and cradling them to my chest. I practically dwarf them with my big arms, but they love it and immediately settle. Marlena is bigger than her little brother, but not by much.

Zeke is half shifted, scales and fins cover his tiny and otherwise humanoid body.

Marlena's own *shedim* form only appears when she's sleeping, which won't be long.

"Oh thank goodness, how do you do that?" Tobias asks, rubbing at his face with a sleepy smile and delicate hand. I'm sure if you looked up the definition of *malakim* in the dictionary, there Tobias would be in all his angelic beauty.

"*Magick.*" I whisper, raising my brows for full effect as I bring the kids over to Caspian. "I'll get these babes to bed, I have a feeling you'll have your hands full with that one, Tobias."

Caspian lays on a soft kiss on his daughter's forehead, then his son's, and he stares at them both for a moment, tears welling in his eyes.

"You're a saint, Arlo, and Bias is fine, please. Come now Cassie, let's get you out of those clothes. No, *not* like that, you stink like a liquor bottle."

I leave behind Tobias and Caspian in the landing, making my way up the carpeted stairs. I pass by pictures of when Tobias and Caspian first started dating, two months after he and *I* stopped. I smile at the sight of Kitt and I photobombing them. The kids snore in my arms when I stop, looking deeper into my grinning face beside Kitt's, both of us holding up bunny ears behind the couple's heads.

On closer inspection I note the date, frowning. Six years ago. There was nothing different about my face, except my cheeks were slimmer than they are now. I look away, avoiding the next span of years where I progressively look shittier, if I'm there at all. The two years before I ....

Before, I went radio silent and barely left my room, which sounds nice right now.

The next set of pictures that pause my step are of Tobias and Caspian bringing the kids home from Garren Castle. They're both smiling, the red headed Marlena is cradled in Caspian's arms and her half brother Zeke is snuggled by Tobias. Caspian's grin is off, lopsided. He never does anything halfway, especially his smiles.

I was supposed to be there.

A year in pictures passes by, full of first steps and birthday cake, toothy smiles and Caspian smiling, smiling, *smiling*. Kitt is there, and Lindsey is too. Quentin makes an appearance before I do, in the background of many festivities which appear to have taken place in the yard outside, which has transformed just like the family has.

When I first saw this place, I thought Caspian was crazy for wanting to renovate it, but he insisted it was home. It was definitely a project, but his parents only live a few streets over. I avoid the last few pictures involving my homecoming and everything thereafter, hurrying as much as I can to reach the top of the stairs.

I tuck Marlena and Zeke into their shared crib, the siblings are only a year apart from each other but joined at the hip regardless. I brush wild red from Marlena's plump cheeks, then do the same to Zeke's inky coils, and at last I tuck a plushie dragon in the space between their bellies.

Marlena's leather wings sprout like a plant in slow motion, unfurling from her back and through the slits in her pajama top. Zeke's scales fade as he snuggles into his sister.

I stand there for a moment, trying with all my might to bury Caspian's words.

It's because of me, isn't it?

I softly shut the door, leaving it open a crack, and sneak to the stairs. I pass by Tobias and Caspian's room just down the hall from the kid's, where Cas' snores leak into the hall and ease some of my tension. The lights are dimmed and the house is quiet, the downstairs filled with the soft bubble from an out of sight aquarium. I trace a finger along the mechanism for Caspian's chair lift, enchanting it with good luck for next time he uses it as I walk down the stairs. When I reach the landing and take hold of the door handle, Tobias creaks down the steps and clears his throat.

"Arlo, wait."

I do, hand tightened on the door knob as Tobias meets me on the ground floor. "They're all settled in." I whisper, giving him a tired smile.

"Thank you, and thanks for bringing Cas home in one piece."

"Yeah, I may have riled him up, I'm sorry for that."

"Sometimes he needs it," Tobias says knowingly.

I release the door handle, rubbing the back of my neck. "I'm thinking Misfits night may become more of a ... family friendly thing, if you wanted to come. I haven't talked to the others yet, but I myself am too old to be frequenting bars."

"Is that so?" Tobias' pink eyes brighten to match his wild hair, one of the witches I know with such colorful magic. "Arlo, did you know there wasn't a single Misfits night while you were gone?"

I shake my head, perfect time as any for tears to strike, but they don't.

"Ah. Well, I'm glad they've started up again. If it's alright with you, I'd love to join you all."

We stand there for a moment, saying everything and absolutely nothing. Then, I dart into the night and close the door to Caspian's family home.

The door to Garren Castle is always open, but only to those who are welcome. Meaning, the door is literally never locked, but try to bypass my wards without permission and your ass is toast. Only a small tingle to the kids who try to sneak out past curfew, enough to remind them the world isn't ready for their trouble yet. I pass through the shimmering magick veiled over the wide double doors, the translucent green visible only to a witch's eye.

The moment I pass through the ward I feel safe, but not at home.

I haven't felt at home in a long time, here nor anywhere else.

The chandeliers are dimmed, the halls empty and cold. Ornamental rugs, paintings, sculptures and other works of art from previous residents decorate the place. Everyone who leaves gives back to Garren Castle one way or another. Dusan focuses our education on not only on textbooks but hands on skills, as such many of us take up a trade.

For me it was painting, and reluctantly teaching. Kitt absorbed every history fact possible while here and took to inking skin after she left. Now she spends most of her days in the museum when she isn't tending bar, tattooing, or doing one of the hundreds of other things she keeps herself busy with. Caspian fell in love with inventing, sound engineering, and later on, Tobias.

I take a detour to Dusan's office, only to find it empty. I stand there for a moment and a shiver puts me back on track. When I pass by my Kitchen, I remember my promise to Felix. I nearly forgot, and I have no idea what to say to him, truly. I reach the base of the southeastern turret and climb the spiral stairs up, up, *up*, until there's nowhere else to go. I pull down the door in the ceiling, revealing another small set of stairs.

I'm tired of hiding up here.

I step inside what once was a simple guest studio. I inhale the cool breeze sneaking in through the open window at the opposite end. I shut the door behind me and Bosko leaves me in favor of his perch. He faces away from me and tuck his beak into his breast, further hidden by his wing. He's pissed I didn't engage with the market guy, but won't say why.

I slide my beanie off and throw it onto the neatly pressed blankets tucked around my mattress, the corners *just* so. A habit that I'll never kick, the need for order was unwillingly ingrained into me. I kick my sneakers off, right then left. I wander to the small bathroom adjoined to the main apartment space, passing by what should be a kitchen but I've filled it with canvases and my drafting table.

I enter the darkness and move to click the light on but am stopped short. A patch of softly glowing skin on my jaw alights my features in the bathroom. I hop onto the counter, knocking my comb and other paraphernalia to the ground. I settle crossed legged, knee in the sink, studying my face with intense scrutiny.

My mark has never shone.

I had given up on thinking it would.

Everyone has one, but only witches can see them. If Tobias noticed, he didn't say anything. Who set it off? Why is it shining *now*, now that I'm alone?

It dies down and I hold my jaw with one hand, the other finds my necklace and holds on tight. Warmth radiates through both palms and I sigh, hanging my head. For a fleeting moment, I think about the person who made my magick sing, and my heart immediately races. I glance up at the mirror and watch my mark come to life once more.

I think about his blue eyes widening with fear, his hands on me, seeking protection. The mirror nearly blinds me.

I think about how happy he seemed to be with me, eyes full of fireworks. The entire bathroom basks in the light of my mark.

I think about how I should've said *anything* besides, *"can't, thanks."* The glowing stops.

It doesn't matter. It couldn't have been him. And even if it was ... I won't ever see him again, and it's for the best. Soulmates are bullshit, and I'm not someone *anyone* wants to be tethered to.

I take a long held piss, wash my hands and face, splashing cold water onto my neck for good measure. I dutifully take my meds, then slide under the tucked covers, disturbing them as little as possible so they're somewhat holding me down. I stare up at the variety of artwork the kids have made me for me over the years, and I smile.

No matter how shit my day's been, the sight of driftwood and shell chimes, pipe cleaner unicorns and tangled dreamcatchers, quilted together banners with '*Happy Birthday Lo*' and '*Best Teacher Ever*' always puts me to sleep.

Saturday

Witch Things

Arlo

Felix and I are out of the castle before the sun fully spills over the mountainous horizon, boots scuffing up dust as we walk the path of the witch.

He didn't complain or question my abrupt change of plans when I woke him, only asked, *'is it cold outside?'*

And it is, unseasonably so.

I'm opting for an edge today, wearing my black leather jacket over a band tee and layers of gold and silver necklaces. My dark pair of jeans ripped up and down the front are tucked into my knee high boots which match my jacket. Felix is dressed warmly in a vibrant knit sweater, wool vest and heavy pants, but his thin figure shivers within moments of leaving the castle.

When we reach the iron gates at the edge of the grounds, I stop where the dirt path empties onto the road. Felix looks up at me expectantly, sleepy eyes brightening. "Today you shall walk in my shoes. Do you know what that means, Felix?"

He shakes his head.

I squat, adjusting my beanie. "Well, you know how on Saturdays I'm usually gone all day?"

Felix nods.

"Well, that's when I do most of my witch things. I try to do it all in one day, and today you will be my apprentice. I want you to see all the good magick can do, and I want you to ask questions along the way. Okay?"

Felix chews on his bottom lip, then nods again. "Okay."

"Do you have any questions before we leave?"

"Am I a witch? Truly?"

I smile and offer my hand to him. His small fingers wrap around my thumb and my heart warms. "Truly, Felix. If you would rather we talked this over tea like we planned, then we can do that too."

"No," Felix says at once, spine straightening.

"Good." I grin upon standing. "But, you're forgetting something."

He tilts his head and I bring my hands together, fingers weaving to cast a simple conjuration. Patches of dark leather lay across Felix's arms and torso, sewn together as they fall from nothingness and compose a perfect replica of my own jacket. Even as Felix spins with excitement the magick does its work, white letters embroidering onto his breast as he turns.

'Felix'

Last but not least, an overly thick beanie knits itself together over his flushed ears. I didn't design this piece, only called for a witch's hat that would suit his personality. I can't help but smile watching blue and white chevron stitches compose the slouchy hat. Gowan calls it cheating, which I can't deny when her hand knit pieces take hours upon hours and my magick can weave something in seconds.

The streets are washed in dawn now, it won't be long before the town wakes from its pre-Game night of festivities. Tomorrow these roads will be thrice as full with scavengers for the day long Game, but the festival doesn't end for a week. I offer my hand to Felix once more, then lead my little witch to my haunts of Levena.

Felix and I are brought through white halls laden with bright windows, white coats, antiseptic burning out my nostrils, and blue scrubs. "Right this way, I'll let Doc know you're here." Doc's medical assistant gestures into the room, like I don't come here every weekend.

"Thanks." I nod to her, then Felix and I filter inside the private medical room reserved for witches. I shut the door behind me and someone else's wards click into place, keeping our errant auras inside the room.

Felix leaps up onto a chair and tilts his head at me. "What was that noise?"

"A ward, like the one I showed you at home. We can't see this one because it's not mine, and whoever designed it did so with the intent of keeping it hidden. During certain procedures a witch's magick can flare out, so this keeps others safe from us."

"Safe from us?"

"Yes, magick is—"

A knock on the door is followed by it swinging open, revealing my old time *behema* friend and savior, Doc. Peppered, textured curls are piled atop their furred head, situated between two wolf ears. Doc grins, a toothy and friendly thing that's always followed by a hug. I stand on my tiptoes to do just that, squeezing tight enough to crack their spine.

Doc is the only good thing about Heartstone Medical.

Doc adjusts the red glasses on their snout, peering down at Felix after we separate. I don't believe Felix has ever met a *behema* before, and to his credit he's rather calm, albeit wide eyed. Doc steps forward, extending a clawed hand to Felix. He stands and takes it immediately, shaking firmly.

"Quite a grip you've got there! My name's Doc, what's yours?"

"F-Felix."

"Felix, what a strong name. Are you here to help me with this problem child?" Doc 'accidentally' back hands me in the chest and I cough in exaggeration. Felix nods fervently with a hint of a smile. "Good! Alright then." Doc picks up my chart from the table and scrutinizes it, for show as they know my history by heart. "Ah, yes. Amputating one leg today, Mr. Rook?"

"What! I think not." I cross my arms and huff. Felix scoots to the edge of his chair, captivated by Doc's antics.

"Oh dear, yes it seems I've the wrong information. That's why it's *always* important to make sure you have the right patient." Doc winks at Felix, then starts to gather the usual from a cabinet. I settle on the exam table, boots swinging over the edge as I slip off my jacket.

"Felix, if you would."

He jumps up and takes my jacket with care, then sets it down where he was sitting and stands by my side. I roll up my sleeves as Doc prepares a tray full of vials, a butterfly needle and tourniquet. "Is something wrong, Mister Arlo?"

"No, not with me. Witches don't get sick, did you know that? Well, most magickal creatures don't, but witches *especially*. Other than allergies, can't stand those. Humans though, and some other beings, they can get *real* sick. Sometimes, an illness takes hold and unfortunately, they wouldn't make it otherwise."

Doc smiles as they listen, tying the tourniquet over my arm with dexterous, long fingers that end in claws. Their preferred form is equal parts humanoid and wolf, giving them the best of both worlds. Sometimes their claws get me, but Doc is pretty good at keeping them filed down. Doc palpates my veins and Felix can't decide whether to watch them or me, gears turning behind those big eyes.

"So ... witch's blood helps them? Is that what you're doing, donating it?"

"Very good, Felix. Yes, it seems to. Doc here is running a few different research programs on the different ways to use witch's blood, so for now it's not an *'official'* way to help, not until it's approved."

"But, if it helps, isn't that enough?"

Doc chuckles, drawing up a fifth vial of iridescent green swirling beside red but never touching, like oil and water. "Why, you are quite clever. Tell me, has your master told you how magick works?" Felix shakes his head. "Come here."

Felix does as he's told, joining Doc's side without fear as my blood fills a sixth vial. "Why is it green? Is *mine* green?"

"A witch's blood *is* their magick. Your heart pumps blood and magick in equal amounts, and magick can take different forms. I've seen pink, green, blue, purple, even. So, if I were to take Mr. Rook's blood and give it to a Human, would it give *them* magic?"

Felix thinks about that, long and hard while Doc loosens the tourniquet. Today's ten vials have me feeling woozy, the loss of magick more so than the loss of blood.

"Maybe, for a little while? But, if it comes from the heart, then, it wouldn't last? Right?"

"Correct, and the residual magick they receive can hurt them, depending on where it came from. Magick ... can you imagine that it has feelings? Now, Arlo is generally a pretty happy guy, right? Happy magick is *good*, happy magick creates and heals. But, if I were to use blood from someone who was angry and scared, I'd be putting *angry,* volatile magick inside someone. Now, what do you think that magic will want to do?"

Felix looks down at his wringing hands, his beanie and hair slides forward. "Hurt them."

"Right. So while in *absolute* emergencies and with known sources, witch's blood *can* be a good thing, but we just don't know enough about it yet to use it for everyone, and Arlo is my only volunteer, which makes the process slow going."

Felix brows furrow and he stares up at me, then to Doc. "Why?"

Doc sends me a searching look, choosing to clean up in silence instead of helping me. I point to my jacket and Felix brings it to me with urgency. I slip it on, but a paw to my chest and stern look keeps me from standing. I take my beanie off and sigh, carding a hand through my wild hair that I only half brushed.

"Did you know there used to be *lots* of witches, Felix?"

He shakes his head, hands shoved deep into his jacket pockets. I glance up at Doc standing near the door, softly smiling. "I'll see you next week Arlo, and it was a pleasure to meet you, Felix."

Felix and I say our goodbyes and after the door shuts, I replace my beanie. "It's hard being a witch, Felix. Everybody wants you, your magick. People have big dreams, and they'll do anything it takes to achieve them, even if it means hurting others. A long time ago, that's exactly what happened. A ... a bad man came to Levena, stole away all the witches. He, well—"

"He took their magic, didn't he? Their ... blood." Felix blanches, and I sigh.

It was so much worse than that.

"Yes, yes he did. Some survived, most didn't, but everybody remembers. He was caught and witches have been better protected since then. But, the idea of letting someone willingly ... *experiment*, for lack of a better word, on us again, most witches can't understand it."

"Well, that's not fair. Doc isn't *the* bad man, and we can help people. Don't they know that?" Felix stands a little taller, and I love him for it.

I smile, standing slowly. "They're starting to, and it may not be fair, but that's ok. For now, I'll keep helping until someone else comes along." I shrug and Felix stares at me for a moment with rare defiance in his eyes, then he nods.

"I'm ready to go now," he says firmly, and I agree.

With each step away from the hospital, my energy returns tenfold in a way that's unnatural, like I've touched a battery. I send Doc a text and quickly put away my phone. Bosko flies in circles overhead, must be he decided to quit pouting and leave the castle finally. Felix hasn't spoken since we left, only glancing up at me every now and then. I wonder what my adolescent years would've been like if I had a mentor to look up to.

Not that I'm a very good one, but someone is better than no one.

"Should I call you Master?" He asks after we turn a corner.

I laugh, rubbing the back of my neck as we approach Kitt's shop. "No, no. Doc is old fashioned, Mister Arlo is fine. We're here."

Felix looks up at a sign jutting out from the red brick. *Kitty's* He smiles wide. "We're here to see Kitt?"

"Hm, I suppose we are. On official witch business though, don't forget." I hold up a finger, feigning seriousness.

He doesn't seem to buy it one bit, but he does as I say regardless. Instead of flying into Kitt's arms when we enter the shop, he stays by my side. She looks up from the receptionist's desk covered in stickers, nursing a cup of coffee like her life depends on it.

Kitt takes in Felix's cool guy stance, his crossed arms and leather jacket that mirrors mine. She grins at his new hat. I wink at her, we texted briefly this morning when I asked permission to bring him.

Kitt sits up, covered in a long sleeved hoodie dress and leggings. Her purple tresses are tied back in a high pony, her hungover eyes are painted in a gray and blue that compliments her plum complexion. She folds her hands together, sunlight filters in through tall windows and her curling horns shine.

"Well, how may I help you?" Kitt asks in her best customer service voice.

Felix looks up to me and I clear my throat. "Arlo Rook, Hedge Witch at your service. I hear you are in need of some enchantments."

And that's about all the three of us can take of proper manners before laughter breaks us apart all.

"Oh my, that was fun. Let's head on back." Kitt hitches Felix up onto her back and I follow her into the parlor, inhaling the incense she has going. Dragon's blood, how fitting. Kitt's parlor is calm and peaceful already, but the thick, earthy fragrance sets the tone. She lays back in one of the many reclined leather inking chairs, stretching out and squashing Felix.

"Hey Lo, have you seen Felix?"

"No, I thought he was with you?" I tease, meandering over to study the hundreds of bottles of ink neatly organized along the center dividing wall. Felix makes indiscernible noises as he and Kitt rough house, eventually he breaks free and bounds to my side with a face cracking grin.

After such a heavy first visit, I knew Kitt would cheer him up.

Kitt joins us, snaking an arm around my waist as her head meets my arm with a solid *thud*. She rubs a horn on my lower bicep and I roll my eyes, letting her do her thing. "Have good dreams about *lover boy*?"

I glare down at Kitt and she grins evilly.

"Alright, which ones need the good stuff?" I turn my attention back to the jars of ink, ignoring the flush taking over my neck.

Felix's curious gaze ramps up the heat. "Lover? Do you have a boyfriend, Mister Arlo?"

I shake my head. "No, I do not. Kitt is being silly."

"Kitt, you *can't* be silly today, this is *serious* business." Felix chastises her in the most firm tone I've *ever* heard from *anyone*, and it takes all my willpower not to laugh. Must be the same for Kitt because she buries her mouth in my sleeve.

"Of course," she says, muffled. After recovering, she points to the bottom shelves. "I've reorganized these like you requested, *Mister* Arlo, and those two shelves are the ones that need it. But I can get by with just these colors if you're feeling–"

I glare at her. "Thanks, Kitt."

She sticks her tongue out at me, then leaves me to it as the front door bell chimes.

I lace my fingers together and crack them dramatically, the veins in my neck and face warm. "How about we do some magick?"

Felix giggles and excitement courses through his scrawny body. His aura pushes outwards and a storm of colors swirl around his figure. Magick responds to magick and I'm curious what Felix's specialty will be, his aura's been constantly changing and hasn't settled yet.

I have a theory, but Gods I hope I'm not right.

Fingers intertwine, separate, then come back together to form a triangle. Some witches harness their magic with focuses or wands, others use the power of the spoken word, but a rare few, like me, call upon the power in our blood with our hands. I rely mostly on my hands, but certain things I use words for. I had to learn everything about myself from the ground up, what worked best and what made me sick from burn out. I often wonder if I'd known how to control this wild power inside me from the start, if I still would have crashed and burned so hard.

If if *if*.

If I do anything right in this world, it will be teaching Felix how to love himself, witch and all.

All of the jars filled with ink need enchanting, but for different reasons. Kitt does many tattoos like mine, ones that can move upon touch, but there are practical ones as well. The glass jars dance above Felix and I's head in a circle, much to his amazement. In truth, I could snap my fingers and the spells would be done, but where's the fun in that?

"And take a seat right here, then we'll get started," Kitt says to someone behind me, then her words are followed by a gasp.

"Oh my, *that's* who charms the ink? I'd like for him to—"

My cheeks burn and thankfully Kitt steps in. "Yes, this is Arlo Rook and his *apprentice*, Felix."

"Oh! I didn't even see you there dearie, well, I won't bother you then."

I glance over my shoulder, spotting a *katan* laid out in a tattoo chair. I give her a halfhearted nod. "Hello there, I'll be finished here in just a moment."

"Oh no worries, I don't mind, in fact I should be thanking you." She laughs nervously, tucking a strand of hair behind her ear.

One by one the jars take on a glow, some are red and others are blue, while a few turn green. "Is that so?" I ask, concentrating on putting the jars away neatly on the shelves they came from, fingers and hands constantly moving.

"Yes, well, I'm getting a reminder tattoo today."

I shake out my hands when the magick show is over, then crack my neck. "I hope it helps. Kitt's the best there is, she does all the hard work."

Before I can turn to face Kitt and her customer, Felix tugs on my hand and whispers, "Mister Arlo, what's a reminder tattoo?"

I chuckle. "Why don't you ask if you can watch?"

Felix bites his lip, debating for a hesitant second. Then he shuffles over, hands in his jacket pockets. Kitt's on her stool, dipping her gun in green ink infused with the telltale sparkle of magick. Her customer lays on her back, forearm resting on the arm of the chair, palm up as she waits.

"I don't mind, Felix, is it?" The *katan* asks.

"Yes, ma'am."

"Come stand over here and listen, all right?" Kitt directs Felix to her side and I lean against a nearby wall, watching the teaching moment. My skin itches to be in the chair again, and I tell Kitt as much.

Before she brings the prepped needle to skin, she glances sideways at me. "Come back in a couple hours, I can fix you up."

"Ah, can't. Quentin and I are going to talk to Gleason this afternoon. What about tomorrow?"

"About *what*?" Kitt balks. I shift to my other foot, waving her on. She glares at me for a moment, then proceeds with her work. "Fine, tomorrow's fine. Bias wants one too."

Minutes pass, stretching into half an hour, and Felix is still as a statue while he watches. Kitt's equipment is enchanted, of course, shortening her work time tremendously. Tendrils of ferns rolled into tight fiddleheads line the *katan's* forearm, laid in a beautiful and vibrant ink but otherwise unremarkable. Felix looks from the tattoo to me, and I gesture for him to pay attention.

"Thea, what would you like to be reminded of?" Kitt asks quietly, leaning back in her chair. She is merely the conductor, relaying the activation words I integrated into the charm. The way she asks, it's like she already knows the answer. She probably does, it's part of the consultation, but the words have to be spoken aloud while the ink's fresh.

Thea sits up, gazing over the fiddleheads in wet awe. "I wish to be reminded every day that I'm happy to be alive."

My eye twitches when the ink swirls to life, spiral heads open and spread their intricate greenery across her sun-touched skin. Many people ask to be reminded of their medication times, who they love or special memories once they've begun to slip away, but I believe this is the first time I've heard this one.

Really, it's not much different than the intention I put behind mine.

Uneasiness settles into my gut as I anticipate Felix's question, but to my surprise, he remains silent. Kitt gives me a curious look, but says nothing as well. Her and Thea square up and go over care instructions, then Thea says her goodbyes and it's just the three of us again.

I don't leave the safety of the wall just yet, instead I watch Felix as he approaches the shelves of ink with a furrowed brow. "He's had a full day." I murmur when Kitt snuggles into my side.

"And you?" She asks knowingly.

I wave her off. "Night, day, it's all the same. Cas hasn't texted me back, have you heard from him?"

"*Ai*, he feels like a jackass, but it sounds like you were one too. You'll hear from him later I bet, once he's found out what you've done."

I rest my chin between her horns and sling an arm around her shoulders. "What's wrong with the bookstore?"

"You're so fucking dense, I swear." Kitt hisses in a whisper. "It's not the *bookstore* that's the problem, it's Q. He's *into* you, Arlo. He's probably thinking, well, you know."

Kitt lowers her voice even farther at the end, even though Felix is fully enraptured by the plants surrounding the ink shelves and hanging upside from the ceiling like they do in the Magpie. He now knows why I insist that plants are important, in the magickal sense.

"*No.*" I gasp, jaw dropping. Kitt elbows me in response. I feign dramatic pain but she isn't having it, she swats me in the stomach for good measure. "He's being *nice*, not every–"

"*Arlo,* all I've heard for a *year* now is Lindsey whining to me about Quentin whining to *her* about how he's hopelessly in love with you. Honestly, you've had no clue? It's kind of obvious the puppy eyes he gives you."

I blink, then rub my face with a sigh. I suppose now that I'm looking at it in *that* light, last night hits much differently. But other than that, I don't see it. "He's hardly talked to me Kitty, last night was the first time we've ever been alone, I think."

Kitt rolls her eyes at me. "Well, he's not exactly alpha material, Lo."

"Alpha material, *Gods* you're so ..." I mutter and absently caress the dragon along my arm. "*Fuck*. There's no living with him without totally fucking our friendship up, is there?"

Kitt pulls her hood up over her horns, the fabric is enchanted to stretch over them when she's wearing it. "Well, that's not even the bad news."

"Hm?"

"Gleason's moved his trip up and he's leaving this afternoon, for good, not just a vacation. We're all to send him off. He sold Thitwhistle's yesterday to Thatch Phantom, right out of the blue. Can you believe he's actually *in* town?"

"Thatch Phantom ... " I echo, and my stomach dips despite the fact I've never met the man. He's a figment of imagination, a philanthropist that's never visited Levena, at least not as long as we've been alive. "The CEO of the Museum?"

"And the Hospital, and the apartment complexes, *and* Scarlet University, yada yada. Crazy, right? I'm supposed to meet with him in preparation for the Game exhibit tomorrow morning, maybe I could talk to him for you?"

My heart pounds at a beat of *Fuck Fuck Fuck* and I've got no clue why.

Felix's head whips around, pupils restricting as my pulse spits and starts. His aura swells to life and bright pink tickles his irises, magick pours around him in shades of cotton candy.

Fuck.

I find my locket and hold it tight, inhaling through my nose and out my mouth. Felix walks over, hands wringing and unaware he's using a *shit* ton of magick right now. I've suspected he's an Empath, and my heart hurts for him. I'll need Tobias to confirm it and the thought of asking him for anything spins my head further.

He takes my hand and looks up at me with wide eyes full of rose color. My heart rate slows tremendously, confirming my suspicion as he unwittingly spreads good feelings and *calm* into my veins. "Are you alright, Mister Arlo?"

I smile, putting all my strength into it. "Yeah, I just forgot the most important rule of doing witchy things."

Felix cocks his head, hair falling and aura retracting as he does. "What's that?"

I hold up a finger, my other hand finds my cocked hip. "Never do magick on an empty stomach."

Felix grins wide and his eyes finally fade to their normal color. "Okay!"

Before we leave, Kitt gives me a long held hug so she can whisper in my ear, "What the fuck was that about?"

"He's like Tobias." I whisper, watching Felix bounce on his heels at the door over her shoulder.

"Oh ... " Kitt pulls back, eyes wide. "Want me to poke Cas?"

I shake my head and squeeze her shoulder. "No, I got this."

She smiles, and it's genuine. "I know you do."

Stars and Galaxies

Thatch

"Coconut water, *really*? I had no idea. And you don't ... *miss* it? The taste?"

Helena laughs, filling the cafe with her bright amusement. "No, not at all, I prefer the sweetness over the tanginess of blood, and it's *so* much easier to find instead of drinking from kinky weirdos. This is it, well, go on then, try it. Anyone would love it, vampire or no."

I peer into the cozy mug that's new to me, inspecting the clear, iced liquid inside. 'Boss' is boldly inlaid in a nice blue against the white ceramic. Swirls, books and coffee cups detail the piece. I was quite surprised to find it waiting for me when I arrived this morning. I hardly know these folk, but they're quite kind. I tip the drink back, relishing in the sweet, if not subtle taste of coconut water.

"Amazing, what will they come up with next?" I say, grinning wide. Helena laughs, as does the stout treant beside her. "Oh, Rhea, if you wouldn't mind, I'd adore some tips for managing this." I playfully stroke at the scruff along my face, then reach into my pocket and jot a few things onto my notepad, specifically the latest blood alternative.

Rhea raises a leafy brow, reaching up with a birch bark composed arm to tug at their own beard that rivals mine ten fold. Theirs matches the wild curls of black sprouting with vines of contrasting white primroses atop their head. "Come see me in a few years, when the hair on your chest thinks about erupting."

I laugh, hand on my stomach. If only they knew how old I truly am.

But that's what I love about this, no one knows *what* I am. I'm just Thatch here. Only Gleason seems to remember me, part of me anyway, and he'll be gone soon. Anyone in Levena who recognizes me, recognizes the name, not the person. Of course, Dusan remembers me more consistently than the rest do, but it's still not *me*. The thing is, Thatch Phantom and *just* Thatch are two very different people.

A rich, mysterious royal from a faraway land who is well known for his philanthropy.

And a bored, *chaotic,* ancient being who wallows in loneliness and good looks.

I leave Rhea and Helena to their work as another rush of patrons flood the cafe, keeping them on their toes at only seven am. I noticed yesterday their breaks don't last very long. I add training the new barista to my mental checklist, and possibly hiring a librarian who can handle things while I'm gone. I can't decide whether to make Rhea or Helena manager, they've both been here for a couple years and are equally capable. There's two bakers as well, but I haven't met them personally yet.

I slide into a booth nestled into the alcove I've claimed as mine, opting to do my work right here in the cafe as opposed to in the back, hiding among the books as Gleason did. To be fair, this nook is separated from the rest, hiding under a window with the curtains drawn. The table is cracked in places and worn, but paint dances around the flaws in the shape of foxes, paws, and swirling vines.

I feel like I can breathe back here, the atmosphere is remarkably quiet and peaceful, almost as if the section is not even part of the cafe. But in all reality, it's not that far removed from the main area. I scratch at my beard and dig through my mess of papers, smiling when I find my to do list. A name is circled at the top.

Arlo Rook.

I've learned his family name from Gleason, and that he still lives in the Castle. I knew that he grew up there, but I thought he would've left after the last time I saw him. He aged out of the system, so the last name must be something he gave himself. I gather my things, haphazardly stacking papers so they'll fit inside my leather binder which I snap shut with difficulty. I slip it inside my backpack, one that hasn't seen the light of day in decades but does its job all the same. I sling it over my back, then take off in search of my old draconian friend.

The chilly streets filled with lazy neighbors are barely warmed by trapped sunlight skirting the ravine and mountains in the east. Garren Castle isn't far from Thitwhistle's at all, and I wonder what it would be like to live in the store all the time. I shove my hands in my hoodie pockets and turn my face to the sky, inhaling fresh air.

Stars, how I've missed it.

I'll have to take a closer look at the cottage today, but from the quick glance I got upon arrival it appeared abandoned and *severely* flooded. I left it under Chauncey's care before I disappeared last time and while I know the centaur is getting up there in years, I can't imagine he died or left his post. Dusan may know more.

I pass through the iron wrought gates that reach for a cloudless sky. Cold fingers escape the warmth of my pockets to trail over the intricate detailing of vines and buds on the cool bars slick with dew. The lights are on inside Garren Castle and the front door is open, but when I reach the threshold I meet an impenetrable force. I frown, extending my palm out until it's stopped by an invisible ward. I contemplate drawing on my limited magick to break it, but I don't want to accelerate my stay or piss off the witch who made it.

I need to save the shreds of magick I'm allowed for the Game, and for staying as long as I can. The ward is warm, incredibly strong and unrelenting.

After a moment of searching, I find a doorbell in the stone pillar to the left of the threshold and give it a push. No sound follows, but a bright and twiggy girl pops out from the front door. She stands on the top step and stares down at me, dressed in rainbow overalls that are a tad too short and mismatched shoes, hands on her hips. Wildflowers are tucked into her striped, colorful socks, and I decide that I *must* try doing the same.

"May I help you?" She asks, much too warily for a child.

I bow at the waist. "How do you do? I am Thatch Phantom, a good friend of your Headmaster, is she in?"

The girl stares me down with apprehension, then decides something. Her hands drop to her sides. "She is, just a moment." In a flash of color she disappears back inside the castle. I wait patiently, kept company by a flock of songbirds attending one of the many feeders and baths decorating the front lawn.

"Who's there?" Dusan's question brings my attention back to the door. She stands there in all her elegance, an odd expression cast upon her beautifully aged face. The years have been fair to her.

I give her a wide smile. "Dusan, you're as lovely as ever. May I come in?"

I gesture to the space between us, but the swiftly changing emotions rushing over her features are painfully familiar and I wonder if I've made a mistake. I know that look. The look of someone who had a dream about you, or they only remember the fuzzy edges of 'what's their name' from 'back in the day.'

Or even worse, they have no clue who you are at all and showing up like an old friend is a definite bad idea.

Dusan stares at me and I curse myself for thinking that for a *minute,* just a minute, that I had people to welcome me home.

I wait in silence, watching the confusion clear from her eyes. She smiles softly and my shoulders relax. She's the only one over the years that's consistently remembered me. Each year the recall is longer and longer for the draconian, and I know there *will* be a day when I have to introduce myself all over again to her and she will have none of the memories we've shared.

Perhaps next time I should arrive as a stranger. I've never been gone this long, and who knows how long it will be next time. It's for the best.

"Of course, Thatch Phantom, you are welcome to enter."

The ward dissipates with her words, but the moment I pass through it conjures to life once more. I turn back, wondering what color it is and who put it there, but Dusan hurriedly embraces me. I hug her, chuckling. "Missed me?"

"Oh Thatch, it's been too long. I ... well, come on in."

I follow behind Dusan as she leads me inside. "You'll have to forgive our security measures, since the Taking, things have been a bit ... *different*, since the last time you visited."

"The Taking?" I ask, slowing her step. She looks over shoulder at me and her brows furrow, contrasting her soft smile. "I've missed a lot, haven't I?" I ask, words punching out of my chest one by one.

"Yes, my dear, yes you have."

We settle into her office and I take a seat in one of the chairs before her desk. Dusan curls up in the one beside me, knees casually pulled up to her chest and piercing eyes set on me. She's dressed a bit more posh than last time, but it *has* been eighty years. I extend my hand to the draconian I first met when she was only a child, and even though thousands of years differentiate us, she's the one who appears as an elder.

She takes it and grips tight. "I've missed you, Thatch. Levena hasn't been the same without you."

I smile, but it's not as easy this time. "Tell me, what is this Taking?"

Dusan sighs, long and heavy. "Remember Leon?"

I rack my brain for a moment, coming up with a *malakim* boy, Arlo's age.

Oh.

I frown upon remembering the day I found him attempting to murder Arlo near the river. I don't forget a thing, but it takes a second to retrieve facts from their well organized and deeply buried drawers. "Of course I do. I brought Arlo home after they ... well, you remember."

Dusan shakes her head. "He got so much worse after that, Leon did... I failed that one. I didn't reach him when he was here, and he turned so far into the dark there was no getting him back. He terrorized Levena, plain and simple. It was Arlo versus Leon for years."

The thought of Leon hurting Arlo again heats my blood. "Tell me, when this happened, did Leon seem ... himself?"

"I–I don't know. I don't think I ever got to the heart of Leon to know who he truly was. The only person who did, well, he doesn't like to talk about it. Why, is there something in play I should know about?" Her vertical pupils constrict, evaluating me.

She knows I'm more than a mysterious royal. Magickal beings that can travel between worlds are rare but not unheard of, so she's never guessed what I *truly* am. I'm not allowed to say it, and no one has entertained the idea, if only because my history has been erased time and time again.

Leon wasn't always a prick, but the last time I saw him he definitely had that look in his eye. The hollowness of the unsatisfied. I chew on her words for a moment. "I don't think so. Sometimes, evil just *is*." She appraises me, not entirely satisfied with my answer. I add, "Oh, before I forget." I sling my backpack that's ripping at the seams onto my lap, then dig around until I find a rather large envelope.

Dusan raises a brow when I give it to her. "I have some of the money you gave me before."

"Well, you're not spending enough then, add to the castle, build another school or something." I wave her off and she sighs, shoulders relaxing. "I've always appreciated what you've done here, and it seems you're doing well. That runt who met me out front was a charmer."

Dusan chuckles as she leaves her seat, approaching the wall behind her desk. "Kleo usually is, she's in a fine mood this morning though. She's rather attached to one of the kids her age, and he's out for the day doing witch things, or so I'm told. Plus, she has prospective families coming to visit her today."

I shift in my seat, zipping my backpack up. Silence falls as Dusan taps the wall, unlocking the false patch of sheet rock which swings open to reveal an eight foot tall safe, which when opened displays neatly organized shelves full of treasures. "Oh? And who might the resident witch be?"

Dusan glances at me over her shoulder, grinning like a cat with a canary. "Arlo, of course."

I tug at the hems of my sleeves, heart quickening. "I, uh, ran into him last night. Quite literally."

"Oh? Did he—"

"No, of course not. You're the only special one." I blurt out with a tight smile. "I asked him to show me around town, but you would've thought I asked him to shovel shit." I mumble, and Dusan laughs softly. She leans against the side of her desk closest to me and crosses her ankles. Her laughter fades and she stares at her bare feet for a contemplative moment.

"He seems different." I try, but she gives me a withering look.

"That is one story I will not tell, for it is not mine, but yes. Arlo is no longer the man you once met." Dusan pinches the thin bridge of her nose.

I stand, taking to pacing. "No, the person I met then was a man clinging to his boyhood. The person I met last night *was* a man, and a troubled one."

"Perhaps, but I think he's moving in the right direction. He's looking for a place to stay, and I believe he completed an interview with the college a few days ago. Of course his impending employment is hearsay, he doesn't tell me much anymore."

I stop pacing and turn on my heel, facing her with a mischievous grin. "Funny thing is, I bought Thitwhistle's yesterday and am looking to fill one of the apartments."

Dusan stares at me, eye twitching. "You ... *bought* Thitwhistle's? Is one of those things like the museum, or the hospital? And don't you already own a bookstore, *Shh*?"

I throw my hands up. "Hey! I'm investing in Levena. What they put my name on makes no difference to me."

It's not like it's my full, actual name, anyway.

She raises a brow. "Mhm."

I chuckle, putting my hands up. "Serious, I'm not changing a thing, the cafe is perfect. Have you been there?"

She nods knowingly. "Yes, Thatch, I've been there. All stars and galaxies."

My cheeks burn. "Well, yes, the artwork *is* wonderful, isn't it? Oh, have you spoken with Chauncey? I went round the cottage yesterday and it was flooded, locked up tight."

Dusan blinks in surprise. "I believe it was last week I spoke to him, he came to town for his usual supply run. I haven't been down in some time, but last I knew everything was fine."

I rub my chin, a solid feeling of *wrong* has my fingers twitching. "Hmm, suppose I'll have to break in then and see for myself."

"Would you like me to come with you?" Dusan raises a white brow, and I wave her off.

"No, that's fine. Honestly, if I have the bookstore to return to that's well enough, I'm more curious about Chauncey than fixing things up." I smile, but it's a tired thing. I want to enjoy my time here, not think about my inevitable departure.

Dusan crosses the room and cradles my face in her heated palms. "Can't you stay this time?"

I sigh, turning into her hand. She asks me this every visit. "Have you found a way to make it so?"

"No, but to be fair, I don't know what you are, why you have to go. Have you learned anything?"

I close my eyes, they're burning. That's not a good sign, I physically *can't* shed tears until I'm close to the end. Dusan is my longest living, and only friend, and I cannot tell her a true thing about me. The laws of the universe are unyielding, so all I can do is lie or avoid.

"No, but I always find my way back, don't I?"

"That you do Thatch Phantom, that you do."

Before leaving, I have one more question for Dusan Garren. She escorts me to the iron gates reaching to a much different sky than I encountered earlier, the early chilled morning has given way to a strengthening, heated day.

With a mischievous grin, I ask, "How have the past few Games been?"

She chuckles, a roarous thing that sparks to life in her draconic gut. "Fine, I guess."

"*Fine*?" I hold a palm to my chest. "Oy, this is no good. Perhaps I can play this year, shake things up."

"You, play the Game? I'd like to see that." Dusan remarks, staring up at the sky with a tender expression. "You'll have stiff competition from Arlo, he's a diehard."

I laugh with my whole heart, quite literally shaking the mountain range a few miles away, tumbling rocks into a ravine filled with goat carcasses thrown by golden eagles. It happens sometimes, I can't always restrain the part of me that is *everything,* the *world,* when my emotions get the best of me. Regardless, I enjoy the moment knowing no one has been crushed by my joy.

"Oh my, this is going to be fun."

Arlo

Rumors have spread in the short time before noon and we have to wait in line at Thitwhistle's.

Outside.

Patio tables with navy umbrellas and white chairs with pretty latticework in the back are arranged along the storefront, carefully arranged so as to not interrupt the full beauty of my mural. All of the brand new seating is full of patrons, and many new faces I don't recognize are mingled in with my neighbors. We're a couple hours early for Gleason's official 'send off,' but I'm glad for it.

I despise crowds, but I care for Gleason, even if he's up and leaving like it's nothing. I've often wondered what it would be like to do so, but I can't imagine anything past the borders of Levena. All I picture are the fields, endless swathes of wheatgrass tall enough to hide even my giant figure. I crane my neck, trying to get a good look inside. I really hope Thatch didn't change the inside too much.

Pixies hover in the air in front of Felix and I and a group of sleepy college kids wait behind us. His hand's been gripping mine nonstop since we left Kitt's, and he's been quiet again. I debate on taking off my jacket, the sun has awakened with a passion. We move a few feet ahead, a big group files out of the place and I peer inside one of the windows in search of the retired owner, only to find a sea of people.

Perhaps this is a bad idea.

Breathe in. Breathe out. It'll be fine.

My phone vibrates and I dutifully check it, finding a text from Cas and Quentin. An unsuspecting email icon wiggles in the upper bar but I ignore it. It's probably spam, definitely *not* a rejection email from the university. Caspian and crew are on their way, along with Quentin, he's able to meet earlier than planned and leaves a smiley face at the end of his message. I turn over Kitt's words and have no clue how to handle this.

We're grown adults, if push comes to shove I'm sure we can live together without me having to break Quentin's heart. He's a good one, but I can't see myself loving someone again. The dark side of my mind whispers *liar* and conjures eyes filled with fireworks and hands tight on my sides, but I swiftly bury the warmth in my gut.

"Mister Arlo, it's our turn." Felix whispers, tugging me towards the door and away from the curious students behind us. I give him a smile and a wink, allowing him to lead me inside. Nothing has changed, but the atmosphere is lighter than usual and the air's charged with excitement. Rhea and Helena are hard at work behind the counter and I finally spot Gleason working the cash register. Felix's eyes are wide and I can only imagine what it feels like to be around so many people, so many *feelings*.

"Let's go over here." I lead Felix over to my corner of the cafe, an alcove with a booth and table detailed with foxes and pawprints which distract you from the runic carvings on the underside. We'll be protected here, give Felix a chance to breathe. The moment we slide into the booth, the weight of hundreds of chaotic energies melt away. The overwhelming scene muffles slightly as well, and when we sit Felix looks up to me suddenly.

His eyes swell with awe and he reaches for my face. "Mister Arlo, what's that?"

I take my phone out with a furrowed brow and look at the screen, then bite my lip upon seeing my mark simmering with a soft glow.

"*Oh*," is all I can muster before Caspian and the others file in, all in good spirits and full of hellos.

Kitt and Lindsey sit on the other side of Felix, holding hands and soft smiles. Gowan takes a seat beside them, the dandelions across her crown blooming as she yawns. Quentin slides in beside me, hands wrung tight between his knees. Caspian wheels his chair up to the open side of the table with a bouncing

Marlena in his lap and bags under his eyes, tainting his sleepy grin. Tobias stares at me for a moment too long after he says hello, then settles next to Quentin with a sleeping Zeke tucked against his chest.

I dare say Quentin is the best dressed out of the group, contrasting the hoodies and loungewear trend between the rest of my friends. His black halter top and light wash skinny jeans are clean and wrinkle free, his neck adorned with the charmed crystal necklace I gave him shortly after we met.

After sobering up, I remembered giving it to him with the intent to ward off assholes. I don't believe he ever takes it off. Quentin's hair is artfully slicked back and his eyes are painted gold, complementing the green flecks in his irises.

He catches me staring, then flushes and looks away with a tiny smile.

Good job Arlo, that's helping.

"How's your Witch Day going, Felix?" Tobias asks, breaking through the idle catch up chatter the others are engaged in. I told him what I could through text and he agreed to help me out.

"Good Mister Bias, I've learned a lot, Mister Arlo is a good teacher, and a good witch." Felix beams at Bias whose pink eyes slide to mine.

"He is, isn't he?" Bias leans over Quentin's side and silky smooth rosy hair curtains his face, brushing against my arm. He whispers to Felix, "Can I tell you a secret?"

Felix nods, eyes wide.

"I'm a witch, too." Tobias presses a finger to his upturned lips, then extends his arm and calls upon his magick which glows a soft pale pink just under his porcelain white skin. As much as I tried to in the beginning, there's no hating Tobias, or Caspian for loving his soulmate. He's a pure and kind soul, nothing less. I think it's more me that's the problem.

No, I *know* that it's me.

Felix gasps, hands over his mouth. He looks around. "But, why is it a secret? Mister Arlo doesn't keep it a secret."

This fucking kid misses nothing, have I mentioned that?

Bias' smile softens and he leans back. "Some of us prefer it that way, but I don't mind if those closest to me know, so count yourself special."

Bias readjusts the tiny *shedim* onto his other shoulder, then musses Felix's hair. Caspian's surprisingly distant from the conversation, giving energetic Marlena his entire cooing attention. He won't look at me and I inwardly sigh. I thought things were fixed.

"Thank you, Mister Bias." Felix bows his head, practically vibrating at my side.

Quentin bumps elbows with me and I avoid Kitt's heavy gaze from across the table. "How're you feeling this morning?" He asks shyly.

I shrug. "Pretty good, but I stopped long before you guys, so not much of a headache." Caspian mutters something about *'being a martyr doesn't help'* and I glare at him. "Doc's was fine, too." I add, much to his chagrin.

No one speaks for a moment, then Quentin clears his throat and looks over to the counter with no line. "Want to get our order with me? We can look for Gleason too, he was at the counter earlier."

I nod, then pat Felix's shoulder. "Could you stay here with Kitt for a few?"

Felix nods, scooting close to Kitt who rubs against his cheek with one of her horns. Quentin and I slide out of the booth and the moment we step away from the alcove, the noise of the cafe intensifies immensely. I check my phone, it's just now lunchtime and the place is full, bookstore and cafe both, not to mention the outside seating.

Rhea and Helen relax against a counter and wall respectively, joined by another barista who's turned away, doing dishes in an industrial sink that rests against the center wall dividing bookstore from cafe.

"Hey guys, seems like the turn out isn't half bad, eh?" I ask, stretching my arms overhead. Quentin slides his hands into his pockets, smiling nervously up at me as my jacket and shirt lifts. Is he watching me more than usual or am I just noticing more?

Damn Kitt, I wish she let me keep on being oblivious.

"Half bad I guess so, but Gleason's happy enough, so that's all that matters. All today's profits go to him, and we get double time today, too." Helena chirps, the vampire leaves the wall to join her treant companion leaning on the counter. "New boss isn't too bad."

"Thatch Phantom, right? Kitt is so nervous to meet him," Quentin says with a shiver.

"Oh, she'll be fine, he's a sweetheart. The usual, guys?" Rhea stands from the counter, gesturing between us with a knowing grin that pulls up the handsome black gnarls in their wooden complexion. The dishwasher shuts off the sink and sets the last coffee mug in the dish rack.

"Yeah, all of us plus Felix," I say, watching the treant and vampire get to work.

"Is that right? Any luck with that last family?" Helena asks over the whir of the espresso machine. I shake my head, frowning. "That's too bad, he's a good kid."

"They always are," I say, and that's that.

I pick out an extra box of pastries to bring back to the castle, loading up with enough baked goods to clear the case. Quentin handles the drink carriers and before we leave, my attention catches on Helena. "By chance, do you know where Gleason went? Or, when Thatch will be back? I suppose he'd be the one to talk to about the apartments."

"Oh? Gleason's just outside, but Thatch is—" Helena's iridescent eyes flash to Rhea snorting, then down to the dishwasher digging around in the pastry case, hood pulled down around their face as they struggle to pull out the empty trays. "Boss, *really*?"

The person stands and my heart palpitates in response to my magick's upcoming symphony. Waves of tightly coiled copper flow from beneath his hood, covering one of his striking oceanic eyes. His mouth's stuffed full of scone, and mocha icing dots his nose. I bite my cheek in attempts to reel in my magick, a few heads turn in response to the mark on my face glowing brighter than a fucking neon sign.

Hello, witches.

And *no*, it's not him. He's not my person, so stop looking between us with those smug grins.

"Oh, hello again," he says over attempts to choke down his food. "You guys missed one." He points to his reddened cheeks full of scone.

"Oh! You already know each other? Why were you hiding then, boss?" Helena asks, and the questions in Quentin's eyes multiply. I rub the back of my neck in anticipation.

"No, he just—I just, *we* ran each other last night." Thatch gestures between us hastily with icing covered fingers, curls bouncing. His eyes linger on mine for a second, but he otherwise avoids looking directly at me. "I did not feel the need to bother you again."

His gaze hardly falls on Quentin, but Quen can't stop staring at the man with a smile brighter than the sun. Wait.

Wait. Thatch.

Thatch *Phantom*.

Oh, *shit*.

I extend my hand over the counter, cursing my past self. I pull out my polite and professional voice. "It was no trouble, and I'm sorry you caught me in a pissy mood. I'm Arlo Rook, and I'm assuming you're Thatch Phantom?"

A split second passes and I wait for him to laugh. This man dressed in a hoodie and sweats, working alongside his baristas, could not *possibly* be the CEO of multiple projects and the mysterious figure who funds half of Levena.

But, as fate would have it, he takes a firm hold of my hand. Sugar and warmth sticks to my skin. He stares right through me and with a mischievous grin he says, "Just Thatch is fine, and you don't need to play nice just because you've found out who I am. You were quite miffed at me last night, and rightfully so I might add. Nothing broken I hope?"

I swallow and shove my tingling hand into my jacket pocket and shake my head. "Honestly, no big deal."

Thatch shrugs, then shakes Quentin's hand after he shifts the drink carriers around. "Quentin Matsdotter." Quen breathes, eyes wide.

"Nice to meet you, Quentin." Thatch claps Rhea and Helena both on their shoulders, leaving sugary hand prints. "You've done well today, I'll clean up after closing. You've still got the tickets for tomorrow, right?"

"Sure do, thanks boss," Helena says and Rhea thanks him as well. Thatch gives Quentin and I a quick two fingered salute, then starts for the back end of the store.

"Wait, Mr. Phantom," I blurt out, veins pounding with the surge of magick trying to break free and reach Thatch. He half turns to look over his shoulder, a devious smile playing at his full lips. "*Are* you interested in renting out those apartments?"

"Just Thatch, and," Thatch *winks* at me and says, "can't, thanks."

Then he walks away, disappearing into the labyrinth of bookshelves.

This is Bad

Thatch

I brace myself against the wall, staring at the long mirror resting against the floral wallpaper of my bedroom. *My* bedroom. That's bizarre to say.

I can't *believe* I said that to him with a straight face. I breathe in and out a few times in rapid succession, then reach for my hood and pull off my top layers of clothing.

I felt the warmth along my hip this time, but I have to know. Hopefully being in the same building as him is enough to trigger it. I turn and pull down the hem of my sweatpants, smiling when I spy the vibrant gash of a soulmark following my padded, unmarred hip bone.

I've finally found him.

I exhale heavily, wiping away my smile with reality. I've truly found him, but I can't *do* anything about it. *Shouldn't* do anything about it. In a week's time, maybe two if I take it easy, I'll be nothing, *gone*, and he won't remember me, *again*.

I've never cared about being forgotten, not really, but I know if I returned and stared into his eyes only to find a stranger there, in *him*, my soulmate, my heart would shatter. It took me decades to return this time and the question that haunts my nights floods my mind.

What if I don't return at all, next time?

I should forget he exists.

I should be happy being alone.

I should be selfless.

I should leave him be.

But *don't* I want to run back downstairs and tell him, 'yeah sure, you can move in.'

A solid knock raps on my door twice and I throw my hoodie over my bare chest, then sprint to answer it. Gleason's there, flushed and wide eyed. "Why won't you rent to Arlo?"

Fucking stars.

"Oh? Is that what he said?" I ask, stepping out of the way to let Gleason in.

He shakes his head, plants his feet. "Not him, and not in so many words. I've told you he's a good boy, he'd treat you well as a landlord. I didn't see you as the type to discriminate, Thatch." Gleason frowns.

I balk. "*Discriminate*? What on earth are you talking about?"

"It's because he's a witch, innit? Why else would you've told him no?"

Oh, *fuck*. I pinch the bridge of my nose. "No, *no*, I'm ... renovating the other apartment before I have anyone move in. And this one too, but it's mine for now." I gesture at the empty apartment that still smells like Gleason, cider and dusty tomes. "Not moving anything or anyone in until I'm done. I'll clear things up with him, don't worry. I know how dear he is to you."

Gleason's frown softens a tad, his shoulders drop. "Ah, I see. I didn't pin you for a bigot, it warms my heart to know I'm right. I trust he'll be allowed to stay then? I know the place is officially yours, but, he's a good one, that Arlo is. Do right by him for me, will you? Silas too, I know he's young, but ... he's got nowhere else."

I nod, charming smile on. "Of course, consider it done. It's almost time, right?"

"*Ai*, that it is. You'll be there?" His arms drop and his crinkled eyes brighten.

I rest a hand on Gleason's shoulder. "Wouldn't miss it for anything."

I had thought about changing into something more dapper, but I find myself standing outside in the same jogger pants and hoodie combination I've been wearing and working in all day. My hair is a mess and a sheen of sweat taints my clothes.

Thitwhistle's is empty and the street is full, Arlo isn't hard to miss but I don't think he's seen me yet. Gleason is surrounded by his community and a pile of luggage, not to mention his air balloon and crew in the street behind him. I wonder how he got permission to take off right in town instead of at the port outside of town. Arlo and his group of friends are next in line to say their goodbyes and I watch with curiosity.

His friends are quite a mishmash of characters, all different races and mostly the same age, relatively, except for the pre-teen boy keeping close to Arlo's side. I didn't see him earlier and I wonder who he is to Arlo. They don't look alike, and from what

I've heard Arlo has no lover. But the way they look at each other and behave, you would think they were father and son.

When Arlo's not looking, his friends take turns appraising him with long held stares filled with warmth and subtle worry. The moment I stepped outside, Arlo's mark flared under the post-noon sun and the pink haired *malakim* stared at Arlo like he had grown two heads. Everyone is born with a soul mark, one of the many things on my list I fact checked to keep up with the times. I'm not sure why this person is surprised at the premise of Arlo having a soulmate.

He doesn't really seem *that* grumpy, and his apology seemed genuine. I find myself wanting to know more about him, my craving at its strongest since we've reunited. What kind of person has he become since I've been gone?

Come *on*, Thatch, you *can't*.

The group says goodbye to Gleason one by one. Arlo hunches over to hug the old bookkeeper with massive arms that wrap around Gleason entirely. After they pull away, I watch Arlo softly laugh on the sidelines while the *qieren* tells a story, the first time I've seen such a thing from him.

During my last visit he didn't laugh, either. Smiled a lot, but never laughed. Even this one is restrained, rough around the edges, but it makes my heart sing all the same. Quentin's watching him, too, and I wonder if they're together. I wrinkle my nose at the thought.

Out of nowhere, Arlo's sharp attention cuts through the crowd and fixates on me hiding near the store for a few heavy seconds. He looks down at the boy who says something, then back up to me with a subtle smile. His mouth moves, but I can't make out what he's saying.

Thatch, you *can't*.

Gleason boards his air balloon, stepping into the gigantic woven basket as the orange and red striped balloon fills with gas and the fabric goes taut. The crowd thickens, pushing together and waving at the well loved Gleason Thitwhistle. Arlo hauls the boy up onto his shoulders and both of them wave in unison. The moment is so damn perfect, I can't help but add a little bit of my own magick to the fanfare. I'll have to draw on it for the Game anyway, and there's no sense in delaying the inevitable. It's only a little bit.

And it's not like I can stay.

I lift my chin and purse my lips, releasing a silent whistle that paints a double rainbow across the sky. Ribbons of color grow stark against fluffy clouds and center overhead our little slice of heaven. The two man crew pull in the sandbags and turn up the fire. Gleason says his final goodbye before taking to the sky, waving to me in the back of the crowd.

"Have a wonderful adventure!" I shout, waving back like a fool. The others repeat my sentiment and the crowd doesn't disperse until the balloon is well beyond the city horizon. I lose sight of Arlo and decide it's for the best that I stop looking for him. I've met him again, he's doing well, I think. I can't ask for more than his health and happiness.

But, I make it three steps inside and crash into Arlo Rook all over again. This time he's ready for me with steady hands and a stunning smile that renders me speechless.

Arlo

Thatch is soft.

I wrangle my treacherous smile, allowing my hands to slowly drop once I'm sure he won't take off. The world flows around us, an indiscernible blur in the background as I fully absorb the man cast in warm daylight before me. Magick ricochets off the chamber walls of my heart and I take a steady breath to contain myself. I study him inch by inch, starting with his luminous, sky blue eyes.

I *know* it was his magick outside. I can see the remains of it in his eyes, but something tells me he's not a witch. He's something far more powerful, but I can't figure out what. There's like a ... shield or something that his magick's pressed against, hiding the signature.

The logical part of me searches him for a mark.

Not a wrinkle tarnishes his face, save for a few lines reserved for laughter, handsomely crinkling the edges of his eyes and lips. I wander over freckles, tiny scars and a beauty spot below his right eye. Ginger eyelashes capture sunlight as he blinks once in time suspended. His carotid pounds underneath a mess of a beard. No mark.

Thatch is soft, firm enough for a hard day's work around the shop, but he's certainly no gym rat. His arms hide beneath the same cotton hoodie he was working in earlier. Thumbs are looped through holes in the sleeves and nails are chewed to the quick, delicate skin angry. No mark.

A matching set of earthy joggers hang loosely on his bottom half and black high tops hide the rest of his skin. My eyes travel back up to his face, only leaving it for a second during my evaluation. Thick copper curls pile out from under his pulled up hood, hiding his neck and ears. No mark.

Who *is* this person?

Time resumes its normal pace and the sounds of a heavily packed Thitwhistle's intrudes upon my ear drums. Thatch blinks again, calm as he lifts his chin. His lips softly part, drawing subtle attention to his cupid's bow.

Fuck.

"Yes, Arlo?" He asks, and it's such a simple thing. Like we're old friends.

I take off my beanie and rake my hair back, then slip it back on and clear my throat. "I don't know, honestly. I have nothing clever, other than I meant what I said, before. I like Just Thatch, and that's who I'd like to show around town, if you change your mind that is, and still need a guide." I absently straighten my jacket, flushed.

Thatch chuckles, scratching at his beard as he stares up at me, contemplating. "I misjudged you, Arlo. I apologize, one can't be too sure of a stranger's intentions, especially when they have such a change of heart."

"Is that what we are? Strangers?" I ask, immediately surprised at myself.

Thatch's mischievous smile fades for a second, then he recovers with vigor. "I suppose so, but I *am* still in need of a guide for the festival. I've obviously visited the city in my brief visits, but I'm curious to know Levena like someone who lives here would."

I laugh softly, but my heart aches. He's not wrong, but I feel ... cheated, in a sense.

"You have only seen the surface, I assure you."

His eyes brighten and he holds his elbows. "You'll do it then?"

He reminds me of a child being told they have prospective parents coming to visit. Eyes brighten like they've never seen a summer's day, and for the first time they can see not only the bright blue sky, but the fluffy clouds that float by in peculiar shapes.

"I'd be delighted, we only missed the first night of the festival, which is just a lot of partying anyway, like you saw. Pre-Game, they call it," I say, and his face bursts with so much fucking excitement I might just—

Oh, *no.*

This is bad.

He claps his hands together and does a little hop, feet barely leaving the ground. His hood bounces back a tad and more bright curls fall out. His ears poke through, they're rounded and he's being too fucking cute right now.

"Okay, okay! Tonight then, is that too soon? I have ... *flooding,* issues to take care of this afternoon, otherwise I'd be ready now. What's first? Ah, I'm getting too excited, I apologize."

I rest my hands on his shoulders, steadying him with a grin even though my nerves are fucking fried. "Tonight works. Did you need help, with the flooding?" My hands slide away from his painfully familiar body once more and it feels so odd. He does *not* feel like a stranger.

But he is.

Not for long, if I have anything to say about it. Why, who knows. I can hear Kitt's *I told you so from here.*

I wiggle my fingers playfully. "I'm pretty good at cleaning up messes, and it would be a good teaching moment for my apprentice, but I don't want to intrude."

Thatch's rounded shoulders relax. "Apprentice? For what?"

I raise my brows, playing dumb. "Pretty sure you're the one who yelled witch for all to see last night, must be you can tell one way or another."

He frowns. "Looking back on it, that was rather foolish, wasn't it?"

I shrug. "We're even in my eyes."

His smile doesn't return in full force, but he nods. "Alright then. Allow me to get changed and close up, then I'll be down. It's just down off the shore, on Leideen Ait." Thatch turns away and I follow him, unable to do anything else.

"Chauncey's place?" I ask, coming to a stop at the counter when a shiver runs through me. "I was just there last week, he didn't mention anything, and we haven't had any rain."

Thatch nods, brows furrowing as he pauses at the archway leading to the bookstore section. He drums on the wall with lithe fingers, considering. "*My* place, technically, he's the care-taker. I haven't been able to find him or get into the house, but when I looked into the windows, I saw water. Dusan said she spoke to him last week as well, how odd. Why were *you* there, if I may ask?"

His place? Dusan?

"Uh, charms. Chauncey likes charms. You know Dusan … and own Leideen Cottage?" I struggle to process how entwined he is in my life without my knowing.

Thatch's grin lights up his entire face. "You'll find we have a lot in common, Arlo," he says, then ducks away into the back. I've been to the upstairs a couple times, back when Gleason was sick with cancer and needed what modern drugs couldn't give him. My magick plays on the threads between life and death. Some come to me to keep them alive, or send them off peacefully.

Of course there's much more to my magick than that, but that's my specialty. All witches have one.

I take off in search of the others waiting outside for me. I had left in such a hurry, only staying long enough after the rainbow erupted to ask Kitt if she'd watch Felix.

When I step outside, I'm surprised to find storm clouds are brewing and the wind's picked up. The Misfits and Felix linger near a stone fountain down the street, one of many. This one has two dragons spitting water into the sky, water clean and considerably deep in the large bath. Sprites dive in and out of the water, clutching coins to their bellies like otters. I catch up to my friends just in time to catch Felix asking Kitt how much longer I'd be.

"Hey, I'm back." I announce, out of breath and heart racing. I brace myself, hands on my knees as I recover. I didn't run but feel as if I did, maybe Doc took more out of me than I thought. I don't feel tired, quite the opposite. Jittery. Magick overflowing and not enough at the same time.

"Mister Arlo, are you alright?" Felix asks, jumping off the fountain's edge.

I wave him off. "Yeah, fine. Just a lil' out of shape is all." Kitt raises her brows but otherwise doesn't question it, Caspian too. I'm anything *but* out of shape and it's not due to any effort. I just *am*.

"Any luck?" Tobias asks from beside Quentin and Kitt on the fountain's edge, opposite Caspian and the kids nestled in his lap. Quentin clasps his hands tightly, looking down at his feet.

"Kinda. He didn't say anything about the apartment, but sounds like I've got myself a side job while he's here." The words border on false, now that I think about it. We didn't discuss payment. *Is* it a job? A date?

No, he told me when we first met he wasn't looking for *that*. Hm.

Nothing sounds quite right.

"That's great!" Kitt says, jumping off the fountain to join Felix and I. The others hang back, the tension palpable. Quentin looks up, he and Gowan both eye me suspiciously.

"You'll be busy," Quentin says, almost hollow sounding, then he stands, recovering his good mood before I can say anything. He rests a hand on my shoulder. "That's good though, right?"

I shrug, rubbing the back of my neck. "I think so. We'll find something else."

And that was the *wrong* thing to say, because Quentin grins wide. "Okay."

A moment passes between us and I tug at my ear, then smile at him and give my attention to Felix. I kneel and brush hair away from his eyes, then straighten his hat. "How are you doing?"

He smiles, but it's fleeting. "I'm having a good day, Mister Arlo. We're not ... done, are we?"

I stand and dancing spots overtake the sides of my vision. I resist the urge to shake my head and take hold of Quentin so I don't fall. I really need to sleep, maybe this should wait ....

Instead I say, "No, in fact, Mr. Phantom has a job for us, right now. How does that sound?"

Felix's brows raise and so does one side of his lips, forming a lopsided smile. "I'd like that."

"'Course you would. Got the pastries? We better drop those off on the way." I jut a thumb over my shoulder, fingers tingling.

"Right here, his arms were getting tired," Bias says, holding up the box with a sagging bottom. He and Caspian fall into our group, as does Gowan and Lindsey who've been quietly conversing with Kitt. The little ones are sleeping, curled into Caspian's lap and unbothered by their father's strong arms wheeling him forward.

We raced once, down Garren Road. Just for the hell out of it, and he kicked my ass. Caspian's upper body is nothing but broad muscle, contrasting his thin legs and hips. He'd been born that way, and I think he's convinced himself that's why he was given up.

That's something we never talk about, orphans, that is.

But you don't listen to someone cry in the dark for years and not have a guess as to what their ghosts are.

Instead, you race them down a busy street filled with the first sun in weeks and people with ice cream dotting their noses, not a care in the world at that moment in time. My bare feet hurrying to keep up with this wide tires, rugged and built for all the adventures he, Kitt and I got into.

We just *were*, and that was enough.

When did it all get so hard?

"Thanks," I say when Bias passes the box over, his attention lingering on my mark. He's done nothing but stare at it and my teeth grind at the thought he knows something I don't want him to. That's his specialty, feelings, *vibes*. He can't help it, I know that, but still. Caspian on the other hand, won't look at me at all. "Alright there, Cas?"

He nods, hands tight on the bars of his wheel frames. Caspian searches me for a moment, then his gaze wanders behind me. "Fine. We'll see you later."

I watch him turn away and my heart slows to an ungodly rate. Bias lingers for a moment longer to lean forward and whisper into my ear, "You were right, but maybe we should do this tomorrow."

I nod, glancing down at Felix watching Caspian with a furrowed brow. "Alright. What's Cas' problem?"

"I ... don't know." Bias admits and I give him a look. "Honestly, he's been like this since he woke up, even to me. It's not just you."

Not *just* you.

"I'll text you in a bit," I say, because I can't pinpoint any other thought. We planned on meeting for dinner there tonight, all of us, but I need to speak to Tobias alone. Bias nods and says goodbye to Felix, then to the others and Quentin. I hold the box of pastries close to my chest, mind whirring so hard I don't notice the others staring at me, or rather the person coming up behind me.

"There you are," Thatch says breathlessly, startling me so hard I nearly drop the box. Felix saves me, suppressing a sly grin as he helps me close it back up. "I thought you'd changed your mind."

The first notable difference are his intensely thick curls, unrestrained and *beautiful*. A shade of amber I've never seen before catches the sun and falls down over one of his eyes, complementing the array of freckles across his nose and cheeks, his features much sharper when they're not hidden beneath a hood.

The hoodie is gone, replaced by a loose fitting long sleeve with runaway leaves across his chest and arms. His bottom half is dressed in light washed skinny jeans, holes in the knees and frayed thread galore. Work boots have replaced his converse, bright pink laces contrast the dark leather.

I remember to speak, clearing my throat. "Ah, no. Um, Felix, this is—" I look between them, remembering what I said to Thatch in the cafe about liking 'Just Thatch.' "Mister Thatch. We'll be helping him today."

Thatch steps around me to shake Felix's extended hand and I exhale heavily, but I'm not sure why. This isn't a *moment* or anything.

"Pleasure to meet you, young Felix. I believe we'll be good friends." Felix agrees and I make to introduce the others, but Thatch beats me to it. "Ah, you must be Kitt. I see our introduction is a day early, but I'm glad for it. Your work in the museum is quite extraordinary."

"Oh my, yes, that's me." She flushes, shaking his hand eagerly. "Thank you Mr. Phantom, I must say you're not what I expected, and I can't take all the credit. Arlo helps me out."

"That seems to be the general consensus regarding my infamy, and no formalities are necessary, just Thatch is fine." Thatch moves down the line, introducing himself to Gowan, Lindsey and Quentin. His hand lingers in Quentin's for a moment longer than the others, but his words are just as pleasant to him as they were to Kitt. "Pleasure to meet you again, Quentin. I apologize for my shortness earlier, I was a bit flustered."

I marvel at the way Thatch speaks, proper and elegant. Timeless.

"It's fine, we were too. Shame about the apartments, but we can find somewhere else to stay together." Quentin gestures between him and me, causing Thatch's smile to fade an imperceptible shade. "I guess we'll see you at Cas' later?" He asks me, full of hope.

"Yeah, I'll be by later. Just might be a bit late is all."

Kitt hugs me, whispering, "You better hit that," in my ear. I swat her arm playfully and scowl. She says a warm goodbye to Felix while Gowan and Lindsey give me goodbye hugs. I've never noticed how much we all touch each other until someone I didn't know was watching.

"Be careful," Gowan says, glancing at Thatch. He pointedly watches a flock of wyverns fly overhead, following the migrating black necked geese to the southern regions. Even from a great distance, the wyvern's wings kick up a breeze through the streets below.

"Okay?" I say, although it comes out more like a question. Why is everyone being weird?

Within moments it's just Thatch, Felix, and I, and the loss of Misfits is palpable in the air. I hold the box closer to my chest, then turn to Thatch. "We have to drop these off, on the way. Is that alright?"

"Of course," he says, eyes full of the sky.

Bosko returns from his endeavors, landing on my beanie with a great waft of heated wind. "Oh, done pouting now?" I ask, to which he preens his feathers and blatantly ignores me.

Thatch's eyes dart back and forth between the owl and me. His handsome face warms with genuine curiosity and I *hate* talking to people, but I want him to ask me all the things that are dancing behind his slightly crooked teeth.

He and I don't speak much though, due to Felix.

Felix walks between us, a spring in his step and questions rolling off his young tongue. At this point, he may have spoken more to Thatch today than anyone else, and it's only been five minutes.

I listen intently as the afternoon sun bathes us in a warmth that severely contrasts the chilly morning we had. I slip off my jacket one arm at a time, ensuring the pastries are safe. Bosko pays me no mind, wings steadying him as my forearms meet the fleeing sun.

"What do you do?" Felix asks, looking up to Thatch whose hands are buried deep in his pockets.

He lifts a shoulder. "I am a caretaker of sorts, but I tend to dabble in all sorts of investments as well. A jack of all trades, or so they say." I catch his eye, then quickly focus on the street before us.

"Where are you from?" Felix asks, eyes never leaving Thatch's.

"The West originally, but my work sends me everywhere, so I haven't been back in some time."

"So, you don't have a home?"

Thatch's lips push thin and a hand escapes the confines his jeans to rub the back of his neck. The collar of his long sleeve is damp with sweat. I had briefly wondered if he ran cold, but he seems to be affected by the swelling heat.

"Well, I wouldn't say that. I consider Levena to be my home," he finally says, quiet and far off.

"But, didn't you say you just arrived?"

"Felix, you're awful interrogative today. Some would consider your line of questioning rude," I say, bumping my elbow into his shoulder. His cheeks redden and he focuses on his feet.

Thatch laughs softly. "That's quite alright, I'm a curious one myself. I visit Levena more than I do anywhere else, and where we're going is the place where I *usually* stay when I'm here on business. Other than a few days dedicated to work, I've never really *seen* Levena. Luckily I have the bookstore until the cottage is sorted, and I can stay longer this time."

"*Oh*," Felix says, bringing an end to his volley of questions. Thatch and I lock eyes again, then swiftly look away. I rub at my chest with my free hand, magick sparks between my ribs. Bosko chirps his annoyance at me.

Garren Castle casts a shadow on us as our path changes from stone to dirt. Thatch's face tilts up to the sky, eyes fluttering shut as he inhales the warmed breeze washing over us. I love this part of town, and this place is especially solitary, peaceful. The deeper you travel into Old Town, the farther back in time you travel. Although Levena is one city, the Old and New sides of it are completely different from the other.

We reach the shield and I extend my hand to it, glancing at Thatch over my shoulder. "I'll have to let you in."

He waves me off, then shoves his hand back in his jeans. "No worries, this will be my second visit to Garren Castle today. I was greeted by a rather mischievous girl named Kleo, and subsequently let in by the Headmaster. We're old friends, you see."

Felix smiles mischievously, then steps through the shield, and doors, leaving us behind.

I bristle, allowing my hand to drop. Old friends? Then, how is it that I've never seen him before? *Surely* we would have crossed paths.

"Oh. Why didn't you say so?"

Thatch shrugs, brilliant curls tossing further over his eyes as he does. "You didn't ask."

I roll my eyes, then gesture for him to enter first. "After you."

He chuckles, then nods his head. "Thank you."

My phone vibrates as I follow behind him, the sounds of unruly kids and tired teachers meet my ears when we step into the castle. I take my phone out, finding a text from Caspian and Bias.

Pain in the Ass: Are you safe? We need to talk.

Bias: Definitely an Empath, will be stronger than me, may need to hide him.

I blink rapidly, then send Cas a message first.

Me: 'I'm fine Cas, at the Castle now. Text in a bit.'

I stare at Bias' message for a long moment and almost crash into Thatch when Dusan meets us at the main landing of the castle. I slide my phone into my jeans, muttering apologies to Thatch.

"Well, what a surprise. Pleasure to see you again Thatch, and ... *oh*, Arlo!" Dusan gasps, hand to her chest. "Are those from Thitwhistle's?"

Every child milling about in the main area *stops*, eyeing me like prey.

I grin, holding up the box. "Of course."

And the wolves descend.

Thatch

I've found myself on a pirate ship, fending off invaders of the uncivilized sort with a saber in hand and a feathered hat upon my head.

"Captain Kleo, we're taking on water!" I shout, causing the crew to panic.

Kleo raises her own sword to the sky, one eye covered by an eye patch and tangled dark hair catching wind. "No matter, I shall call upon the mermaids! They owe me a favor see, said anytime I need them—"

She starts to ramble on with another story that's almost too good to be true (which is most certainly the case), but First Mate Felix shakes her shoulders as the ship quakes.

Wooden planks creak and the ship wavers much too far to the left, then to the right. The flag rips in the wind and actual mist coats my face.

"Kleo, hurry!" Felix cries, launching Kleo into action. She delicately takes off her hat and sets it upon Felix's head, then runs full speed at the edge of the decking and *jumps,* swan diving to her death.

This *can't* be part of the game.

I gasp and run to the edge, taking hold of the chipped railing with blanched knuckles. But of course, a safety net of magickal vines holds a flailing Kleo, slowly lowering her to the ground before dissipating into a green dust. Arlo peeks around the tree trunk holding up our ship, glitter in his hair and a silken red 'tail' trailing the ground behind him.

"Captain Kleo! It's been so long since we last met, are you alright?" He asks in a high pitched tone, full dramatics in effect.

He's amazing.

With the kids, of course. Around them, he's warmhearted and fun, with the right words always there for curious, vulnerable hearts. Felix is a strong Empath, he wandered in my mind by accident on the way over and I had to raise my defenses. I wonder what the boy sees in me, why he's so curious. I suppose most people are, but my gut tells me something more is going on.

Dusan watches with a small group of kids that chose to watch our impromptu pirate play rather than participate. All ages are sprawled out in the soft grass a short distance away, shaded by an autumnal blooming cherry tree.

I'm not quite sure how we got here, but I don't mind one bit.

Kleo holds her nose, making *blub blub* noises as she 'treads water' with her other hand. Arlo waves his hands in the air, causing Kleo to draw in a breath of air. She feels at the imaginary gills that have protruded on her neck. I grin, her acting is superb.

"We need help! My ship, we need patching, could you help me? My crew will die if we don't save them!" She cries.

On cue, the trunk sways harshly and I'm thrown overboard, along with a small fae boy. I catch him in my arms, but a scream escapes my throat.

Vines are conjured to life once more, gently lowering us to the ground. Cheers erupt from the ship above us. I sheepishly look up to Arlo through the mud sloshed onto my face. He bites his lip, hiding a smile as he takes the boy from my arms and slings him onto his hip like he's done it a thousand times before.

He helps me up with his other hand, but there's no time to waste as the ship shudders atop the enchanted trunk. He points at the mud pit surrounding the bottom of the tree, revealing a *very* obvious hole in the bottom of the pirate ship. (was that there before?)

"Let us borrow the earth, it shall help us," he says in a serious, wise mer-woman voice.

I chuckle, but there's no time to waste as Kleo puts us to work. We form an assembly line, I dig into the earth and pass it on to the boy I caught, Olin. He passes it to Arlo at the base of the tree, who reaches up and offers it to Kleo who hastily cobs the hole together. In no time, the hole's patched and the trunk stops swaying. The crew above cheers with such force my ears ring. Dusan and the other onlookers clap and holler as well, concluding our quest for the day.

Arlo, Olin and I leave Kleo and the other kids to their adventures, the boy runs off to Dusan once we reach the halfway point between the pirate ship and her. We stop and I look down at myself, clothes packed with filth. I *may* be smiling wider than I ever have.

"Thank you for playing, I know you must be in a hurry, and now you're all dirty." Arlo mutters, gesturing up and down at me.

"I believe that's the most fun I've had in ages, clothes are clothes, I don't mind at all." I shrug, biting the inside of my cheek.

"Well, it sounds like Felix is going to be playing for a few more minutes, and I might have something that can fit you, if you want. Or we can go back to the bookstore," he says, tugging on his ear.

"I'm not interfering with your plans, are you? If you and him need to–"

He puts his hands up. "No, no, it's fine, honestly. The kid likes you, and he could use a friend."

"Oh, alright then." Heat rolls over my neck and I inhale sharply. "Well, if you have a shirt at the very least, I would much appreciate that."

"Sure thing," Arlo says, then leads the way into Garren Castle.

One of his strides is equivalent to two of mine, but thankfully he takes it easy so I can keep up. We walk near side by side across a barely manicured lawn full of soft, ankle tickling grass and pastel wildflowers. His soul mark catches the sunlight and disrupts the owl upon his head who flutters his eyes shut. I chuckle, hands secure in my jean pockets and eyes wandering the ivy shrouded length of proud brick and mortar.

"How long have you known Dusan for?" He asks, glancing back at me as we approach double purple doors with gray trim.

I shrug. "A couple hundred years or so."

Arlo's hand pauses its ascent to a brass handle. He gapes at me. "A *couple*? But, you, I mean, I just–"

I hold up my hand, suppressing laughter. "It's fine, I know what you mean. I stopped aging before my thirtieth decade." I gesture to the door. "Shall we? These jeans are a bit *chafing*, if you know what *I* mean."

He flushes, then turns back to the door with his mouth opening and closing, contemplating words with brows furrowed. He settles on, "Oh."

I follow behind Arlo, cutting between throngs of rowdy kids running down halls and exasperated caretakers yelling after them to *slow down*. The weekend proves to be quite fun for the energetic younglings. They're all happy, well taken care of, but I can't help wondering why there's so many living here.

Back when Arlo was their age, there was less than half the amount of kids there are now. Is that because of the Taking? As far as I can tell, Felix is the only witch here besides Arlo.

We pass by a set of closed doors and my feet inadvertently stop of their own accord, planted outside the firmly shut entry. I raise a hand and press it to the wood, then a shuddering inhale racks me as thick warmth pours up the muscles of my arm.

Arlo's fingers wrap around my wrist and he tugs me back, something between curiosity and irritation splayed across his face. "You *are* a witch."

"Not *exactly*. I'm a magickal being, not a witch." I nod to my wrist still captured by his strong hand. "You're hurting me."

He releases me as if I've burned him, but his eyes do *not* leave mine. "What were you doing?" Arlo asks, full of doubt. His change of demeanor is surprising, and heartbreaking. His eyes flash to my ears, then scramble all over my figure until settling back on my face once more.

He's seeing me as everyone else does for the first time.

Trying to figure me out. What *am* I?

It hurts.

I sigh, crossing my arms. I dip my head in contemplation, then look back up to him. "Nothing, the energy caught my attention is all. I don't mean to pry, but what is on the other side of these doors? The magick, it's … warm."

Arlo softens at once, a tentative hand thinks about reaching out to mine, but thinks better of it. "Would you like to see?"

I smile, my fingers take hold of his without thinking and I immediately let go, then card a now shaky hand through my hair. "I apologize, excitement got the better of me. I would like that."

Arlo runs his tongue over his bottom lip as he studies me for another moment, then turns away and snaps his fingers before the door's locking mechanism. It *clicks* and he pushes it open, then gestures for me to enter.

"Guests first."

"I won't say no." I admit, shoulder rising and falling heavily. I pass by him to enter a grand workspace. I can't help but fill my lungs with fresh pressed espresso and the thickening electrical storm when our bodies brush against the other just the *slightest* bit.

At first glance, one might consider the expanse to be a kitchen. The rectangular space is filled with cabinets, spice racks and all the modern appliances like a steel stove and fridge. A sink dominates the counters facing the windows, and at the end of the marbled surface is an old school cauldron. I clap with glee and run over to it, then hover my fingers just above the cast iron surface stained with glitter.

It's beautiful, well kept.

Age is hard to discern, but the owl engravings suggest hand-made.

I sigh with content and leave the cauldron, along with its toe to hip length wooden spoon resting against it, the maple wood streaked brilliantly with black. I roam over the paint splatter tainting every inch of the room, then am captured by the wall bordering the backyard.

Faux pirate crews and mermaids are visible through lofty windows. Ferns and other plants dominate most of the vertical space and encroach on the clean, undisturbed glass allowing sunlight to filter in. I stand there for a moment, smiling like a stupid idiot.

I turn around to find Arlo watching me with a soft smile of his own, and there's no way I can stop now.

"What?" I ask, shaking hair from my eyes. I shove my hands into my pockets and approach him. Arlo leans against a length of the counter island opposite an impressive spice rack resting on the wall, watching me over his shoulder with his arms folded.

"Nothing." Arlo lifts a shoulder and his smirks widens. He's mocking me now. I lean on the counter beside him, leaving a good foot between us. I study the jars filled with crystals, spices, leaves and animal parts, both dehydrated and preserved in liquid. Bones line the highest shelf, all various sizes.

"Ah. Nothing can be quite something though, can't it?" I say softly, and he dips his chin.

"It's not very often that I invite someone into my Kitchen. Even the kids, or Dusan, I have to be ... in the mood, if you know what I mean." Arlo admits, voice wavering as he tugs on the gauge in his ear.

He's pretending to study the shelves, so I continue to do the same and spy on him in my periphery.

"Thank you, I'm honored. To be honest, it's been a long time since I've been in the company of a witch. I didn't realize there were ... well, I didn't know what had occurred, while I was gone. So, thank you, for trusting me with your sacred place."

"Well, I don't know about *sacred*, that sounds awful cultish." He mutters.

I elbow him. "You know what I mean."

We stand there for precious minutes in silence. I can't catch any words and Arlo seems content to just *be* with me. At some point in the five minutes we've been standing together, our hips have closed the distance and there are mediocre inches between us. I steal a glance up at him, surprised to find him watching me with intensity.

Every time he looks at me, he *means* it.

"Um, Arlo?"

He licks his bottom lip again, and it's *agony*. His lips are just *dry*, he's *not* doing it on purpose. "Yes, Thatch?"

"I'm still wet."

He laughs. "Let's go, my room is in the attic."

"*Where*?"

Ghost Hunter

Arlo

"This contraption does *not* look safe," Thatch says, eyeing the pull down stairs into the attic warily.

I roll my eyes at him. "It's fine, *go*."

He huffs, then takes hold of the thin railings and stomps up the stairs for good measure. I do *not* check out his ass in those wet skinny jeans, allowing him to reach the top before I ascend. I expect a smartass comment or two, but only find a star struck Thatch, just like before in the Kitchen. He wanders throughout my bedroom, hands out but never actually touching anything. I smirk watching him unabashedly commit all of my things to memory, at ease for reasons I don't care to explain.

I find him some neatly folded clothes from my dresser and perform a quick incantation, smiling when the fabric shrinks in my hand. I turn in time to see Thatch reaching a freckled hand out to the stars and driftwood mobiles above my bed, then pull back immediately when he locks guilty eyes with me.

"It's pretty," he says in a way of defense.

I nod, offering him the clothes. "All the stuff the kids have made me over the years. I'm a bit of a packrat."

"An organized one." Thatch allows. He looks through the clothes quickly, then back up to me with a raised, barely there ginger brow. When the sun hits his face, every lash and hair glows a vibrant amber. "These are my size."

I wave my fingers dramatically, then jut a thumb over my shoulder. "Hedge Witch specialty. Bathroom is in there."

"Hedge Witch? Well, aren't you something. There weren't a lot of those even back in my day." Thatch grins, then takes off for the bathroom. I shake my head, unable to fathom the fact he's at least *hundreds* of years old. I forget about it, then he says something like that or speaks in that elegant way of his, and I think to myself how did I not notice *sooner*.

It feels inappropriate to ask just *how* old he is, but I'm certainly itching to bug Dusan about him. Then again, I want *him* to tell me.

It's not like I'm particularly young. I hit my centennial in the hospital, or so they tell me. I don't remember anything but surviving, and I'm not looking forward to Cas and Kit making up for it next year. Besides vampires, elves, and a select few other races, magickal beings don't live for *that* long. And he definitely isn't a vampire or elf, or anything else I'm aware of.

Witch blood keeps my heart beating longer than the average human's, but I'm only 72% human. Doc tested me twice. Suddenly the studio feels smaller than it ever has and I push open a window, needing fresh air to drown out Thatch's cedar and maple vibes.

Bosko takes off from his perch atop my head and takes my beanie with him, then settles into the hollow taking up his corner of the room. I scowl at him and march over, taming my hair somewhat as I do.

"What the hell is wrong with you?" I mutter, ripping my beanie out of his beak.

"You're a fucking *idiot*, that's what. You're not asking the right questions." Bosko chastises me while preening his wing. "Stay focused."

Irritation creeps through my bones. "Oh, *wow*, his highness deigns to speak to me again. What pray tell, is the right question?"

And just like that, Bosko goes to 'sleep' and ignores me. I curse inwardly, swearing to connect with a new familiar like I always do when Bosko pisses me off, but I never act on it. Like it or not, that damn bird literally saved my life, and he's usually right.

"Everything alright?" Thatch asks, scaring the shit out of me for the second time today.

I spin on my heel and slide my beanie back on, finding Thatch dressed in my favorite long sleeve and dark wash jeans. Protection runes are embroidered into the waistband of the worn denim and cuffs of the emerald sleeves. Heat stirs in my chest at the sight of him in my clothes.

"Yeah, Bosko's just getting into trouble again. All fit ok?" I gesture up and down at his handsome figure and he chuckles, combing hair from his eyes which brighten upon connecting with mine.

"Perfect, thank you. I like the shirt." Thatch rolls his soft shoulders beneath the fabric as he approaches, then his attention shifts to Bosko pretending to sleep. A brow lifts and he scratches his beard. "He's a funny bird."

Bosko chirrups, eyes closed, and I suppress a snicker.

Thatch looks between the barn owl and I with an expression that's quite close to a pout. "What? What did he say?"

"He thinks you're a funny bird, too."

Before long, Thatch, Felix and I are back on the road again with mouths full of hurriedly made sandwiches, courtesy of the castle cook who has a soft spot for me. Bosko's perched upon my head per usual, beak tucked beneath a wing.

I'm finding that Thatch delights in the small things, *all* of them. For someone who's lived for so long, you would think he's seen everything.

He said he's known Dusan for a couple hundred years, but that leaves a lot of gray area for how old he is. Also, I find it incredibly odd that he wants someone like *me* to show him around Levena, considering he's been around Levena for far longer than I have.

I should be put off by the fact he's ... an old man, essentially, but I don't marvel at him any less.

"This is amazing! Is it the bread? *Gotta* be the bread." Thatch exclaims in between bites.

"Sure is." Felix agrees over a mouthful of turkey and cheese. "Freshly made everyday. Kleo and I deliver the week olds to the soup kitchen, and even *those* are good. I'll ask Cook Jean to make you some, if you want."

I smile through the last bits of my sandwich, listening to them talk about how high they could make a sandwich, but not *too* big so that it can still fit inside your mouth. We leave Old Town behind and pedestrian streets become paved roads. The river is a welcoming sight, as are the cottages and small-time farm stands lining the path to Leideen Ait Island. I used to love coming down here, before. Now I only do when necessary, and most times I can get Chauncey to come visit me.

Thatch and Felix walk side by side ahead of me and I wait for a lull in their discussion on who lives where and what farm stands are the best, my little witch is a better tour guide than I. I decide to toe the line, taking a breath before I do.

"So, Thatch, I have to ask, how long has it been since you visited Levena last? Things have changed quite a bit in the past few decades."

I want to say, '*I can't help but wonder why we haven't met sooner,*' but I lock it down.

Thatch's shoulders rise and he casually glances back at me with a sly grin. "I hadn't noticed. Hm, about eight or nine decades, give or take. Admittedly my last visit was cut short, so I feel as if it's been *much* longer."

I would've only been twenty. Or ten.

"Levena is completely different then, I imagine."

Thatch shrugs in that noncommittal way of his and my strides match his. Felix walks between us, looking back and forth.

"But some things never change," Thatch says softly, eyes on the nearing island lingering on the shore at the end of our path. I follow his gaze and my stomach drops.

Willows overhang the shore where a grassy peninsula juts out to meet a circular island. The structures and inner area are hidden by weeping trees and thick woodland. Despite the fact I can't see the cottage, the black presence lingering on the island is plain to my mind's eye, even from this end of the land bridge.

"Something's wrong," I say, looking to Thatch. "Can you feel it?"

He shakes his head, brows furrowed in frustration. "No, what is it?"

"Evil," Felix says, trembling between us.

I rest a hand in between his shoulder blades and he calms immediately. "Why don't you stay here? I'll go check it out first."

"No, I want to." Felix shakes his head quickly, but Thatch doesn't look so sure.

Thatch stares at the island with the most seriousness I've seen yet from him. "I should be able to feel it." He murmurs, nearly indiscernible. Thatch shakes his head and offers Felix his hand. "We'll follow Mister Arlo to the other end of the bridge and he can check it out, if everything is safe then we'll go the rest of the way. Sound good to you?"

Thatch's eyes slide from Felix's to mine and I nod. Felix looks up to me for confirmation and I say, "Let's go."

The water is eerily still and its usually sparkling surface has turned dull and murky. I run my fingers along the split rail fence separating the landbridge from the lake's depths. Kelpies, sirens and other mischievous beings like to visit land dwellers when we're close to the shore, but not for the reasons the old tales say.

Water creatures are all terrible gossips.

A stagnant, negative energy is infused into the fence and I remove my hand, gesturing for Felix to feel it. "What do you feel?" I ask, and he frowns upon touching a length of split rail.

"Lonely, but it's not the same as the house." Felix remarks, hand dropping and eyes falling onto the creeping island. Thatch watches us with curiosity, but says nothing.

"Nothing else?" I ask, and Felix shakes his head. "I will give you a hint, then. I believe we may be dealing with a ghost, little witch."

Felix cocks his head. "A ghost? How can you tell?"

Thatch frowns as we step off the land bridge and onto an overgrown dirt path into the woods. The cottage continues to hide behind the fluttering limbs of the willow trees and their oaken cousins. "This wasn't grown up like this yesterday."

"Hmm, well, one thing at a time," I say casually. Hauntings are no big thing. Thatch wrinkles his nose, leading the way down a weed ridden trail. Felix takes hold of my hand and Bosko leaves his nest upon my head, taking to the woods ahead of us.

"Ghosts are usually created due to two reasons. The first being the person was killed, or wrongfully taken before their time … " I inhale slowly and step over a pothole, overcome with memories. "Or, true to common belief, they had unfinished business. Oftentimes these circumstances are linked, but not always. Now, either Mr. Chauncey has unfortunately passed away, or he is being haunted."

"But, ghosts can't *flood* a house, can they?" Felix asks.

"An incorporeal's ability to break through the metaphysical depends on the … intensity, of their passing, and how long it's been since they've passed. New spirits are often incredibly powerful, and volatile. The fact the fence is affected means *this* ghost is able to travel and corporealize, but not farther than the end of the land bridge."

"What would have happened to Chauncey …" Felix murmurs to himself, lost in thought.

"That's what I'd like to know," Thatch says as we come to a stop, finger raised.

A metaphysical storm of vengeance, anger and fury swirls around the cottage which appears to be thousands of years worn. Dead ivy cracks the stone foundation and walls, water spurts from the fractures and presses upon the towering stained windows. There is nearly more glass than brick and the stained colors are spider webbing dangerously, weeping murky water.

"Mister Arlo …" Felix gasps raggedly, clutching at his chest. I kneel and cup his face in my hands, then murmur a protective incantation and kiss his forehead. His breathing smooths out, but his eyes are wide. "It *hurts*."

"I know, I'm sorry, I didn't know it would be this bad." I whisper and look up to Thatch clenching his fists, staring at the cottage with a furious expression.

"Hey." I call out to him, and he startles violently. "Is there a shield surrounding this place?"

"There's supposed to be. Arlo, I don't think it's a ghost," he says quietly, glancing at Felix. "It wasn't like this before Arlo, I swear I didn't know. I wouldn't have ..." He looks away from us and I stand, sliding my hat back from my eyes. I reach into my pocket, finding my everyday travel stone. I close the few steps separating Thatch and me, widening his crinkled eyes.

"Stay here with Little Witch, I'll take care of this." I take Thatch's sun heated hand and press my amethyst into it, then lean forward and whisper into his ear, lowering my tone so Felix can't hear. "But just in case, say *CasKit* three times, and this will take you both out of here."

"That's not very reassuring." Thatch whispers, pulling back to look at me. His breath washes over my cheek. I fight a shudder, and the urge to push the hair back from his wild eyes.

He's *terrified*.

I almost ask why, but instead I reach forward and cup his cheek like an *idiot* and say, "Hey, *Just Thatch,* I promise, it'll be fine."

Thatch's stormy eyes brighten, like clouds giving way to bright blue sky. His fingers close around the amethyst and he nods into my hand. "Thank you. Try not to get wet." Thatch chuckles and I laugh a little as well, but my hand *won't* leave his face. Felix's stare is suddenly *very* hot and apparent.

I clear my throat, finally pulling my fingers from Thatch's freckled warmth.

I turn to Felix and pull his hat down over his eyes, then grin after he resituates it and looks up to me with a wary smile. "Stay here with Thatch, you can come on the next one. 'Kay?"

Felix nods, not at all bothered. He takes hold of Thatch's hand, like it's nothing, and I fight a smile. "Be careful," Little Witch says, and Thatch echoes his sentiment.

I turn away from them and approach the cottage with intense cockiness and adrenaline surging with the magick in my veins. Bosko returns from his scout and lands on my shoulder when I come to a stop before an old school wooden door with an iron 'o' shaped knocker.

"*Dybbuk*, third possession. Poor old Chauncey was murdered by the spirit when its last host started to fail, the last body's already ash in the wind. That's all I got."

"*Fuck*." I glance back at Felix and Thatch in the clearing, they're talking and both sets of eyes are dead set on me. "Alright. *Alright*. Nothing we can't handle. Are you ready?"

"Are *you*? Been awhile since you played ghost hunter, let alone with an extinct species." Bosko pleasantly reminds me. I reach up and tap the living runes Kit tattooed into my neck long before she ever had the studio. Protection runes for all the time I spent dueling Leon.

"*Hedge* Witch, get it right." I scowl at him, then take a deep breath and crack my neck. "Let's do this."

I take hold of the knocker and harshly bang on the door. "Hey Chauncey, it's Arlo, I know I'm a little early with this week's delivery, but figured since I was in the neighborhood."

The water sloshing behind the windows disappears and a chilling presence occupies the other side of the door. "Arlo, is that you?" Chauncey's form calls in perfect tone, and the door *clicks* open. "Come on in, I've been expecting you."

And here we go.

I step into a pristine, well lit foyer with no sign of the swamp decorating the place just mere moments before. *Oh*, this one *is* powerful. *"May be fifth possession, now that I think about it."* Bosko relays over the telepathic bond between us and I roll my eyes.

"You think?"

The door closes and locks.

I face a chestnut centaur dressed in a white button up with a fine black vest laying over top of the fancy long sleeve. Chauncey's usually pin straight, waist length locks are cropped short, the only indication Leideen Ait's caretaker has changed at all. The black irises and horizontal pupils are the same, along with the vibrant glow of his skin. More color has crept into his bronzed complexion since last time I saw him, subtle enough to be attributed to the sun's embrace.

His large hands are folded behind his back. I form a triangle with my own, thumbs and forefingers meet at my chest. Sparking darkness flows from my fingers when they meet. I lift an edge of the veil between worlds and grin.

"Let's cut the bullshit, shall we?"

"*Oh*, Arlo, you never change, do you?" The *Dybbuk* chuckles, losing Chauncey's tone and taking on a monstrous one of their own. Black eyes flare red, just like I wanted. These beasts can't be killed unless their magick's brought to the surface, and even then it's risky business because they can steal a living body just as easily as a dead one.

Their words though, and this energy, it's oddly familiar.

Don't take the bait, *don't* do it ....

"Let's go for a walk on the wild side, and you can tell me all about it." I taunt, then flip my fingers to form a diamond, which ignites the sparking dark cloud pooling from my hands. The cottage disappears around us and I offer a hand to the *Dybbuk*. The veil tears with a thunderous roar that deafens me.

"We can do this the easy way, or the hard way." I shout over the noise.

Surprisingly, their cool, rough hand slides into mine and a mischievous smile takes hold of their suddenly *wrong* face. It twists into something horrifying and macabre. I'd be lying if I said pissed off spirits taking on their grotesque forms didn't scare me. It's when you think you're invincible that you fall.

I lead the possessive spirit through the veil where the cottage's colors mute and sound ceases to exist. I shoulder Bosko off, willing him to keep Thatch and Felix safe before the veil closes the *Dybbuk* and I into the Other World completely. When we're safely tucked into the other dimension, my brief fear is swept away by pure irritation.

Fuck this guy.

He catches me off guard with his next riddle. "I wouldn't go through all this just to give you a hard time, darling. I wonder, have you missed me?"

That gives me pause. "I don't believe we've met."

The *Dybbuk* grins, revealing rows of blunt, square teeth that can crush elephant bones within seconds. Once their prey is subdued, the teeth elongate so they can rip and tear. Leon loved pets with sharp teeth. Oily black venom spills over the sides of the *Dybbuk's* wide bottom jaw that doesn't quite meet the upper, too many teeth.

"No, but my contractor knows you quite … *intimately*."

Rage, magick, and *slight* insanity screams to be released, but instead of interrogating, I snarl, "*Fuck you,*" then unleash hell.

Thatch

The moment the door shut behind Arlo I knew something was wrong. Less than a minute later, Bosko shot out of a window, shattering it to rainbowed pieces. The bird barrels for Felix and I, unaffected.

"Shit," I say, then mutter an apology to Felix who's squeezing my hand so tight I had lost feeling in my fingers long ago.

The travel stone cuts into my other hand and Bosko lands upon my shoulder, screeching up a storm. "I can't—" I start to say, then the owl *bites* me, taking a chunk out of my earlobe. I reflexively duck and swat at him, but his talons dig into my shoulder. "HEY!"

Blood pours down my neck and the unintelligible cries distort into something understandable. "SHUT UP AND LISTEN!" Bosko shouts in a heavily accented common. "Find Bias, and ... well, find Bias!"

I shake off my bewilderment. "But Arlo said—"

A ripple of cold pressure billows from the darkened, unassuming cottage across the way from us. There's no longer swamp water behind the windows, but a swirling hell storm of black smoke infused with fire. Bosko shifts to my other shoulder, wide eyes set on the broken window spewing chaos.

"Trust me, he needs help."

I swallow guilt for not summoning my own power. How did I not sense such a danger? I trusted Arlo when he said he could handle this. I want to save as much magick as I can. I want to stay a little longer this time. Shame floods me, how selfish of a thought.

I glance down at Felix watching me with intensity, none too concerned by the blood slowly dripping from my ear. "What's Bosko saying?" 'Little witch' asks.

I summon courage. "We have to get help. Do you know how to find Bias?" Felix nods, determined. Nervous, yes, but a new shine overtakes his eyes. "Alright, hold on."

I close my eyes and focus my attention on the crystal biting into my palm. I whisper "*CasKit*" three times, and the world disappears beneath our feet.

It's been awhile since I traveled via stone, but Arlo's herbal scented magick is like a protective, warm bubble muffling the cool wind and pandemonium of time and space being stretched apart. The moment we land, I recognize Arlo's room. I can't help but notice I forgot my wet jeans and shirt on his bed.

Were we really here only a few hours ago?

Felix drags me down the stairs and through the castle undetected. I can't fathom why *only* Bias, but Bosko has my trust. He takes off for the sky, staying close above as we hit the streets.

"It's only a ten minute walk, but we can run," Felix says, then furrows his brow in deep thought. "*Can* you run?"

I can't help but laugh. "Yeah, I can run."

And we do.

Boots slap the ground and humid early evening sweeps through my sweaty curls. Felix runs a few strides ahead of me, but I keep up with him as he dodges down side streets to use 'shortcuts.' They must be, because after what seems like only short minutes later, we come to a stop before a yellow house with white shutters.

Luckily, (or not) Bias is already outside, pushing a child in a double swing and accompanied by Caspian, along with all the others I met earlier. The group stares at Felix and I bracing ourselves on our knees, unabashedly grasping air.

Kitt sprints over, concern written all over her purple features. "What's going on? Where's Arlo?" She gasps, then reaches out to my ear. "What happened to you? Felix, are you alright?"

I wave her off just as Bosko lands on my shoulder, evidence of my plight plain to see on his crimson beak. "Arlo is in trouble, Bosko says we need Bias. The flooding turned out to be a ghost problem, and well, I'm not sure if it's a ghost *exactly*, but he needs help."

Bosko trills in reminder and I nod. "Only Bias. He insists."

Kitt's eyes dart between the three of us, then she nods stiffly. I can tell a hundred questions are bouncing on her tongue, but she says, "Alright. Wait here," then fetches Tobias for us.

I kneel before Felix. "I'm going back, and I think you should go home."

Felix shakes his head, stands his ground. "No, I'm a witch too, I can help."

I scratch at my beard. "Would Arlo want you in harm's way, Felix?"

He crosses his arms and scowls, acting like a true child for the first time since I've met him. "*No.*" He grits out. "I want to help."

"I know you do, but not today, not like this. One day, when you're stronger and know all that you're capable of, you'll be able to. But for today, the way you help is staying safe. Bad guys ... they use people like you, Felix."

Felix blinks. "People like me?"

I nod. "Arlo loves you very much. Bad guys will use anything they can to bring down their opponent, even love. So let's not give them that weapon, okay?"

Felix's arms drop and he slowly nods. "I ... didn't think of that."

Bias joins us, as does a silent Caspian who glares daggers at me. "What's going on?" The Empath asks, arms crossed.

I relay everything that transpired, including bits of information from Bosko which I didn't know until now. Caspian glances between the owl and I with wariness written all over his features. A snow hare rests between Tobias' feet, a beautiful creature that I'm assuming is his familiar.

"How bizarre. Even a *Dybbuk*, that should be no problem for Arlo. Fifth possession may make it tricky, but ... " Bias looks down at the hare who wriggles their nose at him. "Well, let's go, Bosko usually knows what he's talking about."

Caspian takes Bias' hand before he can step closer to me, accidentally bumping his chair's foot boards into the back of Bias' legs. "Bias, I don't like this."

After Bias consoles his lover, I clear my throat. "Caspian, can I trust you to take Felix home?"

If looks could kill ...

"Of *course*. Come on Felix, the kids are out front with the girls, why don't you go play for a minute." Caspian gestures to the curious Gowan, Lindsey, and Kitt waiting with two oblivious toddlers inside the white picket fence.

Felix nods, then throws his arms around my waist. "Be careful."

My hands float in the air above his shoulders, unsure what to do. I settle for patting his back, he's a good kid but I can't understand why he's taken to me so much.

"Everything is going to be fine," I say, sounding more confident than the anxiety brewing in my heart. Felix nods, then takes off for the others.

Caspian stares me down. "Flooding, hm?"

I hold my hands up. "I didn't know there was a ghost, certainly not a *Dybbuk*. I knew they went extinct a few years ago, well that doesn't matter now, but still, I would've never asked if I knew, I swear."

Bias raises a brow. Caspian does too.

"A *few* years ago? You mean, a *thousand*?" Bias asks, raising a brow.

Shit.

I rub the back of my neck. "Yes, that's what I meant."

The Empath tilts his head. Caspian's scowl tightens.

Shit.

Bosko trills, saving me from myself. "Let's go. He says we can use the stone again if you direct your energy, Bias." I offer the amethyst and he takes it. When his fingers brush against mine and a subtle pink hue overtakes the edges of my vision, I *know* I'm fucked. Empaths can't control reading you like an open book upon touching you, which is why most live alone.

Luckily, he remains silent and pretends to be unaffected.

I can't tell if the look on Caspian's face is because he has blurred memories of me, or because my hand is entangled with his soulmate's. Either way, this isn't good. If Caspian remembers me, then it's only a matter of time ....

"Save me some dinner," Bias says to Caspian with a smile, breaking down some of that icy exterior.

"Of course." Caspian mutters.

Bias whispers something to me and rests his hand on my shoulder but I can't discern it over the commotion in my head. I curse myself for being a coward, for not helping Arlo when I was *right* there. Fuck living for a few more weeks if that means Arlo gets hurt. Bosko's talons and the popping of our magickal bubble alerts me to a staggering new reality.

Arlo Rook laid out on a green and white striped lounge chair, on my front porch (not quite sure where the chair came from) with an ... iced coffee? In one hand, and in the other is a mason jar of *gunk*. His face's upturned to the sun, eyes blissfully closed.

The cottage is in shambles, but he's *grinning*.

I sprint the ten feet between us.

Bosko takes off from my shoulder, cursing me. Tobias remains where we landed, dumbfounded at the scene.

"Are you alright?!" I mean to ask in a calm tone, but it ends up a yelped out question. I drop to my knees at Arlo's side. He opens his eyes, and that *stupid* fucking smile widens open seeing me.

But then, his attention slides past me, to Bias.

And his lips push thin.

Arlo stands abruptly from the chair, abandoning his coffee. I skitter backwards to avoid falling on my ass. He glares down to the jar in his hand, swirling its contents as he does. "I don't need help," he says, and I'm not sure to who. Arlo blinks, then offers his hand to me and helps me up.

Bias shrugs. "Tell that to your familiar. Said you needed me, and *only* me. Tell him Thatch, I said that you'd be able to handle a *Dybbuk* just fine, but—"

"It wasn't a *Dybbuk*," Arlo mutters under his breath, then lifts his gaze from the jar to Bias. "Not *just* a *Dybbuk*, anyway."

Bias tilts his head. "What?"

Arlo steps past me, avoiding my gaze, then hands the jar to Bias.

The Empath takes it and when his fingers come to rest upon the glass, he drops it immediately. Bias blanches, staring at Arlo in horror. "*No.*"

Arlo shrugs, glancing over his shoulder at me as he does so. "I told him to fuck around and find out. I've killed him once, and I can do it again, *properly*. Honestly, I'm surprised it took him this long. Old habits die hard."

Arlo turns back to Tobias, reaching forward to envelope the Empath in a hug. Arlo says, "I won't let him hurt you again, Bias. I promise."

"What's going on?" I ask, not in a frustrated scream but a deathly quiet whisper that *feels* like a scream.

The pair pull apart and they both look at me, but it's Bias who answers with terror in his eyes despite Arlo's promise. "The Witch Killer. He's back."

What Are You Laughing At?

Arlo

I t'd be fucking great if I could have one moment without someone checking in on me. Bosko, to his discredit, stands by his sentiment that I need to get over myself.

Nevertheless, Tobias is here now and I might as well take his help, because honestly, I'm dead tired. I *didn't* need his help to contain the *Dybbuk*, I did good, but fainting is a very real possibility for my weakened heart. Between Doc's, Kitt's, fending off an old nemesis and everything in between, my blood is thin and pumping at what *some* would consider to be an alarmingly slow rate. I'm sure if I asked, he'd take the edge off so I'm not as hazy while showing Thatch around tonight.

Because there's no way *that's* not happening.

He, Thatch and I sit beneath a weeping willow nestled behind the cottage, each of us cross-legged and staring at the jar full of *Dybbuk* spirit centered between us. Bosko watches from the canopy above and Daisy rests on Tobias' knee. Thatch looks as if he's using all his restraint not to touch the jar, but I told him *no*.

He reminds me of a cat, in the sense that curiosity will kill him.

"So, he's not *alive,* then?" Thatch asks, scratching at the mess of ginger across his jaw. He's so fucking rough looking, but I don't mind it one bit. I wonder how that scruff would feel scratching against my lips, my thighs.

I shake my head, leaning back on my hands. The moss is cool beneath my palms and I sigh. "No, but he'll keep contracting out his work I bet, at least until he accomplishes whatever he's planning on doing to resurrect. He never was smart, no one can evade death, not forever," I say, voice trailing off as my thoughts muddy.

Thatch's shudder and furrowed brow pulls me out of the storm in my head before I'm lost to it. I like how his brows pull together to form a perfect, singular crease between them. "I can't believe that's a thing, *mercenary* ghosts." He scoffs.

I grin at him, lips stretching slowly and of their own accord. "Ghosts have to make a living, too. Can't blame them for being dead, bored and trapped."

Bias chokes on a laugh. Thatch's pupils dilate in disbelief. When he realizes I'm serious, he rolls his eyes and looks away from me with a frown. "You're unbelievable."

"I've been told," I say, fighting back a chuckle which is a losing battle around Thatch.

His eyes slide back to mine just the smallest bit, and he *smiles*.

"Alright, Cas is going to nut us if we don't get going. Let's do this," Bias says, gesturing to the jar and startling me out of my reverie.

I can't say the smiles won't stop coming, because the first damn one never left the moment Thatch gave me his attention. "Tobias, are you being *vulgar*?"

Bias sighs, raking pink tresses back from his face. He's always had it long, but is constantly exasperated by it. His glasses match his gray sweater and hair hangs over them when he glares at me. "The only time you see me is when I'm surrounded by kids. Can't exactly be vulgar then, can I?"

I don't know why, but I find myself leaning forward to gently clap him on the shoulder. We've never been overly close, just there in each other's atmosphere, Caspian being the frayed thread between us. I don't hate, or even dislike Bias for being Caspian's soulmate, but that doesn't mean I was never jealous of him.

"Well, I'm sure at the family friendly Misfit nights you'll be able to relax a bit more." I promise, and I hope he understands that.

Bias shoulders drop and he gives me a soft smile.

Thatch clears his throat. "So, do we need to ... *cleanse* the area or something?"

I lean back and wave him off. "No, *Dybbuks* are rather simple to dispose of, it's the containing them part that's tricky."

"I wish I could've seen it." Thatch mumbles, sinking his fingers into the moss and leaves before him. "I bet it was ... what do they say ... cool?"

I grin, thoroughly enjoying his adorable pouting. I can't help it, *fuck*. I've smiled far more today than I have in a long time, and the harder I try to bury the telltale quirks of my lips, the more I fail. I decide to not care that I'm smiling. Just for today.

"Arlo is pretty *cool* when he's in action, not gonna lie." Bias supplies, tucking a strand of hair behind his ear. "He took the poltergeist out of our house like it was just ... well, I don't know what, I'm not good at metaphors. But cool, yes."

My ears heat. "I still can't believe you guys played the realtor like that."

"What?" Thatch asks, perking up with moss stuck under his fingernails and moisture tainting his sleeves. *My* sleeves.

I gesture to Bias. "He and Cas got a sweet deal on the place because it was haunted. Like, doors slamming shut and people getting pinched. They failed to mention that they have a certain friend with a knack for sending them on their merry way."

Thatch laughs, the sound reverberates through the forest and for a moment it's like the ground hums with the sensation, but that's just my clouded and incredibly biased mind. "That's brilliant. How did you do it?"

"Do what?"

"The poltergeist? How'd you get it to leave?"

My smile fades a little and I shrug it off. "Oh, that. I asked her if she wanted to play, and we did. Then, she went on."

Thatch deflates. "Oh. A child?"

I nod once. "Yup, younger than Felix. She didn't know what had happened and was upset no one could hear her, play with her. Most poltergeists are kids actually, did you know that?"

Thatch contemplates that and Bias looks between us with a fond expression. "Doesn't it ... bother you? Ferrying people that shouldn't have died?" Thatch asks.

I take my hat off and shake out my hair, then resituate it upon my head. "Used to. But now ... I guess if I'm the last person they see before they go, is that such a bad thing? If it had been anyone else, not that there *are* other Hedges around here, but if there were, they probably would've tried some exorcism thing that would've hurt her. Instead, we played hide and seek. Then, we went for a walk and talked together, and she went on. I don't know her story, and it's sad that she died, but ... death is part of everything, and in that aspect, so am I, whether I like it or not."

Bias looks away from us at that.

But Thatch, clever as he is, asks the one question that throws me off. "Does that mean you can't die?"

I focus on the jar centered between the three of us instead of his inquisitive stare. "I can."

Thatch nods and doesn't ask me how I *know*, because how else *can* you be so sure if you haven't brushed against death before?

Bias and I join hands. I reach out to Thatch with my free hand, eliciting sparks of energy between us. I clear my throat. "The magick in your blood will help us, even if you can't access it."

He nods, glancing at Tobias with a wary look that begs permission. Bias nods to Thatch and doesn't act surprised at the fact Thatch is a magickal being of some sort. Then again, they're holding hands, skin to skin, and I'm sure Bias has had a chance to read Thatch before now. I could ask him what he knows, but
....

Some things are meant to remain a mystery.

Thatch's fingers are scorching against mine. Bias' magick washes into my skin and I shudder at the syrupy cold flowing into my capillary veins under his touch. I open my lips to say thank you, because of course he could tell I'm low on reserves and didn't know how to ask. Bias shakes his head and smiles, so I close my mouth.

The sensation of one hand being cool and the other burning hot, electrifying even, is wildly disorienting.

"Okay, Thatch, all you have to do is repeat after us. *Dybbuk*, you have been found, and are no longer allowed onto this ground. You cannot take solace in the water or on the earth, it's time to find a home of your own, now."

Thatch raises a brow. "That's it?"

Bias chuckles. "Trust me, that's it."

"Alright, let's give it a go," Thatch says, rolling his shoulders back and squeezing my hand tighter, clearly amping himself up.

"Bias, fire if you please."

An orb of rose flames surrounds the jar, sparking and flaring. Magick lazily lifts the object into the air between us. Thatch's eyes widen and his lips part, but he doesn't say anything.

I rub the back of his hand with my thumb absently, then begin. Thatch and Bias' voices join in with mine, igniting the flames with a new passion. Green and soft, *soft* blue intermingle with the pink energy. The jar cracks and splits under the pressure, a solid *tink* echoes around us.

"*Dybbuk*, you have been found, and are no longer allowed onto this ground. You cannot take solace in the water or on the earth, it's time to find a home of your own, now."

The glass explodes.

Hundreds of shards are held back by the orb of fire separating the jar from us. The murky *Dybbuk* soul (I should've *known* it was a *Dybbuk*, they're essentially a swamp in disguise, but who expects an extinct ghost?) thrashes and contorts under our joined words and magick. The viscous, gunk-like substance stretches and snaps in attempts to escape the incantation, but after we chant the verses a second time, the *Dybbuk* evaporates into a few drops of oil, then nothing.

The fire diminishes and I exhale a heavy breath, reluctantly letting go of Bias and Thatch's hands. When I look over at Thatch, I bust out laughing.

Bias does too.

Thatch furrows his brow. "What? It worked, didn't it? I mean, it *was* pretty cool, but honestly not—*what* are you laughing at?"

I smile wide at him, fully basking in the way his windblown hair catches the first rays of sunset through the canopy. His curls are standing *straight* up, like someone took a blow dryer to his face and put it on full blast. His pupils are wide, and his shoulders are lowered from his ears. I wonder if Bias sent him 'good vibes' or if getting rid of the *Dybbuk* put him that much at ease.

"Nothing, nothing at all."

Bias, Thatch and I cut through space and time, thanks to Tobias' magick, mine is dead in the water and the little that remains feels like a limb that's fallen asleep. We land before the gates of Garren Castle, where the stony road gives way to the familiar and worn dirt path leading to the place I call home, but doesn't feel like it.

"Are you sure you don't want to come?" Tobias asks, brow raised.

"Yeah, I'll break the news to Cas."

Tobias shrugs, eyes sliding to Thatch fidgeting beside me. "Alright, but ..." Bias sighs, rubbing at his face in that way he does when he's been up with the kids for two days straight. He levels me with a soft look. "He needs you, Arlo, like once upon a time you needed him. People need each other, and right now, it's his turn. I'm worried about him."

"Hey," I say, stepping forward to hug Tobias when his voice wavers. "I just need tonight, okay? I'm ...."

Tobias nods, fingers tightening in my shirt. His voice drops to a whisper, the words soft but perhaps the most blunt thing I've ever heard from him. "I know, but you can't keep getting mad that people care and worry for you. It's what friends do."

"Fuckin' witch." I mutter, tucking my chin over his shoulder and squeezing tighter. He chuckles, then recomposes himself and nods to Thatch.

"I hope to see you again Thatch, and perhaps under better circumstances, next time, if we do meet again."

Thatch's fingers pause their tugging on his hoodie strings. "Oh, yes, you too, Tobias. Thank you, for the help."

Bias smiles softly at us, then turns away in search of his own home, where Caspian and Kitt and the rest of the Misfits have surely begun to start eating dinner without us.

"Arlo, we don't have to—"

I shift my gaze from Tobias' retreating figure to Thatch.

More specifically, his bloodshot eyes, which are flooding.

And his lips, which are trembling.

Without thinking, I reach out and rest a hand on his shoulder. "Hey, *hey*, what's wrong?"

His eyes widen and shaking fingers reach up to wipe at the tears freely running down his cheeks. "Oh *stars*, I'm–I'm not supposed to—" Thatch steps back, out of my touch. My hand drops as he tightens his hood around his horrified face.

"I—I'm sorry, I have to go. Please, um—" He stutters, closing his eyes as he shakes his head and takes a few more steps backwards, nearly falling. "Please, tomorrow, Arlo."

"Thatch, wait, what did I—" I start, but Thatch takes off running down the street, back towards the island.

I stand there, dumbfounded.

I replay everything, trying to wonder what went wrong.

He was laughing moments ago, in the woods, so it had to be something Tobias or I just said, but *what*?

Well, *fuck*.

I start walking, no clue where I'm going.

Bosko tries to land but I wave him off, shoulders rising. Evening falls properly and people roam the streets, patrons spill outside of restaurant patios as they enjoy late dinners and early drinks. I raise my head, tracking the banners weaving over the street, their sunset colors illuminated by the lamp lights flanking the street sides. I think about the *Dybbuk*, about Leon.

What does he want with me?

Why hasn't he passed to the Other Side?

I bury my hands in my pockets, promptly finding my phone in my right one. I haven't checked it for hours. With a heavy sigh, I do just that.

Six messages from Pain in the Ass.

Three from Doc's Personal.

Two from Kitty.

One from Dusan.

And that damned email I haven't checked.

I settle down at the nearest bench, empty and nestled underneath an iron wrought lamplight. I lean forward and rest my elbows on my knees. I tap my foot, staring at my phone for one more minute. Doc never texts me, or Dusan. I decide on Caspian first.

Pain in the Ass: we need to talk (1:30 pm)

Pain in the Ass: arlo quit being a dick and look at your phone (2:54 pm)

Pain in the Ass: i'm being serious, it's about that guy (3:02pm)

Pain in the Ass: i've been having these dreams and I think he's (3:05 pm)

Pain in the Ass: you better not be late for dinner (4:08 pm)

Pain in the Ass: ARLO ROOK YOU BETTER NOT BE DEAD OR I'LL KILL YOU MYSELF (4:43 pm)

I can't help it. I laugh, then dial his number and lean back.

He answers on the first ring. "What the *fuck*, Arlo? Where are you guys?"

"Hey, Cas. Bias should be there any minute, I'm ... well I'm not sure, but I'm fine, thanks for asking." I glance around, finding myself at Old Town Corners, across from The Uneven Butterfly.

He sighs and I can picture him scrubbing at his face. "I know that you're fine, you're always *fine*. Why aren't you with Bias? Bailing on us for some dick?"

Like you did?

I almost say it, but I don't.

Instead I say, "No, actually, Thatch called it a night. I'm ... I don't know Cas, I just wanted to be alone. It's been a long day between Doc's and that fucking *Dybbuk*, I'm probably gonna head back to the Castle and sleep."

Caspian is quiet for a long minute. I stare at a flock of wyverns silhouetted against the double moons, wondering if they're the same group that flew over Thatch's head earlier.

"Yeah, I bet you're pretty tired," Caspian finally says, a bit softer than he has been.

"Yeah, and you know what tomorrow is. You're not thinking of bailing on tradition, are you?"

Caspian huffs out a laugh. "We're not kids anymore, Arlo. We haven't played the Game in years."

"Yeah, well, maybe we should. Make it *actually* interesting this year."

"Oh yeah?"

"Yeah, Cas."

He laughs and my heart swells. "Alright, sure, why not. Meet you at Thitwhistle's at nine?" Caspian subsequently groans. "Or Phantom's, whatever the hell it's called now."

My stomach drops at the thought of seeing Thatch after he literally ran away from me. "He's keeping the name, but yeah." A pained smile twists my lips, for some reason that fact makes me happy. "Whoever wants to come, and if Tobias wants to join us, I volunteer as tribute for baby wrangling duty."

Caspian laughs again, whole hearted this time. "I'll tell him, he's now sprawled out in the grass with Kitt who's bitching up a storm that you're not with him."

I nod solemnly. "Sounds 'bout right."

"Well, have fun jacking off in the attic or whatever you do in your *alone* time."

"Hey, Cas?"

"Yeah, Arlo."

"I have something to tell you."

"Yeah?"

"I, uh, I applied for a job, at the university, at Scarlet. As a teacher, like Quentin, but for adults, you know? I actually have an email from them, but ... I don't want to open it, Cas. What if you're all right?"

"What do you mean?" Caspian asks, caught off guard.

A couple passing by captures my attention, hands clasped together and laughter rolling from both of them. The shorter of the two beams up at their partner, revealing a bright soulmark that flares against the night. Their partner smiles down, their own mark is visible in the same place along their neck, shining just as brilliantly.

Soul marks aren't *usually* located in the same place on those tethered to each other, but they can be. To the normals, they look like birthmarks, unless you get one of those fancy mirrors. I wonder if the pair know just how vividly they shine for each other.

"What if I can't be ... *fuck*, I don't know, a functioning adult who can have it all without breaking down, y'know? The job, the friends, the home. What if that's not meant for me? What if the reason I've been staying sane is because I'm keeping things small, easy, simple. Or what if this is all that I'm allowed, and If I try to take more than I deserve, then–"

"You're such an ass, we shouldn't be doing this over the phone." Caspian snarls.

I exhale heavily. "Right."

Caspian clicks his tongue. "You don't need a fancy job to have made it, you know this? With that being said, you should check your email. I'm happy for you, and you *do* deserve it. You deserve it all, more than anyone else I know. You've been through some shit, and it's done now. This is your happy ending, do what you *want* to do, not what you *should* do. And I know I've been mothering you, I don't mean to, it's just that ... well, you're my best friend in the entire world, Arlo. I love you, *so* much."

I swallow something heavy, a fracturing heart, perhaps?

"I love you too, Cas. I'm not going anywhere, I promise."

"Arlo?"

"Yeah?"

"Do me one favor?"

"Yeah, Cas."

"Stay away from Thatch Phantom."

Instead of arguing, I say, "I'll do my best, but I won't turn down money right now."

"I thought you said he wasn't paying you."

I can *hear* his brow raising. Fucking Caspian. "Listen Cas, gotta go. I'll text you when I'm on my way in the morning, you better be ready to get schooled."

Caspian grumbles, then hangs up.

"Fuck," I mutter, then check the rest of my messages, because if I don't do it now, they'll be left unread for days.

Doc: Hey, Arlo. Are you busy? (2:37 pm)

Doc: There were some anomalies in your bloodwork, could you come in tomorrow? (3:45 pm)

Doc: Arlo, this isn't optional, you need to get checked out. (5:11 pm)

Well, *that's* not unsettling. I move right on to Kitt.

Kitty: Don't worry about coming back for dinner, you better climb that man like a tree. Or let him climb you, whatever works. (1:38 pm)

Kitty: ARLO what the fuck have you done now?! Quit getting into trouble! (4:32 pm)

I laugh a little, sliding my hat off to rest it on my softly bouncing knee. Dusan's message is the shortest.

Dusan: Felix is home safe. (5:16 pm)

And ... the email.

Caspian definitely sounded like he already knew about the job. Is that why he's been pissy, because he *knew* I was keeping things from him? No, he's been pissy because *I've* been a closed off jerk. I need to fix that.

I open the email.

Salutations,

I hope this email finds you well, Mr. Rook.

First and foremost, I will be honest with you. The gap in your resume had me ... doubtful, to say the least, and while your recent employment teaching at the local studio is a respectable position, it is quite different from teaching in a university. I did not want to tell you in the interview, but I was aware of the rumors regarding your situation.

You surprised me though, Mr. Rook.

I myself have been in your shoes, or a pair quite like them, and I did not expect you to be so upfront with me regarding your past and what you will need in the future to succeed.

After speaking with you in person and reviewing your portfolio, the board members and I have decided that you are a perfect fit for Scarlet University. To be blunt, I admire you as a person, and an artist. I think not only the students will benefit from you, but some of the other faculty as well.

We look forward to working with you Mr. Rook, let's meet before the students return from solstice break, say, two weeks from today? My secretary will be in touch on Monday to smooth out the rest of the details. The accommodations you requested will all be met, which we will discuss further.

Enjoy the festival, Mr. Rook.
Eduardo Liaz
President of the Board of Directors
Scarlet University

I allow myself this moment.

A blip in time to believe the other shoe won't drop, that things aren't *too* good to be true. I laugh wildly, pumping my fists into the air and startling those passing by.

Instead of returning to the castle, I wander through the heart of Old Town, weaving back and forth through narrow alleys.

Whether I intend to or not I'm not sure, but I end up following the route I was planning on taking Thatch. I thought he'd like this part of town, where most of the craftsmen reign. The lake isn't that far off either, it's algae ridden bottom a wondrous nightlight. I pass by Ye Olde Binders and the Abstract Dagger, deciding to backtrack as opposed to passing by Heartstone Medical.

I turn a corner, inhaling the scents from Knead to Know down the way. The scent of tomorrow's bread turns my stomach, and it's then I realize I haven't eaten since lunch. I bury the hunger and my hands into my pockets. I watch Bosko fly overhead, disappearing behind the colosseum that is Rainbow Stadium. While I'm not a sports person, the glaring spotlights and roarous cheer pouring out from the last solar surfer game of the night is heartwarming.

I walk down a path bordering the calm, bioluminescent body of water where the aquatic suburbians dwell, Syorini Lake. The outer roads of Levena are usually quieter than the inner ones and as my boots shuffle ever so slowly across the path, the few people I do see start dwindling down to near nothing. Levena follows a long time, unspoken rule the night before the Game. The inhabitants of Levena are to disappear into their homes by midnight so the Illusionist can work and are not to reappear until dawn.

I look over my shoulder at the almost full double moons hanging heavily over Levena, washing the path and lakeside under its golden and silver rays of light. Bosko comes back around, soaring close to the water's edge and unbothered by the sirens lounging on islands of rock. The nocturnal creatures love to soak up the moonlight, their unabashedly naked bodies beautiful and pearlescent, reflecting the night.

Has he ever seen anything like that before?

I should be thinking about my new job, not Thatch.

I can't help it. I want to point out cool shit to someone who's not there. Someone I *really* don't know, no matter how much it feels like I do.

How much it feels like he's ... *everything* that was ripped out of me a long time ago.

A shiver runs down my spine and I casually look around, but there's only one other being on the path with me. *Great.*

A *selth* follows behind me from a distance, his overcoat collar turned up and doing nothing to hide who he is. His onyx eyes dart away when he catches me looking and the tentacles dangling from his star snout like mouth dance with agitation.

"Fuck *off*, Bob." I snarl, quickening my step.

Bob doesn't fuck off.

He catches up to me, taking hold of my wrist and yanking me to a stop. I sigh, entirely too fucking tired for his bullshit right now. I shake him off and he releases me, but doesn't leave. "The answer is still no, Bob."

"Come *on* Arlo, you haven't even heard me out yet." Bob counters, raspy voice washing over the tentacles draping from his face and onto his chest. His eyes shine, catching the moonlight as he adjusts his beret. "I'm ready to renegotiate."

"Bob, there never *was* a negotiation, and I don't need to hear you out because I'm not using my magick for whatever bullshit heist, hex or whatever the fuck it is guys like you need."

Bob balks, peach toned tentacles fluttering in surprise. "Guys like me? Come on now Arlo, I'd never hurt a fly. No one will get injured, I just need your help to cause ... a little havoc, you know? Nothing fatal, I *promise*."

I roll my eyes and take a step back. "*No*, Bob. Leave me the fuck alone. I don't mix with villains."

He grabs my arm again and doesn't let go, despite my scowl. "5,000 credits." Bob whispers, releasing a snuffling sound.

I scoff. "There's no way you have that much."

A tentacle pokes me on the nose. "How do you know? You never *listen*, just run away before I can get to the good part."

I'm definitely not considering it, but I *am* curious what the fuck he wants for *5,000* credits. Bob is known for crimes so minor and bizarre they're considered practical jokes at best, he *always* gets caught and has seemingly no motive for causing discourse.

I'm too pissed off to stay and listen.

I snap my fingers, snapping the tentacle that touched me with the force of 220 volt, enough to knock a human on their ass and instantly drain what's left in me. Bob flails backwards, yelping. "ARLO!"

I point a finger at him, unable to hide my shake. "*Don't* ask me again, Bob. I'm serious."

"You'll regret this Arlo Rook! Next time, it won't *be* a question." Bob raises a fist from his crumpled spot on the ground. I laugh, turning away from his curses. "Mark my words!"

I collapse onto my bed at five to midnight, not bothering to turn any lights on.

The mobiles of driftwood and charms lazily spin overhead.

I clutch the perfectly tucked blankets with trembling fingers and suck in and breaths that are far too hard to find, then am quickly disturbed by something *wet*.

I sit up with a dissatisfied groan, only to find Thatch's shirt and jeans, the pair he left behind this morning. Was that only just this morning we played pirates and mermaids?

And because no one will know any different, I bring the shirt up to my nose and inhale the wondrous cedar and maple magick that is Thatch Phantom, promptly falling asleep.

Sunday

Let's Play

Thatch

It's happening.

I'm fading, and it's faster than ever before. Is the universe punishing me for attempting to live with purpose?

With potential love?

I *know* now that I have maybe a week instead of the two I was hoping for.

It won't be enough.

It will never be enough.

I need to lock away any notions of living the way I want to.

After settling in for the night, or morning now I suppose, I undress completely.

I stand before the only mirror in the house and stare at myself.

If you've ever wondered what millennia upon *millennia* of years worth of scars look like, I can tell you.

It's horrifying.

Arlo

I'm paralyzed, forced to watch a macabre nightmare unfold.

I don't dream anymore. I had forgotten that it's either *this,* or waking up in odd places.

I also forgot how terrifying they are.

I sit on a river's edge, swinging my bare feet just over the water. I watch a tattered black flag with crossbones catch wind on Newcoin Islet. The galleon will never sail again, shipwrecked upon the craggy cliffs of the island which used to grace the water's surface, but now is a monstrous thing that towers over the sealife below. I lean forward, moving my fingers in different ways to see what happens.

I hurt myself a few times learning magick this way, but I don't have anyone else to ask. Plus, that rainbow I conjured last time seemed to please the fanged nymphs. The same three that always visit me swim lazily a few yards out. I can't remember their names, but I feel like I should. They laugh and call *my* name, teasing me when I accidentally zap myself and cheering when I finally make that rainbow.

A double one, at that.

They seem like ... my *friends.* But their faces are missing, like paper burns on an otherwise beautiful masterpiece of iridescent blue, green and purple scales. I open my mouth to call back like I did once before, but nothing comes out.

My eyes widen and the nymphs scream when my hands fly to my throat, pulling on an invisible force that slowly attempts to kill me. Two of my friends charge towards me and one swims away to the nearby Leideen Ait, for ....

A world shaking headache ensues, encouraging the darkness pulsating at the edges of my vision. It feels all too real, it *hurts*.

For help, that's right, they went to get help.

Air returns to my lungs at the same time a harpoon flies through the air, spearing through my closest friend who combusts into fluttering parchment.

I stagger to my feet and wheel around, finding my first lover.

Not my first love, that title belongs to my best friend. No, Leonidas Forrestal was my *first*.

"You *lied* to me." He snarls, and twin pools of hatred bore into my soul, carving out my heart. An endless abyss of an aura contrasts his angelic wingspan outstretched behind him, gilded tips of white feathers catch the noon sun and block out everything that isn't him.

Everything clicks into place and what's left of my mutilated heart oozes onto the ground. "You're a *witch*," I laugh, despite everything.

"*No*, I'm *not*. But you are! You lied to me! You said that you're not like them! I trusted you Arlo, you're the only one I have!" Leon cries, strands of blond stick to his sweat ridden forehead.

"Leon! Do you even hear yourself? You just used *magick* on me." I corral my tone and the magick burning in my twenty year old veins. I extend a trembling hand to my love, willing him to come to his senses. We had just gotten our own place, and besides hiding my magick from him ... it was good, he *chose* me. The only person who ever did.

"It's you and me, right? I don't know what's going on, but you have to just ... let me help you, we can learn together. I love you, Leo. Do you hear me? I *love* you."

The oily black in his eyes fades to the deep sorrel I know and love. His wings lower as he considers my hand. This particular moment would come to haunt my daydreams and endless waking thoughts, how *close* I was to saving him.

But I wasn't enough.

I never have been, for anyone.

How different would our lives have been?

"*No.*" Leon growls and the darkness seeps back into his eyes. He takes a step back. "I'm not one of them. I'm not like *you*. Stay the *fuck* away from me, I don't *ever* want to see you again."

His beautiful face catches fire, brittle paper set aflame by my confusion.

The edges of my vision catch and fray, beating with how furious my heart is. I always wake up at this point to unfinished memories, a hole where the ending should be. I have Caspian's version of the story, how he found me, but I remember nothing that transpired after Leon rejected me.

But I do remember how I felt.

Angry. So fucking angry. He's all I have. My supposed *person*, and he's leaving me because of something I can't control?

"*No?*" I echo, yanking on the edges of the fleeting night terror. I startle myself, and him. His face shifts back into focus, charred edges coming back together to reveal his shell shocked expression.

I have no idea what territory I'm in anymore.

Did I really say that to him? Is this a memory? Or what I wish I'd done?

Or has Leon moved on from *Dybbuks* and he can taint my dreams now, trying to drive me crazier than I already am?

Caspian's words sweep away the remaining fog. *'It's because of me, isn't it?'*

I grin wildly at Leon, relishing in the warmth pouring from my nose and the pain riding my body. I *feel*, and it's agony, but it's *something*.

"*You're* the problem, Leon. Not me. Quit being a coward and take me right *fucking* now then! Prove to me that you don't want me, because you know what? I. Don't. Believe. You."

My magick fights to be released, begging to maim and avenge and put down, but I stand my ground and raise my chin. Hot copper runs down my throat but I don't care. I fucking *smile* at him, and I'm pretty sure my teeth are coated with the blood escaping my orifices and dripping into my mouth.

Leon's hard, *furious* expression doesn't change when we charge each other at the same time. He roars like the mighty adversary he is.

I *remember* now.

We didn't use magick.

We used fists and boots and elbows and knees.

We beat each other to an inch of our lives, slinging blood into the water where it intermingled with the tears of one unnamed friend and the blood of another.

I lost a tooth, *that's* when it happened.

I broke his arm. Snapped it right in fucking half. I was *winning*.

But then ... oh yes, *then* he cheated.

He restrained me with dark and frigid magick, power I didn't learn to overcome until decades later when we met again, not for the first time, but for the last time.

The world was closing in and I thought I heard boots pounding against the earth, but I gave up. I decided if I was meant to die at my lover's hands at the end of a hard fought battle, then so be it. Tragic, but romantic.

But then, the sun overtook him and there was so much *blue* as the world caught fire.

I awake to a ringing in my ears and the vague feeling that some-one's trying to kill me.

I roll over with a groan and take hold of my vibrating and screeching phone that's about to be thrown across the room. I expect it's Kitt that's attempting to murder me this early in the morning. My eyes widen when I find not only messages and missed calls from Kitt, but our group Misfit chat has exploded along with notifications from the citywide emergency system. Caspian called a few times, along with the director of the museum, and Doc.

Chief's even called me.

"Fuck." I sit up, drowsiness somewhat clearing from my ex-hausted mind. I slept like shit and something tells me today is going to be a long one. I glance over at Bosko's perch, brow furrowing when I find it empty. He loves his sleep, especially after shenanigans like yesterday's ghost problem. The familiar doesn't stay with me twenty four seven, but it's not like him to just leave without saying goodbye.

Another series of vibrations rattle my phone and I scroll through the messages, jaw dropping. I immediately call up Kitt, disregarding the emergency messages and missed calls.

"Arlo! Thank Gods, get your ASS over here!" Kitt shouts over a wave of background noise filled with sirens and people. I stand, frowning down at the damp spot on my chest from Thatch's shirt now on the floor, beside his soaking wet, crum-bled up jeans.

"Alright, start at the beginning." I put her on speaker phone and get my shit together, opting for black leather and combat boots. No rainbow dusters and purple Converse today. I do have a reason for such vastly different looks.

My jacket is my armor, enchanted a hundred different ways to protect me via the runes I stitched into the inner layers, along with being lightly washed with water collected from the last thunderstorm and brewed under a full moon to add a boon to my attacks and heighten my senses. It also wards off physical and magickal attacks, along with any leeching negative energy. I have enough of that on my own.

And the boots match the jacket.

Kitt inhales sharply, reiterating what she's probably repeated a hundred times this morning. "I came in at five to start my shift early and meet Thatch. Your wards were untouched, the doors locked, but it's like a *ghost* came in here and took them all."

I hop into a pair of skinny jeans, remembering I forgot to take my medicine last night. If I take it now, I'll be a zombie. Fuck, just gonna have to remember tonight. "*All* the paintings?"

"Fourteen that we planned on using for the Illusionist exhibit and seven from the Levena exhibit. They took nothing else, the police think it's an inside job and I—"

"Chief knows better than to suspect you." I snap, pulling my beanie onto my head.

"She doesn't, but still, this is my *job*, Arlo, and the paintings, some of them are yours and now they're *stolen*. I'm so sorry, I don't know how I allowed this to—"

"Hey, Kitty, this isn't your fault, just breathe, okay? I'll be right there. Just hold on."

"Okay, okay. I'm here."

I chew on my bottom lip. "Is Thatch with you then?"

"Yeah, he is, but he has no better idea than we do."

I nod, then remember she can't see me. My stomach sinks at the thought of seeing him again but I need to know if he's alright. "Okay. I'm glad he's with you. I'll be right there."

We hang up and I refresh myself in the bathroom, then find the canvas duffel that I usually take on big jobs, the one I would've taken to Leideen Ait if I had known I was dealing with a *Dybbuk*. A fresh pang in my temple takes hold as I sling the bag full of witch shit over my shoulder.

I check my phone again, noting the time. 8:00 AM.

Oh.

Today's the Game.

There are no coincidences in life, and despite the fact someone has broken through my wards (which is impossible) and the museum has been stolen from, I grin.

I sneak out of the castle undetected, not bothering to call the Director back as I'll be there soon. I do call Caspian back, but he doesn't answer so I leave a message. "Hey, headed to the Museum, maybe you're on your way there too. This doesn't change our plans, but I may be a few minutes late. Love ya, Cas."

I hang up and check the emergency notifications. Earthquakes of the 2.8 and 3.2 variety shook the world last night at 2:20 AM and 5:36 AM, signaling an early start to the season. The last emergency message brings me to halt near the shed out back that houses a beast I haven't ridden in years.

"No way." I breathe.

LEVENA EMERGENCY BROADCAST
2:22 AM
OCTOBER 31st
People of Levena,

It has been brought to my attention that the Games in previous years have been subpar, at best. I feel that I owe you the why of it, for as you all know I pride myself on bringing you puzzles and entertainment of the highest caliber.

I have to admit, I did not put these past decades of Games on myself, at least, not in an up close and personal sense. Think of it as freezer meals that you *pop* in the microwave. They'll do the trick, but they're unsatisfying. It is not by choice that things have been this way, and I cannot tell you why.

I cannot tell you who I am.

What I am.

Why I'm really here.

But what I *can* tell you is that I love playing this Game with you, and this year, I've concocted one that benefits the both of us.

If we play our cards right, all those questions will be answered, and the most precious treasure will be awarded to the first person who solves the Game.

One wish.

Now, of course, there's the obvious.

No resurrection.

No striking anyone down.

No forcing people to fall in love.

Ask for anything else, and it's yours. As long as you solve the puzzle.

Await further instructions, and as always,

Let's play, my friends.

-The Scarlet Illusionist

I most definitely am *not* the cause of the burnout on Garren Road.

I slip my beanie under my thigh and cruise through the vehicular streets, the motorcycle between my legs picks up speed along Syorini Road. After powering up the old engine with my magick, it fired right up.

The wind cuts through my bed mussed hair, knotting up the waves. I ride with my legs and arms outstretched, the handlebars curl high off the frame and the second set of foot boards allow me to fully stretch out and relax.

Sunbathing merfae and selkies wave to me from their rock islands on the lake and I lower my hand, waving in a two fingered gesture. The dust on the black gas tank painted with purple pinstripes doesn't go unnoticed, neither does my calm heart. When chaos reigns and the other shoe drops, that's when I do best, *that's* when I feel at home. It's the waiting that kills me.

Waiting for something to go wrong.

Waiting for people to leave.

Waiting for nothing and the possibility of everything is what speeds my heart to an unhealthy and panicked rhythm.

But *right* now?

Right now it's thudding steadily against my chest.

I scrape the foot boards against the road when I lean into the curves following the lake's edge. I scan the skies for Bosko with no luck. We haven't talked since he fetched Tobias for me when purging the *Dybbuk*, and I suppose I owe him a thank you.

I turn right onto the road the museum's located on and after a few blocks, multiple sirens cut at my ears. I park just outside an orange and black striped barricade blocking off thru traffic. I kick down the center stand and a rookie tells me I can't stay here.

I chuckle and before I can say something smartass, Chief is there, resting a scaled hand on the kid's shoulder. "Stand down, Officer. Rook is here for us."

The officer's blood red, vampiric eyes widen, definitely not a vegan. "*Oh*, you're—"

"Arlo!" Kitt calls, squeezing through officers and police cars, dragging Thatch behind her. She throws herself into my arms and I squeeze tight.

"Hey, Kitty. Alright?"

Kitt nods furiously. "Yeah, now that you're here."

"Oh, I don't know about that. It was my wards that failed, after all."

Kitt pulls away from me, wiping at her eyes. Thatch stands awkwardly off to the side, unrecognizable in dress slacks, a freshly pressed long sleeve and black suspenders with gilded clips. It appears he may have tried to brush his hair, but the result is a more chaotic mess than usual. His beard's cleaned up as well, artfully so without taking too much length off.

His eyes meet mine for only a quick second, but it's long enough to see the sky in them is deeply clouded. I nod to him, then the *tannin* waiting patiently, her spiked tail swishing gently behind her. "Good morning, Thatch, Chief."

"Mr. Rook," Thatch says with a nod, surprising me with the formality. "Any new ideas?" He asks, looking between the Chief, Kitt and I. So, that's how it's going to be. I postpone rifling through my memories once again, searching for what I did wrong.

Chief rubs at her long snout with a taloned hand, huffing out small plumes of smoke from her flared nostrils. "We've interviewed the rest of the staff, but that's as far as we've gotten. The surveillance shows nothing, and there's no physical traces. We were hoping you might pick up something."

I nod. "I'll try, but if they were smart enough to make it past my wards, I doubt they would've left a trace. Has the Illusionist theory been brought up yet?"

They all look at me like I've grown two heads.

"I don't think it's a coincidence that this happened on the same day the Illusionist hijacked the emergency system and announced a new type of Game."

Chief sighs. "Well, when you put it like that, Arlo."

I shrug. "Or I'm a conspiracy theorist."

Kitt elbows me. "It's a solid idea."

Thatch tentatively raises a hand. "Hijacked the system? How?"

Chief stares at him, debating how much to divulge. I wouldn't be surprised if Thatch pours money in the police department's pockets, too. "We've no idea. There's no outside I.P, no foreign digital traces."

"How eerily convenient, wouldn't you say?" I add, earning a glare from the *tannin*.

"I'm running on two hours of sleep and a shit ton of leftover alcohol from last night Arlo, fuck off inside and make yourself useful." Chief snarls, forked tongue slipping out to poke the tip of a fang.

"Sheesh, fine." I put my hands up, then gesture to my bike. "Don't touch it, rookie."

The shell shocked officer comes to, sputtering indignantly. I walk away with Kitt hanging off my side. "Coming, *Mr.* Phantom?" I call without looking back.

Two can play at this game.

Whatever game it is we're playing.

"What's that about?" Kitt whispers, glancing back.

I shrug. "Only giving what I'm getting."

Kitt huffs. "So dramatic."

We approach the museum crafted from white marble tinged with a spider webbing of bright silver. Massive arched windows house vibrant stained glass murals which depict scenes of the first scholars who lived in Levena. The masterpieces dominate the forefront of the museum and hide behind great pillars. Kitt doesn't release my arm as we climb the numerous steps leading to open, double doors of oak and iron.

Thatch walks by my side, silent and beautiful under the morning light gracing the last day of October. I think about how gorgeous he would be under the full hunter's moons tonight and hide away my smile. I wish I knew what I did to make him look this way. I want him to smile at me again, talk in that funny way he does and laugh at the smallest things.

We stop before the open doors and Kitt steps aside so I can begin my work. I trace alongside the detailed trim bordering the doors, closing my eyes as I search. "What's he looking for?" Thatch whispers to Kitt.

"Shh." She chastises him.

I find the carved anemone flower hiding in the wood and tap its center. The round piece pops out and I reach inside the hidden compartment, retrieving a bloodstone infused with none other than my own magick. With eyes closed, I close the stone in my palm, searching for any disturbances caused within the past twenty four hours.

Only those with clearance granted by me (or the director, I made them a proxy) can pass through the wards when the museum isn't open, and the common people are allowed in during open hours. Theoretically, there should be nothing between the time when Kitt was here yesterday to do some work, and five this morning.

I find exactly that. Nothing.

"Hm," I say finally, dropping the stone into my duffel. I take out a replacement and put up new wards, anchoring them to the larger bloodstone. With a heavy exhale, I replace the flower carving. "They were never breached."

I turn to Kitt and find Thatch standing close beside her, so close their arms are touching. You wouldn't know they just met yesterday.

"That makes no *sense*." Kitt whines.

"Let's go inside," I say, glancing at Thatch. He smiles tightly at me.

"Actually, the Director needs me for a minute, so, yeah," Kitt says, an obvious lie. She salutes us both and I roll my eyes at her.

I wordlessly head inside.

I don't expect Thatch to follow me. He'll probably disappear and that's, well that's fine.

It's what people do, isn't it?

I walk down an expansive main hallway decorated in crushed red velvet curtains and gilded accents. Small exhibits featuring sculptures rest in the small breaks between side halls. Recessed skylights blanket the ceiling, interspersed between chandeliers which lend further to the lofty space. I inhale the scent of dust, parchment, and cedar, then turn down a side hall, the one leading to the largest showing room.

The new Scarlet Illusionist's exhibit.

"I didn't know you had a motorcycle. Or is it a solarcycle?" Thatch whispers from beside me, startling me just intensely as if he had shouted.

I hold a hand to my heart. "Fuck, Thatch."

He smiles up at me, a devilish thing. "Back to Just Thatch?"

I frown, suffering emotional whiplash. "You started it."

His lips turn down, too. "Did I? Well, that just won't do."

I roll my eyes. "You're complex, did you know that?"

He laughs, and the sound of it echoes throughout the marble halls we pass through, causing me to flush. "I've been told."

"Well, to answer your question, it's a motorcycle with some ... modifications. I fuel it with my magick," I say offhandedly, but the statement perks him up.

"Really? That's inspiring, you'll have to show me."

"Sure." I chuckle, tugging on the gauge in my ear. "Are you ... alright? You, um, you worried me, last night."

Thatch smiles again, but it's softer this time. "Worried you? That would imply that you care for me, Arlo."

"And if I did?"

He stops walking, hands in his pockets and curls in his eyes. "Then that would be fine, Arlo, just fine. But I think the room you need is right here."

I back track the few steps between us. "You avoided the question."

Thatch grins wide, the freckled and warm beauty of it magnified by a skylight pouring the sun's warmth down onto us. I want to reach out and touch him. Why did I ever think I could manage without him? Did we *really* just meet two days ago?

"Did I?" Thatch chuckles, then unburies a hand to reach forward and squeeze my shoulder. "I'm fine, Arlo. I'm sorry for running off like that and worrying you. Allergies, you know?"

"Allergies?" I lift a brow, not buying it one bit. I'll let it slide, for now, if only because his touch warms my skin, even through the leather. "They make potions for that, you know."

Thatch tilts his head. "Do they? Well, I'll have to find a witch who can help me out."

It's my turn to smile. "I think I might be able to find you one."

We stand there, and he doesn't look away this time when I stare into the endless skies dwelling in his face, slightly clouded but not as dull as before. His hand slides down my arm, leaving behind a path of electrified skin beneath my jacket.

"Arlo?" He breathes in the light filtered space between us that's smaller than ever before, hand cupping my elbow.

"Yeah, Thatch?" I reach for him.

"Shouldn't we investigate?" His gaze darts to my lips, then back up to my eyes, not at all subtle and stirring that foreign heat inside my rib cage once again.

"Gods, yes."

BRRR. BRRR. BRRR.

The emergency notification terrifies us both, thrusting my heart into my throat.

"Damn it." Thatch mutters, reaching into his pocket for a phone that's blaring as opposed to the intense vibrating of mine. "Apologies, can't figure out how to turn down this damn thing."

I retrieve mine, scanning the message at the same time he does.

LEVENA EMERGENCY BROADCAST
8:38 AM
OCTOBER 31st

I am pleased to announce the Game has officially begun.

I have borrowed several masterpieces from the local museum, which I highly recommend visiting if you haven't already, the aesthetic there is *divine*.

Now, out of all the paintings I've chosen, I will hide seven for you to find. Why seven? Well, I figured one for each day of the week. Why limit the Game to a *day* when we can have a whole week of fun, *together*?

Also, there is something special about these paintings. There is one detail regarding my true identity in each artwork. If you're clever enough, you won't need all of them to figure it out, perhaps only one or two, but nevertheless you'll have seven clues at the very least.

I have hidden the first puzzle in a new favorite establishment of mine. Where the paintings have been placed are a hint in and of themselves, if you think about it.

I wonder, who shall be the first to find it?

When you have formulated an answer, leave me a note in the Little Library located in Funguy Park. If you've answered correctly, you will be notified in a timely fashion.

Enjoy the Game,

-The Scarlet Illusionist

P.S: I am loathe to admit this shall be our last adventure together, my friends. Let us play one last time, and enjoy it wholeheartedly.

"Well, they seem like quite the melodramatic fellow, don't they? Seems like your theory was right," Thatch says without glancing up from his phone, fingers pressing all the wrong buttons.

I chuckle. "You're not wrong, one year they buried the treasure at the bottom of Syorini Lake and to win, you had to charm a mermaid. Here, let me see."

He hands over the phone, glad to be rid of it and grinning wide. "I bet there were more than a few who tried, despite all the teeth."

"Oh yeah, but if there's one thing I've learned about the Illusionist is how they play," I say, turning down the volume until the phone sets on vibrate.

Thatch raises a brow. "Oh? Well, do tell, maybe we can team up and win this thing."

I laugh. "I already have a team, but you're welcome to join it. Back in the day Caspian, Kitt and I played every year. I thought it'd be nice if we did that again." I check the time on my phone, frowning. "I'm supposed to be meeting them now."

"Oh, well, that's quite alright. I don't want to intrude." He puts his hands up, smile fading.

"No!" I blurt out, starling him and myself. "I mean, that's not what I meant. I *want* you to. I mean, only if you do. I don't really care about the prizes, Caspian gets on my case because I get *too* into the puzzles and then Kitt gets on *his* case for—"

His throaty laugh erases my anxiety. "Okay, I'll join your team. Is this what people do, team up?"

"It's easier to solve a problem with people by your side, isn't it?"

Thatch raising a knowing brow. "Is it now? Does that apply to life, too?"

I feel strange, like I've been backed into a corner. "Well, *yes*."

"Huh." Thatch scratches at his beard. "I'll have to find me a Life team, then. It *is* hard going it alone." His last few words trail off, as if he's speaking more to himself than me.

I want to tell him I'll be on his team. But something traps the words deep inside. I clear my throat and say something else, something simple. "Well, I think since we're here, we should still go look inside the exhibit, even though we know the culprit."

Thatch nods, eyes shining. "Doesn't explain how they got past your wards, though."

I shrug. "Some things are best left undiscovered, Thatch Phantom."

And the sun hides behind the clouds, no longer filtering in through the skylight and warming his face which is too far from mine. Even without the sun, the smile he gives me is unlike any

I've seen before and it brightens my world to a shade that I never want to lose.

I stand in a room surrounded by paintings of all sizes, the largest of which dominate the walls while the smaller canvases rest on easels situated around the space. Squares of dust remain where two frames once rested on the east and west walls, but the remaining missing canvases were of the medium to small variety. They'll be harder to find.

"What do you think?" I ask Thatch who slowly traces around the room, absorbing every detail in the remaining pieces.

He grins at me, back to being mischievous. "This is only my second time here in decades, and when I came in with Kitt this morning we weren't in here long. I have no idea the differences between what they took and what's here. Who even paints these? For there being no one who knows what the Illusionist looks like, there's a lot of portraits of them."

"Well," I say, having already noted a few things of interest. "People who *think* they've seen the Illusionist. For a while it was an open debate on who they were, but then the Illusionist called off a game one year because of it. Since then there have been conspiracy theories and less obvious debates, like painting."

I gesture around us. "So it's kind of a big deal now that they *want* us to find out who they are."

He rubs his chin. "You really think it's the same person, after all this time? What if they're a grandchild of sorts carrying on their ancestor's legacy, how would you be able to narrow it down?"

I blink, considering. "I've honestly never thought any different. I suppose it *could* be a generational thing of sorts, maybe? But I don't know ... it doesn't feel that way to me."

Thatch chews on his bottom lip, trying to hide a smile. I rub at my sternum when Thatch paces back over to me. "If it is one person, why end it now?"

I shrug, having mulled this over since reading the message. "I don't know."

He gives me a flat look. "You really have no idea?"

I elbow him gently, because I feel like that's alright. Right?

"You're like the kid peeking at everyone's papers in class. Why do *you* think?

Thatch shrugs, staring at a piece on the wall. "Maybe they're tired. How long has this been going on?"

I think for a moment. "Over five hundred years. There were some years when it didn't happen, but I bet they're less than ten." I stare at him, his lost in thought gaze is set on a painting of bright green eyes framed by a sunset. Eventually, I say, "I agree."

Thatch looks at me then, exposing the other side of his lips turned up in tired delight. "I guess we'll see. I'm just glad I can be here for this one, I'm either on business or too busy to play."

I squeeze his shoulder and he stiffens, so maybe that moment is gone. That's fine. It's fine.

"Me too, Thatch."

He nods, rigid. "Should we go back to the cafe then and talk with the others?"

"Yeah, I've got what I need."

We walk back the way we came, through halls darkened by the storm brewing overhead, allowing no sun through the skylights. Thatch is quiet, hands in his pockets.

"Are you sure this is alright? I'm not sure your friends like me very much." He murmurs, staring intently at his leather shoes that are a far cry from the black Converse he usually wears.

I laugh a little. "My friends like you just fine, Caspian's just jealous is all."

"Jealous?" Thatch asks incredulously as we travel through the main hallway. "I thought he and Tobias were ..." Thatch thinks better of it and trails off.

"Soulmates?" I supply, stopping before the front doors.

"Yes." He nods quickly, fiddling with his suspenders.

"They are. But Caspian's my best friend, and he's ..." I ponder for a moment. "Protective."

Thatch debates for a moment, chewing on a question I know he wants to ask but is too polite to. We step outside and wait on the raised dais overlooking a now nearly empty street save for Kitt, Chief, and the Director standing together near my motorcycle and the only police car left. The incoming thunderstorm rattles the sky before a crack of lightning rushes through black clouds.

"We were together about a decade ago, but then he met Tobias, and well, that's that."

"Do you still love him?" Thatch asks, eyes darkened like they were earlier, not unlike the horizon.

The question takes me off guard, and I don't want to lie to him, but I also don't want him to think ... well, it doesn't matter what he thinks, does it? Nothing's going to happen.

"I don't know," I say, and Thatch stiffens almost imperceptibly. "I thought I did, but ... maybe I just missed *being* loved. I know I wouldn't have wanted him to choose me over his soulmate. Feelings are ... not my strong suit."

"That sounds like love to me." Thatch mumbles.

"Have *you* ever been in love?" I ask, stealing his boldness. The rain comes down in sheets, creeping up the steps towards us. We're safe under cover, for now.

"I thought I was." He shrugs, watching the stairs dampen. "Same song as yours, different tune."

I want to ask how you can be hundreds of years old and never be in love, or never have met your soulmate.

I want to ask if he thinks he could love me.

I want to ask if he would let me love *him*.

But instead, what I ask is, "Want to go for a ride in the rain?"

That Was It

Thatch

Rain pelts the borrowed leather covering my upper body and I squeeze my eyes shut, arms wrapped tight around Arlo's heated middle as we cruise down Syorini Road. I stopped paying attention to where we were exactly long ago. How he can withstand the rain at these speeds without a jacket is beyond me, but I'm not about to complain that I'm wearing his.

And the rain, it's ... cleansing.

I feel like a madman, laughing maniacally into Arlo's spine.

He's laughing too, leaning back into me. He twists the throttle, ensuring I latch on and sing my joy to the skies. Luckily the thunder and lightning hasn't let up, otherwise the quakes in the earth caused by my stupid happiness would be plain for everyone to hear, and perhaps feel. To them, it would be for seemingly no reason at all.

I told myself last night I would stay away.

But, *fuck*, I can't ....

How long will I be alone for this time?

How long will I be away for?

Will I come back?

And will I regret not spending every fucking minute I have with him?

What if he's not alive when I return, and I miss the *one* chance I had with my soulmate? Even if he doesn't remember me, or realize that I'm *his*, we can be happy for a moment, right?

Right?

"Hold on tight." He warns.

"I already am, how much–"

I'm reduced to a scream when he guns it and I force my eyes open against the rain that's lessening in thickness but not quantity. We're heading out of town, to the north on Vieta Highway. I've never been this way, and that's an odd thing to say, for me.

There's no one on the road and I know I should probably ask why we're going this way, aren't Caspian and the others waiting for us? But I feel selfish right now, and I'm going to let him take me wherever he desires.

Arlo shifts in his seat, looking back over his shoulder at me. I lift my head from his back, meeting his seconds-long gaze before he turns ahead once more. "You can uh, rest your legs up here, if you want." He pats his thigh and if my cheeks weren't already red from the wind, they are now.

The backrest on his bike is comfortable enough, but I don't tell him that. I lean back just enough so I can lift my legs up, wrapping them around his middle. He fucks with the throttle, scaring the shit out of me so I fly forward and wrap my arms back around him too.

"Asshole." I mumble, and he must've heard it over the wind because he laughs.

I sigh, closing my eyes again as I let Arlo Rook carry me away.

I startle awake when we diverge from the main highway and onto a soft dirt road that jostles the bike as Arlo slows down. "Oh, look who's awake." He calls, grinning.

I blink rapidly, lowering my legs from where they're still wrapped around him. I lean back, straightening my stiff spine. "If you had told me I would fall asleep on this machine I would've laughed at you. I apologize, I'm not a very good riding partner, am I?"

Arlo chuckles, cruising slower and slower down the narrowing road. "I didn't mind." He lifts a shoulder, eyes darting away. "Just means you feel safe with me."

"Well, that, I—" I sputter, then try again. "That goes without saying, I think."

He throws a smile over his shoulder. "Good."

We come to a stop at a place I've never been, and the rain has stopped.

How bizarre.

"Oh my," I breathe, clutching Arlo as I absorb the ravine carving out the earth below us. Sparse evergreens dot the rocky cliff sides and the bowl of the trench that extends hundreds of miles to the south and at least another twenty ahead of us. To the distant northeast is a forest I've heard of but never had the time to visit.

Two eagles leave their nest on the opposite side of the ravine and lazily survey their territory, keeping watch for relatively small prey leaving the comfort of their home after the storm. I've always *felt* these enormous birds in the same sense I can feel all the living things I'm connected to, wherever I am, but I've never seen them in person.

"Do you like it?" Arlo asks, gazing at the birds with a soft smile. My hands gently rest on his sides and I grip the wet fabric beneath my fingers. The bike is warm between my legs, almost as warm as Arlo's back pressed to my front.

I clear emotion out of my throat. "Yes, very much. Thank you for bringing me here," I say, pressing my forehead to his spine. We sit there together for a few moments in silence, and because I'm a *somewhat* nice person, I eventually ask, "What time is it? Are the others waiting for us?"

"Well, the plan was changed for a number of reasons. We'll be meeting them at the shop here in a bit." He reaches into his pocket and checks his phone. "10."

"Wh–what?" I blink rapidly. "I slept for almost an *hour* on that thing?"

Arlo chuckles again. "Yeah, that's alright though. We can head back and maybe you'll stay awake this time."

I nod, determined. "Alright, but can we wait a few more minutes? Would that be alright?"

"Sure, I gotta take a walk anyway."

"For what? *Oh*. Actually, me too."

We part ways, dismounting the motorcycle with stiff bones and tight muscles. I look down, taking in my soaked figure and Arlo's jacket blanketing me. The sleeves hide my hands and I frown. I gently take it off, draping it over the back of the bike. I tremble the moment I walk away without it, but it's not bad enough to make a mess of my shoes.

By the time I zip up and make my way over, Arlo's waiting for me, hands in his pockets and boots testing the edge of the ravine. My heart leaps to see him so close to such a treacherous fall. I join him, albeit staying a couple of precious steps away from the edge.

He smiles at me over his shoulder. Arlo's smiles are small things that pull up one side of his lips, and never the same side twice in a row. He has a singular dimple that appears in his right cheek no matter how soft the grin is on that side and I adore it. That kind of smile is present now and his eyes are ... different. Completely open, hopeful, fond.

Physically, too. His pupils are wide and a sliver of vibrant green rings them, pulsating with magick in time to his strong heartbeat.

"Trust me?" He asks, voice hoarse.

"I do." I breathe the moment he finishes.

He holds out his hand. "Come here."

I bite my bottom lip, then do just that. Our souls spark in recognition and I sigh, hungrily committing the sensation of his palm against mine to memory.

"Can I hold you, Thatch?" Arlo asks in a calm, raspy tone which surprises me more than the fact he's asking me to stand on a *cliff* with him.

There's only one answer to that question. "Yes."

I allow him to lead me to the small space between him and the edge. His arms wrap around my middle and his back contorts as he bends down to properly hold me with all he's got, hooking his chin over my shoulder.

I don't dare turn my head to look at him because I think my toes are *right* on the edge and I'm about to ask what the *hell* this is about because I don't really care for heights but *then*—

Oh, but then.

Eagles sweep upwards from below, teasing the cliff's vertical surface and washing us in a great wind. The pair rise, rise, rise, then dive back down again, talons entangled. They plummet back down the way they came, scraping against the cliff. I flinch back but Arlo holds me tight, whispering, "I've got you."

I know.

They ascend once more, but this time their tawny gold wings scoop air in slow motion. The pair dominate the space before us, eliminating everything that's not *them*. The sun tears a hole in the storm clouds hiding the sky. The clouds don't disappear entirely, but there's enough warm light to reveal the gilded beauty of the birds before us.

Birds that are so much bigger than I've sensed and imagined. From far away, the brain can file away their size as a trick of the mind, but up close the lie is revealed. Do they recognize me as the one who shakes their discarded goat carcasses down into the ravine? I've never seen anything more magnificent and awe inspiring, truly.

Air ceases to exist as the larger of the two hovers closer, bringing talons the size of my body mere feet from our place on the cliff. Saucer-like golden irises ringed with silver watch me with intensity and when the creature blinks, the third eyelid slides down and they stare at me through that lens, too.

I feel scrutinized, evaluated, *tested*. For what, I don't know.

A haunting, melodic sound vibrates up the bird's chest, throat and out its beak as it lowers to meet my face. Inches separate the creature and I.

I don't breathe.

Feathers press against my forehead.

And a grand magick courses through me, one comforting and bright and everything I'm without. I gasp, shuddering in Arlo's unrelenting arms. He has me.

Then, a voice. One that I'm sure is meant only for me. *"He needs you, and you need him. You have to change, Thatcher. This is what he would feel like."*

I bite back a sob because I've been *trying*.

All I've been doing for *thousands* of years is rebelling against the chains that bind me to the universe. I *want* to change.

"Despairing is not the answer." The golden eagle, a universal being who is most definitely more than it appears, gives me a

dose of my own medicine, leaving the riddle inside my heart before it flaps its wings once, twice, and a harsh third time.

The eagles leave just as quickly as they came, diving into the chasm before soaring back out to their nest. I look down to find a feather clutched in my shaking hand.

"Are you alright?" Arlo asks, pulling us back from the edge one step at a time. "They can be intense, I should have warned you." He loosens his arms in case I want to leave.

I don't.

I hold the feather tighter. "That was ... wonderful, Arlo, thank you."

He nods, chin rubbing against the top of my head. "I met them when I was younger, at a time when I really needed someone. They sent me Bosko and some life changing bullshit advice. I've ... I've never told anyone about them, except for you, now."

I turn in his arms to gape at him. He doesn't appear phased. "*Bullshit*? I think some might consider that an insult, Arlo Rook."

He laughs. "Well, if they were wrong, perhaps it would be. But, bullshit as it was, I needed to hear it."

"So, they *do* know what they're talking about, then."

"Mhm," Arlo says, looking down at me.

He wants to kiss me.

I *want* to kiss him.

But once we cross that line, there's no going back. No *holding* back.

And I'm not that selfish that I'll have him falling in love with someone that's going to disappear. Speaking with the eagles has cleared my mind and despite every fiber in my being telling me not to, I press a hand to his chest and gently push my person away.

"We should probably get going."

Arlo lets me go.

His warm smile lessens a shade, but his disappointment remains otherwise well hidden. "Yeah. Yeah, they're all waiting for us." Arlo shoves his hands deep in his jean pockets and gives me a tiny smile, barely meeting my eye with flushed cheeks.

If there was ever a moment to kiss him, that was it.

I smile at him with all the brightness I have left and we leave the cliff's edge in favor of the motorcycle. "Where is Bosko, anyway?"

"Off doing old man things, I imagine." Arlo grunts, waving vaguely. "He likes his alone time just as much as the next person."

"Ah, I can see that," I say, then immediately string together another question to fill the silence before it turns even more awkward. "Why the shop? That's Kitt's parlor, right?"

Arlo shrugs. "A few of us want tattoos, so we figured why not get inked while we discuss strategy? It's not often we're all free at the same time during the week."

I raise a brow. "And are *you* getting one?"

"Yeah, I had an idea for one last night, and Tobias wants one, so I'll do his." Arlo chuckles at me when I raise a brow. "I have a few, you know."

I scratch at my jaw. "I noticed. I didn't know you knew how to do that. May I ask, why are you doing his and not Kitt?"

Arlo retrieves his jacket from the backrest, then slips it back over my shoulders. I sigh with relief and fall into the movement too easily, subsequently cursing myself. Getting into his clothes is *not* keeping my distance.

But it feels so nice.

"I'm sure you noticed Tobias is an Empath. Some people are easier to touch than others, I guess. He calls Kitt a rollercoaster of thoughts, whereas I'm a brick wall."

I chuckle. "Sounds about right."

He slings a leg over the bike and starts it up. The beast roars to life and I grin the instant it does. I bite at my ridiculous, uncooperative lip and sit behind him, holding onto his sides with less force than before.

"Ready?" Arlo asks over his shoulder, words almost lost to the bike's music. His face hides beneath a curtain of slightly curled black flowing from beneath his hat.

"As ready as I'll ever be."

He twists the throttle and I squawk, throwing my arms around his waist so I don't fall off. "Hold on," Arlo calls over the wind, full of mischief.

I *may* have bitten off more than I can chew.

"So, when you said strategizing, what you *really* meant was partaking in herbs and stabbing yourself thousands of times."

Arlo glances down from his fixed stare on the wall of ink bottles behind my head. He's sitting backwards in a gleaming steel and leather tattoo chair, chin resting on his crossed arms as Kitt stabs into his back. Half burnt joints hang out of both of their mouths. The group nestled into the leather booth behind them smoke on a long handled glass pipe and pass around jokes.

I'm the odd one out, per usual, standing by myself with the ink bottles and plants dividing the parlor. The ride was beautiful and I stayed awake this time, but I kept my feet on the pegs and my hands to myself as much as possible. The air between us has settled back to the same awkwardness of yesterday, but it's pleasant nonetheless.

Caspian scowls at me every few minutes, but even that's lessening with each passed bowl. He and Tobias both are here, their children are with a sitter until this evening. Gowan and Lindsey sit on one side of the couple, Quentin sits by himself on the other side. No one has offered for me to sit, and I'm not entirely sure they knew I was coming.

Well, except for Kitt. She hugged me the moment I walked in, unbothered that I was soaking wet. Arlo quickly remedied that, drying us both with a quick spell that warmed my body for a few precious seconds.

"No better way to clear the mind," Arlo says, wincing when Kitt tugs on his hair, needle safely above his skin.

"Stay *still*."

He throws up a hand. "I didn't move!"

Kitt wrinkles her nose. "Sure looks like you did."

Arlo rolls his eyes and that subtle smirk makes a reappearance when he looks my way.

I roll my bottom lip between my teeth, trying to hide my grin. "Definitely looked like you did."

Quentin wanders over to the pair, followed by Tobias and Caspian. They peer at Arlo's back, a feat I cannot accomplish without sweating. To say he is broad and muscled is an understatement. He's not finely rippled, but bulky and thick in a way that would be suited to a lumberjack or something.

I knew he was ... *intense*, I mean, he towers over me and cuts an imposing figure *with* clothes in. Not to mention I practically swam in his jacket, that's proof enough the size difference between us.

"Where'd you come up with that?" Quentin asks hesitantly, pushing up his violet framed glasses. Kitt lifts her gun and Arlo reaches back to hand Quentin the joint, which he takes.

"Had a dream." Arlo mutters, focusing on his smoke rings with distraction clouding his eyes.

The joint makes its way to Kitt, then to Tobias beside her, and Caspian at the end. Caspian finishes it off, then packs *another* pipe in hazy silence as the others start to talk about the Illusionist's messages. My goodness, do they ever stop?

Caspian glares at me accusingly like he read my mind. "Do you *partake*?"

I shrug. "I've never tried it before."

Everyone *stops* talking.

Arlo looks genuinely surprised, as does Tobias. Caspian doesn't seem to give two shits, staring impatiently at me after he extends a glass pipe inlaid with purple swirls across the distance. The shape reminds me of a spoon.

"Do you *want* to?" He asks, perhaps softer than before, if that's possible for him.

Gowan and Lindsey join my side, giggling. Quentin comes over, standing at my other side with a hesitant grin. I rub at my beard, contemplating. "Sure, why not," I say, stepping forward to take the offered peace pipe, quite literally, and the lighter that comes with it.

"Question," Tobias murmurs, eyes dulled to a deep pink that borders on red. "How are you so *old* and have never tried herb?"

"Old?" Quentin asks, glancing between us.

I focus on the pale green herbs waiting in the glass. "A few hundred years or so. Maybe five? Stop counting after a while." I joke, but no one laughs. I suppose to them, I should look like Dusan, considering it's her roundabout age I'm giving. It's not an answer I can give truthfully, considering I met Dusan when she was a hatchling. Dancing around it will have to do. "Dunno, just, never had the chance, I suppose."

I nervously look up, finding multiple open mouths. Only Tobias and Arlo aren't overtly surprised by my age. Caspian tries not to let it show, but I can see that it throws him. Interesting, I figured Tobias would've told him everything there is to know about me. It makes me wonder if Tobias didn't pick up on as much as I thought.

One can only hope.

"What else haven't you tried?" Lindsey asks softly, the warmth of her body pressing against my side in such a casual way I don't know how to comprehend it. Is this what friends do?

"Oh, lots of things probably. You mean vices, I assume?"

"Don't camp on it, tell us after." Caspian orders with mild annoyance, gesturing to the pipe.

"Oh, right," I say, even though I'm not exactly sure what 'camping' *means*, but I assume it's because I've been holding onto the pipe for a few minutes now.

I bring the flame to the finely ground herbs and inhale deeply like I saw the others do, releasing my finger on the hole in the side of the piece once I think it's filled enough. I should've done that *much* sooner, a thick cloud storms down my throat and into my lungs, illuminating the tired cells that have pumped air through my broken body for much longer than the time I've mentioned to these people.

I double over coughing, holding up the pipe for someone to take before I drop it. Quentin does, using his other hand to awkwardly pat my back.

"Not bad for a rookie." Arlo allows, chuckling underneath Kitt's needle which earns another tug to his hair.

I'm not sure how much longer we stand there, passing around peace and calm and *everything is good,* but it's the most at ease I've been in ages, and not because of the herb. Well, not just because of it. I feel like I've stepped inside the door to Arlo's world instead of looking in from the outside, like last time. I'll never be as close as I want to be to him, but this is good. This is nice.

We talk about ridiculous things, meaningless things. Mostly food, which is when I discover Caspian is the cook out of the group and if you ask him, the others are hopeless.

Finally, we talk about puzzles.

"It's almost noon and no one's found the first painting yet." Quentin remarks, checking his phone.

"Because they're looking in the usual places." Kitt lifts from Arlo's back for the last time and wipes his skin, then sets down her gun. She stretches her arms overhead and her tail darts back and forth while she yawns. "That's not gonna work this year."

"That's true. The past few years have been easy, made everyone go soft." Lindsey agrees, and I chew on my lip. It's so bizarre to listen to them.

"What would you know, you've never played!" Kitt raises a brow and Lindsey flips her off with the sweetest smile. Kitt makes an obscene gesture involving her tongue and split fingers, flushing the elf's cheeks bright red and earning disapproval from her friends. She rolls her eyes, then winks at her lover before giving Arlo her attention. "You're all done, you know the drill. If you fuck around like that next time, you can find yourself a new artist." Kitt warns, full of love.

Arlo leans back, groaning as he does. "Sure, sure. Thanks, Kitty." He stands, then leans down and rubs his cheek along one of her horns. She blushes and hugs him, grumbling. I want to ask *why* he's not putting his shirt back on when he walks around the chair to join Tobias' side. "Still want one?"

Tobias smiles at him, slow and wide. "Yeah, let's do it." Tobias kisses Caspian's cheek. "I won't be long, love."

Caspian grumbles something, reaching up to capture Tobias' face. He plants a hard kiss on his lips and I don't miss Arlo looking away, disguising his action by asking someone a question.

Oh, *me*. He's asking *me* a question.

"What?" I ask, and he *smiles*, which does *not* help the goofy feeling in my stomach.

"You're baked, aren't you?"

I giggle, pushing hair away from my eyes. "Yeah, man."

Arlo raises both brows. "*Yeah,* man?" He laughs, and it's so full. "Alright, we'll be about thirty minutes or so. You good?"

I give him a double thumbs up which feels strange but I allow it, if only because I can't help it. "So good."

He watches me for another second, then places a hand on Tobias' shoulder. Arlo turns, revealing an esoteric sun on his right shoulder blade, but the rays stretching across his dark skin aren't yellow, or black, but blue. A sky blue that contrasts his skin in such a vibrant way I didn't think ink could achieve.

I want to trace every line of ink and plane of muscle. There's plenty of both.

Arlo leads Tobias out of the common area, past the front desk, and into one of the rooms on the opposite side of the building. I watch him leave, enraptured by how he smiles at Tobias and the muscles in his back flex.

Gowan rests a mossy hand on my shoulder, causing me to jump. "I brought pastries from your place, or what was left of them. Pretty busy over there."

I do a little dance, definitely *not* shrieking. "*Please* tell me you have scones."

She laughs, short blades of grass and tiny bellflowers bloom along her neck and on the part of her shoulder exposed from her shawl. "Sure do."

I frown. "*Wait*, did you say busy?" I lower my tone conspiratorially. "Should I be there?"

Gowan shrugs. "Your baristas seemed to have it covered. Have you had a day off yet?"

"No." I frown, then immediately grin at her. "They're lovely. Did you know vampires can drink coconut water?" Gowan opens her lips but I get ahead of myself. "I know! Right?"

"Oh boy." Lindsey whistles, earning an elbow from Kitt who joins our group at the ink and plant wall. "He's like a puppy, *please* tell me you see it."

"A terrier, maybe." Caspian rolls over reluctantly, bringing forth a box of said pastries. I can hardly restrain myself, settling for two scones instead of the five I crave. I haven't eaten since last night. I don't *have* to, but I love food. I think I trick my mind into feeling things like hunger and thirst while I'm here, because it's the only time I indulge.

I *must* be high because Caspian's looking at me with something other than a scowl, but that can't be right. Quentin's between him and I, so that's good. "Oh. My. *Stars.*" I moan over a mouthful. "Gowan, you are now my favorite person."

The dandelion fae giggles. "You're pretty nice too, Thatch."

"So, do you have any tattoos?" Kitt asks me, her arm slung around Lindsey's shoulders and ink smeared across her cheek.

"*No*," I gasp, eyes wide. "Should I?"

"Definitely." Caspian remarks, smiling for the first time that I've been allowed to see. It's almost *too* wide.

"Don't listen to him," Quentin says, but his eyes are bright as he adjusts his glasses. "So no tattoos, you haven't smoked before. Have you *drank*?"

I wave him off and devour another scone, disguising my lie in pastries. "*Pfft*, of course."

Lindsey leans forward and studies me before bursting out with, "You're totally lying! No way!"

"*Yes* way! Hook me up to Tobias, I'm not lying. Never drank a day in my life. *Woah*, okay, that's *not* what I meant by hook up, okay I'm just going to stop talking now."

Caspian stares at me, unimpressed.

Kitt shrugs, then kisses Lindsey on the temple. "No better time than the present. They'll still be a bit yet, but Arlo'll be pissed that he missed out on popping your cherry."

I choke on a third scone that I *swear* I have no idea how it got into my mouth. "*Yes*, let's piss Arlo off."

"Oy," Quentin mutters, rubbing his forehead with a sly grin.

Even Caspian looks amused, but Gowan does not.

"Don't listen to them, Thatch, this is the kind of decision you *don't* make while baked," Gowan says, glaring at Caspian and Kitt. "They are the worst at getting people into trouble."

I grin manically at her. "Get one with me."

She balks, the other two ladies squeal. "She can't tattoo us at the same time."

"Aha!" I point the remainder of my scone at her. "So you're *thinking* about it."

Gowan rolls her bright yellow eyes. "You go first, and if there's still time, I'll go after. We're supposed to be looking for the Illusionist, remember?"

"That's a brilliant plan." I nod once with enthusiasm.

"This is gonna be great," Caspian says, earning a swat to the arm from Lindsey. They hiss at each other and I giggle.

"You sure about this?" Quentin asks me, chewing on his bottom lip.

I give him the same double thumbs up that I gave Arlo, then dive for the comfy leather chair before someone else takes it. I smile brightly at Kitt, feet bouncing. "Ready! Can we smoke again though? This is probably going to hurt *a lot,* right?"

"Already on it," Lindsey says, packing a bowl as she leads the group over, surrounding the chair like they did when Arlo was in it. Do they want to keep me company? That's nice.

"Okay Thatch, three things. You have to stay still, you have to know what you want and where," Kitt says, gathering together some binders from an ivy ridden bookshelf nearby. "Here are some ideas." She plops them into my lap and I stare up at her, mouth agape.

"*I* have to pick?"

Quentin barks out a laugh, but Kitt scowls at me. "Maybe *this* isn't a good idea." She mutters.

I put my hands up, then hurriedly reach back down to grab the binders before they fall. "No! I really do want one, I might not get another chance for a while, because you're the *only* person I'm letting *near* me with that thing." I nod to the device sitting innocently on its rolling table beside the chair.

Kitt softens at that. "Fine, fine, but don't sue me if you change your mind."

"You make it sound like Arlo can't just zap it off if he doesn't like it." Caspian grumbles, writing on a small notepad in his lap. I want to tell him I have one like that, too.

Kitt waves him off. "Can't rely on magick for everything, Cas."

I point at the *hundreds* of pretty glass ink bottles. "Aren't those magicked?"

She glares at me and I snicker, amusing Lindsey.

"What's the third thing?" I ask, rifling through the binders.

"Oh, do you want it to move, be a reminder tattoo, or ... I don't know, change color or something weird?"

I nod, half listening. I notice a small infinity sign at the corner in most of the design sheets. "What's that?" I ask no one in particular.

Gowan peers over my side to look where I'm pointing. "That's Arlo's signature."

I look up to her, raising a brow. "The same as what's on the banners?"

"Close, but his has the dot underneath the bottom." Caspian adds without looking up, writing faster than before.

I study the insignia again, noting the spot I missed before. "So, he designed all these then?"

Kitt nods, clearly proud. "Yeah, those are his older works there, before the parlor even opened. I may have convinced him to let me borrow his sketchbook a time or two."

I flip through a few pages, then one stops me in my tracks. I point to the third out of the four on the page, confident. "I want that one."

Everyone peers over. Caspian looks up but can't see from his chair behind the others. It must be a bummer to be on the outside looking in, so I lift the book up so he can see. The look on his face is one I cannot describe, but he nods to me before returning back to his work.

"That's a good one." Caspian mumbles, and that seals it.

"I like it." Quentin agrees.

"Me too," Lindsey says, absently braiding a section of Gowan's hair. "Arlo will like it."

They all touch each other so much, a casual ruffle of the hair or pat on the back. Hugs are often, too. Arlo squeezes shoulders, and he's *so* good at it.

Gowan smiles, a gleam in her yellow eyes. "It's minimalist, won't take long to do. Maybe I will get one after all."

Kitt gives her nod of approval, the corners of her dusky purple lips softly turned up. "I think it should go over your heart, unless you have another place in mind."

"Oh, sure," I say, slipping off my suspenders. I unbutton my shirt, like it's *nothing*.

It's not until I slip it off that I realize my error, and the consequences rain down all at once.

"Oh, Thatch," Lindsey gasps.

Caspian drops his pen, scowling.

Kitt murmurs, "My Gods."

Gowan sprouts a cluster of white flowers across her crown.

Quentin clenches his fists, looking furious.

I sober immediately, hurriedly sliding my shirt back over my shoulders. I bow my head as I button it closed, failing to line up properly but I don't care right now. How could I have forgotten? I'm *such* an idiot. "Actually, I um, I should probably go check on the cafe, you said it's busy, right?"

"Yeah, really busy." Gowan breathes, playing right along in attempts to save me, but her eyes are just wide as the others.

"Thatch," Quentin says, reaching out when I shove out of the chair. I flinch violently, swinging the suspenders hanging from my waist. "Hey, you're alright. We didn't see anything, you hear?" He gestures between them all, brow pinched.

I look between him, Caspian, Lindsey, Gowan and Kitt.

I shake my head and smile halfheartedly at them. "Tell Arlo I said goodbye, and that ... I think you guys are on the right track. You have to look somewhere the Illusionist has never been before." I walk backwards, hands up. "Thank you, for the smoke, and ... well, thank you for including me. Thank you for everything."

I have nothing else to say.

I flee, desperately wishing for a hood to pull down over my face and Arlo's jacket enveloping me once more.

The mid-afternoon sun filters in through the numerous store-front windows and beats upon my back. I'm elbows deep in dish water and my muddied thoughts when a familiar voice sounds from the other side of the counter behind me.

I swallow something heavy, dry my hands off and make sure to pull my hoodie sleeves down past my wrists, before turning to face Quentin. I give him a smile. "Hey, Quentin. Gowan need more scones? They're on the house, I did eat three or four of hers."

Quentin smiles back, shoulders squared, stance tall. "No thanks, I was actually wondering if you could help me with something. I'm looking for a book."

"Oh, sure. I'm not completely familiar with the selection yet, but there's a computer back here that I can use. Well, once I figure it out. Follow me," I say, gesturing to the hidden aisles of books.

The circulation desk rests on the opposite side of the dividing wall that houses the sink and appliances for the cafe. Green velvet upholstery and dark brown leather provide cozy lounge chaises and reading nooks, accented with silver embroidery.

Arlo's touch lacks in this area, but the occasional black or gold feather flutters across the dark wood of the towering book-shelves. Aisles stretch into a seemingly endless labyrinth, offering anonymity. A few private niches and group friendly reading spaces are tucked between the aisles, often not revealing patrons until you're right upon them. My favorite area is the least occupied and hides in the far back, under the stairs that lead to the apartments.

Quentin waits patiently while I struggle to boot the computer on, then find the right browser. My brows furrow, the desktop is a mess and full of icons. He peers over my shoulder. "Oh boy. You should have Caspian take a look at that dinosaur."

I look back at him. "Dinosaur?"

"Yeah, that's like twenty years old."

I wrinkle my nose, muttering, "I must be the dustings of a fossil then."

He chuckles nervously. "True."

"I think Caspian most likely would rather do anything other than assist me, but thank you for the advice. Ah, here it is. What book are you looking for?"

Quentin blushes, pushing up his glasses. "Well, I feel bad now seeing how much of a hassle this is for you, but I don't *actually* need a book."

I turn from the computer to glare at him head on. "Oh."

He adjusts his glasses. "We could really use your help, with the Game, you know? And Arlo's worried about you." Quentin shifts on his feet. "Your business is your business, you know? I don't know what happened to you, but ... you don't owe us anything, or have to feel weird. I think you're really nice, and the others do too. Caspian's an ass, but that's just him."

I cross my arms, having to look away from his elegant features. He has one of those faces that can bring forth your deepest secrets and crack your heart open. Quentin should be with Arlo. He won't disappear. He's kind, and I know he would love Arlo so much better than I ever could.

"I appreciate that, Quentin, thank you. I don't—" I pinch the bridge of my nose and sigh. "It's been a very long time since

I've ... made connections, I guess you could say. Making friends is not a strong suit of mine."

Quentin blinks in surprise. "I don't think I've ever seen you make an enemy, not yet, anyway."

I chuckle darkly, an unfamiliar feeling. "People liking *you*, and what you can do for them ..." I finally drag my eyes up to his. "And those who are a true friend, are two *very* different things."

Quentin nods solemnly. "I think I can understand that."

We stand there, staring at each other.

"*Oh*, also, Kitt wanted me to tell you that she'll be empty bright and early tomorrow morning if you still wanted to get that tattoo, if not that's fine, too." Quentin nods quickly. "But anyway, I'll, um, I'll go now. Oh, also this message is from Tobias, they're having dinner at six tomorrow, if you wanted to come. Stop by and eat some grilled food, surprise a good mood into Arlo. We'll all be there, talking theories."

And *fuck* if that doesn't spark my interest. "Did you come up with anything?"

"Well, *we* didn't, but someone found the first painting about an hour ago, in Arlo's studio. It's been all over the news and social media, a few people have already submitted their guesses that it's *him*. Can you imagine?"

I chuckle. "I might be able to."

Monday

Never Said I Was Sane

Thatch

This is ridiculous.

I frown at my damp high tops.

A fog has descended upon Levena and the few people traveling the puddle ridden streets at this early hour are nearly hidden by the thickness of it. The stillness of the air permits one to temporarily forget that a festival currently dominates the night and a mysterious madman plays a game that's doomed to fail.

I seriously debate turning back. I'm thirty minutes early. The windows are dark, the sign above my head is unlit and a chill has settled into my bones.

Then the bell *tinks* and a pair of black boots join my toes. I look up, finding Kitt glowering at me. "Quit acting like you're special. You want one or not?"

A startled laugh escapes me and I nod. "Good morning, Kitt. Scone? Coffee?" I lift my hands, one holds a white box and the other a drink carrier with two hot coffees. I went off memory, I think she likes hers intensely sweet and over creamed with a hint of caramel.

Kitt raises a brow, taking the carrier from me. "Thanks. Come on in."

The lights are turned down and a few candles are lit, dimly illuminating the haze from previously smoked herb and an unfamiliar incense burning at four points in the parlor. It's not humid in here like the outside world, but I can't hear or see any fans. Also, the layers of smoke are undisturbed.

Kitt brings me over to a different chair this time, one on the opposite side of the ink bottle wall. It's the only tattoo chair back here and there are a few couches, along with a bookshelf, on this side of the parlor. Kitt sets the coffees down on a counter, gesturing for me to do the same with the scones.

She takes a drink and I do as well. A corner of her lips gently turns up after she takes a sip. "Alright. This definitely makes six in the morning better."

"I'll let the owner know," I say, then set my coffee down and face the chair.

There are no windows encased in brick to let the outside world peek in on this side of the parlor, but the skylight above is wide and spews light onto the seat waiting for me. I stand before it, clutching the hem of my sleeves.

I had changed the moment I got home yesterday, not feeling like myself until I was under soft pants and a heavy hoodie. Admittedly, I'm wearing the very same pair. I'm not a morning person, and rolling out of bed was a feat in itself.

Kitt works behind me, organizing supplies on a stainless steel rolling table. "Same place?" She asks.

"Y—" I clear my throat resolutely. "*Yes.*"

"Black or color?"

"Black is fine."

"This is the part where you get settled in. I've got special herb from Arlo if you want it."

"Did you—"

"No, this is out of my own stash."

"Oh. Alright, then. Will you smoke with me? I don't want to alone."

"Sure," Kitt says offhandedly.

I glance over my shoulder, and she returns my attention. Her face is carefully neutral, not betraying pity. I know what she's doing. If she doesn't treat me like glass, I won't break, maybe. She's probably seen and covered a good deal of scars in this business.

"I'll go get some. Just slip the hood and your left sleeve off, I should be able to get to your heart just fine like that."

"Alright."

Her boots clack away and I decide if I'm going to do this, I'm going to *do* this.

I rip off my hoodie and long sleeve all in one go, then throw the ball of clothing onto a distant couch. I sit in the chair and lean back against the cool leather, sighing as I do. This is fine.

It's fine.

It's just a body.

It's *just* skin.

Boots echo and I scurry off the chair, retrieving my clothes and untangling them quickly. Kitt's footsteps stop, waiting on the other side. "*Please* don't tell me you're masturbating in there. That's gross."

I bark out a laugh, holding my clothes tight to my chest. I sit back down and spread out the hoodie across my right side and part of my left. My left arm, shoulder and pec are exposed, along with some of my ribs, but it's enough. Enough to show my damage and enough room for her to work. I want this.

I *need* this.

"No, I'm not," I say, code for 'you can come in.'

When Kitt enters, I focus on the hanging plants overflowing from triangular metal planters situated on the center wall, arranged in staggered rows. Whereas ink bottles and plants dominate the other side, only plants do over here. Tools clatter softly on Kitt's work table when she rolls over to me on a comfortable looking stool, pulling her table with her.

I slide my gaze from the wall to the pipe in her hand. After taking it, I finally meet her eyes. She's scowling, eyebrows furrowed. "Quit being weird."

I shake my head, then take a long inhale from the pipe with much more ease than I did yesterday. "I'm not being *weird*. And I never understood the negative connotations that came with that term," I say after exhaling.

"Weird can be pretty good, can't it?" Kitt allows.

"I think so."

We finish the pipe in comfortable silence and I roll out my shoulders, feeling much better than when I first sat down. I lean back, tucking my left hand behind my head. "I'm ready."

Kitt nods, then ties back her slightly knotted hair with a leather band. She leans forward, scrutinizing a series of wide, hypertrophic scars that extend from my shoulder and across my untrimmed chest, then jaggedly taper off at my sternum.

They are the earliest, besides my burns, and smaller scars lay over top the already constricted and oftentimes, painful skin. The evidence of a fire that changed my life peeks around the edges of fabric laying across my stomach.

I stared at myself in the mirror again last night for an unhealthy amount of time. There are so many stories written across my body, some of them bury others.

"There's not much to work with, is there? You know, what, it's fine, really." I start to sit up but Kitt gives me a look, essentially freezing me with the ... *Arlo-ness* of it.

"I thought you said you wanted a tattoo."

"Well, I *do*, but ... you can't really tattoo over ... *this*? Can you?" I gesture to my chest, neck heating.

Kitt rolls her eyes. "You're not a snowflake in this regard, Thatch. I've tattooed over plenty of scars before, just strategizing, that's all." There's a tightness around her mouth that contradicts her casual words.

I laugh nervously. "Strategizing? Is my body a battle ground?"

There's that look again.

"*Right.*"

Kitt taps her chin and a smile slowly comes to life, matching the idea flaring behind her eyes. "You don't care *how* I do this, right?"

I shrug. "Not really. I just want to be able to say I have a tattoo, and as long as it's *that* design."

She reaches up to scratch at the base of her horn. "Alright. I've got an idea, but first, you gotta get rid of some of that." She points to the ginger hair curling on my chest in uneven, weird spots between my scars.

I gasp. "No! Anything but that!"

And we both laugh, softening for real this time.

Kitt gets started on shaving my vulnerable chest, surprising me with a few different size razors. One the width of my finger erases the hairs between the raised debris of claw marks. I watch her brow furrow and strands of hair escape from its tie, falling around her horns and into her face one piece at a time. The herb settles into a nice buzz, amplifying the sensation of Kitt's skin on mine.

It's not a sexual feeling. But it has been a *very* long time since someone touched my bare skin, save for the occasional handshake or things like that. I didn't know how much I missed it. *Needed* it.

Kitt washes the razor in warm water, then goes back to work shaving above and below the marks. Whatever she's planning involves the entirety of the scars. I clear my throat softly, eyes closing. "Ever heard of a Leviathan?"

Kitt pauses mid-stroke, then starts again. "Like ... the sea god from myth?"

I chuckle a little. "Is that how people describe them? Well, they *did* have a flair for dramatics."

Kitt taps the razor in the bowl again, then does nothing.

I open my eyes.

She's staring at me. "You're saying the *Leviathan* did this to you?"

I shrug, fighting back a shiver from the water trailing down my ribs. "Just this part." I gesture to the claw marks, cheeks flushing. "And where it continues over my back. Being eaten is *not* pleasant, let me tell you."

"*Eaten*? But, how did you–" Kitt sputters, unable to find words.

"Well, they were a pretty big creature, I wasn't digested right away. Swallowing someone whole, with a *sword*, isn't a good idea, for future reference. Took me a while, but I cut my way out. Like in the stories, you know? All based on me, I assure you."

Kitt shakes her head, smiling a little. "Just ... wow."

"Right?"

Silence falls again as Kitt situates the new design on my chest, then presses a warm washcloth to the transfer paper. "Why were you fighting?" She asks, focused on her work.

"Oh, well, that might be connected to the *'god'* thing. There were a few cities on the coast that Leviathan terrorized, and later convinced the people to feed them human sacrifices in exchange for not causing chaos. I suppose after a few years of oral history twisted in Leviathan's favor, the story might've been changed. But, couldn't have all that, so, I—"

Words are abruptly stolen from me as I attempt to tell the true story. I recover quickly with a half truth, hoping Kitt doesn't notice. "I took matters into my own hands."

"That's ... *crazy*, Thatch." Kitt gives me a stern look, a hundred questions waiting in her unbelieving, violet eyes.

I wait for the 'what are you', or the 'who are you' and the 'where did you come from?'

But she doesn't ask any of those things, so I simply reply with, "Yes, well, never said I was sane."

Kitt laughs softly, reaching for a hand mirror on the table. "In this group of Misfits, that's not a bad thing. What do you think?" She holds it up, reflecting the proposed design back at me.

The smile that spreads across my face is slow, at first. I try to hide how happy seeing the transfer ink on my skin makes me, but it's no use. I look up to Kitt with a face cracking grin that hurts my cheeks.

"It's perfect," I whisper.

Kitt nods, biting her lip. A part of me wonders if she knows what Arlo is to me. "Good. I think so too. Alright, this is the fun part."

I nod, relaxing into the chair as best as I can while Kitt loads up her needle gun with black ink. "How long have you been doing this for?"

Kitt hums, bringing the needle to my rough skin. "I've had the shop for about seven years now, but I've known how to ink for much longer." The needle penetrates my skin in rapid fire movements and I grimace. Kitt raises a brow, waiting for permission to continue.

I nod, and she does. "So you work here, *and* the museum?"

"*And* tend bar at the Magpie every other weekend, more if I can," Kitt says without looking up. The pain has dulled from startling to irritating, the vibrations constant and stinging. She wipes my skin between strokes, careful and quick. That hurts more than the needle itself.

"Why so busy?"

Kitt presses her tongue to the inside of her cheek, squinting as she crosses over a tightened area that's painful to begin with. When she wipes away blood and excess ink, pain strikes with a fresh new blade.

I inhale sharply through my nose, entering a certain state of mind, one I frequently escaped to while that nightmarish *rasha* carved me up for insane purposes.

"Well, I like inking, history, and people. Hell, I'd solar surf for sport like Lindsey does if I had the time. The shop will be forever, but maybe one day I'll trade the museum for a new hobby. The bar's just fun. Besides, there's a loft in *Etz Hayim* with our name on it, once I've got the money saved."

"You and Lindsey, you mean?"

"Yeah, she likes the city, I do too. There's an apartment here for when we want to get away from it all. We'll have our place overlooking Levena, all glass walls and bioluminescent chandeliers, drink champagne and be rich snobs."

I laugh, and she does too. "Sounds nice. So, she's a ... what did you call it, solar surfer?"

"Yes! You've never heard of solar surfing?"

"I'm afraid not," I say sheepishly.

"Oh man, I'll get you tickets, clear your schedule. We'll get Arlo to go and the rest of the gang. She's brilliant, have to have thighs made of steel for that sort of thing, which she *does*." Kitt grins mischievously and I blush. "Her day job is working at the credit union, though."

I file away that tidbit for later. Always good to have a friend at the bank.

"So, um, how is Arlo? Was he ... upset?" I wince at her withering look.

"I think he's more upset that you haven't written him back, not so much about you taking off yesterday. Worried more than anything else."

I raise a brow. "Written him?"

Now it's Kitt's turn to be confused. "Yeah, he sent you a message yesterday, or said he did."

"Well if he sent it just yesterday he's got to be more patient, the post doesn't—"

Kitt busts out laughing, lifting the needle away from my skin. "Oh my *fucking* Gods, Thatch, a text, he sent you a *text*. I gave him your number. You didn't get it?"

"*Ohh*. Yes, my phone stopped working yesterday. Just *poof*, went black." I exaggerate with a hand movement and popping my lips.

Kitt only pauses snorting long enough to manage, "Did you charge it?"

I tilt my head, drawing out the word with a furrowed brow. "*Charge?*"

Kitt gently knocks my forehead with a horn and my heart swells unbelievably. "So you're telling me that you've been eaten by a *literal* sea monster and were clever enough to escape, but you're not clever enough to work a *cellphone*?"

I roll my eyes, but the laugh bubbling within me is uncontainable, intermingling with my friend's. Through the haze of joy, that *one*, singular thought replays over and over.

My *friend*. I have *friends*.

Or I can, for a few more days.

Wolf Boy

Arlo

I'm starting to think I should've listened to Gowan and called off today.

I dismount my motorcycle at quarter to eight, a little over an hour before the studio opens for the day. On a normal morning, I would be the only one here for a few minutes, followed by the rest of the teachers who arrive at eight, among them Gowan.

But I'm not alone this morning.

A swarm of waiting people push off their vehicles or break their well formed groups scattered around the small square of a lot that's tucked into the back street. My name's called in thirty different directions in tones ranging from outraged to enthralled or worse, desperate. The morning fog blends everyone together, who coordinated the gray theme?

I panic, throwing my arms up over my head and conjuring a visible shield when the crowd shows no signs of calming down, encroaching on my bike. I envision it being crashed to the ground and my heart stops for a long few seconds, catching in my throat.

"Hey! Back *off*!" Gowan shouts, pushing her way through the crowd. "Back. *Off*." She reiterates, standing with my quaking shield to her back. "You can come back as civilized people when the studio opens, and not for harassing Arlo, either. I've got the Chief of Police on speed dial."

Gowan pulls her phone out of her pocket and dials Chief right up when no one takes a step back, letting the speakerphone do the work. "Chief here."

"Hey, Chief. I've got an angry mob here at the studio. Could you–yeah, that's what I thought! Scurry! Yeah, Chief, I'm here. Bunch of scavengers bothering Arlo. Do we need a patrol? No, that's not necessary. I think they'll back off now."

I release a sigh. Being watched by an officer, even if they're supposed to be protecting me, does not sound like a good time. I allow the shield to fall and my fingers tingle intensely, like I've been gripping a buzzer for hours.

"*Fuck*." I mutter, shaking out my hands which does little to abate the sensation.

"You alright?" Gowan asks, taking my trembling fingers in hers.

"Yeah, fine. Thank you. What did Chief say?" I squeeze her gently, then release her hands and straighten. I reach down and take my forgotten beanie from its place on my seat, then slide it over my head. Despite the fact the fog's chilly and my bones are cold, sweat runs down my back.

"Let Chief know if it happens again. She's going to make a general announcement later on about not harassing the locals during the Game." Gowan rubs a hand up and down my back. "Sure you wanna do this?"

I stare at my bike longingly for a moment, then nod to her. I didn't sleep well last night, terrors filled with Leon and me battling to the death ran on a loop every time I closed my eyes. Not to mention when I was awake, I kept staring at the lonely text message in the thread between Thatch and me.

Me: Hey, are you alright? Kitt said you got sick and went home. I'll visit you later, if you want, just call me and let me know.

It's not often I can admit this to myself, but being alone today is not a good idea. I sling my arm around Gowan's petite shoulders, one is covered in a hand knit sweater. "Sounds to me you're trying to get out of work today."

She groans, and we walk together to the back door leading inside the studio. "It's *Monday*. Who wants to work on a Monday?"

"True, true." I release Gowan to punch in this week's code, then lead the way inside. The back room is all tables, chairs and storage cabinets. The only central area is the kitchenette, a tiled area off to the side with a fridge and the whole works for cooking a hot meal.

Gowan starts for the coffee pot, and I flick on the overhead lights hanging from the high ceiling. Despite the fact there are no paintings back here, the walls are just as white and brightly lit as the work and showrooms outside the innocent looking wooden door separating us from the rest of the two story building.

I hate white walls.

Gowan inherited the studio from her grandmother, who admittedly let the building go. It took a lot of work on Gowan's part to get the place into a decent state, let alone ready to be a studio once more. She's done a fine job. The thought of not coming here three days out of the week barbs my heart.

"How many classes do you have today?" She asks.

I count off on my fingers, pausing near my empty locker. "Two morning and two afternoon, plus I have my one-on-one right after lunch. You?" I shed my jacket and hang it on the hook inside my open locker. Gowan's space beside mine is full of clothes, shed moss, dried up petals and bits of yarn.

"This morning's the field trip," Gowan says, pouring us both a cup of coffee.

"Oh boy." I cross the room and take my blue mug from her, indulging in that first sip of perfectly creamed coffee with a hint of sugar. "Glad I'm not part of that. Quentin's leading the class, right? I can't imagine any class of his being too wild."

Gowan nods, staring into her coffee. "True. We're still going to meet Kitt for lunch at *Shh* after?"

I nod, considering. "Yeah, as long as we're back by one. Are you sure about this place?"

"We've already crossed off Infinite Library, the Illusionist has hidden clues there before. *Shh* Elves is the oldest bookshop and has never been involved in a Game. It doesn't hurt to take a look around, besides, no one is ever there anymore. You've always said—"

"I know, I know. The point of the games is to explore the city. Alright, like you said, doesn't hurt to look." I dig into my pocket and pull out my phone. Doc wrote me about five minutes ago, and Kitt did not long after.

But no Thatch.

Kitty: morning. see you at lunch?
Me: Yup. You're up early.

I switch over to Doc, feeling bad for ghosting them for days.

Doc: Arlo, if you don't answer me I'm calling Kitt.
Me: Hey, Doc. What's up?

A phone pings at the same time the back door opens.

"I'd be better if you'd answer your *phone*, Arlo Rook." Doc snarls from the doorway, phone in hand and fangs slightly bared. They're dressed in a knee length, plaid skirt and a plain white blouse, freshly showered.

I sigh, waving them off. "Sorry, sorry. In case you haven't heard, I've been busy."

Doc stands beside Gowan, furred arms crossed. "Arlo, this isn't funny. I don't make it a point to harass my patients. You know this. So either you know what I'm going to say, or you're a prick. Which is it?"

Gowan looks between us, thorns sprouting and receding along her hands. "What are they talking about, Arlo? Is something wrong?"

I rub the back of my neck. "No, nothing's *wrong*. Honestly Doc, I just ... well, there's no excuse. What's going on?"

Doc's eyes flash to Gowan, then to me. "I think this a private conversation, Arlo."

Well, fuck. That's promising.

"I'm sure whatever you have to say is fine for her to hear."

"No, that's fine Arlo, I'll go get things ready," Gowan says, squeezing my arm before leaving. "Don't forget to restock studios one and two, if you get a minute."

Then it's just a *very* pissed off *behema* and I.

Doc removes their glasses and rubs at their face. "You've had me worried sick, Arlo. I thought you were dead in a ditch somewhere."

I let out a disgusted laugh. "Thanks for having for faith in me, Doc."

"Oh knock it off, that's not what I meant. After you sent me that message I went digging, and when weird numbers started showing up and you didn't answer, well."

I blink. "Doc, I'm fine, honestly. What's ... what's not right?"

Doc glares at me. "So you *did* see my messages."

I put my hands up. "We've already established I'm an asshole."

Doc sighs as they replace their crimson glasses. "How has your magick been, Arlo?"

"Oh, fine?"

"*Fine*?"

I give in a little, shrugging. "Well, it's been ... *tingly*, or almost jittery maybe is the right word. More ... well, just *more*, if that makes sense. I didn't really use any yesterday, not like the day before. I put up a shield this morning which seemed to take the edge off."

Doc frowns. "And how have you been sleeping?"

I tense up, the white walls do nothing to combat my paranoia. They were different from the others, but Doc didn't arrive in that prison disguised as a medical center until the end. I know I needed help, but that place almost finished me off. I'm just glad Doc red flagged the policies there, stopping anyone else from getting hurt like Loch and I did.

Doc's the one who suggested I work at the studio, teaching art to students like me. People who need something to feel like they're alive. A jolt rattles my heart again at the thought of giving that up. I won't be able to work here *and* at the university.

But I'm *supposed* to move on to bigger and better things, right?

"Alright until a couple nights ago. The uh ... the dreams are back, and I can remember more but less at the same time? If that makes any sense. Why? What does that have to do with my blood tests?"

"And when did they start? The day you used your magick reserves? You restrained a *Dybbuk*, correct?"

Doc's starting to scare me, if I'm being honest. Sweat trickles down my neck, and I shift on my feet. "Yeah I did, but I slept like a rock that night. It was the next night that the first dream started, last night."

"The day you didn't use much of your magick."

"*Yes* ..." I nod. "Doc, what the hell?"

Doc takes to pacing, rubbing their peppered chin. "I don't know. But what I *do* know, according to my research on bodily witch limitations and your test from a few days ago, the percentage of magick flowing through your veins was near fatal levels. Very well could be today, too."

"Near *fatal*?" I take a step back.

Doc nods, continuing their slow steps. "Witch hearts can only withstand so much power used at once Arlo, heart attacks and aneurysms are a very real threat if you push yourself too far, use everything you have and then some. On the flip side of that, certain circumstances can cause situations like yours."

I put my hands up. "I've never pushed my limits before. I've never even come close, and sending a *Dybbuk* to the Otherworld isn't enough to do that."

A painful itch wracks my brain, reminding me of my dream. If that really happened, then I have pushed myself, once.

Doc smiles sadly at me, finally stopping. "I know. The amount of magick within you on a good day is too much for a regular witch. Imagine yourself as a pressure cooker right now, Arlo. If you don't release some of the magick building up inside you, you're going to suffer the same fate as someone who exerts too much. Your heart can't take it. I don't know why this build up is occurring, but I have a few theories."

I rub my temples, mind racing as I process their words. Honestly, that's *exactly* how my magick feels. Volatile and ready to explode. The only time it's been tame the past few days is when I used too much and when I was around Thatch.

"What are your theories?" I murmur, eyes closed while I work out a headache.

"*Well*," Doc's voice hits a high note, "something similar happens to many races, especially in *behema* and other shifter races like the *tannin*, when the alphas go into heat. Their essence intensifies to dangerous levels and the treatment is for their partner to act as a conduit. It's really–"

"No offense, Doc, but I'm not a shifter, wolf boy ... an alpha of *any* sort!" I cut in immediately.

Doc huffs. "To be fair, Arlo, we don't know *what* you are."

I roll my eyes. "28% unknown DNA doesn't equal shifter, and even if it did, that's not enough for my ... *primal* instinct or whatever to kick in."

"Yes, well, *anyway*. A few questions can clear this up. Have you met anyone new in the past few days? The first encounter may have caused influx of magick and would've been when you started to feel different–"

I groan heavily, burying my heated face into my hands. "Doc, *I'm not* going into heat! Next theory!"

Shh Elves is a dark academia lover's paradise.

The bookshop is the official supplier for Phoenix University students to pick up their textbooks, but they never do. *Gadol* skulls and the giant land snails that accompany the macabre decorations rest inside numerous glass terrariums, tending to scare off the normals. If that doesn't do it, the occasional shrunken head or ancient and *very* explicit tome titled 'Monster Relations Through the Ages: How to Make it Fit' might do the trick.

Those who remain are the bizarre, the peculiar and the interesting.

I stand before a case of baked goods housing much more curious pastries than those served at Thitwhistle's. Thatch should *definitely* sell red velvet truffles with little axes sticking out of them and cakes in the shape of snakes. The moon elf baristas are a harmonious team, both sing to the folk rock pouring out from the surrounding speakers as they prepare our coffees.

I lean down and whisper to Gowan, "How have I never been here before?"

"Pretty neat, isn't it?" She says, grinning up at me.

"It really is. Do you know who owns the place?" I ask, peering into a terrarium with snails that have bright yellow shells and black dots.

Gowan shrugs, further exposing her bare shoulder. "No idea."

The cafe is the first area you walk into, a decent sized space with plenty of dark leather couches to rest in and accompanying fireplaces to warm your cold marrow by. Azure brocade curtains are pulled over diamond shaped windows, the silken fabric reminds me of the ones in Thitwhistle's, how the silver and blue threads weave together in a mockery of the universe.

A wide and pointed arch sits opposite the front door and leads to the books. The trim surrounding the frame consists of a deep bookshelf that stretches impossibly high and puts the books at curious angles, highlighting their ancient spines. I have to assume those are not for sale.

Beyond that, more bookshelves await, rows upon rows of them.

"Hey guys, sorry I'm late." Quentin rushes in the door behind us, all windswept hair and a formerly tucked in flannel that's now a mess. His frames are wooden today.

I chuckle upon seeing him. "Did you *run* here?" He shrugs, cheeks flushed. He definitely did. "I'm glad you made it, I ordered you a coffee, three cream and sugars, right?"

Quentin beams at me. "Perfect, thank you. Where's Kitt?"

"Back here!" She yells, hand sticking out from the other side of the arch shelf.

"*Shh*!" The elves chide and pin her with a glare. After, one with electric blue hair passes me our drink carrier full of coffees. I smile, mouthing a '*thank you.*'

Talking with inside voices is fine here, they don't expect you to be silent. But Kitt doesn't have one of those. That's probably why we haven't been here before.

The androgynous and admittedly handsome elf winks at me and I flush, giving them a hurried smile before I leave in search of Kitt. The number scrawled onto my cup doesn't go unnoticed, and my stomach does a nauseating flip. I can only think of Thatch, he's overtaken my thoughts since I've met him, and there isn't room for anything else.

I find Kitt halfway down a narrow aisle of tall bookshelves in the back, lounging on the middle rung of an elephant ladder with a book in her lap, her tail swishing back and forth. She grins at the sight of Gowan, Quentin and me, even though we just saw each other a few minutes ago.

"How did you get up there so fast?" Gowan asks.

"Magick." Kitt wiggles her fingers over the book in her lap.

"Whatever. Here's your muffin," Gowan says, retrieving said muffin from the box in her arms and passing it up to Kitt. "Have you found anything?"

Kitt shakes her head, then takes a bite of her muffin. "Nope," she says over a mouthful.

"I had an idea," Quentin says, taking his coffee. Gowan claims hers, and I do mine, then tuck the empty carrier under my arm.

"Based on what Arlo said, all the paintings left behind depicted the Illusionist with green eyes, so we know that's not true, and that's a clue in itself. So, I think it's safe to say the brown eyes in the first painting are not the true detail. They wouldn't give the same clue regarding physical details twice, right?"

I take a sip of my coffee, thinking. Kitt groans overhead. "Quentin, you're worse than Arlo is with these puzzles."

He grins. "That's fine with me. I want to win."

"Oh? What would you wish for?" Gowan asks him, causing Quentin's pale cheeks to flush adorably.

"I'm not telling. Isn't that the *one* rule of wishes? You can't say what it is or it won't come true." His last few words roll together in a mutter.

"Quen," I say, squeezing his shoulder. "You are *much* too good for this world."

He rolls his eyes. "Whatever, think it's lame if you want, I'm sticking to it."

"I don't think it's lame, I'm serious. If there were more people in the world like you, it'd be much more fun to live in."

Kitt clears her throat. "Okay, okay. I do think you're right, Q. The painting is abstract, so the only other discernible details are ears, which are non-pointed. I highly doubt a human is the culprit."

"There's more round ear folk than just humans," I remind her. Besides Thatch, I know of a few other magickal folk that have round ears or simply glamor them as such. "And there may be something we're missing, and the ears aren't the true detail."

"But there's nothing else." Kitt throws back.

"That's not true." Gowan pulls out her phone and looks up pictures of the painting posted online.

The news and social media has focused on the Game, the first painting, me, and the ravine's latest quakes which creep closer to Levena every year. I've never understood why Levena was built so close to the fault line, but to be honest I haven't looked into it much. They were never something to worry about before, but this year they just might be. The season runs from the end of summer to the first snow, so we still have a few more weeks to go.

Gowan passes her phone around, and we all get another good look at it. The painting isn't one of mine, I don't do abstract work, but I do know the artist personally. They're the person I'm meeting after lunch.

We've never really shared theories, but Loch has stuck to his guns after all these years that he saw the Illusionist. With Loch's condition, I'd be surprised if he made it to the one-on-one this week with everything going on, honestly. I did send him a text and let him know the studio was busy, but we could still have our private session if he wanted.

I haven't heard back.

"The colors splashed behind the face, maybe they mean something," Gowan says, gesturing to the splash of orange and red watercolor silhouetting the half a face. "They *did* hide it in our studio. It'd be hard to ignore the paint if you think of it that way."

"Your studio, you mean," I say, earning a murderous look.

"You've put your blood and sweat into that place, Arlo. Let's not go over this again, I don't feel like growing thorns, and if I *do*, I'm definitely stabbing you."

I chuckle, tossing the carrier in a nearby bin. "Fine, fine. It's a good idea. We'll have to wait for more clues, the color could signify anything. I only have a few more minutes, I'm going to have a look around."

"I'll come with you," Kitt says, climbing down the ladder.

She and I split off one way, Quentin and Gowan disappear down a different row of bookshelves. The sections are organized alphabetically and by genre. Kitt and I roam the fiction section, specifically mythologies. My heart quickens erratically and my shoulders rise unwillingly.

A gentle force tugs me through the next row. I hover over the nondescript books with careful fingers, eyes closed and steps slow until I'm drawn to a stop. I caress the worn spine and gently tug it off the shelf, brow furrowing when I read the complete title.

'Watchers: Who Were They and Where Are They Now?'

I turn around quickly, sensing a pair of eyes on me and foreign magick inspecting my wards and protections. When my own magick rises to the surface, ready to find the source, the stalker disappears.

"Let me know if you see anything about Leviathans," Kitt says a few paces down the row from me, scouring the shelves and unbeknownst to my plight.

I glance down at the book in my hand, waiting for the force to return, but it doesn't. I come up with a smartass remark to distract myself from the paranoia rising in me.

"Why? Ew, please don't tell me Lindsey is into you pissing the bed. That's just too much—"

"Arlo!" Kitt wheezes so loud I expect a *shh*, but there isn't one. "Don't be *gross*. No, I'm not ten anymore. I'm thinking of doing a new exhibit, but I need to do some ... research."

I tuck the book under my arm, careful not to spill my coffee, then wander over to her. I look for a minute, then call upon my magick to find a book the easy way. Before I can lift my hand and perform the movement, a book comes flying out of a shelf above us.

"Shit!" I throw my hand up, palm out, slowing down the tome's trajectory.

"*Shh*!"

"Yeah, yeah." I mutter, taking the book once it's in arm's reach.

I hand it over to a wide-eyed Kitt. "Did you just do magick without ..." She whispers, leaning in conspiratorially.

I sigh. "It's a witch thing, don't ask."

"Not enough room in my brain to argue with you. Thanks," Kitt says, giving her attention to the book. She opens it and rifles through the first few pages, then her eyes dilate farther than before. "*Woah*." She breathes.

"What?" I ask, leaning down to look over her shoulder. The book is open to the fifth page where an illustration reigns, detailing a massive snake like beast with bared fangs larger than a treant. On the sixth page beside it are 'fun facts' regarding the Leviathan story.

"I didn't realize how old the story is. Whenever you told it to Cas and me, it felt like it could've happened yesterday." Kitt remarks, caressing the illustration. Her words bring back happy memories filled with shadow puppets and long nights when we really should've been sleeping.

I chuckle. "Then I couldn't tell it anymore because *somebody* kept wetting the bed. What time period does the story originate from? I honestly can't remember where I heard the story, one of those old wives tales things."

Kitt stares at me, aghast. "I think scary mythologies and old wives tales are two different things, Lo. It says here the Leviathan was first described by the Atlantean societies to the northwest ... two thousand years ago." Kitt's voice trails off and she stares at the page, unseeing. I note the illustrations of the Leviathan providing fish from the sea for the coastal peoples, a fearsome god who was endlessly generous.

"You alright?" I ask, squeezing her shoulder.

"Mhm." She nods quickly, breaking out of her funk. "Yeah, yeah, totally, just, *wild*, right? I'm gonna buy this, you ready?"

"I'll be right there, I wanna do one more quick look."

Kitt smiles at me with something odd in her eyes, then takes off with the book clutched to her chest.

Weird.

I meander to the end of the row and turn down another, peeking for witches. But when I come round the corner, I crash into a breathless Quentin. "Fuck!" I grit out, luckily my coffee was empty and the book under my arm is unharmed. "Why are you running?"

Quentin shushes me, finger over his lips. His other hand *slowly* reaches down the front of his pants.

"Woah," I say, holding my free hand up.

But when Quentin pulls out a small, rolled up parchment, the magick within me flares like it did for the Watchers book. I take him by the arm and pull him close to me as he unrolls it.

"Where?" I whisper, and Quentin nods down the row at Gowan who looks a lot like she's keeping watch.

"We found it in the religion section, but look." Quentin points to the painterly style artwork that I recognize but the artist I cannot recall. The person in the painting is androgynous and really could be anyone, their hair is a cacophony of colors spread directly from tubes of paint with a palette knife. Their skin is light brown, and their eyes are red.

"Their ears are round," Quentin says.

"Which means you're right, the colors in the first one are what's important. They wouldn't give us the same clue twice."

"Unless the hair's a clue." Quentin frowns.

"I don't think so, but we'll keep it in mind and add it to the list. We better call Chief." I pull out my phone, noting the time and a new message from Loch. "Shit. Could you? I'm supposed to be at the studio in five minutes."

Quentin nods, spine straightening. I do a quick illusion spell, hiding the parchment in plain sight in his hands so he doesn't go stuffing it down his pants again.

"So, first a studio, now a bookstore run by punk elves." Quentin whispers as we walk to Gowan together.

"We'll talk some more tonight at dinner. I might be a few minutes late, I have to visit Doc after my classes."

Quentin's brows furrow. "Everything ok?"

I adjust my beanie. "Yeah, just some witch things. I'm good."

Gowan stares at me when we regroup, but doesn't say anything. If anyone can keep a secret, it's Gowan. Granted, she doesn't know the specifics of what Doc and I talked about, but she knows something's up. I'll tell everyone tonight when I know more. Probably.

I swallow something heavy, wishing I could pick Thatch's brain about it.

And that thought just brings up Doc's absurd alpha heat theory.

Yes, my magick acts funny around Thatch. But it acts funny around a lot of magickal beings, and since I don't know *what* Thatch is exactly, that's to be expected. The small voice of reason in the back of my mind argues that it's never felt like *this* before, that Thatch is different, but I bury it for now. He obviously wants nothing to do with me.

I'm the one who insisted on the tour after we met again.

I'm the one who offered my help with his cottage.

I'm the one who almost kissed *him* in the museum.

I'm the one who offered him a ride in the rain.

I'm the one who can't stop thinking about him.

I'm the one who tried to kiss him *again* with great eagles as our witnesses, only to be softly pushed away.

No wonder why he's not writing me back.

It's fine.

Honestly, that's what I expected, why I let myself hope for anything more is beyond me. I had just thought ... maybe someone was picking me.

"Alright, Arlo?" Gowan asks, grounding me.

We're walking down some street I vaguely recognize. I shake my head, pulling together shreds of how we got here. We're close to the studio. Did I say goodbye to Kitt and Quentin? Yes ... or, I think so?

I groan, hugging something close to my chest. Oh yeah, the book. The closer it rubs against my heart, the better I feel.

"Yeah, I'm okay," I say, although I haven't been truly okay in a very long time.

The studio is overrun with 'interested artists.'

I sneak away to the upstairs where Loch waits for me. I open the door and step inside, finding Elochian Adrastus sprawled out on the floor. Six opalescent wings are spread out beneath him, sparkling like the edges of the ocean under the chandeliers above us. I've never told him, but his wings remind me of a dragonfly. A *shedim* probably wouldn't want to hear that though, especially one as self conscious as Loch.

"Arlo," Loch says without looking over at me, his voice deep and distorted like it was taken out and wrung through a voice modulator, then put back in his lean chest. He's dressed in the usual suit and tie, fabric black and white with an emerald green detailing in the most subtle of places. "They've gone mad."

I lay down next to Loch and stare up at the ceiling with him, heads together. I fold my hands on my stomach, mirroring his. "Tell me about it. I'm glad you came. *I* nearly turned back when they stormed the castle this morning."

Loch snorts. "*You*, turn away from a good fight?"

"Wasn't in much of a fighting mood, if you catch my drift."

Loch nods once. "I do."

"I think we've figured out your painting."

Loch slowly turns his head and looks at me. His prominent, hooded eyes are a soft brown, his jet black hair falls around his head like a halo. His skin is a lighter brown than mine by a few shades, besides the lighter areas stretching along his neck, face and farther under his clothes. Thin lines of gold are inlaid into his high cheekbones, highlighting his elevated status.

Shedim are an older race and there are many different tiers of demons. Loch is of the most revered sort. That's fine and all for someone who *wants* the power that comes with such 'noble blood,' but Elochian hates it. He dislikes dealing with people on a general basis, let alone leading the demon chapters of the Northern Regions. But it's a position that was promised to him the day he was born, and he was raised for nothing else.

"Oh?" Loch asks, genuinely curious.

"Well, Quentin, did."

Loch's chest stops rising for a moment. "Who?"

"Quentin, a friend of mine. He comes to the Magpie from time to time. The one I told you about?"

Loch twirls long tresses around his finger. "Oh, right, the grade school teacher square who's not such a square."

I chuckle. "Yeah, that's the one. Anyways, what can you tell me about the color scheme you used?"

Loch pauses his twirling, then resumes as his gaze shifts to the ceiling. "It felt right. Everything else was like the edges of a dream. I could remember *seeing* them, but over the years the harder I tried ... the more it slipped away. You know how it is."

I nod, because I do.

"But, those colors. I've always associated them with the Illusionist, and not because of the festival's hoorah song and dance." I snicker at his wording which earns a scowl. I gesture for him to go on, and he does after another moment of glaring at me. "When I think of them, I think of red and orange and *fire*."

Loch sits up quickly, all six glass-like wings open like a babe yawning after a long nap. I've always wanted to touch them, but that's a line you can't cross with any winged people, not just Loch. Unless you're a partner, of course, then I'm sure it's greatly welcomed.

"Arlo."

I sit up and my fingertips tingle with an intensity that jars the funny bone in my right arm. I ignore it in favor of saying, "Loch."

"I want to paint."

I try not to show my excitement, but I do, and Loch notices. Loch has been visiting me in the studio for six months, although we've known each for years, and he's only wanted to paint *with* me once. Otherwise, we sit and talk, or sit and say nothing. It's just a place for him to feel safe.

I've helped a few people like Loch and they eventually join the group classes, but I don't think Loch ever will, and that's okay. I like our time together, and hearing him say he wants to paint lights my heart up. "Okay, let's paint. Any ideas?"

Loch shrugs. "Something *blue*."

I stand and offer a hand to him, which he takes. Wings flutter as the *archshedim* rises, exposing swirling black tattoos inked over hundreds of thousands of chitin scales. At first glance the microscopic scales appear blue, but they're actually an oil slick of green, blue and soft purple at the edges.

We gather some canvases and set them up on easels that are dusty at best and centered in the modest room. Tapestries line the walls in here, leaving no evidence of white paint. Loch doesn't like white walls either. I take out my phone and turn on a band we both like, something I can imagine the moon elves jamming to as they make coffee.

Loch undoes his suit jacket and throws it haphazardly near the door, then rolls up his sleeves. I take off my rainbow duster and toss it in the same direction, then gather my supplies. I'm feeling watercolors today, and when Loch said blue, of course I thought of Thatch's eyes.

The thought of painting any part of him pressurizes the strained magick ricocheting inside me. *Fuck*. I'm not an idiot, and it's getting harder to deny that my magick reacts to Thatch. Just the idea of him writing me back is ....

I shake out my hands, breathing heavily as I stare at the empty canvas.

"Loch, do you mind if I use some magick?"

He peeks around his easel, buckets of paint sit at his feet. His hands are covered in sky blue, brilliant splashes taint his fine suit. "'Course not. Are you alright?"

I nod. "Yeah, just a witch thing."

Loch gives me a look. He's better at breaking me than Kitt is. But he doesn't demand solutions or provide an endless spew of advice. He doesn't try to fix me. If I expect truth from him, then I have to offer it in return.

"There's too much, or something like that. It's making me feel weird. Doc says I need to 'vent it' or I'm going to explode."

Loch snickers. "Doc knows best, whether we like to hear it or not."

"Yeah, well, I'm not liking the theories, so there's that."

Loch grunts, then goes back to painting. He knows if I want to talk more, I will.

I don't, at first.

I exhale and call upon my magick which erupts like an immediate waterfall when I bring my fingers together. I twist and bend and carve through the air, conjuring light cantrips that hover above us, simultaneously dimming the atmosphere. The music from my phone amplifies and an illusion blurs out the edges of the room, replacing tapestries with far off mountains and grand lakes with crystal cities resting along the shorelines.

I roll my shoulders out, feeling marginally better. A steady stream of magick will be needed to keep this up for the hour we're together. That should be enough. I usually feel tired right after conjuring and can only keep something like this going for twenty minutes, but right now I can't even tell there's a draw on my supply.

I'm still a little shaky but marginally better, so I pick up a brush and do my best to push away everything that isn't

Thatch's eyes. It's easy, so *easy* to bring them forth and get lost in something that isn't even here.

"I don't think I've ever seen your illusions so vividly before. What technique are you using?" Loch murmurs after a while.

"Same one as always. Like I said, weird magick shit."

"Weird magick shit." Loch echoes thoughtfully. "There's a slogan there."

I chuckle. "Doc thinks I'm a wolf boy."

Loch coughs. "Sorry?"

"He compared me to an alpha in heat, Loch. If I don't get my rocks off with the right person, I'm gonna croak, or something to that effect."

Loch is silent for a few minutes. A new song comes on, one of my favorites. I find it in me to murmur words about a blue healer, capturing ginger locks cast over watery eyes. Loch speaks without looking around his easel, and his next words are so soft they're nearly lost to the music. "*Shedim* call it *khawbar*. It's when our inner spirit awakens, a part of us that sometimes is never found because it's shared with someone that is your fated. If you never connect with them, it never comes to life. It's rare, for demons."

I swallow. "I didn't know that."

"It's a weird demon thing." Loch uses my own words against me and I chuckle. "A lot of species have something similar, it's not limited to just shifters. Maybe because Doc is a *behema* their mind is closed to other ideas. Have you talked to Tobias?"

"*No.*"

"Ah."

"Tobias is ... he has a lot on his plate right now," I say, because I don't want to ask Tobias what he knows. I don't want to know things about Thatch that Thatch hasn't told me himself. And if I start asking about the *malakim* equivalent to fated mates or whatever, that will *definitely* look suspicious.

"Excuses are like assholes Arlo, everyone's got one."

I Exist

Thatch

I stand before a yellow house with white shutters.

Arlo isn't here, and everyone's staring at me.

I inhale, hold in the crisp autumn evening, then exhale and take the first step off the paved driveway.

Leave crunch under foot and *shedim* children squeal from a double seated swing as Lindsey pushes them high into the air. Kitt leaves her side, sprinting over to me. She slings an arm over my shoulder, rubbing her horn against my cheek. "Hey, Quentin said he invited you, I'm glad you came. Come say hi to the Misfits."

I smile at her, unsure what to do with my arms. I had changed into 'real' clothes and freshened up before I came, trading my sweats and hoodie for a jeans, long sleeve and suspender combination. I changed my footwear also, those leather shoes were *awful*. I settle for burying my hands in my pockets.

"Yes, well, can't pass up free food, right?" I say, wincing. "I mean, that's not the only reason I came, I, well–"

"You're adorable when you're flustered." Kitt laughs, bringing us to a stop before a picnic table occupied by Quentin, Gowan, an unfamiliar fae, Caspian and Tobias. Lindsey and the swing isn't too far away, the children seem to be very interested in me and scream to be set down.

I wave awkwardly to everyone, receiving smiles, hellos and waves in return. Caspian nods at me wordlessly, but I'll take that over glaring. "Good evening, thanks for having me."

"Hi, Thatch. I like your suspenders." Quentin says, smiling nervously.

"And I like your bowtie." I gesture to his glittering silver bowtie.

He beams. "Thanks."

I swallow heavily and take a casual look around. "Where's Arlo?"

"Oh, he's on his way now." Kitt waves in the air, an amused gleam in her eyes.

I nod, then address Tobias and Caspian. "Is there anything I can help with?"

Caspian shrugs, rolling away to meet a distressed Lindsey with overflowing armfuls of kids. Tobias smiles at me. "Sure, the grill is almost done, but there are a few things inside we can bring out."

"Great." I say, despite the pit growing in my stomach.

Time to get this over with.

Tobias leads me inside the yellow house which immediately feels like a home the moment you walk in. Cinnamon, apples and something faint that I can't put my finger on fills my nostrils, warming my lungs. The soft trickle of water and a kid's show playing somewhere in the house greets me, along with a litter of toys along the halls I follow Tobias through.

"Right in here is the kitchen, we just have a few things to bring out. Mostly pie, that goes pretty quickly around here." Tobias says, gesturing around us as we step into a modest, farmhouse style kitchen. All milky white cupboards and soft blue trim, along with ceramic crocks and cast iron hangers that hold an endless supply of ladles, spoons, spatulas and measuring sets. A set of double windows situated over a flower box are open, releasing the scent of baked goods into the night.

I smile weakly at Tobias. "I think it's about time we had a talk."

"Of course." Tobias takes a seat at a small breakfast nook. He nods to the chair beside him, so I dutifully sit. "What would you like to talk about?" He asks, head tilted and hands folded in his lap.

"Well ..." I say, unsure how to start. What if he doesn't know anything and I'm opening a can of worms?

"I know that you're an Empath, and I've been ..."

Tobias chuckles. "Ah. Wondering how much I know about you?"

I bow my head. "Yes."

"I don't make a habit of sharing other people's secrets, unless they put someone else in danger. And what I learn through touch is ... vague, generally. But, that was not the case with you." Tobias leans forward, serious now. I tilt my face up to him. We're in secret sharing distance, but not touching.

I hold my breath. Has someone finally *seen* me?

"There is nothing beneath your skin. Your presence, it's ... cold. Non-existent, one might say. I'm not one to pry, but why are you like this? Is it a defense mechanism? Are you malicious and have things to hide?"

His bluntness surprises me. Everything he said cracks me down the middle.

I'm ... *nothing*?

I look away, tears burning my eyes. I sort through words, trying to find cracks in my free will. In the end, what I manage is a strangled whimper.

"I exist. I do, I *exist*. You have to believe me. You have to *remember* that I exist."

All at once, the flood gates open, and I don't care that they're a direct contradiction to my words. I exist, but for how much longer?

Tobias pulls me into him and I allow it.

I allow his arms around me.

I allow my tears to fall into the silk of his shirt.

I allow the feeling of a friend to sink in, one more painful time.

I sob like I haven't in ... I'm not sure how long, but Tobias holds me all the same, steadfast as I clutch his shirt.

Somewhere beyond this bubble of Tobias keeping me safe, footsteps approach, then retreat. After a few more minutes, the tears dry and the circles rubbed into my back slow down until Tobias gently releases me. I sit back, wiping my eyes.

"Thank you." I mutter, unable to meet his pity filled gaze.

Tobias nods. "Of course. Do you feel better?"

I laugh, and it's a broken sound that startles me. I never sound like that. "We'll go with that."

Tobias nods again, lips parting with a question. Then he looks away, chewing on his cheek. I love him for it. All of these people, I'm falling in love with who they are and how big their hearts are, all in different ways.

"I don't know *why* I am the way I am. I just am, and there's nothing I can do about it." I whisper, and the words slip off my tongue like poison. "Can we ... can we go back?"

"Sure. Gowan just came in to let us know that Arlo's back. Let's go surprise him." Tobias says, and his soft smile follows mine after Arlo's name is mentioned. "Here," Tobias reaches forward and wipes the remaining tears from my cheeks, then gently musses my hair somewhat into place.

I wonder if this is what a father feels like.

"Thank you, Tobias."

"Bias is fine, dear."

We wander back through the house, pies in hand. Tobias stops me before he opens the front door. "If you need help, Thatch, we can do that. Arlo, all of us. That's what friends are for."

I don't meet his eye when I say, "Okay, I'll think about it."

Tobias lets it go and opens the door, revealing a chorus of raised voices and good natured arguing. He rolls his eyes. "Ready for the animals?"

I chuckle. "Ready."

I follow behind him, fighting the grin that overtakes me when Arlo calls out to Tobias. "Bias! *Please* tell me that's apple. Cas said you didn't make it this year, but I *know* you wouldn't do that to me. Right? *Right?*"

I step out from behind Tobias with said apple pie warming my hands. I grin at a moonstruck Arlo, reveling in how his throat bobs upon seeing me. Arlo stands abruptly from his place at the table beside a snickering Kitt, hands twitching at his sides.

"Hi, Arlo. I hope you don't mind that I'm here," I say sheepishly.

Arlo stares at me. His lips open and close, words tumble behind his teeth. A grin creeps across his handsome features. Everyone watches him gaze at me with something akin to happiness and I've never felt more stripped bare.

"Thatch, you're here."

"I'm here, Arlo."

Arlo is trying to murder me.

We sit together on a bench. Kitt sits beside me and Quentin takes up the other side of Arlo. The stretching picnic table blanketed in red and white plaid is fully crowded. Caspian and Tobias bring over the last of the food from the grill.

Our thighs are touching.

He's one of those people who tells stories with their hands. They frequently brush against my back as he waves in the chilled air behind me, or alongside my forearm when his fingers settle on the miniscule bit of plaid between us. I don't know if I've ever heard him talk so much at once. He's *smiling*, and his eyes shine in this light like I've never seen before. Gold and emerald specks quite literally dance in his irises and he catches me staring for a few seconds too long multiple times.

To be fair, I've caught him staring at me, too.

His leather jacket is gone, resting on the bench between his hip and mine, revealing thick arms fully adorned with ink and another loose tank top. I've noticed whenever someone asks him a question, his fingers tend to find the dragon along his wrist. He'll briefly sweep over it in one direction, then the other, and that's all, but he doesn't ever look at it when he does. Maybe he doesn't realize he's doing it at all.

To say he's happy to see me is an understatement. It's infecting the others, drawing broad smiles and laughter out of everyone. I almost feel like a *real* part of their Misfits. Conversation and witty remarks flow like a river as opposed to a murky swamp. None of them look upon me with pity, but I've caught Kitt staring at me a few times with burning curiosity.

I feel equal parts warmth at the idea that I make Arlo so happy, and guilt of the same fact. I should be withdrawing, pulling back, not getting closer. I'm going to hurt him. His soulmark softly glows, catching my eye repeatedly.

The stars are a gorgeous backdrop for our night, strands of warm bulb lights crisscross over the yard, illuminating the twilight atmosphere perfectly for our feast. I listen to those around me chat with contentment, watching the dynamics unfold with curiosity.

Arlo makes sure to give each of his friends attention, but Kitt, Caspian and Quentin especially thrive under it.

Lindsey and Kitt have no problem flaunting their relationship, while Caspian and Tobias keep close to each other, but not much else.

Their children often find their way into Arlo's lap who dutifully fawns over them and Caspian looks upon Arlo with such fondness I find myself more ... *jealous*, (yes alright I'll admit it) of him than Quentin.

Those wide smiles from Caspian cause Arlo to fluster or distract himself with conversation, whereas the plain adoration from Quentin is lost upon Arlo, or it seems that way. He talks to Quentin like he does to every one of his friends. Arlo said he doesn't feel that way for Caspian, but it appears old feelings die hard.

"So, Thatch, have you ever visited during the festival before?" Kitt asks, distracting me from Arlo wrestling a giggling Marlena off his shoulders.

I face her and Lindsey. "Regrettably, no. But from what I've seen thus far, it seems like a grand time, although I'm not sure what all the fuss is about. This Illusionist seems like a drama

queen, to be honest. All this stealing and hiding and theatrics."
I wiggle my fingers, stretching out the word.

Gowan giggles from her seat across from us, as does the glad-
iola fae she brought with her tonight. Both fae are in full bloom,
which I find deeply fascinating. Canary yellow dandelions decorate Gowan's mossy skin, while soft white gladiolas drift past
Iris' grassy shoulders. Iris' long, blue hair curls between the
flower heads, leaves and stems with hidden roots.

"All the *fuss*?" Arlo starts, to which Caspian and Kitt simultaneously groan.

"*Now* you've done it." Lindsey agrees, leaning on Kitt's
shoulder. She watches me with a mischievous grin that matches
Gowan's.

"Alright, alright. Let's eat before Lolo pitches a fit." Caspian
says, passing around the platter closest to him.

I raise a brow at Arlo. "*Lolo*?"

Arlo glares at me after he passes Marlena off to Tobias. "Don't
even. I'm mad at you."

"No! Why?"

He nods solemnly. "This is unacceptable."

I press a hand to my heart and look to Kitt for help, she only
puts up her hands. "Arlo is *very* passionate about the Scarlet
Illusionist."

"*You're* the one who runs a museum with not one, but *two*
exhibits dedicated to them." Arlo reminds her.

She rolls her eyes. "Whatever."

I chuckle. "I thought it was the games that you enjoyed,
Arlo."

Perhaps it's a trick of the light or his soulmark glowing
brighter, but I swear his cheeks are deeply flushed. "I do, but
you have to admit, dramatics or not, the mind of a person that

can make such puzzles, well, yes, fine, I find it admirable. Go on, let's hear it."

My face warms with a vanity ridden smile. "Oh? What will you do when you find this person?"

"Yeah, Arlo, what *will* you do? *Please* tell me you've already picked out a ring." Kitt clasps her hands together, faux begging.

A roll meets her forehead with superb accuracy.

"Arlo!"

I bust out laughing, as do the others.

The playful bickering softens as platters make their way around the table. I load my plate to overflowing with vibrant salad, stuffed mushrooms, something fried, cheese maybe? No one speaks of the Scarlet Illusionist or the Game again, but that's alright. It's been a long time since I've had such a large meal. I eat until I can't anymore, but I put my fork down much sooner than anyone else does.

"Thatch," Arlo whispers.

I shiver upon locking eyes with him. He raises a brow at me, searching my face for *something* with darkened eyes. He reaches down between us. My breath hitches, then returns to my lungs when he retrieves his jacket. Without saying a word, he slings it across my shoulders and I melt into it. He nods, satisfied, then goes back to eating.

"Um," I say, brilliantly.

He glances over at me, a chunk of roasted squash stops before his parted lips. He doesn't look away. "I had plans, you know. Want to tag along?"

I nod, perhaps too quickly. "Yes, of course. Where?"

Arlo chuckles, glancing at Quentin first, then the others. "You guys want to take him to the Magpie with me?"

"*Oh* boy," Quentin says, leaning back to clean his glasses with the hem of his button up.

"*Yes.*" Kitt says resolutely, followed by a nodding Lindsey.

Gowan confers with Iris who agrees enthusiastically. "Sure," Gowan says.

"Well, it's getting late for these chicks and it's going to be an early day tomorrow." Tobias announces with a yawn, stretching his arms overhead. "You can go, Cas, if you want." Zeke whines from his place in Quentin's lap, while Marlena snores from her spot between Lindsey and Kitt.

Arlo stands abruptly. "I'll take them in, Bias."

Caspian reaches up and takes Tobias' hand, then kisses his knuckles. "Relax for a bit *ahuvi*, Arlo and I got this. If you want to go, I'll stay."

"Oh?" Tobias smiles at his partner, pleasantly surprised, then leans forward and kisses him on the lips so softly, they barely meet. Caspian's cheeks pinken, then he mutters something and takes off after Arlo waiting with a kid dangling from each arm. Arlo winks at me, and I flush.

Caspian's hands pause on his wheels and he looks back, catching me grinning like an idiot. "You're welcome anytime, Thatch Phantom." Caspian grits out, and I can't tell if the words are meant to be comforting or a threat.

"Thank you, Caspian, I appreciate that."

Caspian nods, then he and Arlo disappear into the house.

I turn to Quentin. "Quentin, I wanted to speak with you."

He startles. "Oh, okay. About?"

"I wanted to say thank you, for inviting me, and coming to see me, yesterday." I reach back to pull my hood up, forgetting that I'm only wearing a long sleeve and Arlo's jacket. I hide my hands in the leather sleeves instead, fingers desperately gripping the cuffs.

"And I wanted to apologize, truly, for how I behaved the other morning. If you're still interested, I *am* looking for tenants."

Kitt chokes on something and I turn back to her in alarm, but she waves me off. Lindsey rubs her back. "Are you alright?"

"Oh yeah, she's fine." Lindsey supplies with an unsettling grin.

Tobias sighs heavily, then throws back whatever Caspian was drinking with a grimace. I nod warily, then give my attention back to Quentin who's a few inches closer than before, occupying half the space Arlo was.

Quentin blinks those owlish, grass green eyes at me. "Thank you for the apology, but it's really not necessary. Arlo can be a bit, *much*, so I understand the need to sass him sometimes."

I chuckle. "I've noticed."

"Like you've ever sassed him, Quen." Lindsey adds.

"*Well,*" Quentin sputters.

"Come now, children. Quentin doesn't *have* to because he doesn't antagonize Arlo like you all do." Gowan chides in a peaceful tone, causing Iris to smile up at her.

Iris asks something, her fingers cut through the air in movements I haven't used myself in quite some time. Common is the only language I frequently use, and it's not like there's *time* to refresh on the ones I don't. I'll have to dig through my mind and fix that.

Kitt laughs wildly at my side, startling me. "No, no, they're not together."

Quentin wrinkles his nose, looking down into his drink. "We're friends."

Oh.

Tobias shifts uncomfortably across from us, pink hair loose and hanging around his face. I clear my throat, itching to get us all out of these treacherous waters.

"So, why *does* Arlo like the Illusionist so much?"

Gowan smiles softly. "Who doesn't like a little mystery?"

Iris agrees, and I pay more attention when she speaks, catching more this time. "He won a long time ago, didn't he?" Iris asks.

I glance between them all. "Is that so?"

Kitt nods, picking at a nail with a frown. "Yeah, when we were younger."

The mood is turning *incredibly* somber, not the direction I was hoping for.

Gowan stands, offering a hand to Iris after she does. "I say we end the night here with a dance. Thatch, do you play anything?"

Tobias stands from the table with a small smile, eager to leave behind the conversation.

I blink at Gowan. "Why, do you have a cache of musical instruments? I'm good with the kazoo."

Laughter breaks the ice, warming everyone's heart but Kitt's, she stares off distractedly.

Quentin nods at a storage shed hiding alongside the house. "You're not far off. I play the drums, Kitt the bass, Gowan the guitar, and Lindsey's good at the sax. Caspian's our vocalist, and Tobias is known to pick up a lute every once in a while. Iris, do you play?"

She nods. "I'll take a guitar if you have an extra."

Quentin stands from the table, waving off Tobias. "We'll get them, Bias." He looks to me, the only one still seated, and gestures for me to follow him.

And I do.

We walk together, leaving the chattering picnic table behind. "Um, I'd like that, by the way." Quentin murmurs.

"Hm?" I ask, distracted by distant fireworks erupting high over the opposite side of town. Do they go on every night of the festival?

"To look at the apartment, with Arlo." He says quietly. I trip over ... nothing. Quentin steadies me all the same, a small hand on my shoulder. "Alright there?"

I nod quickly. "Yes, sorry. The fireworks." I say as way of explanation, bringing forth a tiny smile to his face. He's handsome and has proven to be kind, leading me to wonder *why* they're only friends. "Yes, come by tomorrow."

"Alright. Oh actually, that won't do, and tomorrow I'm ... how about lunch on Thursday? Arlo's free then, and so am I."

"You care for him quite a bit, don't you?"

It's Quentin's turn to fall over nothing.

"Well, he's, he's my friend, and a very good person. Who doesn't like Arlo? He can be grumpy sometimes, but, well, it's all a show. I'm sure you've figured that out by now."

We reach the storage shed, but neither of us move to open the unlocked, sunflower yellow door framed by white. I force a smile, hoping it reads as genuine. "I have no romantic plans regarding Arlo, if that is a concern for you. I ... I can't stay long, so that would be,"

I shake my head, reaching up to rub out an incoming headache. "It couldn't happen. Not that he feels that way, or that I do, I just–"

Quentin laughs, a cracked thing that breaks my rambling.

I blink. "What?"

"Nothing, it's, well, you're ... so *normal*. When I first heard about you, I thought you were this ... well, I don't know what, but you're ... you're pretty nice, Thatch."

I chuckle quietly. "Well, I don't know about that. What fun is there in being normal?"

He grins at me, then it fades. "Thank you, for ... *that*. But Arlo doesn't see me that way."

"Oh, I thought–"

He gives me a pained smile. "That I didn't know?"

I shrug, retracting my hands inside my leather sleeves just a little. I can't believe I'm having this conversation with someone about *my* soulmate, but ...

I can't ever be with Arlo, no matter how much I want to. Admitting that fact to myself brings painful memories of the last lover I dared to have centuries ago. I don't ever want to come home to a lover who doesn't remember me. By the time we reconnect, if we do, I'm torn away again.

I put myself through it three times in my cursed immortality, and no more.

I can't imagine how it would feel to experience all of that with *my* person chosen by the universe. The very universe that abandons me time and time again has promised someone so breathtaking, so wonderfully loyal and kind, only to hold them out of reach. Arlo and I weren't lovers before, only friends, and that was tortuous enough to leave behind the first time.

It's not fair to either of us.

I sigh, coming back to myself. "He might surprise you."

Quentin shakes his head, then opens the door. "No, he hasn't looked at anyone like this in a long time. I don't mind that it's not me, I'm lucky to call him my friend."

He steps inside and I follow him into a large room, every wall is blanketed in well kept musical instruments. "What do you mean?" I ask, letting curiosity get the better of me.

"What?" Quentin asks, flicking on a light switch.

"You said 'like this.'"

He halts his step towards a disassembled drum set packed away in leather cases, glancing at me over his shoulder. "Like the way he looks at you. I've only seen it regarding one other person, and ... well, it's dim compared to this."

I laugh nervously. "*That* sounds ominous."

Quentin smiles at me, then returns to his drums. "Whether *he* knows it or not, Arlo cares for you, Thatch. Like *that*."

I scratch at my beard. "Oh, well, that's ..."

I trail off, unsure how to put my predicament into words.

"Here, take these." Quentin says, offering me a way out, and I take it.

After several trips, he and I stand in the shed for the last time so I can pick out an instrument. A thin sheen of sweat coats my forehead, my curls stick to all parts of my face obnoxiously despite the autumnal air that's chilled considerably even in the last hour. Caspian and Arlo still haven't returned. I worry Caspian's throwing me under the bus, but there's little I can do.

Then again, if Tobias can't reach the truth of me, then I doubt Caspian will remember me. His disdain for me is more likely to be due to his over-protectiveness of Arlo.

I point at one of the very few remaining instruments now that we've essentially moved the inventory outside. "I'm pretty good with one of those."

Quentin chews on his bottom lip, staring at the dusty thing for a moment. "That's Arlo's, but he doesn't play it anymore, so ... I'm sure he won't mind if you do."

Arlo

"Feeling alright, Cas?"

Caspian breaks his stare into the aquarium. He gives me a smile, but it's lopsided. "Yeah, fine."

I sit beside him on a blanket and toy covered couch, studying his features cast in a gentle glow from the tank's lights. Splashes from Zeke's earlier swim session are beginning to dry, still wet enough for boot tracks and tire treads to leave their muddy mark. I don't feel right going back out there and leaving Caspian in here, something's off with him.

I rub the back of my neck. "Have you still been having bad dreams? We never did talk about it."

Caspian's pupils restrict, and his breathing quickens, both reactions last less than five seconds. He looks away from me. "Something like that. It's fine, really. With the final solar game coming up, they're pushing me on this latest project. Once the season's over, everything will go back to normal." His last few words trail off, the heaviness in them makes me wonder if he's talking about *just* work.

I reach out and take his hand, startling him a little. He recovers, then squeezes my fingers. "Caspian, I've got your back, you know? If you need anything, I'm here. I mean it. This friendship thing, I hear it works both ways. You've gone above and beyond for me for so long, let me do the same for you, okay?"

Caspian's smile returns, and it's wide and full, no half-assness about it. It doesn't last long, but I'll take it. "Thanks, Lolo. I love you, you know?"

I nod, then lean forward and press my forehead to his, reaching around to clasp him on the back with intent. His hand thuds between my shoulder blades and he holds onto me like he hasn't in a long time. "I love you too, Caspian."

Air bubbles in the aquarium, softly disturbing the kelp transplanted from the farms near Market Street. The soft whir of the other points of the oxygenation system rustle the pondweed growing from the silty bottom. The expansive tank is like a mini world crafted from the Levena River itself, perfect for *shedim* of *mayim* descent. Marlena took after her other biological parent, a more traditional demon in the sense of the word, possessing leather wings and smoky blood.

"I'm sorry, Caspian."

Caspian pulls away from me, surprised. "For what?"

I shrug, looking at the tank like that explains it. "I wish I had been there, when they came home. What a fucking shitty thing to do, pulling a stunt like that right before they–"

"*Hey*," Caspian orders, fixing me with a stern glare. He takes hold of my shoulder. "You're here now, you're Uncle Lolo and they love you. We all do. Now get out of here with that, it sounds like they've started to get the instruments out. Can't let your boy suffer for too long without you." He grimaces at the thought.

I roll my eyes, pushing off the couch. "He's not *my* boy, and I don't think you can say that about someone that's hundreds of years old."

"Is that all?" Caspian mutters, dodgy again. "Just ... be careful, okay?"

"Of hundreds of years old boys? Yeah, got it Cas."

"I'm serious, Lo. Please, for me. I like him, but ... there's something about him that I can't put my finger on, and it makes me uneasy. And no, I'm not being 'asshole Cas,' I'm being serious." Caspian crosses his arms, leaning back on the couch.

I give him a soft smile. "Okay, Caspian."

I leave Caspian to his devices and mull over his words, more specifically how close to home they hit. *There's something about him that I can't put my finger on.*

Maybe tonight I can crack open Thatch a little more.

I open the front door and am greeted by the harmony of a well put together band, of what genre I can't say. Perhaps if folk rock and bluegrass had a love child?

My heart rages in dreaded anticipation and recognition. Surely that isn't ...

I approach the Misfits playing together with quiet and slow steps, finding relaxed bodies perched atop picnic tables, in trees and the spaces in between.

Quentin hammers on his drums, the long tousle of black atop his crown falls over his face, nearly obscuring how he's biting his lower lip and experiencing nirvana. Gowan and Iris stand together off to one side of him, playfully dueling with guitars and flirty winks.

Kitt's sleeves are rolled up as she strums upon her bass expertly. She sees me and smiles nervously but doesn't stop playing. Lindsey plays beside her, fingers tapping and cheeks full of air as she bellows upon her saxophone.

Tobias sits on the picnic table with his back to me, perched on a small corner where food and drinks were pushed out of the way. I can't see his face but I can tell by the way he's playing his lute that he's in heaven.

And Thatch. Oh, that man is almost enough to bury the bad dreams.

But sometimes, there's nothing anyone can do.

Thatch sits in a crotch of the tree keeping them all company, leg hanging down and swinging gently as he fiddles upon a violin. *The* violin.

His eyes are closed, face tilted up towards the sky and catching moonlight. He sways back and forth and lovingly swipes the bow across strings that have been neglected for years. They can't be the same ones that were on it, they would've snapped by now. His lips are pursed and brows softly furrowed, a scene I wish I had the heart to play.

What song they're all playing I have no idea, or perhaps they're playing their own distinct harmonies and somehow end up perfect, *cohesive*, without trying at all.

It's a moment, a happy one, but that *one* instrument shatters my nerves and ruins it. I should've gotten rid of the thing. I stand behind Tobias who nods at me with a flushed smile. "Sing," He says, then falters upon realizing I'm *not* good.

I glance at the others who catch on, too. Thatch however, is absorbed by his music. I *want* to enjoy it, I do, but when I see that *fucking* violin, there's only one person I can think of. So, I do something uncomfortable.

I say, "No."

Magick claws at the walls of my arteries and veins, furious and terrified of someone who haunts my terrors. Someone I killed long ago and who has the nerve to *fuck* with me beyond the grave. The music crashes to a violent stop and I push air in and out of my lungs in rapid succession, overcompensating in attempts to corral the volatile energy pulsating outwards around me.

So much for emptying my reserves at lunch time. I was half capacity and rising at Doc's just before I came here. I'm *definitely* regenerating much quicker than I ever have. I need to get this magick out of me *right* fucking now.

I close my eyes and focus on even words. "Tobias," I call in a gruff voice, turning away from the heavy stares on me. I take a few steps towards the driveway, not having to wait long for Tobias to join my side.

"Arlo, your magick, it's like a fucking solar storm right now, what's wrong?" He whispers, resting a hand on my shoulder. He immediately drops it, encountering my grief. *Such* grievous anger.

"Who thought getting that thing out would be a good idea?" I whisper.

Tobias shifts his feet. "Does it matter? You don't play it anymore, Thatch wanted to join us, impress you, I think. What's wrong with it?"

I hunch over, bracing my hands on my trembling knees. The edges of my vision ebb and flow harshly. "That violin was never *mine*, Tobias. It was," I suck in air, determined to spill a long held secret. "That was the only thing Leon ever gave me, the only thing I ever kept. That's *why* I don't play it. I should've told you ... but I couldn't get rid of it."

"*Oh*, Arlo."

"*Fuck*, Tobias, take some of this away from me, it's too much." I reach out blindly, nearly collapsing under the weight of my exponentially pressuring magick. My other hand clutches my chest. My heart, it *hurts*.

"Arlo, are you alright?" Thatch asks from just behind Bias, fists shaking.

I open my mouth to send Thatch away but blood streams out my nose. What the *fuck*? Memories, or dreams, whatever the *fuck* they are, haunt me and I gasp for air.

"Give us just a minute, Thatch." Tobias says, sliding his hand underneath my hair and grasping my bare neck. The sensation of giving away energy is much different than receiving it. Especially giving it away willingly, a privilege Leon didn't let other witches have. He took and took and *took* some more.

Leon, *Leon*, **Leon**.

Frost penetrates my veins and my magick fights against the current flowing between my heated body and Tobias' cool skin. The sensation of losing magick is always cold and hollow, but this is like straight up ice *daggers* slicing apart my circulatory system.

"*Fuck,*" I grit out, "it doesn't want to go."

"Arlo, I can't, your magick is too much, too much." Tobias cries, releasing me.

"Let me try," Thatch says firmly, and before I can tell him to stay where he is, he rests a hand on my spine, over my shirt.

Despite the fact we're not skin to skin, the effect is immediate.

Thatch echoes my gasp. His glacial fingertips spread out and dig into the muscles of my upper back. I tighten my grip on my knees and fucking *moan* as my magick gratefully seeps into Thatch, practically dancing to its own tune as it *thumps thumps thumps* into his body and spirit.

The light touches we've had until this point have been electrifying, something I've attributed to my attraction to him, but there's no denying now there's something between us.

Something *more.*

Thatch's hand slips away.

I barely restrain a groan at the loss of his touch. The sensation is like two magnets unwillingly being pulled apart and my magick cries out for him, I had received a … energy of sorts, a whisper of something that's heavy and cold, but not unpleasant. A cool balm to the heat rushing me, and my soul wants it back.

"Better?" He asks breathlessly, taking with him the last of the energy.

I straighten, body still trembling a little but with adrenaline, not magick. I focus on Thatch, finding him like the day I met him. Once pale and exhaustion ridden skin is bright and warm, the soft bags under his eyes are smoothed out and his lips are no longer cracked. His irises are no longer that dull gray but a vibrant blue that promises happiness.

But he's not smiling.

He doesn't look angry, or happy, or … anything.

He looks at me with … nothing.

I nod slowly, unsure what to say, what to ask.

Why are you looking at me like that?

What are you to me?

What am I to you?

Why are you so close but so far away?

"Good." Thatch says quietly, head down as he glances sideways at Bias. Thatch's tight shoulders relax when I don't press him for answers, but only a shade. No questions, then. Not right now.

Bias's pink brows furrow as he looks between us, obviously waiting for me to lose it. When I don't, he shakes his head. "Oy. On that note, drinks? Is that still happening?"

"Agreed." Thatch and I say at the same time.

I don't ask what happened to the violin. I hope someone burned it.

Burn The Bar Down

Arlo

The streets are thick with those off work or searching for clues to the Game. Even though the next painting won't be revealed until tomorrow, that doesn't seem to be stopping anyone. Or maybe they're *awake*, inspired by the Game to explore their city. I've always said that's the real point of the game.

"I'm glad you came, Tobias," I say, glancing over my shoulder at him. My shoes scuff pavement.

"Oh? Why's that?" He smiles, an arm slung around Kitt as they walk behind us. Gowan, Iris and Lindsey bring up the rear behind them, talking excitedly. Iris has never been to the Ethereal Magpie either. I feel guilty that this is the first time in a *long* time that Tobias has come

"It's *Malakim* Monday," Quentin says, walking between Thatch and me.

Thatch perks up at that, giving Quentin a shy smile. Thatch has been eerily quiet, only politely nodding or answering when spoken to. I feel better than I have in days, and he looks better, but somehow things seem *worse* between us. I did kind of lose my shit, but I can't make heads or tails as to what's going on anymore.

I can deal with nothing romantic, that's fine.

I only want ... I want to be his *friend*.

I want him in my life.

"What does that mean?" Thatch asks.

"Angels get in for free." Quentin smiles at him, soft and not at all nervous. Before I had gone and ruined everything earlier with the music, I could tell Thatch was feeling more comfortable with everyone, and that was mutual. He and Quentin especially seem to get on well.

I check my phone and a sly grin comes to life when I see Loch's message.

Loch: Figured since I made you listen to Doc's bullshit advice. To answer your question, yes, I'm tending bar.

Me: Did you happen to bring the painting?

The dots bounce up and down a few times as the others talk around me.

"What're you laughing at?" Quentin asks.

"Nothing," I say quickly, shoving my phone back in my pocket.

He raises a brow, but Kitt saves me. "I'm so fuckin' glad I don't have to tend tonight. Thatch, we're dancing, you know this, right?"

Thatch sputters. "Oh, I don't know about that, I'm not–"

"Don't you *dare* say you can't dance. We've already been through this with *way* too many things." Quentin points a finger at Thatch, surprising me.

Thatch flushes. "I *can*. It's ... been awhile, that's all. I'm not, well, how do I put this ... " He taps his chin, and I can't help but smile at him.

"Not up to the times?" I offer.

He gives me a stern look. "Yes, because I'm old, Arlo. Haha."

"Well, if you break your hip, we got two witches who can fix you up." Tobias shrugs.

I give Thatch a look of mock surprise, pressing a hand to my chest. "Thatch, what have you done? Tobias *and* Quentin are sarcastic now."

I get a swat upside the back of the head, Kitt, of course. "No sassier than you."

"*Ow*."

Thatch laughs a little, the first time since dinner. "You guys are something else."

"So are you," I say, which was the wrong thing.

He smiles thinly at me. "Thanks, Arlo."

We turn down a small boulevard with a false ceiling of wooden lattice work that supports a heavy canopy of climbing ivy, moonflowers and other plants. Small, warm globes float along the space, powered by their solar batteries. Thatch's eyes widen as we walk at a slower pace than we have been.

Brick buildings and multi-level cottages flank both sides, some front doors are open, allowing the last smells of dinner to escape into fresh air. The soft *whirr* of the vertical turbines nestled at the top of the buildings intermingles with music pouring from some of the residences. I search the skies for Bosko, but no luck.

"I've never been down this way," Thatch whispers, like we're in a special place.

"It's beautiful, isn't it? Not where you expect a nightclub to be," I say to him, noticing how we've somehow ended up at the back of the group.

Thatch blinks rapidly, pulling my jacket tighter around himself. I won't ask for it back, and I think he's forgotten he's wearing it, honestly. "Wait, on *this* street?"

I chuckle, nodding. "Yeah, we're almost there."

Kitt leads the charge, bypassing a set of stairs leading up to intricately crafted double doors. Thatch briefly looks at the front doors as we pass by, then to me, and back to Kitt. She walks up to a mural on the side of the brick building, the second to the end of this block. There's a decent separation between this building and the one to our backs, but they're both owned by Elochian.

She taps bricks in the pattern Loch decided upon when we put this into effect ages ago, although the stones weren't always painted. Courtesy of Shroom and Pus, fellow air spray graffiti artists whose skills rival mine. Now *that's* who the Illusionist should've talked to if they wanted to hide paintings in Levena, there would be no one better.

After she taps the last brick, the illusion falls, revealing a nondescript door. Thatch stands on his tiptoes trying to look around the others, so I gently cup his elbow. "Come here," I whisper, leading him closer.

He looks up to me with surprise, then softens and follows me. We stand behind Kitt and the door swings open, revealing a *shedim*. While the patrons in the Magpie may be diverse, Loch's security is composed of demons only. Not his choice, like most things in his life.

"Cards." The red skinned *shedim* asks gruffly, one of his horns is sheared off and the other curls back like Kitt's does. A thin tail swishes back and forth behind him, slow and steady. He's the bouncer most nights, Jon, I think?

Thatch tugs on my sleeve. "Arlo, I don't have a card."

I reach into my back pocket and take out my leather wallet, then find my card. A plain, black business card with a gold insignia in the center. Mine is special, there's no limit to the number of guests I want to bring. I hand it to Thatch and he turns it over and over in his hands.

"We can share. I made these years ago for Loch."

"Oh, okay. Why?" He asks, focused entirely on me. I nod to the bouncer, surprising Thatch. "Oh! Sorry, sir, here you go. Is that what I do? I just give it to you?" He thrusts the card out, nearly punching Jon in the gut.

Kitt snickers from ahead of us, partially blocked by the bouncer. She yelps and I'm assuming Lindsey smacked her. I cover my grin as Thatch stares up at Jon, mouth agape.

The *shedim* raises a thick brow, lip twitching as he takes the card from Thatch. "Haven't seen you here before. You'll fit right in."

"Oh. Thank you?" Thatch straightens, voice rising and hands settling on his hips.

Jon taps the insignia, causing it to glow once. He hands it back to Thatch who takes it *very* carefully. "Go on," he says, nodding to both of us. When I pass by, Jon reaches up and squeezes my shoulder, tugging me close. "Not sure how you did it, but Boss is on the floor."

I clap his shoulder, smiling. "I didn't do anything, but I'm glad."

Instead of sitting at the bar, we find an empty round table and accompanying booth in a corner. The tank, raised stage and bar are all in open view, but we're set far back and are as private as we can be on the main floor. There's a second floor, but that's for vampires, werewolves and other blood inclined creatures to satisfy their urges with either volunteers or someone they've brought.

With consent, of course. Loch doesn't run *that* kind of place.

I catch Quentin and Thatch before they sit down. "Hey, want to help me with drinks?"

They both agree and I lead the way over to the bar, fighting a smile. I don't know why, but I have a good feeling about this. We weave through the dance floor, Thatch is swiftly distracted by the lights and people, but Quentin keeps him from getting lost.

"This place is wonderful." Thatch remarks, grinning as the three of us come to a stop at the end of the bar. The neon lights dance across his face and illuminate his blown pupils. His curls bounce every time he whips his head around to stare at something or someone.

"So, Arlo, I was thinking–" Quentin starts, then abruptly cuts off as the bartender complains.

Perfect.

"I can't *believe* you convinced me to work in this shithole."

Elochian Adrastus sets to work on a tray of drinks across from us, practically snarling at me. Silk black sleeves are rolled up and three buttons are undone, revealing a hint of the tattoos on his chest and lightly defined arms. The globes above us reflect the lines of gold inlaid into his cheeks and the subtle blue powder painted across his eyes which match his wings. His raven hair is neatly plaited into easily thirty different braids, all woven together and snaking down his back.

All six of his wings flitter in a constant state of nervousness, almost knocking the bottles behind him over which makes his anxiety worse. I know if he had the choice, he'd hide them all the time, but the runes tattooed onto them keep him from doing so at will like other *shedim* and *malakim* can.

"To be fair, it's *your* shithole. I have a couple people I want you to meet, if you're up for it," I say, lifting Loch's eyes up to mine from the shaker in his hands.

Loch stares at me, then his eyes *slowly* slide to Quentin and widen. His nostrils flare and a sly quirk takes hold of his thin lips. "Ah, the not square."

"Square?" Quentin straightens as if hit by lightning. He looks between Loch and I quickly, not at all subtle. He swallows whatever else he was going to say and slides his glasses up, then reaches over the bar. Loch stares at his outstretched hand, wings freezing. I watch the flight response come to life in his eyes, but he takes Quentin's hand.

"Elochian Adrastus."

"Elochian ..." Quentin breathes, mouth dropping as he finally puts two and two together. Yup, that's the look.

"That's my name," Loch says, a hint of amusement coloring his endless tawny eyes. All his wings flutter open and closed once, then relax. No more anxious flitting.

Thatch brushes up against me and I look down to find him smiling knowingly at me. "What?" I whisper, and he shakes his head once.

"Nothing at all."

"Right! I'm Quentin, Quentin Matsdotter."

"Matsdotter ... the author?" Underneath Elochian's smirking, cool guy facade, there's a hint of curiosity and awe.

Quentin pales. They're still shaking hands. Well, not so much shaking as holding the other firmly. Quentin's knuckles have turned bone white. "Oh no ..." He whispers in horror.

"You're an author, Q?" I ask, grinning at him.

Quentin drops Loch's hand, looking at me like a deer in the headlights. "Oh, um, I used to, but it was a long, *long* time ago, and the content is, *well* ..." His voice pitches high, and his ears burn red.

"Perverted and obscene." Loch informs me, nodding seriously.

I choke on a laugh. "*What*?"

"Thatch!" Quentin squeaks, *begging* someone to save him. "This is Thatch!"

Thatch chuckles, stepping past me to shake Elochian's hand. "Thatch Phantom, how do you do?"

Loch cocks his head, shaking Thatch's hand firmly. "Have we met before?"

Thatch's smile disappears, so fast I nearly miss it, but then it's back on like nothing happened. "No, but perhaps you've heard of me through my ventures. It's a pleasure to meet you. Adrastus, you said?"

Loch nods, pleasant but wary. "Well, a friend of Arlo's is a friend of mine."

Thatch smiles at him. "Indeed."

Thatch has many, *many* smiles. The one for me that's rarer by the day. The one that's a mask. The one that's genuine and heartfelt. The one that's hiding secrets beyond words.

The smile he's wearing now is a mask. I can see how it doesn't reach his eyes and how he chews his cheek through it. Without thinking, I reach down and gently press my palm to his lower back. I expect him to pull away, but he immediately leans into my touch and lets out a breath, shoulders falling.

We're pushing and pulling, never staying in contact long enough.

We talk to Loch for another moment, well Thatch and I do while Quentin short circuits, then we take the drinks back over to our table. Quentin scurries ahead of us and Thatch elbows me gently. "I saw what you did there."

I shrug. "I have no idea what you're talking about. Loch's my friend, Quentin's my friend. Thought, hey, they should be friends with each other."

"And that has nothing to do with Quentin's mark glowing?" Thatch asks, surprising me.

"What? It is? Where?" I crane my neck as we approach the table, but Quentin's sitting down. I haven't seen his, I assumed it wasn't visible.

Thatch chuckles. "No idea, but the look on your face was adorable. You're kind, Arlo."

I roll my eyes. "Tell anyone and we'll have problems."

Thatch slides into the booth and just as my ass hits the seat beside his, Quentin starts in. "Arlo!" He whisper-shouts, "Why didn't you warn me!"

I tilt my head innocently. "What do you mean? About what?"

"You could've *told* me you were taking me over to the *shedim* prince!"

Kitt laughs. "Oh man, Loch is tending tonight? C'mon Linds, we gotta go give him crap."

I point a finger at her. "Not too much. I think before we came over he was about ready to leave. I told him to come over and drink with us, but I'm not sure if he will."

"You *knew*?" Quentin asks the *qieren*, aghast. Kitt decides that staying to pick on Quentin is *much* more entertaining for the moment.

Gowan smiles, leaning against Iris' side. "What's the matter, Quentin?"

"Nothing's the *matter*, I just would've ... dressed. Differently. That's all." Each word is carefully punctuated and Quentin gestures up and down to himself, then adjusts his glimmering bowtie. He hurriedly rolls up his sleeves. "No one expects to find an *archdemon* behind the bar." He mutters to himself, ears still red.

"You're handsome, Quentin," Thatch says warmly, and my heart swells for reasons unknown. He fits into our group like he's always been there, swiftly taking hold of my friend's hearts.

"Agreed." I add, then hold up my drink. "To Quentin's bowtie."

Thatch is next, followed by Bias and the girls. "To Quentin's bowtie."

"I hate you all." Quentin groans.

I take a long drink, then grin at my friends. "By the way, who else knew that Quentin is an author?"

"Of porn." Thatch notes sagely, studying his half gone drink. I never told Loch what to make for him, but Thatch seems to like whatever it is. The rest of us are creatures of habit and drink the same thing every time.

"Oh. My. *Fuck*." Quentin mutters, then throws back his whiskey.

"*Porn*?" Kitt squeals, leaning on the table across from us.

"I've read some of it. He's pretty good," Lindsey says, taking the cherry from her cup and *popping* it into her mouth. She starts work on the stem, much to Kitt's delight.

"Why didn't you tell us, Quen? We wouldn't be good friends if we didn't support you," Tobias says, reaching into his pocket for his phone. Quentin grabs his wrist, but Gowan's already got it pulled up on *her* phone.

"The Adventures of a Spice Trader and the Monsters They Fucked." Gowan reads off, nodding her approval. Thatch hides his giggles behind his hand, and oh my, that's cute.

"A ten novel series, each one featuring a different monster. Wow, go Spice Trader." Kitt adds to the chaos, peering at Gowan's phone.

I laugh, pounding a fist on the table. "Monster porn!"

"Honestly, the best kind of porn." Iris agrees, giggling.

"STOP saying porn." Quentin pleads, cheeks a deep scarlet.

"What's wrong with porn?" Loch asks, standing nearby our booth and ready to run. Well, he *looks* suave, arms crossed and muscles flexing, but the subtle look in his wide eyes and trembling wings give him away.

Quentin blanches. "N-nothing! I was only, oh my Gods ... I was trying to make it through school, and romance books pay well! That's all."

Thatch leans into me with a true smile. "I'm having fun. Thank you."

I chuckle, bending down to his level. "We've barely gotten started."

"I know, but this is nice. Feels like a family." Thatch admits, a shade quieter than before.

I rub the back of my neck. "That's because it is one."

"Yeah," Thatch says, then throws back the rest of his bubbly red drink in one go. I don't know if I've ever heard him say 'yeah,' besides when he smoked with us, that is. It's always *yes*, or something equally proper.

I turn my attention to Loch, feeling like I've made Thatch uncomfortable. Again.

"Decided to join the cool kids?"

Loch scoffs. "Only making sure you're not going to burn the bar down."

"You have insurance," I say, tipping my drink to him before I finish it.

After that, things flow normally. Loch pulls up a chair and sits on the open side of the table, quiet at first but eventually opening up to our banter. Quentin's nerves ease and the pair keep catching eyes. Thatch remains pressed up against me and his smile returns, one that ranges between genuine and half there, to half lost in thought and vacant.

I tell myself that I'm being paranoid, that I'm not the reason why he's upset. Regardless, my head assures me it *is* my fault for acting like such an idiot earlier. Of course he would be uncomfortable. He chose to come with us though, so there's that.

Thatch pounds drinks faster than Gowan does, and that's saying something. She may be small and docile, but she can handle her alcohol. Not sure if that's a fae thing or a Gowan thing. Kitt keeps up with them, clearly wanting to let loose tonight. Iris sips on her drink at a soft pace, like myself and Lindsey. Tobias has switched to water and herbs.

I pack another bowl, the sensation from the herbs something I crave more than a drink. Thatch had instantly relaxed after the first round that Bias prepared, so I hand him my pipe, giving him the green hit. Thatch grins dopily up at me, cheek rubbing on my arm. "I should've picked this up *centuries* ago."

"Yeah?" I ask, laughing breathlessly.

"Yes, it's ... I dunno, makes everything quiet." He gestures to his head in a roundabout way.

I nod. "I know what you mean. After ... " I clear my throat, lowering my voice and steering us away from *that*. "I've tried a few different medicines, for my head, you know? Only one works, and even that one is ... I don't like taking it, but I do, because I'd be hopeless without it. This I use because it fills in the gaps, makes me happy, and because I want to. Because I can."

"Are you not happy without it?" Thatch asks, nudging impossibly closer.

"It's not that." I search for the right words, unsure how to put it. "It's like you said. Makes everything else quiet. Gets me out of my own way, you know?"

Thatch nods. "I do."

I stare into his eyes. "Are *you* happy, Thatch?"

He blinks in surprise. "Oh, I'm ..." I wait for the lie prepared on the tip of his tongue, but then he lifts a shoulder and smiles honestly. "I'm happy right now."

I release a small chuckle. "Me too, Thatch."

"Work is going to *suck* tomorrow." Lindsey whines loudly, breaking us from our moment.

"I don't know why you don't just take the week off, between championships and work you're exhausted, my sweet," Kitt says, rubbing her horn against Lindsey's cheek. Kitt only uses words like *'my sweet'* when she's extra sappy, or in other words, drunk.

I nod to Thatch who lets me out of the booth and he stares up at me after I stand. I take my beanie off and throw it down where I was sitting, then reach into my pocket and dig out a leather cord. I tie my hair back, then roll my shoulders out.

"The candyman?" I hold my hand out to Kitt over the table.

"*Oh*, boy," Tobias says.

Kitt grins, more mischievous than a gremlin. "*Fuck* yeah."

"What's happening?" Iris asks when Kitt climbs *over* the table, taking my hand as she jumps down.

Tobias smiles at her, signing his answer. "You're about to see how witches dance."

Thatch glances between Bias and I, unsure. That look makes me want to dance even more. Maybe if I act a fool, he will too.

Kitt tugs me towards the dance floor and I give Thatch the biggest grin I can muster. "Come break a hip with us, old man."

Thatch

Once again, Arlo's trying to kill me.

He managed to trick me onto this crowded dance floor.

Mist falls down in clouds, sparkling in the neon lights that are remarkably different from the soft globes overhanging the bar and seating area. These lights are wild and bright and vibrant, hues ranging in every color of the rainbow. Arlo *shines* under them, dancing horribly with Kitt to some indie rock band that the crowd goes wild for.

They're going wild for Arlo, too.

The 'candyman' is an adorably ridiculous move that involves Kitt and Arlo swing dancing wildly, taking up the entirety of the dance floor for a few minutes as they enact a grand routine that's obviously ingrained into their muscles.

It ends with Arlo sweeping Kitt into his arms. She sticks her legs straight out and he spins her in a circle, then *tosses* her into the air like she's nothing.

I wonder how many drinks I've had, because *what*?

The cut of Arlo's muscles awash with mist and sweat, flexing under the lights, nearly distracts me from Kitt's marvelous front flip. Of course, she lands on her feet and they both cheer, fists pumping in the air. I holler and our friends do too, the crowd roars.

Arlo immediately searches for me and how can I *not* give him the smile he's looking for?

I hold my hand out to him and he takes it, pulling me close to him with concern written all over his face. The air knocks out of me when our chests bump together. He doesn't release my hand and when I entwine my fingers with his, Arlo softens. His other hand *gently* takes my waist as he bends down to hold me properly.

"You alright?" He asks, his whisper more of a soft shout.

I blink up at him, surprised. "Yes, of course. Why?"

He opens his mouth, then decides against whatever he was going to say and shakes his head. A small, playful smile takes hold of him. "Dance with me?"

"Oy, you *are* trying to murder me, Arlo Rook. Fine, but no acrobatics. I'm much too old for that, as you keep reminding me."

Arlo laughs, the sound so wonderful and cleansing that the entire room fades away. He already has a tender hold on my hand and waist, I stand on my toes so he doesn't have to bend so far.

New melodies join the band one by one, our friends. The band of string instruments are joined by Quentin's harmonious thrumming on the drums and Kitt's confident picking on an elegant bass. Gowan and Iris are there too, playing guitar. Lindsey dances on the stage in a way that mesmerizes not only Kitt, but most of the club. Tobias sings with a treant and *katan,* his countertenor hauntingly beautiful. The oak of a man and small statured woman singing with him are rumbling contrasts to his tone.

Arlo and I meld together as we sway, push apart and pull together. He gently rubs his jaw alongside the top of my head and I lean into him, hardly dancing anymore. Arlo holds me, and I hold him. The music, the people, the lights, the mist and *everything* that is life and wonder, it flows in glorious swells around us. I've never felt so *alive*, so connected and present.

"Look." Arlo murmurs into my hair, nodding towards the stage. I follow his gaze, gasping when I see Tobias. He's singing, face flushed and a sheen of sweat upon his forehead. Pink tresses flow around his waist and he's smiling. The evidence of parental exhaustion and the burden that is life are still there, but illuminated *and* overshadowed by his bliss.

But that's not what takes my breath away.

Six wings silhouette Tobias' figure, rose feathers outstretch high into the air and catch multi-colored droplets of water. Random, small eyes of bright rose gold are nestled into his feathers, brightening and dimming with his voice, blinking open and closed. An enormous, fluffy and pink cloud surrounds the stage, increasing in size until it trickles down to our level.

"He's an archangel," I whisper, awestruck.

Phones appear throughout the crowd and small flashlights peek up at Tobias, but he doesn't care. His focus is on the music, not hiding who he is. "Has he ever done this before?" I ask, holding on tight to Arlo. He pulls back a little, hands settling on my hips.

"No. I didn't even know he could sing. And this, well," He gestures at Tobias' wings, "this is a rare event. I ... it's my fault, I think. Everything's been about me for a long time, and I'm trying to fix that."

I smile up at him, then try to gnaw it away. "Your friends are allowed to care about you. It's a give and take, you know? You all have a turn at crashing and burning, picking each other up. And it seems like Tobias *is* happy."

Arlo nods, the song finishes and the crowd erupts. The cloud deepens in color and spills across the bottom floor, warming me from the inside out. Magick infused with happiness and peace and *love*, hits me like a drug. I waver and Arlo's grip tightens on me, giggles spread around us.

"Happy is an understatement," Arlo says through a laugh.

I laugh too, but it turns into an obnoxious giggle that I can't stop. Another song starts and we sigh, catching our breath. I admire the way his eyes flicker between gold and green, like a candle in the wind. His soulmark glows in the same fashion, a soft wave of gilded light just for me. He was made for me, and I for him.

Arlo searches my face, for what I'm not sure. Finally, he reaches up and cups the back of my neck, grounding me to the earth. "You *look* at me, Thatch, like it means something. Like *I* mean something. I can't figure it out. And I can't decide if it's because I'm an idiot ... or if you won't let me in."

"You *do* mean something to me, Arlo. A great many things." I squeeze his shoulder, feeling as if he's punched me in the gut, and look away. "You're not an idiot," I whisper.

Arlo's fingers dig into my hip and the crowd moves around us in waves, obscuring us in plain view from the world. I inhale deep and slow when he captures my chin, tilting my face up to meet his. His eyes are no longer hazel, but full of endless pastures at the peak of summer. The magick within him begs to be released again, the soft purr under his skin vibrates against my cheek and wants to say hello. I cannot deny how good it felt to take on some of his energy.

"Thatch." Arlo breathes in the space between us. I stare into his eyes, unable to do anything else. "Let me in."

My lungs catch and I fall forward.

My head thuds into his collarbone.

I wrap my arms around his waist and he immediately blankets me with his own, protecting me from all the forces tearing us apart. Can he feel them? The magnetic pull between us and the dividing cut of the universe?

I grip the back of his shirt, spilling partial truths into his heated chest like a coward. "Arlo, this is doomed to fail. I have to leave soon, and it's not fair to either of us, starting something we cannot finish."

Arlo's chest rises and falls evenly under me. One hand slides up my spine, gripping the back of my neck as softly as he does my jaw. He rests his chin atop my head and we sway in place. He won't ever let me go now. I've fucked up by falling into him. By being impossibly mortal. I've tasted what my life could be like and I don't want to give it up.

I hate this so *much*.

The music continues around us.

Kitt laughs as she dips Lindsey, forgoing the band.

Quentin's gone.

Gowan and Iris dance not far from us, foreheads pressed together.

Tobias sings about a sweet man named Caspian with a heart of gold. I wish he was here to see it.

Another round of mist falls upon our heads, thick with the scent of sweat, liquor and Arlo's perpetual espresso fragrance. The tattoo over my heart aches. I want to show him the ink and introduce him to the worst parts of me. With a passion just as strong, I *never* want him to see my broken body.

Arlo's thumb sweeps back and forth over my neck. He tips his head down and whispers into my ear, "We're here now, Thatch."

I leave the comfort of his chest, lifting my chin. We're a breath width apart and our noses brush when someone bumps into us. Do we do this? Do we break our hearts?

"Arlo, I'm *serious*. It's not a ... *choice* for me, when it's time to go."

"So am I." His soulmark ignites, a beacon that proves his point.

And everything becomes too much.

"Take me home, please." I ask breathlessly, fingertips pressing into his chest.

He doesn't ask questions, or argue. Arlo only nods, leading me out of the chaos by the hand. "Alright. I have to grab something from the bar, then we can go."

I hold on tight to his hand and don't let go.

Besides the brief moment when he stopped to magick something from behind the bar, we haven't stopped holding hands. Words are hard to come by and for the most part we walk in silence. The night is cold, and I'm grateful for his jacket. I tried to give it back once, but he wordlessly shook his head. Eventually I break the silence, after the clock towers along the way chime ten.

"Arlo," I exhale, tugging on his arm to stop his long and easy steps.

His thumb brushes over the back of my hand. His soulmark brightens, tugging on my heart. "Yes, Thatch?"

"I don't want to hurt you," I say, barely stringing the words together.

He pulls me to his side, studying my face. "Thatch, are you in danger?"

I shake my head, unable to resist the force drawing my forehead to his arm. "No, it's not like that."

Arlo stiffens and I can feel his head craning slowly to the left and right, surveying the area. "Then why do you *have* to leave? Are you ... promised to someone else?" I huff out a laugh, shaking my head. "Indebted?"

"No."

Arlo doesn't say anything for a moment. The warm, ghostly touch of magick sweeps over my cheek, emanating from his arm. I lift my face from his body and loosen my fingers from his grip. He doesn't release me, though. Then again, I'm not trying very hard.

"You *can't* tell me why, but you *want* to?" Arlo affirms.

"Correct."

He looks away from me then, and a pang of loneliness hits me. Arlo grips my hand tighter, gazing back at me with a new determination in his eyes.

Oh, no. He thinks he can *fix* me.

I pull away from him then with intent and he allows me to go, brow furrowed. I put my hands up, taking a small step back. I need to pull myself together, this is getting too ... *real*. "Arlo, no. It doesn't work like that."

He puts on a good show of being affronted. "I didn't say anything."

I give him a look. "You didn't have to."

He chuckles, then it fades. He gestures between us. "I ... I thought you didn't want this. Me."

Although he's switched the topic, I don't think he's giving up on the idea. I sigh, pretending to let it go. I comb a hand through my hair, looking away. "That's quite far from the truth. All I want is what I cannot have."

Arlo closes the distance and slowly reaches for my hand with both of his, but sparks arc between us and electrify my veins.

I inhale sharply, and a gasp escapes him. "I'm sorry," He says, releasing me immediately.

I take his hand again. "It's alright. You're not hurting me, just surprised me. Your magick seems to like me."

"You have no idea," Arlo breathes out. He stares at our joined hands, the light from his birthmark intensifies when he looks back up at me. "Can I ask you a question?"

I inhale, preparing myself for something I cannot answer, then nod.

"Can I take you out on a date? Tomorrow night?"

I blink once. Twice.

"*What*?"

Arlo chuckles, reaching up to brush curls away from my eyes. His fingers slide down to my jaw, holding me like he did before. I lean into his palm without thought and he smiles tenderly. "A date. It's what two people do who are interested in each other. I would like to take you on one."

"I know what a *date* is, Arlo." I mutter, closing my eyes. I breathe in, out, absorbing the warmth of him, storing it into my mental files for the years I'm alone. The memory of this will never be enough. "I don't want to hurt you." I repeat, because it's like he never heard me at all.

"I may not be ancient like you, but I am an adult. I want to spend time with you. When it's time for you to leave, then I'll be here. Waiting for whenever the infamous Thatch Phantom returns, that is ... if you want me when you return."

That sounds too good to be true.

I open my eyes and find him looking at me with such fondness and pure honesty that it terrifies me. He truly means it. I reach up and place my hand over his on my face.

"I might not be able to come back," I say before I can't. "I'm not sure if *I* can handle loving and leaving you, Arlo Rook. You just may break my heart." Heat burns my throat and eyes, I sniff.

"Hey," Arlo murmurs, fingers sliding past my jaw to bury in my hair with a firm grip. His body aligns with mine, his free arm wraps around my shoulders and he's so *warm*. We've pulled apart and come together so many times already, just tonight. Our bodies know where they're supposed to be.

Tears run down my face, a burning reminder of my impending end.

I lift my head from his chest. His lips are parted and eyes a soft hazel, the magick within them calm and pleased at my closeness. When he sees my tears, he wipes them away and exhales heavily. "Okay. I understand, I do. We don't have to, I'm sorry for pushing you—"

"Stop." I press a finger to his lips before he can say anything else. "I *want* to be broken, but only if you're the one cracking me apart. I ... I want to go on a date with you, Arlo. I want to do this until we can't. If ... only as long as you are aware that this is ... temporary."

He smiles, and it's so *fucking* bright.

I've lost my mind.

The Others won't be happy with the mess I am after this is through.

Arlo leans down and this is *it*, he's going to kiss me, and this time I–

He kisses my forehead, upturned lips brushing against skin and curls. His fingers weave through my hair for a tenuous moment, then his hands slide away from my body ever so slowly as he pulls away. "I'll pick you up here at four. Sound good?"

"Um?" I look around, confused. I have no idea where we are, nothing is familiar even under the full double moonlight. "You're not *leaving* me here, are you?"

Arlo chuckles, then links his pinky around mine. He leads me to the end of the alley which spills out onto Garren Road, depositing us just behind Thitwhistle's. My cheeks flush against the cold and I bury my face into the collar of Arlo's jacket. I'm glad he hasn't asked for it back yet, I'm hoping to add it to my stash for next time.

I have to believe there will be a next time. He does.

But then again, he doesn't know anything other than the small scraps I've managed to give.

Arlo walks me to the front door, then brings my hand to his lips and kisses my knuckles. Air thins when his smile brushes my skin. "Until tomorrow, Thatch Phantom," he says, then releases me and walks away.

"Until tomorrow, Arlo Rook," I softly call after him, watching as he goes.

He really seems to want *me*, in whatever capacity he can have.

Perhaps I should borrow some of his courage.

Only after he disappears do I realize that he slipped something into my hand. I turn over my palm, revealing a tiny, *tiny* folded piece of paper. I unlock the door and step inside the darkened cafe. I don't bother turning on any lights as I make my way through the place. Each step upstairs weighs me down more and more. I come to a stop in a small hall, before the door with a '1' above the keyhole, then glance behind me at the apartment labeled '2'.

With a certainty I haven't had in a long time, I decide Arlo will never have to go without his own home again, even if it's not with me.

Instead of entering the apartment right away, I lean against the wall and slide down, occupying the hall as I work out the puzzle he's given me. The edges of the paper are hard to find at first and work in opposing directions, but after a while I manage to unfold the sheet to its original size.

It's blank, save for a circle centered in the paper. I press it like I would a button, which swiftly transforms the sheet. It stretches out and thickens, the texture roughens underneath my fingertips, exposing vibrant blues, reds and oranges.

I press a hand over my mouth, using my free hand to caress over Arlo's impression of my eyes. *My* eyes, their true color. Does Arlo really think I'm this beautiful? I take in gasping, shaky breaths, then stand and let myself into the apartment, canvas tight to my chest. I wander through the darkness until I'm standing in the center of my room. Ever so carefully, I set down the canvas beside my bed.

I undress, dress, then undress once more. I lay in bed, naked under the fairy lights I strung in *my* room. The place that for a little while, is mine. I roll over and study Arlo's painting, hugging his jacket close to my bare chest. I shift my gaze to the pile of paintings leaning against the opposite wall. Such simple things. I hope they're enough, that Arlo can understand what I'm trying to tell him. Not that it will change anything, but someone will *know* who I am. I've never been able to tell anyone, not even Dusan, but Arlo, I *need* him to know.

I've planned my departure many times, but this, *this* feels like I'm organizing my own funeral.

With less difficulty and Kitt's berating tech advice carved into my mental files, I send my first text. I spend ten minutes typing and erasing, then hit send before I can change my mind again. Silas sent me a message regarding his shift tomorrow and I *have* to remember to ask Arlo about him. Rhea and Helena wrote to me as well, using smiley faces to say hello. I respond with a 'See you in the morning' to all three of them, then wrinkle my nose at the time. 11:50 pm.

It hits me then.

This will be the last Game.

I'm theorizing that if I do come back, it will be *at least* eighty years before I return, *if* I do. My magic diminishes each time as well, and honestly? I want to stay alive as long as possible. I wish I had never put on the Game this year so that I could spend more time with Arlo. Three weeks opposed to one doesn't sound like much, but it is to me. I don't know if he'll be alive the next time, and even so, I can't survive falling in love with him and losing him twice.

I can't even do it once, but I will try.

Me: Thank you for tonight, and for everything. I told Quentin you two can have the second apartment, I meant to tell you, but, well, I forgot. Bring in your things anytime, we'll figure the details out later. Good night.

Tuesday

Turn Down The World

Arlo

Tuesdays are for brewing.

The door to the Kitchen is open and a menagerie of children keep me company. Somehow, I think they know. The last day Arlo Rook, 'Hedge Witch Extraordinaire,' (courtesy of Kleo) concots potions and enchants objects in Garren Castle is coming soon.

I woke up to an elegant and formal text from Thatch which jump-started my heart and in turn awoke the beast that is Rapidfire Endless Thoughts. I wrote him back in the same, grammatically correct fashion and accepted his offer.

He hasn't written back yet.

Quentin has, and he seems ecstatic. He confirmed they talked about the apartment last night and was hoping I would say yes. He didn't tack emojis onto his messages like he usually does, but the words seem sincere. I can't see why he wouldn't be excited.

Bosko hasn't returned, and I'm starting to get worried. Really, a few things have me worried today, but I'm trying my best not to think about Leon crawling back from the dead or haywire magick.

With the long-handled spoon that Thatch admired just days ago, I poke around rapidly melting cubes of shea, coconut oil and lavender. I trust my hand conjurations, but for this I utter a soft incantation designed to give the user a sense of calm and a slight muffling of their surroundings. I read once that there's something to be said about the power of words.

Sometimes all you need is a few soft words to center you. Other times, entire secrets can be told in silence.

This is the same base I use for all my 'Turn Down the World' products, but I do something different with this batch. I add some orange oil, along with a few pinches of thyme and clover. I watch the oils, herbs and threads of green magick dance together, reminiscing about Thatch's joy at seeing my cauldron.

He's said multiple times witches were everywhere last time he visited, but I never thought to ask if he was friends with any. To be able to identify every nook and cranny of the cast iron behemoth like he did, he must've been in the same circles at the very least.

"What are you thinking about?" Felix asks, sitting patiently on the counter.

My stirring briefly pauses. "Do you know who crafted my cauldron, Felix?"

Small, dirty fingers pause their rearranging of the spice rack (I pretend not to notice). Eyes peek over the counter, and legs dangle from its surface. The children lingering near the windows and outer reaches of the room creep in for a story.

I dramatically recall the day I truly became a witch, and my heart doesn't hurt when I tell it.

"Arlo! Arlo! Where are you?"

"Go away!" I cried, huddled against a tree trunk.

"Don't be rude! (He actually called me an asshole, but we'll leave that part out) *Tires and roots don't mix!"*

"I said go away, Caspian!"

"Best friends don't let best friends cry in the woods." Caspian called, grunting as he wheeled his chair through gnarled debris with difficulty. I felt bad but didn't get up.

"I'm not *crying." I sniffled, wiping my nose.*

He found me, like he always did.

He glared at me, full of love.

"I don't care if you cry, Arlo. You're supposed to."

I looked away from him. "Leon says guys aren't–"

"Leon's a bully. (let's keep it kid friendly) *Guys can cry just fine, better than some girls, even." Caspian locked up his brakes and knocked his foot boards out of the way, then settled on the ground beside me. He groaned a little, but I didn't offer to help him. He doesn't like that. I wanted to tell him it's alright to ask for help, sometimes. Or at least I think it is, because I ask for his help all the time.*

That's what friends do.

We sat together in the thicket behind Garren Castle for a while, listening to the birds, crickets and distant hum of children in the distant yard south of us. My legs were pulled up and I laid my cheek on my knee, doodling in the dirt with a stick. Caspian constructed a log cabin out of twigs. He kept getting three layers deep before the house collapsed and he would have to start over again. But, he kept trying.

With a tiny smile, I made a diamond with my fingers. This one I knew very well, it was the first conjuration I learned. Every-one makes weird shapes with their hands, or at least I thought so, and one day when I did it, well, magick *happened.*

A thin thread of green snaked up through the leaf litter be-tween Caspian and me, interweaving through his newest cabin in progress. He didn't notice at first, but it slowly hit him that the cabin wasn't falling. Caspian grinned over at me, handsome under the waning sunlight. "I love your magick, Arlo."

"Yeah?" I said, nervously smiling at him.

I did that a lot that year. The last time we lived at the Castle together. We weren't kids, but we weren't adults yet, either.

He nodded quickly, bouncing his chin length, brunette locks. We were opposites then, my hair was short and his long. "I do, and Kitt does too."

My eyes widened, heart beating out of my chest. "Kitt knows?"

Caspian was the only person I'd trusted the secret of my magick to. I thought I had done so well hiding it, and it's not that I don't trust her, but ... did he tell her? If she figured it out, then Leon can and he'll–

"Hey, hey, I didn't tell her. I promise. Your eyes, they ... glow, sometimes. The last family she was with, one of them was a witch, too. That's how she could tell."

"My eyes?" I pressed my fingers into my eyes, as if that could stop it. "Are they glowing now?"

Caspian reached over and cupped my cheek. "Yeah, but they're beautiful."

"*Arlo*, quit being gushy!" Kleo demands and is subsequently shushed by a kitchen full of kids, friends, and Dusan. Kitt waits in the entry, grinning at me. I lock eyes with Caspian, noting his handsome five o' clock shadow.

What am I doing? Oh, right, pouring the balm into jars.

"There's a point to all this, I promise. You have to hear a story from the beginning, dear Kleo. And friends can touch each other's faces without it meaning anything romantic."

She rolls her eyes and remains dutifully quiet.

"You know what I think?" Caspian said, leaning back against his tree and I mine.

I leave out a part that would be uncomfortable for everyone involved. He didn't kiss me then, no, that would come many, many years later, but I've never forgotten what he said to me.

The part I leave out was a cautious question and answer, words barely spoken in fear of breaking everything. In a way, they did. It was the beginning of the end.

I had asked, "Caspian, do you think I'm beautiful?"

And with his rough hand cupping my face he said, "I do, Arlo."

I thought it would happen. I leaned forward and everything. It felt like a moment. I should've known then, but I still hoped against hope and let him kiss me years later because he had always wondered what it would be like to kiss a guy.

Not what it would be like to kiss me, but a guy.

I was safe.

A friend.

And a kiss turned into something more when it shouldn't have.

But, we were young and dumb. I don't regret all of it. I regret how I treated him after he left me.

I leaned forward, and he leaned back.

He smiled at me, and it was lopsided. An anxious tell I hadn't caught onto yet. He was nervous, unsure. To this day I don't know what stopped him. I blamed it on the magick for a long time, I thought he was lying about liking it. With a heart made of spider webbing glass, we pulled apart and leaned on our separate trees.

Anyways.

He said, "You know what I think?"

And I said, "What do you think, Cas?"

"You need a special place."

I gave him a look.

"A place where you can be you," Cas went on to say, back to smiling properly.

I snorted, because back then, it wasn't safe for people like me to exist. "You've seen the posters around town. Last thing I need is some AWO family to come in and see me throwing spells."

"Then they wouldn't be worthy to adopt you if they believe that bullcrap. It's not so bad here, you don't need to be adopted by bad people who want to hurt you." *(*He actually said burn you at the stake, but, you know)

I smiled at him. How could I not?

"True. I do like it here."

"There's the spirit," *He said, reaching over to squeeze my shoulder.*

And I thought that was the end of it, but the next morning, Kitt yanked me out of bed. She rambled on a mile a minute about Caspian needing me right *now.*

Bleary eyed and barefoot, I followed her down the stairs, the halls, until we reached the doors. Those doors there. *The doors that hadn't been opened in decades because the locking mechanism was ancient, and no one could figure it out. At the sight of them open, I woke in a cold rush.*

"What's this?" *I asked Kitt, and she smiled at me.*

"Go on."

I walked inside, expecting cobwebs, dust and mold.

What I found were none of those things.

Well, there was a little dust.

At the end of a counter island that would eventually suffer endless spills, minor explosions and paint, Caspian waited for me with a gloved hand resting on a cast iron masterpiece. A cauldron.

His hair was a mess, singed in some places. One eyebrow was gone, replaced by a smudge of angry pink skin and soot. The floor around the cauldron was blackened, and his tools lay in a corner. How he managed to construct the cauldron and break into the locked room all in one short night is beyond me, even to this day.

Caspian grinned at me, dirty lips cracking his face apart. "What do you think?"

"I ... "

I stepped forward, feet heavy. I reached out and traced a finger along the rim of the cauldron, the cool metal eased the tension in my shoulders. No matter how hard I tried to hide it, a smile warped my face. Caspian remained silent as I marveled over his handiwork, then reluctantly wandered around the room.

"It's a special place," I said finally.

"For you." Caspian added with Kitt's hand entwined with his. They both smiled at me knowingly. A place where I could be unafraid to be me.

"For me." I confirmed, breathless.

I dip bottles in wax, sighing. "The moral of the story is this. We all belong somewhere, and we all deserve to exist. We all deserve a place that's ours. And I—" I *barely* meet Caspian's watery gaze and clear my throat, shifting gears. "I want you to remember above all else, never forget who your friends are. Never let them go."

And with that, Kleo promptly runs out of the room, silent and fat tears streaming down her face. Felix runs after her as do some of the other kids, all the while Dusan reminds them not to run in a stern tone. I stand there blinking, unsure what I said to upset her. I've never made a child cry before.

Dusan dismisses the rest of the children and nods to me with a '*don't worry yourself*' look, then strides out of the kitchen.

Caspian rolls up to me, jostling me in the shins with his chair. "You bastard. I came in here to yell at you and you gotta bring up shit like that."

"*What*? Yell at me! What for?" I yelp and swat at him, looking to Kitt for help. She grins at me, a carrier full of drinks in her hands.

"*Oh,* wouldn't you know it that Tobias is an overnight internet sensation," Caspian says, waving his hands through the air with a false scowl.

"*Oh,*" I whisper, feeling guilty now. "Listen, I didn't ask him to go all archangel and get a crowd of people horny."

"Arlo's right, and to be fair, Bias wasn't even drinking at that point." Kitt adds, passing a drink to Caspian, then me.

"Yes, well, his phone won't stop going off and there's all sorts of people gawking at the house. Can you put some look-away wards up?" Caspian asks with mock annoyance. He looks better than he has in days, and his rough edges are softer, despite his griping.

I scoff. "Fucking people. Alright, I will later."

There hasn't been another *archmalakim* besides Tobias in the Northern Region of Min for a few years now, and even in the southern regions they're quite rare. The ancient celestial rules dictated there would be an archangel for every thirteen *shedim*, and an archdemon for every thirteen *malakim*. Tobias hasn't ever shown his wings in public, and I've been wondering how soon the consequences would rear their ugly head. He and Loch are each other's opposites, their anchors.

There's a reason Elochian stays hidden. He can't hide his wings, so he hides all of himself as much as he can. But he didn't last night, and he had fun, or it looked like he was. We all did, really.

When Cas opens his mouth, I cut him off.

"Tobias knew what he was doing, Cas. I *especially* loved the part when he was singing about how sweet you are for all of Levena to hear." I croon, batting my eyes at him.

"Shut it." Caspian's ears turn red and he groans, rubbing away his treacherous smile.

"Oh, *that's* it, isn't it? Aww, poor Cassie, everybody knows you have feelings now." I chuckle, teasing Caspian's hair. He swats me away playfully, loosening up further. I turn a little bit more serious, shrugging off my next words. "Maybe he was done hiding. Have you talked to him about it, or did you just come right over here to bitch me out?"

Kitt snickers. "Tobias filled that place with so much fucking magick last night they had to air it out. He's passed right out still, Cas and I took the kids to daycare."

Caspian sighs, allowing the rest of his hard exterior to fade. "I know. I worry for him, that's all. I don't want .... "

"Listen." I take his hand and squeeze gently. "He won't get hurt again, because he's got you, and us. Tobias won't be alone again, and no matter what happens with Leon, I *promise* Cas, I'll keep you both safe. All of you, the same way I know you all look out for me."

Caspian smiles at me and the harder he tries to hide it, the more it comes out to play. It's been so long since I've seen him at ease and eyes clear. "You're awfully mushy today." He remarks.

"*And* happy moment ruined." I playfully shove at his face and we all laugh.

The three of us drink our coffees together, chatting about nonsense and the upcoming solar surfing championship while I clean the Kitchen up. Between Caspian working the technicalities of the sound systems and planning half-time's performance, *and* Lindsey surfing in the actual game, we spend a bit of time discussing it.

Regardless, it doesn't take long for Kitt to cause trouble.

"*So*, how's Thatch today? He seemed to have fun last night." Kitt elbows me, grinning. "How do your toes feel?"

"Well." I set my cup down on the counter, rotating it as I pick my next words with a sly grin. Thitwhistle's stamped on logo catches my eye, and my heart warms. "We're actually going on a date, tonight. And ... he told Quentin and me we could move into the free apartment. But we're going to wait until the festival is over before we move in, I think."

Caspian's brows rise to an unnaturally high state, and Kitt squeals. "That's awesome! Where are you taking him? Oh, fuck yeah, Arlo, this is gonna be great. It's about time you got out there."

"Fuckin' Gods, Kitt." Caspian grumbles. "He doesn't have sunshine coming out of his ass, calm down."

She punches his arm. "Neither do you."

I chew on my cheek, debating on telling them Thatch said it's only temporary, that he's doubtful he will return. That he can't say *why* he has to leave. He looked terrified at the thought of departing and said no one is hurting him, but I'm not sure if I believe him. One step at a time.

Of course, Caspian beats me to it, in a way.

"He's leaving again." Caspian states, flat and even. "That's what he does, isn't it? Comes and goes?"

My jaw clicks. "I know this, Caspian."

He stares at me, long and hard, then shakes his head. "I have to go. I'm late enough as it is."

"Yeah, you go engineer those speakers!" Kitt calls after him.

"Not how it works!" He flips her off, wheeling out of the Kitchen and very obviously avoiding the cauldron. Well, the good vibes lasted for ten minutes.

"He does *not* like Thatch." I mutter before taking a sip of my coffee.

Kitt scoffs. "Too bad, the rest of us do. You do. That's what matters."

"So why does it feel like I'm choosing Thatch *over* Caspian?"

"You're not, he's just being an overprotective dick," Kitt says, then takes a sip of her coffee. She gently sets her cup down, treading warily. "He does have a point though."

My shoulders curl in. "I know. We talked about it, Thatch and I. He says he has to leave, and that he doesn't ... he doesn't have a choice."

Kitt balks, taken aback. "What?"

"I know. He can't tell me why, either," I say, and she raises her brow. "I know how it sounds, but I think—I think he's telling the truth, or as much as he can. I think he's in some kind of trouble, Kitt."

Kitt frantically starts twirling a lock around her finger, staring off into deep thoughts.

"*Kitty.*" I cross my arms. "What do you know?"

"Nothing." She puts her hands up, plum complexion blanched to a pale lilac. She definitely knows something, and it's not good.

"You're a terrible liar, Kitt."

Kitt sighs, reaching up to scratch her horn. "It's not my story, Arlo. I can't, I'm sworn to secrecy. After how skittish he was, I'm not going to betray Thatch's trust like that."

Irritation crawls through me, and I stare at her. I love and dislike her for this. "Can you at least tell me if he's ... *okay*?" The thought of someone hurting Thatch so bad that it deserves a *story* infuriates me.

Kitt looks away, holding her elbows. "I don't know if someone is hurting him *now*, but ... he's been hurt in the past, that much I can tell you. Like, a lot of times, Lo. A *lot*."

Irritation is swiftly replaced by barely restrained rage. The overwhelming force of it knocks the breath out of me. I hunch over, gripping the edge of the counter. Not anger towards Kitt, but at the idea of someone hurting Thatch.

"How do you know?"

Kitt spills bits and pieces, voice wavering. "He came back to the shop on Monday, for his tattoo. When it was just us, so no one else would see his body. Please, Arlo, just ..." A light bulb goes off behind her violet eyes.

"Here." Kitt reaches into her pocket and types something out on her phone, then my own dings. It's a link to an article named, '*Leviathan and The Malefactor.*'

"Leviathan?" I ask, remembering the book she picked out at *Shh* Elves. "What does the Leviathan have to do with Thatch?"

"Just read it. There's ... there's a lot more to Thatch than either of us know, Arlo. I think he's telling you the truth, that he has to leave. Why, I don't know. But, maybe together we can figure it out." Kitt takes my hand, eyes glistening.

I stare into her face, searching for answers.

"Okay. We'll help him, together."

When I say on time, that means I'm usually five minutes early.

It drives Caspian nuts, but Kitt operates the same as I do.

I kick the center stand out from beneath my motorcycle and silence the purring engine. A few clicks ensue as the new solar batteries kick on, absorbing the light of this beautiful evening. Thitwhistle's is open for another hour, those leaving work and meandering through the streets take great advantage. A thick line weaves out the door like it did a few days ago, filled with the old and young, families and friends.

A few solo patrons like myself wait outside and I recognize a few friendly faces. Ren waves to me, their horns shine under the sun and curl back from their face. The cheesemaker waits with

Atinola, petite and dainty beside the built like a brick shit house florist.

Atinola stretches her muscled green arms overhead, yawning wide and exposing her tusks. "Arlo," The orc grunts, unable to shake her drowsiness. "You're a sight for sore eyes."

"Thanks for meeting with me." I extend my hand to Atinola, and she shakes it firmly.

"No problem, but are you sure you don't want to barter more for—" Atinola starts.

I wave her off, grinning like a fool. "No, no. Trust me, it'll be perfect."

Ren opens their arms to me, cane in hand, and I hug them carefully, having to bend over quite a bit to properly embrace the faun without causing them more pain then they're already in.

After saying hellos, I pull a vial of Night Shift tincture out of my inner duster pocket and hand it to Atinola, then reach back in and take out a jar of the Turn Down the World balm I made this morning, along with a vial of Chronic Relief for Ren's curved spine infringing on their nerves.

Bags of holding have nothing on my jacket.

I offer the balm and vial to Ren who smiles warmly in response, their smooth cheeks pink. "Everything is ready," Ren says, tucking a lock of warm blond behind their slightly pointed ear, velvet nose wrinkling. Ren and Atinola lead the way inside, Ren's free arm looping through Atinola's. I duck my head under the doorframe and follow the longtime friends.

"Great, we shouldn't be much longer," I say, peeking over Ren's shoulder.

I spot Thatch immediately, working behind the counter with Rhea, Helena and someone I don't recognize but is most *definitely* a witch. The aura surrounding them is a white magick that pulsates in steady, short waves. I know most of the witches in Levena, registered and those underground, but I've never seen him before. I stumble a little but otherwise, keep my cool. Not that the lanky e-boy seems to be much of a threat, but you never know.

We're only a few orders away from being next and poor Thatch is working a mile a minute, loading up boxes with a tired smile while Helena makes drinks. Rhea darts in and out of the hallway to the left of the cafe counter, bringing more food out from the kitchens.

The youngest barista works in perfect tandem with the others, taking orders and working the register. His hands jerk every now and then, followed by a routine downward twitch of his head. His eyes are completely hidden by thick white hair which hangs down to his chin, waving back and forth over his face as he involuntarily moves in place.

Ren nods, catching me staring. "We'll be waiting for you."

And then we're there, standing before the witch. Thatch's head is stuck in the pastry case while he fills a large box for a group of bouncing children and two tired parents.

The witch raises his head, exposing a pale chin and nothing of his eyes. A set of black earbud wires drift between locks of hair, disappearing underneath an all black band t-shirt. It's hard to tell exactly how old he is, but I can't imagine he's past sixteen. His hands tremble, but his twitches subside as he focuses on us. The power emanating from him is overwhelming, moving in shorter, more intense waves.

Oh, fuck.

He's a chaos witch.

I've never met one before, but Leon thought they were the holy grail.

"How may I help you?" He asks, voice hoarse and low like he's been screaming.

Ren and Atinola place their orders, then say their goodbyes before moving to the pickup line. I clear my throat when the witch nods to me. "I'm just here for the owner."

Thatch yelps, dropping the box in his hands. Before I can raise my hand, the other witch's head jerks down and to the left. His hands blanket over his ears and he *hums* loudly, the sound reverberating through his chest and bordering on a whimper.

The children squeal as airborne pastries hover back into an open and waiting box. The witch tucks his chin into his chest as his magick reverses the accident in slow motion, absorbing the chaotic energy Thatch created. The parents watch with fresh eyes, their exhaustion swiftly evaporating as rare and young magick unfolds before us all.

The witch's hands pull down from his ears and he uncurls on himself. He takes the neatly assembled box floating over Thatch's trembling fingers, then sets it on the counter and *gently* pushes it towards the family. His fingers twitch and he hums piercingly again, then mutters, "Sorry," and backs away, head bowed. The hair hanging over his face brightens, illuminated by the brilliant white glow of his hidden eyes.

His shoulders slump as he turns to Thatch. "Can I take my fifteen?"

Thatch sighs, combing his fingers through his hair. Up close it's easier to see the sickly pallor has returned to his skin, like my magick infusion never happened at all. "Of course, and don't be sorry Silas, I startled you, after all. You've been doing very well."

The witch nods, then glances back to the retreating family, and lastly to me. The hint of an arched, white eyebrow and icy blue iris peeks out from under his shaggy hair, then he turns away and escapes into the bookstore section of Thitwhistle's.

Thatch wipes his hands on his slacks, then straightens the russet ascot around his neck. He's dressed in a long sleeve button up and a different pair of suspenders then the ones I saw before, leather with brass clips. A cute little green apron adorns his front, and I quickly have to shut down *that* line of thinking. His hair might have been combed at one point, but it's been raked and pulled on numerous times.

"Arlo, is it four already?" He asks, coming around the counter with a breathless smile. He looks to a starry clock on the wall, wincing at the time. Quarter past. "Oh my, give me just a moment."

I chuckle, moving slowly to take his hand. He immediately takes mine and I repress a sigh that *some* would consider to be swooning. "No rush, Thatch. Can I help?"

A smirk comes to life, erasing some of the tiredness from his features. "Why, know how to make a good coffee?"

"Oh get *out* of here! We've got this, boss." Rhea calls in a deep tone, grinning at us from the pastry case.

Thatch fidgets with the hem of his sleeve, eyes darting to the books section. "Are you sure? It's still terribly busy—"

"Go on." Helena agrees, waving us off. "We've got the kid."

"Oh, alright then. If I didn't know any better, I'd say you were trying to get rid of me." Thatch relents, reaching behind him to untie his apron. I gesture for him to turn around and he does, but not before I catch a glimpse of his adam's apple working up and down.

"They are," I say in all seriousness, earning a scoff from him.

He points a finger in the air. "No sass from you, Arlo Rook."

A laugh cuts through my chest before I'm even told of its arrival.

"I'm afraid that just won't do, Thatch."

Date Night

Thatch

"Care to tell me where we're going?" I ask, although I really don't care one bit. We're together, and that's all that matters to me. I'm allowing myself tonight to live, to be with him. I deserve a stolen moment with him. I've done all that *They* have asked of me.

Arlo's fingers have a gentle hold on mine, feather light but unwavering. The evening settles around us with a pleasant chill that defies the all encompassing sunset washing over Syorini Lake to our left. Leaves interrupt the foot path we stroll down, they crunch under foot and twirl in the soft breeze that ruffles my hair.

When I saw Arlo's motorbike outside the shop I thought we would be going for a ride, but he said not yet. He's been awfully dodgy about why he drove over instead of walking, but oh well.

"Don't ruin the fun, Thatch." He tells me, and I laugh.

"Fine, have it your way. I'll be happy as long as there's food involved."

Arlo studies me for a moment, then breaks into quiet laughter. Before I can ask what, he reaches forward and wipes something from the corner of my mouth. "You just munch on scones all day, don't you?" He teases, then licks icing from his thumb.

I sputter indignantly, raising my chin when I turn my heated face away from him. "*Please*, one must consume more than scones. But yes, I do tend to *graze*."

Arlo chuckles, elbowing me gently. "There will be food, don't worry. But first, I thought we could do something a little … *different*, and we'll definitely want to do it before we eat."

Well, that doesn't sound good.

"Different?" I ask, wondering what the hell I've gotten myself into.

"Do you happen to know what the Aviary is?" Arlo rubs the back of his neck, hand wading beneath curled waves of soft black. His signature beanie is nowhere to be seen, allowing his hair to catch the wind freely. The same rainbow duster he wore Friday night covers his shoulders, the vibrant colors absorb the golden sunlight beating down on his figure. He stands between the blinding sun and me, protecting me from the worst of it.

A familiar necklace hangs at his sternum, a locket in the shape of a compass. I've caught sight of its chain a few times now and the necklace itself once, but that was during our collision. The urge to reach out and cradle the pendant is strong, but I resist. He watches me, expectant eyes a warm, golden brown that matches his brilliant skin.

Oh, right, he asked me a question.

"Oh, um, it's a place for solar surfing, right?"

Arlo blinks in surprise, then smiles, clearly pleased. "Right, it's like a community center for people to borrow boards or fly their own. Have you ever been?"

I shake my head. "No, but Kitt said Lindsey's a professional surfer. She actually gave us tickets, you know. Said that we'd drag you kicking and screaming if we had to–"

I frown, releasing his hand.

He grins, and it's *evil*.

"No. Nope. Forget it." I raise my arms, creating an X-shape to ward off Arlo's pleading eyes and manipulative lower lip.

"We're already here, look." Arlo whines, pointing to the sky.

Dozens of triangular sails catch the sunrise, admittedly beautiful and mesmerizing. Surfers tempt death above us, cutting through the atmosphere on metal apparatuses that resemble longboards. I can 'get hip' with those, but not when they're *flying*.

I cross my arms, frowning at him. "I can't believe you thought this was a good first date idea. You should be ashamed of yourself."

Arlo drops the pouting act and steps closer, brushing against my crossed forearms. I raise a brow, unprepared for whatever he is about to say. He chews on his bottom lip for a moment, looking me up *and* down.

Great fuck, where did *this* Arlo come from?

In a low purr, he asks, "Sure there's nothing I could do to change your mind?"

I cannot deny the strangled noise that escapes my throat. I set my jaw and lift my chin, unable to tear away from his heated gaze. He pins me in place, patiently waiting for an answer. I shake my head. "Nothing at all," I manage three choked words, that's it.

Then, he does the most unfair thing.

He gently cups my elbow and brings his lips down to my ear, soft waves brush my cheek as he does. Arlo Rook lowers his tone and his words rumble into my body with such impossible ease it's *unfair*.

"Please, Thatch?" He asks, and how can I deny him?

"*Fine*. Do *not* make me regret this."

I don't know what I was expecting. The circular skyscraper was constructed during this latest industrial age and as such is of modern architecture. All plain, wide windows and shining metal. A stark contrast to the unique older residences and businesses dotting the freakishly distant ground below us.

I was fine in the graffiti decorated elevator car that took us up a *hundred* stories.

I was fine stepping onto the last floor and into a common area carpeted in a pleasant navy blue and walled in with *nothing* but glass, except for the solid inner walls that surround the elevator shaft. Along the solid walls are benches, young folk, and racks upon racks of solar boards. At the northern and southern ends of the circular floor are wide halls that respectively lead to the Take Off and Landing Zones.

I was fine *until* we stepped into said Take Off Zone, the journey from the elevator to here was really a blur. The wide bay houses a massive rectangular exit that's quite plain, finished with sliding glass doors. Arlo's voice and a soft hand on my shoulder cuts through the fog in my brain. I startle, jostling the board clutched in my white knuckled grip.

He looks genuinely concerned for me. "Hey, why don't we just go get some dinner? It's not everyone's thing, I was just teasing you."

"What? No, *no*, I want to do this. It's just. *Heights*, you know?" I wave my hands to emphasize the word *heights* and Arlo bites his lip, veiling a smile. "Maybe I could ... ride with you?"

Arlo lifts a shoulder. "Nah, these don't work that way. Besides, sometimes you have to face your fear on your own two feet, but that doesn't mean I won't be right next to you the whole time."

I sigh, exasperated. "Does that still count when my two feet are relying on a contraption to keep me aloft?"

"We'll see, won't we?" He laughs, magick thrums in a low vibration across his skin as he does. He must feel it or notice, but he doesn't say anything about it. He's *got* to know.

I nod, straightening my shoulders. "Alright. Let's do this."

We shuffle behind a group waiting ahead of us, a gathering of friends by the looks of it. They laugh and pick on each other, waiting for the doors to open and release them into the world. A buzzer sounds and a green light flashes overhead the exit. The doors slide back, offering an edge to nothingness. The friends chant and scream, simultaneously laying their boards down at the precipice. Metal noses overhang into the atmosphere.

One by one, they strap their lead feet to the front of the board.

The boards remind me of a dinghy, complete with a triangular solar sail. The special golden fabric is thick and weaved into geometric patterns crafted for catching the sun's energy. These sails appear well made, providing efficient paths for the energy to travel and meet the various different engines on the heel of the boards.

As the group's sails unfold, their engines purr to life, a pleasant sound not unlike Arlo's bike. The riders slip on their goggles and take hold of a horizontal steel bar jutting out from their masts.

Then they thrust into the sky.

Arlo's hand brushes against my lower back and I look over, finding a soft smile waiting for me. "Ready?"

I grin, full of trepidation and admittedly, excitement.

In response, I lay my board at the edge and strap my foot in.

Arlo follows in kind, grinning to himself as we work. "Sure you haven't done this before? Seem to know what you're doing."

"No, but I'm quite good at observing, love." The endearment slips out unbidden, and I flush intensely, but he doesn't tease me for it or shy away.

Instead, he laughs softly.

"I've noticed," he says, full of mischief. Arlo reaches into his duster and retrieves two sets of goggles. He dons one pair, and I take the other. "Let's fly." He engages his board's power.

And we do.

There *may* have been a scream at the beginning, but it's easier than I ever imagined. The scream morphs into something joyous and heart breaking, melding with Arlo's laughter as we soar up into the sky. I take back what I said before, *now* I've never felt more alive.

"Lean back! Easy!" Arlo yells to me, demonstrating. He gave me an impromptu lesson on the way up here, but explaining with words is nothing compared to *actually* doing it. I did sign a waiver, didn't I? I remember that clearly now.

But I do as he says and go easy, tilting the nose of my board to the sky. The taut and billowing sail catches the sunrise, casting my body in impossible gold filtered rainbows. Gusts of freezing wind cut through me, electrifying my nerves as it whistles between Arlo and I.

We climb into the sky, rising higher and higher until Arlo shouts, "Hey, Thatch!" I look over and he's grinning at me like he hasn't a care in the world, an echo of the actual first time I met him. He pulls his sail in and lays back, closing his eyes.

He falls.

And falls.

Surprisingly, I don't lose my composure. I laugh instead, because that mischievous grin is a terrible tell. I think about trying the same trick but decide on not being a total idiot and aim for a nose dive instead.

I shift my weight onto my toes and plummet towards a lazily spiraling Arlo, then whoosh past him with alarming speed. I even out before the inertia is too much, and it's not long before Arlo catches back up to me.

He reaches for me with his free hand, fingers wiggling.

With my heart pounding out of my chest, the sun in my eyes and wind rushing through my ears, I take it and hold on with all I have.

Once again, Arlo and I walk the streets of Levena. No matter what I do, my wind swept hair won't relax, matching Arlo's own wildness. I've managed to avoid giving him the satisfaction of being right, until now.

"What was that you were saying about solar surfing being a bad first date idea?" Arlo asks, the lamplights flanking the pedestrian streets illuminate his smug grin.

I roll my eyes. "I'm not entirely certain you're not trying to kill me." I hold up my fingers, counting off his transgressions. "First, you ask me to banish a ghost with you, then you take me on a wild motorcycle ride and push my toes over the cliffside.

I've drank, smoked *and* gotten a tattoo. Oh, and don't forget the dancing, my hips are still sore from that one."

He chuckles. "And now I've taken you into the sunset. Whatever will you do with me?"

"Oh, I just don't know." I admit, meaning it in more ways than he can ever imagine.

"So, a tattoo, huh? Anything good?" Arlo rubs the back of his neck, his free hand casually slides over my shoulders and he pulls me close to his side. I nuzzle into him and enjoy the color creeping over his cheeks.

"Yeah, Kitt helped me. I suspect you already know that, though." I raise a brow at him, and he shrugs.

"I knew that you went back and got one but no other juicy details. Gotta say, I was hoping I'd be the one to pop your cherry." Arlo's face screws up, and I snicker as he attempts to recover. "I mean, for tattoos, you know. Fuck, do you even remember your first lay?"

The whiplash startles a laugh out of me, and I lightly hit his side. "I'm old, not *senile*. I have an excellent memory, I'll have you know. Now I'm not one to kiss and tell, but he was twenty eight and a rather nice young man like myself."

Arlo laughs too, stealing my nervousness. "Is that so? Well, I do apologize."

I clear my throat. "And you?"

His arm tightens around me, and he leads me down a small boulevard not unlike the one the Ethereal Magpie rests on, trees and gardens intermingle in the wide spaces between the buildings. "It was alright. I've certainly had better since then, even if it's been awhile." His last few words hit a strident note, and we shift against the other.

"Well, that's ... yes, me too."

My cheeks heat. How did we end up on the topic of sex?

Arlo's hand slides from my shoulder down to my hand, squeezing gently as we come upon a series of storefronts with their doors open. Strings of glass lighting overhang front patios, providing the perfect atmosphere for a late night on the town.

A striking *malakim* with enormous black wings and freckled skin busks in a small plaza set between the buildings. A small crowd is divided between watching him, fully enraptured, and dancing like there's no tomorrow. He plays a tune on a lute using a prosthetic hand composed of gears and shining brass. Blond curls bounce as he skips in a circle with a tall male dressed only in trousers, music unhindered by their wild dancing. His partner's face is adorned with scars and an intricate golden tattoo trails down his black, exposed chest.

Both of them wear wide, loving smiles which break long enough for the two to embrace the other in a deep, passionate kiss. Before they separate, an oversized black fox streaked in neon blue runs between their legs, yipping all the while. Everyone laughs, but there's sadness lingering in the group's eyes.

As to why, the answer is visible only to my eye, and my heart races at the realization. A soft iridescent aura surrounds the edges of their figures. They aren't from this world.

They're like me, in that respect.

An anomaly.

The side of me I can't control, the one that is duty and balance and a compulsion to *right* the universe, fights to take over. *No*, I don't want to do this now. If I send them back now ... I'll have to leave, my 'mission' will be complete. I'm not ready yet.

"They're pretty good, huh?" Arlo asks, glancing between me and the street side party. I nod, making the decision to track them down later. If I can touch one of them, it'll be easy to find them again. No godly hands tug on me in protest at that plan, so I open my lips and test lies.

"Will you come up with me? I'd like to tip them." I reach into my pocket and pull out a few dollars, fresh from this morning's trip to the bank. Lindsey said credits are common currency these days, but I like cash.

He grins. "Sure."

We slip through the crowd waiting patiently for the musician to start again. The bard himself drinks water, flanked by the fox and his male companion. The fox tilts their head at me and I receive a … *flirtatious* grin from the bare chested male. There's no tip jar, so I clear my throat which draws the bard's attention. He smiles at us, possessing the most intense otherworldly aura out of them all.

"You guys take tips?" Arlo asks, hand on my shoulder. His tone is clipped but not unfriendly, perhaps even less gruff than when we met. (again) "Music was awesome, haven't heard anything like that around here before." Arlo's fingers gently dig in and I glance up at him, wondering if he's caught onto something.

But multiple dimension theory hasn't been explored in this world quite yet.

"Oh no, we don't need any money." The bard laughs and his silent companion mirrors Arlo, resting a protective hand on his musician. "Thanks, though."

"Will you be here for long? I'd love to hear you play again." I ask, hoping it sounds casual.

He shrugs. "Yeah, for a few more days, but we didn't really plan on the show, just …" He waves his metallic hand about in a vague gesture. "Sort of happened. We're only passing through."

"It's never planned, *ahuvi*. The moment you pull that lute out, you know what happens." The taller male bends down and presses a smiling kiss into his partner's blond curls, surprising me with the Old Common. That narrows down the world they came from to about six.

I reach into my pocket, finding the small pad of paper and pencil I keep with me during my stays. I flip past notes of what's changed in the years and things I want to see again, then find a blank page and rip it out. I write Thitwhistle's address on there and my first name, then hand it out to them.

"Before you go, feel free to stop by for some coffee and something to eat. There's books, too. I'd love it if you came by and played. I open fairly early."

The bard reaches out, grinning.

His fingers brush against mine, and his smile fades. He takes the paper, pupils restricting. His tucked in wings ruffle, then he pulls his grin back on like nothing happened. "You know what, I think we will. What's your name again?"

"Oh, I'm Thatch, and this is my, um, this is Arlo." I gesture to Arlo who's watching me with an intensity that causes me to look away. Thing is, I stumble upon a similar look on the warrior's face. "And what about you two?"

After they give us names that are most certainly fake, we part ways, and Arlo leads me to a quiet patio down the street, tucking us underneath a white awning that declares the place *'Ren's'* in black script.

Tension returns to my shoulders while I await Arlo's questions. He definitely picked up something. He must have so many of them, I'm wading into dangerous territory the longer I stay around him. When will he figure it out that–

Arlo lifts my hand to his lips and presses a gentle kiss to the back of my knuckles, staring into my eyes with an unreadable expression upon his face. He straightens, and I prepare myself to tell more pretty lies when his lips part. "Are you still hungry?" He asks.

I nod so fast, he laughs.

I'd give anything to hear his laugh again and again. A memory will never be enough.

"Alright, just in here," Arlo says, releasing me. He opens a simple, glass door encased in white and leads the way. I follow him inside, finding an old world hiding behind the modern storefront. Weathered shiplap boards make up the walls, holding up open shelves full of cheese rounds, plants and glass.

All kinds of glass bottles, jars, and vials decorate the place, the different colors catch the light from one of the candelabras overhead and reflect onto other surfaces. Packing crates stand in pretty pyramids, creating ingenious rustic displays. Wheels of cheese, charcuterie boards of the ordinary type and those shaped like animals, embroidered cloth napkins, and all the other goods that 'Ren' offers are organized upon them neatly.

At the back of the store is a long counter with stools pulled up to it, eerily similar to a bar. Bottles of wine and spirits even line the wall behind the counter, along with mason jars. Arlo sneaks around the end of it, heading for a closed door. Our footsteps echo throughout the dim place, and I glance over my shoulder, spotting a sign on the front window.

The open side of the sign faces us, so the store must be closed. The door was unlocked, but still ....

"Arlo, what are you doing!" I yell in a whisper, earning a mischievous grin cast over his shoulder.

"Having dinner," he says, waiting for me with a hand on the doorknob. At the look on my face, he relents with a chuckle. "Don't worry, a friend of mine owns the place."

"Honestly, mysteriousness does *not* suit you, Arlo," I say, rolling my eyes when I approach his side. He leans down, smile widening.

"I beg to differ." Arlo taunts, then his head whips up and he focuses on something behind us. I turn, finding nothing. "Someone's here," he says, brows furrowed and arm lifting, offering his side to me.

"What? I don't sense anyone." A shiver runs down my spine at the reminder that I couldn't sense the *Dybbuk* either. A problem that I'm sure is a punishment from the universe. I step into the space Arlo offers.

He scans the store before us, intent and quiet. Nothing appears out of place to my eye, but he hyper focuses on the light switches on the right side of the room. He takes a step towards them, pushing me behind him.

Then the lights go out.

Something long and metallic smashes into the back of my knees.

I fall forward, crashing into Arlo with an *oof* as he meets me on the way down. I reach for him but my wrists are caught and expertly bound by something cold and slimy. I oddly start to panic, trembling in the dark like a child, but Arlo doesn't resist.

"Thatch, are you alright?" Arlo asks, calm and even, which makes me feel a little better.

I force myself to take a breath. I'm not *actually* bound, I can escape. It's not like before. "What's going on?"

Before he can answer, an enormous crash sounds in the darkness and the domino effect is horrendous. Glass shatters like the pitter patter of rain and heavy weights *thud* onto the floor. That'll be the cheese, I bet.

"*Well*, well, well. I told you—"

Someone curses in a language I'm not familiar with, their voice raspy and masculine. The impending monologue is further interrupted by a responding series of beeps.

Arlo *sighs* with heavy exasperation.

"*Ahem*, I told you that you'd regret the day you turned me down, Arlo Rook." The voice continues, closer than before and bringing with it the smell of low tide and something spicy. Cloves? "Floyd! The lights!"

All at once, the lights kick back on with such an intensity I worry for the bulbs of luminescent algae above our heads, waiting for them to burst. When I take in our kidnapper, I'm at a loss for words.

Arlo's not, though.

"Fuckin' *Bob*." Arlo groans with such annoyance I wait for a vein to burst in his forehead.

"You *know* each other?" I ask, glancing between a dashing *selth* in an overcoat and the android now standing behind Arlo and me. That must be who hit me in the legs.

"Unfortunately," Arlo admits, glaring at Bob standing atop a mountain of collapsed crates, wood split and nails poking out.

Bob clears his throat pointedly, hands raised high in the air and a maniacal grin quirking his tentacles. "I have you right where I want you, Arlo! Now you have no choice but to aid me in my quest to–"

Arlo cackles and I raise a brow, more amused now than scared. "Imma take a wild guess and say that the trap wasn't intended for *me*," he says through a sly smile coming to play on his lips.

Bob's onyx eyes widen and he adjusts his hat nervously. "Of course it was! Who else would it be for? Hmm?"

Arlo flattens him with a look. "I'll give you credit for using kelp cord, it's unbreakable by physical means. Magickal, however." Arlo's golden eyes alight with a pale green ringing his irises and he triangulates his fingers, barely touching upon his power. The cord comes apart and my arms fall forward. I rub my wrists, then take Arlo's offered hand.

We stand and he wraps a protective arm around my shoulders, glowering at Bob. "If you knew it was me coming, you would've had some protections against magick. I was fine ignoring you, but now you've pissed me off and interrupted my date. I've told you time and time again, I will *not* help you."

The droid behind me, Floyd, I think Bob had called it, taps its humanoid pointer fingers together nervously and catches my attention. It's rusted and worn, an old model that would've been around last time I was here, back when droids were first invented. There's an intelligence behind those horizontal pupils and golden irises, revealing ... *something*.

Bob's face drops and the tentacles waving around his face stop moving, curtaining his frown. And yes, he did try to ... what, *kidnap* us? But the disappointment crushing his face is awful, and he's obviously not very good at this sort of thing.

I clear my throat and look up. "Um, Arlo?"

"Sorry about this, Thatch." He mutters, body vibrating beneath my fingertips.

"It's alright, but ... can I ask him a question?"

"Yeah?" He says, confused.

I warily glance towards Bob climbing down the crate mountain, holding Floyd's hand as not to fall. He trips on his overcoat anyway, falling into a big heap with the poor droid. I take a few careful steps towards them, avoiding glass and wood splinters. I extend a hand to Floyd and help them up, then the droid pulls his master up as well. Blood trails down a scratch on Bob's cheek.

"Bob, is it?"

"What's it to you?" The *selth* grunts, then cowers when Arlo steps closer.

"I was just wondering, what, um ... oh, how do I put this ... "
I tap my chin, smiling at him nervously. "Could you tell us your
master plan? What were you trying to achieve?"

Arlo chokes on something and I throw an elbow, pinning him
(hopefully) with a most serious glare. His cheeks flush, and he
covers his upturned lips with the back of his hand. With a huff,
I turn back to Bob.

"Well, it's like this, you see." Bob starts, glancing between
Arlo and me. He gestures to the storefront with a frown. "I've
been coming here for years. The best Dragon's Cheese in the
entire northern realm, where they get it from I have *no* idea, have
to special order it every time, but it's worth it let me *tell* you."

"Wait, wait. You have a problem with *Ren*?" Arlo asks with
more curiosity and less anger than before. Bob looks away, doing
nothing to hide the color creeping through his fair tentacles and
face.

"Well!" He says, crossing his arms. "If they wouldn't have
served me *poison*, I wouldn't have one! I don't take kindly to
people trying to *kill* me, Arlo. Like I said, I only wanted to cause
a *little* trouble, make Ren think twice about trying to assassi-
nate the great Bobulous Tenicii the Third, Master Conniving
Extraordinaire—"

Arlo puts up a hand. "Yeah, yeah, we get it." He looks to me
with a frown. "I know Ren, they wouldn't hurt a fly."

I absently tug on a curl overhanging my eye. "When you say
poison, you're *absolutely* sure?"

Bobulous Tenicii the Third scoffs, hairless brows furrowing
as he begins digging through his pockets. With an 'aha!' he
thrusts forward a small bundle cradled in his hands. "What else
would you call *this*?"

Arlo puts up his hands, glaring at me. "You started this, you
get to open the creepy bundle of joy."

I roll my eyes at him, something I've done too many times to count this evening and not enough. "What a brave witch you are. Fine." I reach forward and unwrap the simple linen wrapping, noting the delicate floral embroidery along the hem. Familiarity sinks in, I saw a few cloth napkins somewhere earlier done in the same style.

As I unfold the last layer, an unmistakable salt and brine scent greets my nose and I sigh with relief. Nestled in the fabric is a perfectly round wheel of roquefort Dragon's Cheese, such a rare find that I'm positive Bob has no idea what he's holding. The veins running through the pale white wheel are a vibrant blue, crystalline in appearance. Definitely alarming to someone who doesn't know what they're looking at.

"You've *got* to be kidding." Arlo groans into his hands, then gently claps my shoulder. "You wanna take this? I'm going to put the store back together."

I give him a knowing smile, and he ruffles my hair in response to my smugness, then turns away and bodily glows to life, setting to work on cleaning up the chaos around us. Bob glances between us, still unsure what's going on.

Leaving it unwrapped, I push the cheese closer to Bob's chest. "Bob, it's not poisoned, I promise. That's roquefort Dragon's Cheese, ever heard of it?" I ask quietly.

Bob's tentacles snuffle as he concentrates, one takes the initiative to rub his hidden chin. "Roquefort's a cave system, innit? What's that got to do with cheese?"

Debris gingerly lifts from the floor and flows back to where it belongs, like how Silas' magick worked earlier. Whereas he gains energy from corralling chaos, Arlo has to expend energy to do so. Regardless, Arlo doesn't seem to be lacking any magick. He's got quite the opposite problem.

And I think he's starting to catch on that his newfound power is due to me.

So many questions, so many discussions coming to a head.

"Right, well, there's a flock of Cold Drakes that live there in harmony with the neighboring dairies, exchanging their milk for the aether crystals growing in the farmer's fields." I can sense that I'm losing Bob, so I backtrack.

"Anyway, the cheese produced there is one of a kind, understand? This here," I point to the crystalline blue webbing through the cheese round, "is not poison, but the proof of an incredibly valuable block of cheese. Ren probably intended this as a gift for you, and I dare say they hold you in high regard, seeing how they gifted you something of such quality. Were you two ... friends?"

Arlo returns to my side, surprising me with how quickly he righted the store. He takes my hand in his, and it's like nothing ever happened.

Well, almost.

Bob turns the cheese round over and over in his hands, staring down at it in silence for so long I wonder if he'll answer at all. "Maybe? I mean, who wants to be friends with this?" Bob frowns, gesturing up and down to himself, tentacles snuffling. My heart tightens and I squeeze Arlo's fingers.

"But they smiled at me a lot. Well, they smile at everyone, but ... I don't know, it's silly, isn't it? I'm glad you didn't help me, Arlo. Poor Ren." Bob's last few words trail off, and he sighs.

Arlo chuckles, surprising us all when he reaches forward and squeezes Bob's shoulder in typical Arlo fashion. "I'm glad Thatch took the time to ask a question I should have long ago."

"Arlo, are you in there?" A voice calls, soft and airy.

Bob pales immediately, hurriedly wrapping the cheese up and stuffing it into his pocket. "We're back here!" Arlo calls, grinning at Bob and I.

"Oh please Arlo, *please* don't—" Bob cuts off, face turning red when a blond faun enters the room, using a cane to keep their slightly hunched figure upright. They're wrapped in a burgundy shawl and a tender smile. I like them immediately.

"Bob! What a delight, I haven't seen you in so long, I was starting to think you wouldn't come by and see me anymore." The faun I presume to be Ren looks between us all. Their smile fades a tad as they try to puzzle together what's going on. "Hey you two, I just wanted to check in on your dinner, see if you needed anything."

"Oh, we ran into Bob outside and stopped to have a chat, got a bit distracted and wandered in here, admiring all your works of art," Arlo says easily, relaxing the *selth's* hunched shoulders.

"Yes, this is Arlo!" Bob affirms, causing Floyd to hum and smack a hand to their face. I hide my chuckle behind my hand.

Ren giggles. "Yes, I know Arlo. He's nice, isn't he?" Ren says, smiling at Bob much brighter than they did with Arlo or I. They look down at their shifting cloven hooves, then back up to Bob. "Would you care to walk with me, Bob? The stars are out, it's rather nice."

"Yeah, sure, *yes*, I mean. If that's what you want to do." Bob nods quickly, disturbing his tentacles.

"I do, I've missed you. We need to catch up," Ren says, offering Bob their arm.

Bob links his own through and awkwardly waves to us over his shoulder, allowing Ren to lead him outside. "Thank you," He mouths, and I'm quite sure this isn't the last we've seen of Bob.

Well, for Arlo, anyway.

I wipe my hands on my slacks and sigh while Arlo rubs the back of his neck. When I meet his eye, we both start laughing.

"Well, that was *something*. How long has that poor *selth* been asking for your help?" I pinch his side gently and he yelps.

"Longer than I care to admit. He's not the brightest and honestly I just assumed he wanted to cause trouble because that's what he does. Another instance of being too caught on myself, I suppose." He mumbles the last part and I slide my arm around his waist, squeezing his side gently.

"Can we eat now?"

Arlo kisses the top of my head like it's nothing, and I die a little. "Yeah, we can eat now."

My Leva

Thatch

Through the back door is a cozy porch protected by a pergola. The wooden rafters are home to a number of hanging plants and another algae bulb chandelier. The hanging bulbs are centered overhead a small round table and two chairs, where dinner and candles await.

"You've outdone yourself," I say, unable to breathe past the butterflies.

He grins nervously, pulling out a chair for me as he does. "Yeah? It's nothing fancy, everything's local and most of it's from Ren one way or another. Quickest way to tour the city is to eat your way through it."

I take a seat, watching how the chandelier casts pink light upon his features as he sits across from me. "I quite like that idea."

After that, it's bizarrely easy. We eat, and Arlo insists on feeding me half the dishes himself, but I don't mind at all. The candles lick away at their wax, spilling over onto the small space between us. We talk about mundane things like Arlo's new job and whether or not he wants to leave the studio, and I tell him just how dirty Quentin's novels are, because I definitely started the first one.

Arlo throws his head back and laughs, warming the night around us with the carefree sound. When he leans back in, his fingers brush against mine on the brocade tablecloth. Sparks fly, and I don't pull away from the harsh vibrations riding his skin. "Learn anything interesting?"

I chuckle, hooking my pinky with his. "All I can say is that I wish I had a tail. Multipurpose, those things are."

"You should stock them in the bookstore, on a *very* high shelf. Books, not tails." Arlo rests his chin on his hand, smiling so hard I wonder if it'll ever fade away. I hope not.

"There *is* a section for that kind of thing, you know. And I'm happy to."

"Is that so? Read a lot of books from there?"

I roll my eyes, cheeks flushed. "And if I had?"

The rest of Arlo's fingers find mine, and his gaze never wavers. "Then I'd consider myself lucky to be in the company of someone so educated."

"Exactly." I laugh again, the heat spreads down my neck and further. When was the last time I laughed this much?

"Can I ask you something?" He asks, and I stiffen.

"Of course."

Arlo licks his bottom lip, cheeks darkening. "Your name, is it ... well, you know."

I laugh, caught off guard. "You really think Phantom is any type of family name?"

"You never know." He flushes deeper and I grin, feeling especially powerful right now. I can give him this.

"Alright, I'll share this secret with you. Thatcher Gaillot is my real name. I chose Phantom as a ... homage of sorts." A heavy breath leaves my chest. I half expected the name to be restrained, and I wonder why I'm able to tell him.

Arlo leans closer, as do I, and there's little space between us. He ensures I'm looking at him before whispering, "Thatcher Gaillot. I like it, is that alright?"

Now it's my turn to suffer under the heat. "You may call me that if you like, while we're in ... intimate company. May I ask *you* something?"

"I'm assuming it's the same question."

I nod. "Yes, why Rook?"

His eyes track our joined hands. "Do you know what Arlo means?"

I shake my head.

"Between hills, or as Dusan thought, between worlds. When I got older, the meaning of that name became very apparent. My purpose as a Hedge Witch is to move between worlds, that of the living and the dead. A rook is strong, steadfast, able to move in any direction. That's what I wanted to be. A strong point for those who needed me."

I can't help but chuckle. "Your intention is much more significant than mine."

He squeezes my hand. "I don't think so. Your name means something to you, and you chose it."

A distant clock tower chimes, ringing me back to reality. I look around for a clock but find none. Arlo reluctantly pulls out his phone, checking for me. His brows rise. "*Wow*, it's almost eleven."

"It is?" I ask, slightly panicked. "Oh my, I didn't realize how late it is. Do you mind if we start walking back? I have to get up early and train Silas."

Arlo nods, not at all bothered. "Of course."

We clean things up with the help of Arlo's magick, then he leads me back into the night. For a while it's only the ambient noise of the city around us, distant music and the hum of a place full of life.

Arlo clears his throat, squeezing my hand as he finds words one at a time. "So, how old is Silas, anyway? I've uh, never met a chaos witch before."

Is he *curious*? I smile at him, holding his hand with as much sure force as he holds mine. "Fourteen, but he acts like he's twenty. You know how that goes." I bite my lip, immediately trying to correct my course. Arlo doesn't say anything, but he tilts his head. "You probably had to grow up fast on your own, right?"

He stares at me for another moment, then studies the path before us. A trolley goes down the line beside our sidewalk, lit up by strands of soft golden lights that wrap around the doors and windows. "Yeah, but I wasn't on my own. I had Kitt and Cas, and … well, I had them."

"True, but still …. "

Arlo's gaze cuts back over to me, brow raised in question.

I pull at my ascot. I've had to retie it several times, the first being after I dived a hundred stories for this man. "It's just … I can't imagine it's the same. You were together out of necessity, and you needed someone to *choose* you. You didn't have anyone to call you theirs, and vice versa. Besides, they … they were adopted, right?"

Arlo's quiet again for a long time and I wonder if I've overdone it. Eventually, he sighs. "To be honest, I felt alone a lot, even when they were there. I've always been that way, though. Alone in a crowd, right?" Arlo teases, but there's no heart in it. "I wouldn't trade them for anything, though."

"I wouldn't either. I ... I never stay in one place too long, you know? Hazards of the job. Makes it hard to have friends."

"You've never told me what you do," Arlo says, not unkindly.

"Oh, a consultant of sorts. An overseer, if you will. All very classified my dear, but I will say that it's taken me some amazing places, at the very least." I admit wistfully. I haven't always disliked my work, that much is true. An eternity alone, that eats away at someone nearly as much as the fact that your makers don't care about you.

Arlo chuckles, but he doesn't say anything more about it. I want to ask him about Silas again, but I won't push it for now. I don't know why it's so important to me that Arlo watches over him, but I just know he needs to.

"Where's Bosko? I'm surprised he didn't ride third wheel." I tease, gesturing around his head.

"Oh, still doing bird things I imagine." Arlo remarks distantly. "He's getting old, you know? I don't like it when he just takes off without a goodbye, but I can't expect him to be at my beck and call, can I? Familiars don't work that way, but ... he's all I got."

And for reasons unbeknownst to me, I say, "You've got me."

I scream internally. I can't promise that, can't *say* that. This is a fun distraction from an inevitable end. He can't have me, no matter how much I want to give myself to him.

Arlo stops walking and tugs me into him. I *oof* into his chest, unable to stop the giggles pouring from me after we collide. I look around, finding us outside of my place.

"How do you do that?" I ask, out of breath from laughing.

"What?" He asks, tilting his head innocently.

"I never realize we're here until we're ... *here*. All I can see is you."

"Is that so?" Arlo smiles at me like I've hung the moons, which I have *not* done, but I've visited them both a time or two.

"Absolutely," I say, unable to come up with anything clever.

"Here, give this to Silas." Arlo reaches into his pocket and pulls out a jar and a small, folded up piece of paper. He hands me the jar first. "It'll quiet things down for him. Just rub it in like lotion."

"Oh, Arlo." I take it, smiling.

He waves me off, blushing, then offers the piece of paper. "Before you go, I have something for you, too. I meant to show you how to drive the bike after dinner, but you know. Cheese-makers and villains, all that jazz."

I squeal with glee and take the triangle shaped paper, inspecting it with intense curiosity. Obviously, I love puzzles. "This is much more my speed. I'd most likely crash your bike and cripple us both. I'll leave the daredevil theatrics to you."

"Oh come on, have more faith in yourself than that. I think you could handle it." He tries to show me which flap to start with and I slap his hand away. He laughs out an "Okay," raising his hands. His eyes simmer bright green, distracting me a few times until I double down my efforts.

After a few minutes of sticking my tongue out and squinting, an action I did *not* realize I committed while solving problems until Arlo pointed out how cute I am, I finish the puzzle. A three dimensional flower head rests in my palm, but there's an extra piece. A tab of sorts sticks out of the center.

"What's this piece? I can't figure it out." I ask, looking up to Arlo.

He's watching me with such a tender expression my heart skips a beat. Arlo reaches up and brushes hair away from my eyes, then leans forward and whispers, "Pull," in my ear. I shiver when he leans back and hurriedly pull the tab so he doesn't catch my flushed cheeks.

A bouquet erupts from between the folds of paper, stems extend and petals unfurl, taking my breath away. The flowers outshine the lamplights around us, green carnations lay with full stalks of lavender and nine roses, each dyed a different color. Smaller sprigs of wildflowers fill out the arrangement, finished with a copper ribbon around the neck. The tone matches my hair quite closely.

"Arlo, this is ... oh my." I hug the bouquet to my chest, grinning up at him.

Arlo cups my cheek, thumb rubbing back and forth over my warm skin. "I thought you'd like them, a friend of mine helped me out, the owner of the store next to Ren's. It's not too much?"

I shake my head quickly, overwhelmed. "No, they're *perfect*."

"That's good, real good," he says, nodding quickly. His cockiness has left, replaced by something more vulnerable and honest. Arlo's eyes lift to mine, a beacon in the dim night. He rolls his bottom lip between his teeth, humming as he considers me.

For once in my life, I don't let life *happen* to me.

I beat life to the punch.

With my free hand, I trace up his arm and the back of his neck, then settle deep into his waves of shining and curled soft black. I tug him into me with more force than intended, he falls onto my parted lips with a grunt that transforms into a moan.

He straightens, pulling me with him as his wonderfully large, heated hands take hold of my hip and lower back. I whimper into his inviting embrace, brought onto my tip toes within seconds. I throw both my arms around his neck, holding on tight to the bouquet as I do.

I need to be closer to him.

I slip my tongue past his and he gently takes my bottom lip between his teeth, eliciting a shiver from me. Goosebumps tease my arms and electricity zings down my spine as Arlo's magick flows down my throat and soaks into my lungs. I breathe in the involuntary response he's having. If he was purposely transferring magick, I'd be on my knees.

"Thatch," Arlo pleads, fingers and lips full of firm need.

What he's asking for I don't know, but I want to tell him he can have it. I know now that whatever this man could possibly ask for or want, I would give it to him, regardless of how much it hurt. With a certainty I haven't had in a long time, I throw away the debate.

Who cares how much it hurts after? I would be a fool to pass my love on by.

Arlo Rook kisses me like he's dying, imparting electrical waves of magick onto my lips. My body responds of its own accord, greedily inhaling everything he has to give me. His magick is warm and comforting and *home*.

He slides his hands beneath my shirt, fingers brushing over age old scars. Suddenly the magick overwhelming my senses is too much, powering through me like a tidal wave that will surely flood my heart. He's still not actively transferring, but there's so much *need* within him.

"I'm here, my *leva*." I murmur, pulling away long enough to regrettably breathe more air and less Arlo. Our foreheads press together and his breath pants onto my lips in heavy bursts. I try to find some composure, but that's a lost cause.

Arlo cradles my jaw in a trembling hand, eyes darkened. "Thatch, my magick, it's—it *wants* you. *I* want you." He whimpers, and the lamplights around us flicker.

"Hey, I'm here, you have me."

He whines and shakes his head in an odd way. If I didn't know better, I would say he's drunk, but he hasn't drank at all. He does it again, rubbing his sweaty forehead against mine.

"*Mm*, I think I need to go home." Arlo draws his words out. "Or this is going to get *very* messy." He giggles and I pull back, cupping his face in my hands. I get a good look at his hazy, dilated pupils. Thin, metallic green rings encircle his black irises and his cheeks vibrate beneath my palms. I chew on my cheek, trying to figure out what to do.

I go the easy route and play dumb. "Arlo, what's going on with you?"

Arlo groans, nuzzling into my palm. "I'm a wolf boy. You smell *really* good, Thatch, like maple and crunchy leaves and clean *fire*. My magick, it's singing to you. Did you know it does that? Can you hear it?" He drops to a whisper. "I didn't even know it could do that. Why do you do this to me?"

I breathe with my entire chest, trying to decipher his words through the haze of magick induced lust between us. I always want him, but whatever his magick is doing to the both of us is an aphrodisiac like nothing I've encountered. I understand most of what he's saying, but *wolf boy?*

I slide my hands from his face down to his fingers. He pouts until realizing I'm reaching for his hands. Arlo smiles wide and I chuckle, unable to hold back. "Alright, you can give me some of your magick, I'm ready now. You'll feel better."

Arlo frowns. "It hurts, doesn't it? Tobias said it hurts. But you, you didn't say anything."

I nod, treading a thin line. He must not know that he's been perpetually vibrating with energy since Ren's, his magick constantly leaking into my skin as we held hands.

"Because I'm made for you, and you were made for me. I can handle it. You understand?"

Arlo beams, squeezing my hands tight. "I understand."

A sudden force weakens my knees. Engulfing surges of magick *hot* with love and happiness and belonging and

Thatch

and Thatch

*and **Thatch***

Arlo

"Thatch!"

I sit up with a start in the darkness, unsure where I am or how I got here. Thatch's name echoes around me and I shake my head, absorbing my surroundings as my eyes adjust. I'm in my bed, alone in the attic. Everything's in its place, except for a piece of paper on my bedside table, pinned down by my phone and the contents of my pockets.

My jeans are nowhere to be seen and I'm down to my boxers.

I scrub a hand down my face, then reach over and attempt to unlock my phone, but it's dead. I take the note, then snap my fingers and bring forth a small cantrip of light so I can read it.

Arlo,

You had a magick overload whilst transferring to me and sort of passed out. I brought you home. I'm fine, no worries there. I'll be busy the next couple of days, but feel free to write me if you'd like. I had a good time, thank you for everything.

Yours,

Thatch

P.S: I couldn't find your charger, I apologize. Your bike is out front.

I put the light out and lay back, holding the paper to my chest.

My thoughts immediately wander to his words before I passed out. *"Because I'm made for you, and you're made for me."*

He really said that, didn't he?

I sit up again, this time with a driving need to solve the mystery that is Thatch.

With purpose, I swing my legs out of bed and search around for my duffel bag. I rip out my phone charger and get that plugged in, then dive back into the bag for the book that called to me in *Shh* Elves. I'll read this until my phone charges, then I'll read the article Kitt sent me. I'm going to help Thatch.

Problem is, the moment I start reading, an unnatural force drags me back under and I fall asleep with the book in my lap.

Wednesday

How It Ends

Arlo

I awake with a racing heart and pulsating, blurry vision.
Great.

I roll over on a cool floor and groan in response to stretching muscles made of jello and exhaustion. I open my eyes to find Kleo staring down at me, silhouetted by the dusky morning outside the wall of windows behind her.

I don't startle, if only because my body won't cooperate.

She tilts her head at me, her twisted hair tickles my face. "That's not your bed."

I brush her hair away with a heavy hand. "No, it is not, but to be fair, you are not in *yours,* either."

Kleo straightens and I wait for her hands to rest on her hips defiantly, but she sighs, and I'm not sure if I've ever heard her sigh like that. Not out of exasperation that she's not getting her way, but ... hopelessness.

I reach out to her. "Help me up?"

She raises a brow. "How about I'll start the kettle."

My hand drops and I nod solemnly, hair scrubbing against the floor which I hope is halfway clean, last I knew it was. "Probably a good idea. I'll squash you."

Kleo rolls her eyes, turning away with a hint of a smile.

I sit up with extreme difficulty, grunting and groaning like 'an old man,' according to Kleo. My suspicions are confirmed when I rub the back of my head and take in my surroundings, the Kitchen. We work together, producing two cups of steaming green tea, sweetened with honey and topped off with lemon slices. We settle into the nook by the windows and sip our tea while the sun threatens to make an appearance.

We used to do this often. Kleo only sleeps for a few hours, no matter the circumstances, and has been that way since she came here. For a long time, I would sleepwalk through the castle and find myself accompanied by Kleo wherever I woke up. I'd rather wake up in odd places and with a broken back than endure the night terrors that possess me the other nights.

We would have tea together, and then she would confess her troubles. But sometimes we would say nothing at all, and she wouldn't move an inch for hours, as opposed to the constant fidgeting and bouncing she tends to do.

I haven't done this or had terrors in a blessedly long time. But now I'm doing both.

"Why ya' sleepwalkin' again?" Kleo asks when the tea reaches the halfway mark in my neon pink mug and the sun has risen a few shades. Outside the closed doors of the Kitchen, Kleo must've shut them, the Castle murmurs to life.

I lift a shoulder. "I hear stress is an awful thing."

She nods. "I couldn't sleep last night. At all."

I take a sip of my tea, then set the mug down on the table. We never did get a chance to talk after she ran out of my story crying yesterday. "Felix?"

Kleo brings her knees up to her chest, tucking herself deeper into the over-sized chair opposite me. She clutches her bright pink mug, frowning down at her tea. Kitt had gone through a pottery phase, long enough to supply both my Kitchen and the actual one.

"He won't tell me he's a witch."

I inhale sharply through my nose and rub at my heart. "He will, Kleo, when he's ready. It's hard being one, you know. It's not all fun and games."

Kleo's eyes rise to meet mine over her mug and she doesn't lift her head. "I know that. I see you."

That catches me off guard. "Hm?"

She lifts a shoulder, looking back down to her mug. "Stress is an awful thing."

I laugh, a bellowing thing that echoes throughout the Kitchen. I clap a hand over my mouth, eyes just as wide as Kleo's. A grin cracks her melancholy, and we both laugh, although much quieter than my initial outburst.

I lean forward and rustle her hair, already wild and sticking up everywhere. I'm reminded of Thatch and I wonder what he's doing now. The ghost of his lips on mine haunts my nerves, and a shiver runs down my spine at the thought of kissing him again.

We sit together for what must be another hour. I'm in no hurry to move other than to fix up the blinds as the sun stretches across the backyard with a vengeance. A shower is in order, but for now we have another cup of tea, and Kleo goes on about her latest adventures. The usual bravado is lacking, and the next time a beat of silence hits, I feel another confession coming.

"There's something else." Kleo mutters.

I reach out, offering my hand across the table. "What's wrong, Kleo?"

She takes what I offer and sniffs, holding on tight. "I ... I was adopted."

"*Oh*, honey, that's a good thing, come here."

I release her hand and open my arms. She scrambles from her chair and throws herself at me, arms around my neck and violent sobs breaking against my shoulder. I hold her tight, rubbing circles over her shoulders.

"I—I don't want to *leave* him."

My hold on her tightens, and a memory blinds me.

I don't want you to go Kitt!

This must've been how Kitt felt leaving me behind.

"Listen, shh, listen. I know you don't, but he's going to be so happy for you, just like I am, and Felix will find his home, and you two will still be friends. That will never change, Kleo. Breathe, honey, breathe."

"But what if he doesn't and he's alone and I'm not here to protect him and what if—"

"Hey, shh, Kleo, breathe in, there you go. He's safe, and he's loved, and he loves you. His future isn't yours to worry about, okay?"

Kleo nods rapidly against me. Tears and sweat and hair stick to my bare shoulders. I don't remember it, but I must've changed into my tank and sweatpants sometime in the night. Did I take my meds? Fuck, when *was* the last time I took them?

Kleo's sobs steady out into something coherent and I pet her hair. There's endless thoughts and worries ripping apart my head, they swirl into darker and darker territory, bordering on depressive and self loathing, but I try. I *try* to push them away, for her, for right now. None of Leon's hatred filled words crawling across the past, no empty hole where my heart should be.

"When are they coming?" I ask.

Kleo sniffs. "In the morning. You'll be there to say ... to say goodbye, won't you?"

"Of course I will." I give her one last squeeze, then gently set her back on her feet. I tuck her hair behind her ears and wipe away her tears, then give her a tentative smile. "Are they nice?"

Color sweeps over her cheeks and she shrugs, bashful. "They played pirate with me, the others didn't do that. But Mister Arlo, they already have seven kids. *Seven.* That's so many."

I chuckle. "You'll have your own crew. How about this," I grip her shoulder gently. "If you'd like, the three of us can talk together. You, Felix and me. We'll make plans and I'll talk to your parents myself, keep you and Felix in touch. Okay?"

"Parents." Kleo whispers, staring past me. "I have *parents* now."

"Yeah honey, you have parents now."

My room has been ransacked.

Or I ransacked it, which is more likely than someone breaking past my personal wards.

I wade through heaps of clothing strewn across the floor, scowling at empty drawers left open and my mess of a bed. After a few minutes of searching, I locate my phone, powered off but plugged in. Within seconds of turning on, the notifications roll in without stopping for a full minute. My breath catches at all the people who tried to get a hold of me this morning. It's only eight and the amount of phone calls I've missed are absurd.

Caspian.

An unknown number.

Doc.

Thatch.

Elochian.

Quentin.

Chief.

Gowan.

Tobias.

Lindsey.

Lindsey.

Lindsey.

"Fuck." I mutter, scrubbing a hand over my face.

I sit on the edge of my bed and call Thatch first. He doesn't answer, but I leave a message. "Hey, Thatch. Thanks for bringing me home. Give me a call later."

Caspian doesn't answer.

Kitt doesn't answer.

Doc's rings twice, then goes to voicemail. The gnawing black hole in my gut widens, inviting worst case scenarios and guilt to roam free.

Chief answers on the first ring. "Arlo Rook. Question, is it possible for you to go a *day* without causing trouble?"

"I'm not awake enough for this, Chief. Cut to the chase." I grunt out. A beat of silence extends and worry seeps into my bones. "Don't tell me someone's dying."

"No one's dying, but another painting has been found."

"*Okay?*"

Chief growls something in the *tannin* tongue, then switches to common for my benefit. "I'll be blunt with you, Arlo. This Game is getting out of control. People are going mad out there trying to figure it out, it's only a matter of time before someone gets hurt. I've already had more charges in the last week than I have all quarter, Kitt included."

I register Kitt's name but the accusation floors me. My free hand clutches the crumpled blankets beside me. "You think *I'm* doing this?"

Chief inhales sharply. "Arlo, we know for a fact several of the stolen paintings are yours, and the one found today *is* yours. Not to mention Loch's involvement and the location of—"

Chief goes on and on. I rub out the incoming headache settling in my temple. Last night was a beautiful dream with Thatch, and today is a fucking nightmare.

"I've got nothing to do with this, Chief. And even if I did, I'm not responsible for people not using their heads, Kitt included. Have you ever known me to be a liar in all the years we've worked together? Not to mention the *decades* I spent saving your father's ass time and time again during the Taking."

I don't like pulling out the '*I saved the city for you*' card, but this is bullshit. I wait for Chief to argue with me, but she relents. "I'll be glad when this is all over. I don't have enough manpower for this."

"Where's Kitt now, Chief?"

"Last I knew, home with Lindsey. Not too happy about the trespassing charges and spending a few hours behind bars, but what can you do?"

"*Trespassing*?"

"She was in Old Widow's Peak, Arlo. I could've slapped her with a felony or two."

The *temple*? How did she get that from the painting we found? "Fucking hell, how did she get up there?"

"Exactly my *point*. What'll be next, the tallest branch on *Etz Hayim*? And imagine this Arlo, there's idiots dumber than you guys out there." Chief whispers dramatically.

I scoff. "Which painting was it?"

"Something depressing. Someone looking at the river, I think. Everything's blue."

Intuition churns my gut and I grip my phone tighter. "Talk to you later, Chief."

Then the sun took over and everything was blue.

My blood heats as I recall the night terror. I know exactly which painting it is and where I have to go. I scrub my face with my hands and groan, then snap out of it. I send texts to everyone, debate on calling Thatch again, then move onto the bathroom and all it entails.

I find fresh clothes, mildly annoyed when I can't find my leather jacket but don't dwell on it. It's probably on my bike. I gather my shit and stand in the center of the room. Something is out of place, or I'm forgetting something, but I can't put my finger on what it is.

I'll remember later.

Bosko returns with flair, and I'm more relieved to see him than I care to admit.

He lands on my shoulder and I stop, squelching into the mud path running along the riverside. A storm must've hit last night, everything is soaked, and my bones are cold. Although it's nearing noon, the sun is nowhere to be seen, and the day holds a general dreariness.

I reach up and stroke his head, the ball of anxiety that's come with his disappearance eases and I don't have it in me to be irritated with him. "Hey, bird. Where you been?"

"I do have a life, you know." Bosko replies in typical Bosko fashion, and I laugh. "Have you solved your soulmate's mystery yet?"

I swallow something heavy. All this time, the subconscious knowledge has tumbled in the back of my mind, waiting for me to pull it out and examine it. There's no other explanation for my soulmark glowing when he's around, the heavy influence he has on my magick, and the *rightness* there is when we're together.

He said so himself last night, more or less.

"Because I'm made for you, and you're made for me."

Which means he knows, too, probably has this whole time.

Part of me wants to be angry with him, but at the same time, I understand. He doesn't want to start something we can't finish. How many times has he tried to fight the chains that bind him, and has given up hope on breaking them?

But he hasn't had me to help him before.

And I won't let him go easily.

Bosko nibbles on my ear, drawing me to the present. "Yeah, I've figured out that he's my soulmate."

Bosko makes a noise in his threat, clearly displeased. "Gods help me. That much was obvious, or so I thought."

"You *knew*?"

"Of course I did, your face was glowing!" Bosko trills.

I pull on the gauge in my ear, groaning. I resume my journey, heart thumping as we leave the main road. "Then what are you talking about? What is there to figure out?" I trip over a stone. "Do you know what he is? Why he has to leave?"

Bosko takes off from my shoulder. "Can't say, can't say. Better hurry up and play."

"Play?" I call after him, but he doesn't come back.

Kitt and Caspian wait for me near the shoreline that leads to a cottage I visited just days before with Thatch and Felix. It's hidden by the trees, so I can't tell if Thatch is there. He wasn't at Thitwhistle's, and neither was the bard we met yesterday. I bury the urge to call or text him again. He said he'd be busy today, but a sinking feeling won't leave my heart alone.

"There you are, about time," Caspian says, not half as menacing as he's trying to be. The bruising under his blood shot eyes calls for a week's worth of sleep, and his congested, hoarse voice makes me wonder if he's sick. "Why are we here?"

"Morning Cas, how're you today? I'm splendid, thanks for asking."

Caspian groans, rubbing his thickening scruff. "Fuck *off*, I called out of work for this."

I mock him, and Kitt swats us both over the back of our heads. I glare at her, pointing an accusing finger. "Chief spanked my ass this morning over you. What the hell were you thinking climbing up there?"

Kitt rolls her eyes. "I was thinking that shit's getting serious, and if we want to solve this, we need to step up our game. You're busy with lover boy, and everyone else is being adults or something like that." She gives Cas a pointed look and he crosses his arms. A shot of guilt courses through me, I've been so wrapped up in Thatch that the Game has taken a surprising backseat to everything else.

"Oh, I'm *sorry* for having a life. In case you couldn't tell, climbing old ass fucking churches isn't in my skill set." Caspian pats his legs, glaring at Kitt.

I pinch the bridge of my nose. "Alright, alright. We're all bitchy and whiny this morning. Kitt, next time you need to trespass, ask for some fucking help, maybe from your *witch* friend? Cas, quit being a dick. You *wanted* to play this year."

"Yeah, well, maybe I don't care who the Illusionist is. Have you given thought to the idea we might not like what we find, Arlo? What's if he's a murderer or something? I wanted to have fun with you guys, but it's not fun. Not anymore."

Kitt and I stare at Caspian, thousands of half formed thoughts fly through my brain at hyper speed.

"Caspian, what's really going on?" I ask gently, reaching for his shoulder. I try to recover the armistice we formed just a couple days ago.

He flinches back.

"Nothing! I'm just fucking tired, alright? And this place is creeping me the fuck out. How can you stand to be here?" Caspian glares at me but I'm caught up on one word.

"What if *he's* a murderer? What makes you think they're a guy?"

Kitt looks between us, chewing her lip.

The blood drains from Caspian's face, but he keeps up his glare. "Nothing, just slipped out. Look, you guys can count me out, I don't know why I bothered to come down here, I got shit to do."

Caspian disappears via a transportation stone and Kitt goes after the place he once was, but I stop her. "No, let him go."

"He's not good, Arlo. You can't just let him–"

"I know he's not, but staying here isn't going to help. When he's calmed down, I'll go find him."

Kitt's brows furrow and her eyes dart back and forth across my face. "Why? Why does it bother him here? There's nothing but open land and the water. You can't even see Thatch's cottage. Where are we going to find a painting down here, anyway?"

I exhale, long and slow.

"This is where Cas said he found me, Kitt. When I faced off with Leon for the first time."

Kitt's hands fly up to her mouth. "*Oh*."

I release clenched fists and shove my hands into my pockets, walking towards the water's edge. "Yeah. Figures the one dying has less trauma about a place than the person who found them." I wince, releasing an arm to wrap around Kitt's shoulders. "Fuck, sorry, I wasn't thinking. Gods, I'm an asshole."

Kitt says nothing, swallowing hard as she stares into the water. Her arm slides around my side and she sighs. Silence overtakes us, and I curse my loose tongue. "I'll visit Caspian later, I promise."

"Don't joke about that shit, Arlo." Kitt chides, looking up to me with a frown.

I nod. "I won't, I'm sorry."

She nods too, overlooking the lake with no end in sight. "So, why are we here now?"

"Doesn't it look familiar?" I ask, gesturing to the water.

Kitt nods slowly. "The painting. I didn't recognize the place at first, but I do now. The ship on Newcoin is in the painting, and Leideen Ait, you can see both if you stand just here."

I nod. "I'd have to say our next painting is around here somewhere." I ruffle her hair, drawing an exasperated smile from her. "By the way, how did you guess the last one was at the temple?"

Kitt chuckles. "Oh, that? Look at it upside down, the Old Widow's peak is in the background." Kitt studies the water, nose wrinkling. "What do you think the clue was in yours?"

I scoff. "I have no idea. I painted it after one of my terrors, and I just … there was so much blue, I had to get it down." I frown, reminded of what Loch said. The orange and red captured him and he *had* to get it down. "The blue. Besides the location, the blue means something. I'm sure of it."

"But *what*?"

I shrug. "I have no idea." Honestly, the Game has been the least of my concerns the past couple days.

"Do you think it's in the water?" Kitt asks, peering closer.

"Find out?" I ask, then push her off.

"Arlo Rook!" Kitt screams, furious. "You'll pay for that!"

Moments later, I'm yanked into the water right with her.

Despite our state, we laugh.

A shine from beneath us catches my attention, nestled into the bedding of kelp and seagrass tickling our legs. "Kitt," I breathe, gesturing to it.

She grins. "Race you to it."

I smile right back, feeling like a kid again. "You're on."

Thatch

The willows weep onto my companion and me, showering us with the remnants of the recently passed storm. Dew and precipitation blanket the island much thicker than it does on the mainland. Drops of fragrant water linger in the thick hair along my cheeks, my beard having grown an inch after only a day of not shaving. Despite Arlo's magick infusion during our kiss last night, I feel and look like shit.

I'm fighting the *harsh* pull of the universe, more than I've ever had to before, and it's the bard's fault.

Not that he can help it.

He stands beside me with a cup of coffee in hand, his blond curls catch the breeze swaying the branches overhead. His companion waits with the black fox, back in the cottage, where I'm sure both are snooping through my half packed things. Can't blame them for that.

Sapphire eyes track every minute movement I make, and he taps his mug with a metallic finger, charcoal feathers rustling as he considers his next words. I take a sip of my own coffee, freshly brewed from the new machine inside. After hours of painstaking work, the cottage is sparkling and ready to be lived in. Only a few personal belongings of mine remain, but I'll take care of those next.

He says, "They call you a God, where I'm from."

I laugh. "Do they? Well, you'll be able to straighten them out, won't you?"

The bard frowns. "After everything, how can you not be?"

I sigh. "Because Gods can do whatever they like, and I cannot."

Screams and laughter across the way break the tension, melded with water splashing. I smile, unable to stop myself. The bard peers through the weeping branches, finding his own smile when he spies a witch and his friend hauling a treasure from beneath the depths. I hoped that by leading Arlo back to where it all began, he would remember me on his own, but I'm starting to think he never will.

"That's why you brought me here," The musician says, watching them climb out of the water.

I swallow back the tears clawing my throat and breathe deeply through my nose. "I need to see how it ends, if he figures it out. Please, I need a few more days, and then we can leave. I know you need to find–"

The bard rests his hand on the back of my neck, gripping firmly as he gives me his steadfast attention. "We can wait. Saturday is the last day, right?"

Like a ton of bricks, his words collapse my spirit and seal my fate.

I knew my visit was coming to a close, but the finality of three days rips out my heart. The sunshine warmth of Arlo's lips on mine creeps to the forefront of my memory. I want him, I need him, and I'm *leaving* him.

A coughing fit ensues, something that started early this morning. The blood splattering my hand is new, however.

See You In The Morning

Arlo

Heart pounding out of my chest, I knock on the white door of the yellow house.

Caspian throws it open and for a moment, I'm convinced he's going to shut it in my face. But, he wheels back and pulls open the door farther, avoiding my eyes. "You didn't text."

"You would've ignored me or told me you weren't home." I step inside, noting the eerie silence. The halls are dark and a cold atmosphere greets me. So cold that I instinctively blink, engaging my magick. I search the area now veiled in unnatural light green for spirits, but there are none. "Where's Bias and the kids?"

"Working in his office, daycare." Caspian rolls into the living room and I follow him. He hurriedly gathers papers and shoves them in a once open notepad filled with his scrawly writing, then slams it shut. "Needed some time to myself." Caspian adds, but there's no heat to it. He rubs his forehead, then truly looks at me for the first time.

I stand at the opposite end of the living room, wondering if we've always been this distant and I never noticed, or if something's happened. Sure, we've talked more than we've ever had lately about *feelings,* but none of it sticks. Has it always been this hard?

What have I done to make Caspian constantly so angry with me?

Honestly, I've come to realize I've wronged him in a lot of ways.

I clear my throat and jut a thumb over my shoulder. "I can go, if you want. Just uh, wanted to tell you that Kleo was adopted, she's getting picked up tomorrow morning, and I think it'd be cool if you could come see her off. Kitt's coming, not sure about the others. But it's fine if you can't. Just ... wanted to keep you in the loop. Y'know?"

Caspian's shoulders fall in. "Of course I'll be there." He gestures for me to sit, and I do, perhaps a bit too quick to be considered casual. He finds his wooden transfer board leaning against the side of the couch and uses it to slide out of his chair and onto the cushion beside me.

Cas sighs, raking a hand through his hair. "Are they decent people?"

I remove my beanie and rake through my hair, then replace it. "According to Dusan they are, I haven't met them myself. Kleo says they have a lot of kids."

Caspian snorts. "Sounds perfect. How's Felix about it? Was he more like you or Kitt when I left?"

"What, you mean bawling like a baby or stoic and mature?" I jostle him and he rolls his eyes, allowing a small smile. "She hasn't told him yet."

"Ouch." Caspian wrinkles his nose.

"*Yeah*, that's my night tonight. Gonna make some dinner for the Castle, all that good stuff. Kitt's coming, just saying."

Caspian chuckles a little. "Is that an invitation?"

"I'm makin' chili." I offer, knowing it's his weakness.

Caspian huffs out another laugh, then shakes his head. "Thanks, but I'm probably going to sleep the minute you leave." He taps his knee a couple times with an impatient finger, contemplating. "Did you ... find anything by the river?"

I grin wide. "Can't resist, can you?"

He glares at me. "Just wondering what the latest wild goose chase is."

I take out my phone, happy to have some level of normal bickering between us. I show him the pictures I took after Kitt, the painting and I had dried off and before we turned it in to Chief. "It's another one of Loch's."

"It is?" Caspian takes my phone and flips through the pictures, brows furrowed. "So let me guess. You're going to the cemetery next." He mutters, rubbing his chin.

"First thing in the morning, you could come with." I offer, but he shakes his head again. Caspian's eyes narrow and he drags his gaze over me, lips pressed thin.

Finally, he asks, "Where's Thatch?"

I wasn't expecting that. Telling Cas that Thatch and I kissed last night, I had a magick meltdown, and now Thatch won't call me back, doesn't seem like a good idea.

I settle for a shrug and half the truth. "No idea, working probably? Despite what you think, I do have a life."

My teasing falls flat and Caspian stares at me, jaw twitching.

"*Yes*, Cas?" I ask after our stare down commences for a full minute, anticipating shouted frustration, mild irritation.

Anything other than Caspian's next cautious, world shattering words.

"You seriously don't remember him, do you?"

"Remember him?" I lean back, fingers digging into the couch cushion for purchase. "What are you talking about?"

"*Fuck*." Caspian breaks eye contact, rubbing his face with a murmured curse. "You can be so thick sometimes, Arlo."

And that's how I know he's truly worried and not just being a dick, because he never calls me Arlo. I release my death grip on the cushion and reach for his shoulder. "Cas, what's going on? Just talk to me, please. We're all worried about you."

"*You*, Arlo, you're what's wrong with me." Caspian snaps, jerking away from me.

I inhale sharply, reeling in my quick to rise frustration. "Explain any time now."

"I don't like the idea of you living in the same building as him. Yeah, Quentin told me, thanks for that. I don't want ... I don't know who you *are* lately, and obviously neither do you. Ever since he came back ... I've been *waiting* for you to turn him away, but you don't!"

When I'm angry, I don't shout and shake with fury like Caspian does. I bathe in the feeling. I lower my tone and stiffen, preparing to pounce with barbed words, but not just yet. I have questions, and I'm not so hot headed that I can't focus.

"And what exactly is wrong with Thatch? Everyone else likes him. *You* said he was welcome here two days ago, you're not making any sense. What's changed?"

"Because no one remembers him!" Caspian slams a fist down on the couch between us, furious eyes boring into mine. The scent of rage and alcohol swarms the air between us. How did I not notice he's been drinking, *again*?

"*Cas*," I whisper.

"I've been silent, waiting, waiting, *waiting*! I don't want to be the one to pop your happy fucking bubble, but fuck! This has got to stop, or it'll all end with you—"

"*Caspian*, what the fuck—"

"But I *do*, I remember, because the last time I saw *him,* he was carrying your burned up carcass into the castle, then left without a word, never to be seen again. I don't know what he did, or why you or nobody else remembers, but I *don't* trust him, Arlo. Keep your friends close and enemies closer, right?"

Icy dread washes over my nerve endings. "What?" I ask, but it's so small that the fire in Caspian's eyes dies. "Are you talking about .... "

Magick and countless emotions pound in waves through my veins and my body shakes of its own accord. I dig, *deep*, into my memories, and find nothing. I've never been able to find the truth. There's the sense of familiarity I've had since the moment I met Thatch, but nothing else.

Then, my body convulses with an unbidden memory.

The world was closing in and I thought I heard boots pounding against the earth, but I gave up. I decided if the way I was meant to go was at my lover's hands at the end of a hard fought battle, then so be it. Then the sun overtook the world, and there was so much blue.

A voice floated around me, full of unfamiliar malice. "You're going to regret that."

"Who the fuck are—" Leon's voice cuts off, and his body hits the ground.

Gentle hands slide under my shoulders and legs, accompanied by soothing words and a cool touch that eases the pain wracking my body. "Shh, it's alright Arlo, I've got you. Hold on, leva, just hold on."

My head falls onto a rough, bare chest, and I fall into nothingness, surrounded by love.

Caspian reaches out for me. "Arlo?"

"You didn't find me." I flinch back, shaking harder now. My lungs struggle to cooperate. "Right? When was this?" I whimper, needing to hear him say it. I don't trust my own mind.

"The year we turned twenty." Caspian whispers, full of regret.

"That's ..." I start, but I can't find *words.*

Half formed thoughts chase each other relentlessly.

Thatch said the last time he came to Levena was around that time.

Did he ... *make* me forget him?

He knows Dusan, and she knows him.

I have no idea what kind of magickal being he is.

Did he purposely crash into me at the Market?

Has he known that we're ... *connected*, for far longer than I could've imagined?

Is he going to make me *forget* him again?

Why?

And ... is Caspian right?

I want to say that he's not, that the holes in my memory can't be filled with Thatch. That whole summer is hard to reach, but especially that day at the river. The doctors blamed it on the trauma, *I* blamed it on the trauma.

Would Thatch ever hurt me?

Everything did go downhill for me after that year, but *why* isn't something I've been able to pinpoint. Yeah, there was Leon, but fighting him for decades gave me purpose. I was the witch who stood up for others, he *made* me that. And you can't explain away mental illness, you can't *make* the chemicals fuck up.

The doctors said—

They said—

I fall forwards, shivering and not *breathing*.

I reach out for Caspian, but he's not there. His voice sounds around me and my head narrowly misses the floor, cradled by a large hand. I vaguely recognize his body on the floor beside mine, but everything's disappearing.

Soft words fall into my ear, but I can't make them out. I convulse again, the violent shakes give way to constant trembling, and I can't *breathe*.

A muffled river of emotion barrels through me, breaking my bones and snapping my spirit into thousands of splintered pieces.

A voice breaks through.

Tobias.

He cups my face, pulling me above the surface. "Breathe, Arlo. *In*, yes, that's good, *hold,* and *out*. In, *in*, Arlo, there you go, now hold onto it, and let it out. I've got you, you're safe."

He says something else, but it's not meant for me, blending into the background and much more irritated than the words he gave me. His hands are on my shoulders now, gripping *firm* and anchoring me to reality. His magick whispers *safe safe safe* through my skin, greeting my capillaries and washing further, caressing my arteries until the promise passes through my witch's heart.

The cracking of my world slows down as we breathe together for what feels like an eternity.

Kitt can't come.

Doc's hounding me about my latest round of blood work, something about a nuclear reactor about to explode.

I tried calling Thatch and he didn't answer.

I can't stop thinking, reevaluating.

I have a swarm of children keeping me company, along with a completely at peace Dusan. I have an endless array of questions for her, but I made a promise. The kids were waiting for me when I walked in the castle door, giving me no quarter. Bright, expectant smiles clash with the maelstrom inside my mind and I don't have the heart to go back on my word. Even a group of the reclusive teens have come out of their hiding spots in the castle.

Kleo and Felix bounce happily on a granite counter in the actual kitchen which is full of stainless steel appliances, hanging cast iron pots and pans and endless cupboards. My mind is a whirlwind of noise, thoughts and a million other things that threaten to take me under with each passing moment.

I try my best not to let it show, but of course Felix notices. I tend to overcompensate when the ants invade my skin and mind, my storytelling voices hinge just a *bit* too high, or my words fall out too fast.

Felix rests a hand on my arm and I still, exhaling heavily. He takes my hand and guides it to my necklace, reminding me of its weight. I breathe.

He smiles at me. "Hey, Mister Arlo."

"Hey, Felix," I say breathlessly, catching up with myself. The chili simmers, releasing a smoky and spicy aroma around us. Now all we can do is hurry up and wait. I push away another breath, then give him a smile. "Have I ever told you about the time I met a unicorn?"

"Yes, he was eating the garbage and you chased him down three streets before getting your hat back, one that Kitt, to this day, claims she did *not* throw away." Felix drones, rolling his eyes in a way that is suspiciously similar to how Kleo does it.

"Oh come on, you could've said no!" I pout, admittedly impressed with his impression of me. I ruffle his freshly cut hair, he had a visit yesterday which ended in a no call back. A chorus of dissatisfied 'Arlo!' rings around me and I chuckle halfheartedly.

Dusan leaves her perch, a stool near the windows facing the backyard. Her vertical irises dilate and her smile is downright mischievous as she comes around the counter island, followed by children. All those present gather in our corner of the kitchen, eyes bright and smiles wide, even the older kids.

"How about *I* tell a story about Arlo?"

I give her a look, wondering if she can sense my irritation with her. "Which one?"

Dusan waves me off, then casually *pushes* me out of the way so she can sit between Felix and Kleo. "Oh don't look so put out. I have good stories, too."

I scoff, leaving her for the gigantic stove taking up the opposite side of the space. I remove the lid from a pot that's half as tall as I am, then poke around the chili as Dusan recalls a tale I haven't thought about in quite some time, not until Thatch asked me about my name.

"Almost a hundred years ago, I found a little boy with hazel eyes and a knitted, albeit smelly old hat that kept falling over his brow in my office." Dusan begins, and I smile, despite myself.

"How did he get there?" Lunaria asks, a vampire that's nearly aged out.

"Well, I suppose he must've walked right in and made himself at home. Some say he was born from the stars, others say he wandered in from the Dragon's Claw, a place between worlds."

I roll my eyes at the embellishment and turn from dinner, only to find the kids are completely enthralled. I swallow my protests and lean back against a counter in silence. The truth is never pretty, and the kids need as much pretty as they can get. They don't need us to tell them how shitty the world can get. They're here, abandoned or forgotten for one reason or another, they know that.

"What did you do?" Felix asks Dusan, then glances over to me. I wink at him and he tries to do the same, but ends up cross-eyed. I give him a thumbs up for effort.

"Well, I gave him a bed, same as I did for all of you. He was a *talker*, but he was respectful, and I thought, 'Well, this one will be mild mannered, won't he?'"

Snickers and giggles follow that statement and I feign offense. "Hey! I wasn't *that* bad."

Dusan levels me with a look, and I sheepishly tuck my hands into my pockets as she continues. "It was early in the day yet, so he wandered around in his new home and made a friend, ate a meal and told the cook how they could make it better."

My ears burn and Kleo grins at me.

"But *then*," Dusan proclaims, startling those closest to her. "It was time for bed. Any guesses as to what happened?"

"What! What happened?" A child asks.

"Well, I was laying in bed and could *not* sleep. There was all this giggling coming from the dormitories, so I had to investigate. I *cracked* open the door, and what I found took my breath away." Dusan presses a hand to her chest in full dramatics, leaving the kiddies hanging.

I chuckle softly, at the time I had no idea she was watching.

"Arlo had directed all of the lamps at the wall and was doing the—"

"Shadow puppets!" Several voices cry out together, causing us all to laugh.

"Yes, he was telling stories and casting shadows, even then. And no matter where you go, you'll have his stories and mine to keep you company." Dusan ruffles Kleo and Felix's hair simultaneously, then hops down from the counter and hugs a few of the children who come her way. "Now, who's setting the table?" Dusan smoothly gathers the herd out of the kitchen and to the dining room across the hall, effortlessly leaving Felix and Kleo behind.

"Hey, Felix?" I call, turning both his and Kleo's heads. "Could I talk with you two for a minute?"

"Are we in trouble?" Felix glances over at Kleo who stares at me, face pale.

I can't help but laugh a little. "No, and I don't think you get in trouble enough for that to be your first thought, not really."

"She does." Felix points at Kleo whose nervousness breaks into annoyance. "And brings me down with her."

"I do not!"

I turn off the stove and take up refuge in the sitting area, then wave them over when they don't follow. There are no waning rays of sunlight breaking through the windows today, just the threat of another storm on the horizon. It's not quite night time, creating that fever dream, in-between atmosphere when the day masquerades as eternal twilight.

The plants at my back curl and wither. I frown.

I've been hexed. I suppress a sigh at the idea of *another* obstacle rolling before me today. Felix and Kleo share the booth opposite my rickety stool and a round table lies between us.

"Felix, there are several things I want to tell you, and so does Kleo. You are not in trouble, and everything is good. Understand?" Felix hastily looks between Kleo and I, the boy not at *all* looking like everything is good.

I extend my hand across the table to him, prepared this time when his magick ridden skin brushes against mine and his fingers entwine strongly with mine. I send out love and warmth and *everything is ok,* and he nods slowly.

"Kleo, do you want to go first?" I ask, and she raises her bowed head. She looks over to Felix with glistening eyes and a shy smile.

"Felix, I know you're a witch. I'm not mad!" She adds, hands up when his eyes widen. "Well, only because you didn't trust me enough to tell me! We're best friends, we tell each other *everything*."

Felix releases my hand, capturing both of Kleo's own hands in his with a renewed fire to his eyes. "I do trust you! I ... It's scary, Kleo. I don't want to scare you, ever."

"You could *never* scare me, egghead. Think of all the bets we could've won with your superpowers." Kleo knocks his head with her own.

Felix grins. "Like ... reading minds?"

"*No* reading minds," I cut in, startling both of them, like they forgot I was there. I raise a brow at a sheepish Felix. "That's an invasion of privacy, Little Witch."

"Right." Felix adds, glancing at Kleo with a hesitant smile. "So ... you're not mad?"

Kleo shakes her head. "No, I'm not *mad*. But, there's something else, too." Kleo looks over at me and I nod, giving her a reassuring smile. She gives Felix her attention again, chin wobbling. "I was adopted on Sunday, Felix. I'm leaving tomorrow and I'm *so* sorry I didn't tell you and *please* don't be mad, I'm so scared and I don't—"

Kleo's words string into an incoherent babble and Felix wraps his arms around her, holding his best friend as tight as he can. She hugs him back, and I say nothing, closing my eyes as they murmur promises and *'it's okay'*s to the other. I relive my goodbyes to Caspian and Kitt. I was a mess for both of them, but Kitt especially. Whether it's because she was last or we were closer at the time, I don't know.

When the young friends sniffle and pull apart, I open my eyes and arms.

They immediately come over for a hug, and I hold them both tight. "No matter what happens, no matter how far you two go from each other, you will always have this. These years, these memories. I won't make big promises like things will always be the same, because they won't. But I *can* promise you that you will always have this, and if you work hard, each other. Understand?"

Both nod and hug me tight, then we *all* wipe our tears because I'm crying too now, damn it. I wish Cas and Kitt had come. I wish Thatch would answer his phone.

When Felix and Kleo settle back into where they were, he asks questions about her new family, and she asks him what it's like being a witch. That's where I cut in.

"Felix, that's the other thing," I say, getting his attention. "I've been talking with Tobias and we both believe your specialty is what's referred to as an Empath, that's why you ... *get* people so easily, understand their feelings. Especially through touch. Does this sound right to you?"

Felix nods without hesitation. "Yeah. I've noticed it more since Sunday, it's ... getting worse." He chances a look at Kleo and she takes his hand. I don't miss the way he addresses his magick intensifying as *worse*. "I can hear things, I can't help it."

That takes me by surprise. Teleth work is its own specialty, widely varied, and as far as I know not even Tobias can fully read minds. I internally groan at the thought of contacting Arche, the only complete Teleth I know.

"We can work on that," I say to Felix, giving him a warm and hopefully comforting smile. He relaxes a little. "I suggest that you spend time with Tobias. We can still do witch things together as you like, but I think he should be your mentor. He has agreed to speak with you about it, if you're interested."

Felix nods slowly, mulling it over. "Okay. I'll think about it." He focuses on Kleo, squeezing her hand. "For now, let's celebrate. I'm happy for you, Kleo. Truly."

Like an unwelcome nightmare, hollow, drugged out words from the night of Caspian's wedding plague my thoughts. *I'm happy for you Cas, truly.*

The darkness creeping in at the edges of my mind intensifies, bringing with it cold feelings that I haven't experienced since ... *before*. I need someone. I need help.

I escort Kleo and Felix to the dining room and manage to serve dinner without drawing attention from Dusan, successfully pulling on my mask and going through the motions, then disappear to the attic. Bosko's gone again and the room is abysmal. Empty despite the fact it's full of my neatly organized things.

I shed all my jewelry, finding a once clear crystal orb pendant now full of darkness, the remnants of the hex placed on me trapped inside its confines. I throw the necklace across the room, then sit on the edge of my unmade bed, drowning in the darkness with no sight of land. I dig through my pockets, retrieving my phone before my hands are no longer my own and the nothingness paralyzes me, convincing me that reaching out is *wrong*.

I dial up Thatch, only to receive a 'this number no longer works' message.

Before I suffocate, I call Doc.

They answer drowsily on the fourth ring, just shy of me hanging up.

"Arlo, to what do I owe the pleasure?"

I try to find words, but all I can manage is a strangled sob. I draw my knees up into my chest and press my face into my thigh in attempts to muffle the sound. A rustling sounds on the other end and a soft, indiscernible voice.

"Arlo?" Doc asks, much more awake now.

I turn my face enough so my lips are free. "Doc, it's bad again. My head, it's ... not good."

"Imagine that. You haven't been sleeping, probably haven't been eating properly, and you're all worked up over your *not*-soulmate. The city's after you, and so is an old enemy, not to mention your magick is haywire. I imagine your head's *pretty* fucked up, Arlo."

I fucking *laugh* through hot tears. "And this is why you're my therapist."

"One of the many titles I hold, my friend. Can I come over?"

I chew on my lip, glancing at the time. "I don't think I can be alone right now."

"That's very—"

"Yeah yeah, I don't have a praise kink so knock it off."

Doc chokes on something, and the tension releases from my shoulders. "Must you always be so vulgar?"

I smile. "Always, Doc."

Thursday

Basket Case

Arlo

"My wife is going to be wondering where I am, and when I tell her that we slept together and you *dragged* me out to a graveyard in lieu of breakfast, she's going to be *very* upset."

I laugh, boots sinking into the mud as Doc, Quentin, Elochian and I walk down a narrow trail leading to the Netherspring. There's only one cemetery in Levena, and it's full of graves that range from days old to centuries. I don't like coming here alone, the only spirits that linger here are the ones that have lost their way, fighting the pull of the other side.

Of the inevitable.

"Slept?" Quentin sputters, glancing between the gigantic *behema* and me. Elochian on the other hand looks unimpressed, hiding beneath a black ensemble with a hood pulled up over his head. His wings are on full display, like always, catching the sunrise and reflecting rainbows onto the cheeks of those around me.

My mind hasn't stopped running since I woke up, but I don't feel *right* on the verge of a breakdown, just staring it in the face. I rely heavily on sarcasm to smooth over the edges in my exhausted tone. "Oh, come on Doc, *live* a little. Besides, we'll get breakfast on the way back, and you can bring her home some." I promise through a yawn.

"Oh yes, then turn around and go to work on two hours of sleep because your bed is not built for someone of my stature." Doc counters, yawning which turns into a growl.

"You were in college once, I'm sure you can manage." A cold shiver runs down my spine when we step off the trail and officially on the property. Visages of resident ghosts watch us from their respective stones, and if I didn't have my wards prepared they'd be rushing me, demanding help or vengeance. Of course, the others can't see them, but I can.

They're so *loud*.

In truth, Doc and I fell asleep on my floor after a late night therapy session and the discussion of retrograde versus post traumatic amnesia. While the possibility that Thatch might not have purposely made me forget him is comforting, that doesn't explain why he acted like he didn't know me at all. There's also the fact that Caspian's memory is foggy.

Bosko rides upon my shoulder, quiet and comforting as he speaks what I don't want to admit and desperately need to hear. *"He's the reason you can't remember, you know this in your heart, but I don't believe it's intentional. You need to speak to him, and keep in mind he's done this hundreds, if not thousands of times. Comforted those who have forgotten him, all the while he's the one who is lost."*

I exhale a shaky breath and reach up, stroking his feathers. *"Thank you, old friend."*

"Why were you two sleeping together?" Quentin asks, hiking a shovel over his shoulder and startling me out of my thoughts. I hide a grin at his work outfit. Jeans and a nice sweater, loafers.

"Arlo gets bad dreams and Doc knows all the right ways to make them go away," Loch says dryly, dispelling my swelling cloud of emotions.

Doc stares at him, lip twitching and baring a hint of fang. "When did you get *mouthy*, Elochian? I knew going on a field trip to the cemetery with two basket cases was not a good idea."

"But we're your *favorite* basket cases," I add with mock cheer.

Doc grins, all teeth now. "That you are."

I elbow Quentin gently, needing a distraction. "So, what are your theories on the painting, Q?"

"M-me?" Quen asks, pressing his free hand to his sweater vest covered chest. Elochian studies the cemetery coming to life through the fog, hiding a smile as he listens to Quentin. Doc cleans their glasses on their flannel.

"Yeah, you." I chuckle, taking the shovel from him. We weren't exactly sure what searching for a painting at the grave-yard would entail, but a shovel didn't seem far fetched.

Quentin nervously glances at Elochian, the artist behind the painting, then focuses on his feet. "Oh, well. I've always thought it was someone who stayed behind after their loved ones were gone. Being the last, you know?"

"That's not far off from how I felt when I painted it, Quentin," Loch says, sparing Quentin a stiff smile. "Did you know the name of it is—"

"Survivor's Guilt," Quentin adds hurriedly, eager to please.

Doc raises their brows at me in question, and I shrug like I have no idea what's going on, happy to listen to the pair talk. I think about what Thatch said in the museum about the Illu-

sionist being tired, and an idea strikes me. Why haven't I asked
the others this?

"How many of us think it's the same person from the very
first game, or that it's a family affair passed through the genera-
tions?" I ask, and it's a couple minutes before someone answers.

"I never even thought about it being the same person. I assumed it was something passed on through the years." Doc
remarks, eyes narrowing as we approach the northern edge,
housing stones with dates that stretch hundreds of years and the
bones of the settlers who first moved here.

"It's the same person," Elochian and I say, tripping over each
other's words.

"I don't know, that's a lot for one person to do," Quentin
starts, sheepishly looking between the three of us. Loch nods
for him to continue, and he does so with such enthusiasm it
overwhelms me.

"I mean, think about *just* this year. How much work has to
be done in what, four hours or less each night? Not only a heist,
but hacking the system, planting the paintings, and everything
else I'm not thinking of because there's got to be so *much*, and
that's for this year. It *can't* be one person, and if it was, why
would you do this year after year? That's a *long* commitment."

No one says anything until our boots reach well tended sod
and ankle height, eternal wildflowers. We stand before the headstone Elochian took inspiration from. He brought to life the
masterpiece almost a hundred years ago, long before he and I
met. I forget sometimes he's nearly twice my age.

Elochian's throat works as he stares at the nondescript stone.
We face the blank side and the morbid, curious side of me wants
to break the moment and walk around, read the name of who's
buried here. I know the story, but Loch has never told me the
man's name.

The *shedim* who was chosen to grow up with him, take the brunt of his punishments and protect him with his life. It's a common practice for celestial nobility, but I've long suspected the person was a lover in the end, if not a very close friend in addition to their duties.

And in the end, he kept that promise, laying down his life for Elochian.

"We're here," Loch murmurs, nodding to the stone with his hands in his hoodie pockets. He shakes his head, frowning. "Arlo, what significance does the temple have? Why go from there to here?"

His question borders on raspy desperation, throwing me. I didn't expect him to truly want to solve this, but something like wild emotion runs behind his dark eyes. The Game is harvesting emotions and feelings relentlessly this year, tearing out my friend's hearts and laying them bare for all those who care to witness the dissection of their lives.

I'm not immune to its effects.

"I'm not sure, that was all Kitt. She said it was in the attic, dusty like it had been there for years." I admit, taking a firm hold of Loch's shoulder when I notice his wings trembling. He relaxes under my grounding touch but doesn't acknowledge me.

"Not a pious person, then." Doc adds, stroking their snout. "Can we get another look at the painting?"

Quentin pulls out his phone, unlocking it to reveal the painting as his last open screen. We all look over his shoulder and I *accidentally* push into Elochian, bumping him into Quentin's side. Quentin rolls his bottom lip between his teeth, but neither of them show any ambition to move. I focus on the task at hand and study the painting, something I've been haunted by in person.

A man wearily sits upon the grave stone before us, dressed from the waist down in trousers and boots that ride up to his knees. He's hunched over, blurry face buried in his hands and surrounded by a halo of red that drips into the stars beyond him. He might have been beautiful once, like his fine clothes, but his body is broken and discolored, clearly sick.

"It's ... evocative, Elochian," Doc finally says.

We all lean back and separate by mere degrees, as if the scene will take shape before us and blood rain will fall. Loch nods slowly, unbothered by our reactions. "Three nights after I saw ... *them*, I had a dream. I had to get it down, and this is what happened."

"A nightmare." Doc murmurs.

Quentin stares at Elochian with a renewed intensity that washes away his nervousness. "You really saw them, didn't you?"

Loch doesn't break his gaze from the headstone, brows furrowing. "Sometimes I wonder if I ever did, or if the ghost I saw was me."

His hoarse voice drifts off and I take a gentle hold of Elochian's shoulder. "I believe you, Loch."

Loch snorts, gaze shifting to me as he relaxes under my touch. "No offense, but you're not any more sane than I am."

All three of my so-called friends laugh, and I can't help but join in.

I clap my hands together. "Alright, alright. We have a send off to attend, let's look around and see what we can find."

Loch pairs up with Doc, and Quentin goes with me. We meander to the northwestern region while the other two take the northeastern and I dodge spirits the whole way. Voices rise in the distance from several groups of the living, other puzzlers come to do what we're doing. Time to hurry it up.

"Doing alright?" Quentin asks, and not because of the ghosts, he knows that I'm used to them. I wasn't always, but he wasn't around for that.

I smile at Quentin with all the energy I can muster right now. "Yeah, fine. Just ... busy in the head, you know?"

Quentin nods solemnly. "Yeah, I do. You know I'm here if you need me, right? I know we're not as close as you and Cas, or you and Kitt are, but we're still friends, right?" He looks over to me with a shy smile.

"Oh Quentin, of course we are." I abruptly take hold of him and squish Quen into a hug. He yelps into my chest and the sound transforms into a laugh. "Thanks Q,"

I open my lips to admit more, but Doc calls, "Over here!"

Quentin and I sprint over to the beast and demon standing before a freshly dug grave. A large, ornate and weathered stone stands guard at the head of the hole, half the text has crumbled away. A few rows ahead of us is the headstone we were congregated behind earlier.

"The man in the painting must've been facing this," Doc explains, gesturing to what's left of the words of the stone we stand before, one I've never noticed.

'In Remembrance of — -
Savior of — and friend to all, —-
Thank you — for your continued —-
Rest in Peace —-'

A small canvas rests not in the hole, but at the base of the crumbling stone. One so old, I'm sure it's pre-Levena, whatever that is. There's no history on what came before the city. If only Tobias were here, but then again, touching a memorial stone probably isn't pleasant. I've been here many times, but this stone ....

I kneel down and gingerly pick the canvas up, reminded of my date with Thatch. A solar surfer rides the sunset, figure composed of orange, red and golden scribbles that extend down into the earth, tethering the person to the ground, even from such a height. Warmth and ... hope, perhaps, radiates from the painting, but the connections are what catch my eye and dampen the figure's freedom.

"What the hell does this mean?" I mutter.

Everyone looks at me.

"If you don't have a clue, there's no way we do," Quentin says.

I give him a stern look. "Need I remind you that *you* found the second painting, Kitt found the third, and I only found the fourth because she helped me. This is a joint effort, here."

Quentin flushes adorably, and Elochian clears his throat, shifting his gaze from cute Quen to an incoming hoard of puzzlers. "We can debate later, let's go." Elochian grits out, his distorted voice more strained than usual.

"Agreed." The rest of us say, quick to leave the cemetery.

I'm not off the hook that easy, though. I find myself at the back of the group, alone and walking slow. Cold stabs into my external ward and I roll my head, glaring to the right. I lock eyes with a spirit retaining a loose visage of its former self, its form no more than a transparent cloud of pale green. Not a permanent resident, then.

"Yes?" I ask, crossing my arms. "If you need something, all you have to do is ask politely. Touching someone without consent has consequences, you know."

A garbled voice fights with itself, echoing in my head painfully. I refuse to let it show, especially since Quentin and the others are watching me now.

"Leon wantsss to play." The spirit hisses out a giggle. Twin pools of neon green blink into existence, taking shape vaguely where their head would be.

My heart throbs and my hands drop into fists at my side. I give the spirit my full attention, summoning an angry orb of magick into my hand. A banishment spell. I skip all the things I would try first to minimize the draw on my heart.

The spirit retreats a few feet but I extend my free hand, curling my fingers in. A translucent rope conjures to life, barreling for the ghost and pinning it into place. I chuckle darkly, trying on the tone of Retired Hero That Doesn't Give A Fuck.

It fits nicely.

"Then tell him to quit being a coward and visit me himself."

I yank on the rope, simultaneously thrusting the orb forward into the spirit's body. It screams, an awful, petrifying sound that rattles my bones. I haven't forced a spirit to the Other Side in a long time, but this one can fuck all the way off.

The smoke emanating from the spirit's forced departure is visible to the physical realm, the only evidence to the crowd now gathered that I'm not dueling air. I stagger forwards and Elochian's arm slips under my shoulders, steadying me.

"Arlo, what the *hell* was that?"

Quentin stands guard on my other side, glaring at the crowd that Doc attempts to redirect. I groan, leaning on Loch heavily which draws Quentin's attention. "Do they all look like that, Arlo?"

I blink at him. "Y-you could see it?"

Quentin and Elochian trade a look. "Yes," Quentin says, a little unsure. "Were we not supposed to?"

"Fuck." I grit out, standing on my own two feet after a minute. "No, definitely not. If Leon has the power to corporealize spirits from wherever he is, he's not far off from returning."

Loch awkwardly pats me on the back. "Maybe it's time you talk to Gaia."

I wince at the Necromancer's name and shake my head. "I'm not going to bother her, not yet. If things get worse, then I will, but not a day sooner."

Loch doesn't push it, he and Quentin stick close to my sides as we leave the Netherspring behind. Doc's gaze burns into my back the whole way, waiting for me to crumble under the old, traumatic memories that I've shared with Gaia, Tobias, and all the others.

I straighten my shoulders and walk just a bit taller.

Doc and Elochian separate from us at the main drag. Loch offered to return the painting, and Doc headed home to their wife. Quentin and I walk the streets together, talking about everything and nothing for a little while. We don't talk about ghosts, enemies, crushes or anything of real importance.

But when a beat of silence hits, I turn bold.

"Hey, have you by chance talked to Thatch lately?"

Quentin blinks at me, wordlessly trying out Thatch's name like he's having trouble placing the man. "Thatch?" He tries out loud, stretching out the name, then his eyes widen and he nods quickly. "Oh, Thatch, no, not since the other night, when we all went out?" His words rise into a question, like I'm supposed to know.

"Yeah ..." I'm unable to shake off an unsettling feeling.

"Oh! That's right. Loch and I stopped in yesterday afternoon for coffee, but I didn't see him. Sorry, I haven't been getting much sleep lately, brain's a little fuzzy."

We turn down Garren Road and my stomach twists for an altogether different reason. Kleo's departure. "Coffee, hm? Loch never goes to coffee with me." I tease, changing the subject.

Quentin laughs, adjusting his pink frames. "Yeah, he likes our booth, says it's quiet. I think he'll be going back again, which is good, right?"

I doubt it's the coffee Loch likes. I smile at Quentin and slide my arm around his shoulders, pulling him in for a hug. "Yeah, it's good, Quentin. Real good."

When he and I arrive at Garren Castle, Kitt, Lindsey and Gowan are standing outside the open front doors with coffees and tired smiles. The fact I've been up for hours already disorients me to the notion that it's early morning for them. We all hug and say our good mornings.

"Where's Cas?" I ask Kitt after she finishes rubbing her horn on my shoulder.

She grunts something under her breath, then says, "He came and went already, said he's gotta get ready for tomorrow."

I huff, not believing it one bit. I woke up to a slew of guilt filled texts from him, apologizing profusely and asking if I was alright. I sent him back only two words.

I'm fine.

"I'll be glad when the season is over." I notice the boxes of pastries in Lindsey and Gowan's arms, growing hopeful. "Thitwhistle's busy today?"

"Yeah and no," Gowan says, while Lindsey stares into space. "He wasn't there, by the way." Gowan adds, moss thickening along her neck.

If I were more dignified, perhaps I'd feel ashamed of the way I instantly slump. Kitt knocks my shoulder with a horn. "He's probably sick."

"Maybe," I say, glancing back at a spaced out Lindsey. "Alright, Linds?"

The elf startles, blinking exhaustion ridden eyes. Is *anyone* sleeping lately?

"Yeah, just, thinking about tomorrow. Last game and all." Lindsey offers, smiling halfheartedly. Her blonde hair is pulled into a messy bun, a very not-Lindsey look, especially when paired with her jogger sweats and hoodie.

"Why don't we take a nap after this, we both have the day off for once," Kitt says, leaving me for her girlfriend. She kisses Lindsey's forehead and takes the boxes from her, earning a genuine small smile from her lover.

"That'd be nice."

Kleo's parents are not what I expected, and in all the best ways.

Gareth, Nienna, and Eilae Krisgella have seven children between them, four from marriages of old and three from their new partnership. Kleo, Felix and all seven Krisgella children occupy the pirate ship, accompanied by the children who live in the Castle.

Instead of being offended or overwhelmed by a party of emotional adults they've never met before sending off their new daughter like Kleo is our own, they welcome us with open arms.

Gareth has endless laugh lines, callused hands and kind eyes. He radiates eternal patience, something he'll need for Kleo.

Nienna is the moons reincarnate, all bright and wise and elegant. She greets each of us with a hug, asking first if that's '*quite alright.*'

Eilae is nothing like her seemingly docile partners, but an explosive ball of cheerful energy that the children eat up. She's currently Captain Felix's First Mate, fending off pirates with Kleo as the new Captain steers them to safety.

"They're such good friends," Gareth notes, nodding to Felix and Kleo. Then, he looks between Dusan and I. "Ms. Garren told us how important Kleo's relationship to Felix is. We'll be staying in touch so they can visit each other, even after he's adopted."

A burden tumbles off my shoulders. "Oh, that's—that's good."

Nienna laughs softly, gently touching my arm as she does. "We can see more than just Felix will miss Kleo. Rest assured, our farm is just outside of Vieta, you're all more than welcome to visit Kleo any time. As long as you don't mind paw prints or mud."

"I think we can deal with that," I say, watching Kleo bound over with one of her mothers with a broad, honest smile upon her face. I hunch over and throw my arms around Kleo, squeezing tight. "Hey, kid. I'm gonna miss you, but your parents said we can all visit.

How's that?"

"Really! Oh Arlo, did you know that Octavian has goats and Milred–"

And on and on it goes. I listen to Kleo tell me all about her new life, all the while keeping an eye on a child sneaking away from the pirate ship to go sit in the woods alone. Felix.

The bell rings when I enter Thitwhistle's, finding the cafe surprisingly empty save for a few college students actually studying near a hearth. Silas and Helena are working, the former wipes down tables while the witch does dishes, headphones in and back turned to me. I approach the vampire and give her a tight smile, heart shredded with fear.

"Hey, Helena. How's it going today?" I ask, interrupting the peace in the cafe.

She smiles and it doesn't quite reach her eyes. She twists the washrag in her hands as she speaks. "Oh fine. Quiet day, which is nice after the week we've had."

I nod, pretending like I care about small talk right now. "Yeah, the festival's almost over, though, then it'll go back to normal."

"Yeah, almost over." Helena nods, turning away.

I follow her to the counter, glancing at the witch elbows deep in dish water. "Is Thatch around, by chance?"

"No, he won't be in today." Helena's brows furrow.

Something clicks in my mind.

I inhale slowly, corralling my magick before I implode. I did a few charms on the way here to vent some energy, leaving good luck for travelers on the trolley lines and graffiting small protective sigils onto signposts. Regardless, Rapidfire Endless Thoughts and Pissed Off Magick is a bad mix.

"Will he be back at all?"

Before she can answer, Silas approaches whilst drying his hands, drawing attention to his long, pale fingers and nails painted black with white runes drawn on them. Helena excuses herself to the kitchen without saying goodbye. That's fine, this boy and I need to talk.

His eyes are hidden by a curtain of white hair and he's dressed in minimalist, all black attire and combat boots. Silas tosses the dish towel over his shoulder, then reaches up and taps one of the earbuds in his ears, presumably shutting off his music. Silas stares at me for a moment, hands open at his sides. With the same rawness as the last time I heard him speak, he asks, "Did you read the book?"

"Wh-what?"

He sighs, rubbing the side of his head. "Obviously not. He says you're this genius that can figure it out, but I'm not so sure."

"Where is he?" I lean over the counter and Silas tilts his head, not making a move to get closer.

"He told us all yesterday that he was leaving, wouldn't be coming back. 'Everything's taken care of,' he said. Let me guess, he's ghosting you." He leans forward conspiratorially. "He says you're supposed to help me, but to be honest, not sure how much help you're gonna be after all this."

There are so many questions, but I settle on the one that can be answered the easiest. "Who are you? Why does he want me to help you?"

The witch lifts both shoulders up to his ears, rocking back on his heels as he does. "No idea, I'm just another teenage runaway, no one special. He thinks witches should stick together or something weird like that, but personally, I don't give a shit."

Silas twitches, involuntary hunching his left shoulder up and tucking his ear into it. He grumbles, looking away from me. At least, I'm pretty sure he was looking at me from under all that hair. "But when I noticed some ... *things*, it didn't take long to realize Thatch isn't who he says he is. Not that he can help it."

"What *things*?"

Silas hums lowly, then says, "Ah, that's not for me to say." He mimes zipping his lips shut and irritation heats my blood. "Don't look at me like that, it's not *my* fault. You want answers, you go read that book and listen to your friends, *then* find

Thatch. It won't be the whole story, but at least you won't be flying blind when it's time to talk, before it happens, you know?"

I pinch the bridge of my nose, blowing out a breath. "Kid, I'm having a *bad* day. I suggest you knock off the mysterio act and tell me what's going on. Before *what* happens?"

Silas tilts his head again, far enough that white locks fall and expose one icy blue eye watching me with an intensity that no boy should have. "Before he leaves and isn't *allowed* to return until we're both dead. Think about it, where is the only other place Thatch is fond of here in Levena?"

I search and search and *search* my catastrophe of a room, unable to find the book. I can't even remember the name of it now. I *know* that I fell asleep with it in my lap the other night. Where *is* it?

I pull up the link to the article Kitt sent me, only to be directed to a crashed site.

I call her, but she doesn't answer.

I try Caspian, but he doesn't answer.

Fuck it.

Forget You

Thatch

I walk through the cottage, fingers tracing shelves now bare of personal knick knacks and shined up dark wooden trim that contrasts cream walls. I pull soft purple curtains back from the windows, allowing the afternoon sun to stream in and warm the bones of this place. I did my best over the years to make it feel home, but it's not meant for me. I won't be able to come back to it, and this place needs to be lived in, loved.

The road cutting through the universe is where I belong.

I lean against a counter in the kitchen, watching dust and other particles dance in the rays of light washing the plank floors in warmth. I haven't left the island since bringing the bard here and it's the first time I've been alone with my thoughts since then. The trio had left before I awoke, leaving a note saying they would be back Saturday morning. Perhaps they think I need time to sort my affairs, but there's not much left to do.

Someone is *very* close to solving the Game and it's likely we'll be leaving much sooner than Saturday.

I pull Arlo's jacket tighter around my perpetually cold bones, burying my nose in the collar and inhaling his scent. I replay our kiss over and over again, hoping it was a good enough memory to leave him with. With a sigh, I decide that it's time to stash the jacket with the rest of my things. I should feel bad for stealing it from him, but it may very well be all that I'll have left of him.

I comb a shaking hand through my knotted curls, wincing when snarls trap my fingers. I pull my hood back up after accidentally pushing it down, needing to hide under every layer I possibly can today. I reach inside the jacket and pull out a small jar with the herbs Kitt gave me, Arlo's pipe that I found inside the jacket, and a matchbook. I quickly pack a bowl, something I've become quite fond of the past couple days, a passion my new friends and I share. My stuff is better than theirs, though.

I open the dutch door leading from the kitchen to the back yard, a lawnless garden flanked by fruit trees and traversable only through a path of stepping stones. I shut the door behind me, then light the herbs and exhale smoke rings into the cool air. I smile, thinking about how impressed Arlo would be if he could see me now, then cough and am humbled immediately.

I wander with intention through the woodland hiding the cottage. I smoke and absorb the island as it exists in this moment of time, noting how a soft breeze jostles the colorful leaves above me. Mushrooms dot the landscape, thriving under the damp atmosphere. Squirrels chitter and crows call to each other as they follow me. I finish my pipe upon reaching a pebble blanketed beach occupying the eastern shore of Leideen Ait.

An odd chunk of bedrock stands tall in the center of the beach, seemingly plucked from the deepest seas and dropped here. Shells, fossils and tiny rocks compose the sedimentary giant, accompanied by swirling marks burned onto the ancient surface. A shimmering, rainbow aura surrounds the stone, the only indication of the portal lying in wait.

I press my hand to the only lifelong constant I've had in this, or any world. Air whooshes from my lungs when my palm connects with the cold stone that has an identical sibling in every dimension, all made for people like me. Now, I'm the only one left who can use them.

"I know, it's almost time." I whisper to the innocuous stone, pressing my forehead to its surface. I cough, splattering blood across it. I grimace, wiping my mouth with the back of my hand. It has nothing to do with the smoke and everything to do with my impending end. I leave the stone to its vigil over the river and set to work.

I cross the beach and roll over an inconspicuous fallen log dressed in moss and time, revealing leaf litter and pebbles from the nearby shore beneath it. I wave my hand, releasing pent up magick that's only been released in short bursts, all for the Game. Arlo's magick has sustained me thus far, if it weren't for him I would've been dragged away by now, but I can't *use* his energy.

A rumbling ensues beneath my feet, then planks of battered wood rise to the surface, pushing pebbles and sod out of the way until a trap door swings open and thuds back against the ground. I stare into the hole that contains all my personal possessions, except for the jacket along my shoulders.

I shake out my arms and exhale heavily, then drop into the darkness.

By the time I ascend from my stash, twilight has fallen and rain thrashes the river, forcing overhanging branches to dip under the surface. Without Arlo's jacket my teeth chatter and the storm does nothing to improve my pathetic state. I tug my hood down over my face and sprint to the cottage, stumbling over branches and across the slick ground.

Howling wind rips the fabric back and I wince at a new onslaught of rain pelting my face. There's no beacon to lead me home, the cottage's windows are darker than the slivers of sky visible through the canopy. When I trip into the wide clearing housing the cottage, I tuck my head down and squeeze one eye shut, running as fast as I can. I hop onto the first step leading to the front door, only to crash into a drenched figure.

I scream, but it's short lived.

"Thatch." Arlo Rook grits my name like it physically pains him.

Scalding hands take a firm hold of my shoulders. I throw my head back and stare up into darkened eyes, chest heaving. He's *here*. I can only imagine what I look like right now, dressed in my rattiest sweatpants and hoodie, beyond exhausted and wild eyed.

I can't *breathe*. I thought I wouldn't see him again. Things ended as well as they could have, and now ....

"Arlo, why are you here?" I ask, trembling.

Arlo's eyes flare to violent neon green, lighting up the rain separating our faces. His steady hands leave my shoulders, sliding up either side of my neck until resting on my cheeks. His thumbs swipe back and forth across my wet skin, warming me from the inside out. With a tender expression that dares me to try and lie to him, Arlo Rook asks,

"Thatch, who am I to you?"

My lungs catch on freezing rain and I reach up, blanketing his hands with my own.

"Mine, Arlo. You're mine."

Whereas our first kiss was chaste and sweet and heartwarming, this one is fierce and strikes with such a violence it rivals the lightning cracking overhead. The world quakes when I wrap my arms around Arlo's neck, yanking his desperate body closer to mine.

His hands slide under my thighs, lifting me effortlessly and without breaking the kiss. A swirl of emerald is the only indication when Arlo's magick tears the front door open, the cracking sound intermingles with the storm.

I don't care. I kiss him until I can't breathe, and then he's there to offer the air I desperately need and can only receive from him.

A wall slams into my back and I grunt into his mouth, earning a moan in return. I roll my hips and his fingertips dig into my thighs, the sensation is intensified by the slide of his tongue against mine.

I dig my fingers into his hair and pull, exposing his neck to me. I leave the comfort of his lips to place open mouth kisses along his beautiful soul mark glowing just for me, illuminating the darkness between us. I move further down, whimpering when the skin over his pulse vibrates with intensity. Magick hums beneath my tongue.

"Thatch," Arlo pants into my hair, "don't you dare give up, and don't you *dare* try to leave without a proper goodbye."

"Arlo—" I start, then am swiftly cut off when Arlo's lips overtake mine. He nips my bottom lip and gently tugs. I moan, unable to do anything else. He pins me in place with a fiery stare that I cannot break away from, nor do I want to. I don't want to argue and spend our last moments trying to convince him what I know to be true.

In a few days, or tonight, even, the Game will be over and I'll be gone, ferrying the anomalies to the world they belong in. And then the next, and the next, and the next.

Instead, I grip the back of his neck and pull his forehead to mine. "Okay, Arlo. Okay. I'm not giving up."

Arlo searches my eyes, then hoists me up and pulls us away from the wall. "Where's the bedroom?" He asks gruffly.

A nervous laugh falls out of me. "Um, upstairs?"

Arlo nods once and kisses me, much softer than before. "We don't have to do anything, Thatch. I just want to be with you, whether it's kissing or sleeping or staying up late and staring into each other's eyes for hours like they do in the movies."

I giggle, then press a barely there kiss to his lips. "Bring me to bed, Arlo." I whisper, and he does. He climbs the stairs with me in his arms like it's nothing and I rest my head on his shoulder.

"Which room?" He breathes the question into my hair and I shudder.

"The first," I whisper, directing him to the master bedroom I haven't slept in. Can't sleep in.

Without another word, he steps into the room and lays me down on the freshly made, king size bed. He straddles my hips and looms over me, bracing himself with a hand beside my head. With his free hand, he caresses my scruffed cheek with his thumb.

I stare up at him, chest rising and falling rapidly.

Arlo studies my face, licking his bottom lip as he considers his next words. When he speaks, he looks away from me. "Are you sure this is alright? It's ... been a long time, for me. I can't guarantee I'll be any good."

Arlo huffs out a baseless laugh and I slide my hands beneath his wet shirt. His eyes flutter closed, adding to the heady feeling swelling in my bones. I can't believe that I make him feel like this. *Me.* His erection slides against mine, both of us separated by clothing and trapped between closely melded bodies.

Such small words keep replaying in my head. Us. Our. *We.*

"That makes two of us, but I think we'll do just fine." I murmur, brushing my nose against his. Arlo kisses me through a nervous smile and I can't help but smile too. He leans back a little, eyes flicking to the lamp on the bedside table.

"No lights, please." I shake my head, anxiety swelling for the first time.

"That's fine," he says, then rests back on his heels. He takes hold of the hem of his shirt, slowly peeling it off his body. Even in the darkness, the shape of his broad hips and mountainous shoulders are plain to see. There's hardly any light coming through the windows at all, restrained by the storm. Arlo takes a gentle hold of my hips and looks up to me. "Can I undress you? Is that alright?"

I bite back a whimper at his soft, clear words. They're just words.

"Yes, but ... no questions about ... about what's underneath, not now. Later, if that's that okay?"

"Of course." Arlo nods once, but he doesn't move. Lightning breaks the sky and briefly lights his face, perfectly displaying the way he chews on his bottom lip. Do *I* really want to do this in the dark?

I want to gaze upon his face, capture every detail and burn it into my memory. But to do that, I have to reveal *my* imperfections.

"Thatch, are you sure—"

Arlo

Thatch silences me with a breathtaking kiss, murmuring promises onto my lips. "Yes, I want you, Arlo, I want this. I'm nervous, that's all."

I gaze into his eyes, searching for a lie, but only find honesty. "You're safe with me, and I won't judge you for anything. You're beautiful to me, and nothing is going to change that."

He softens, trembling lips brush against mine. "I know."

I lower my nose to his jaw, nuzzling his thickened beard as I go.

"Mm, Arlo," Thatch whispers my name like final rites when I reach the hollow of his throat. He arches up into me, rocking the outline of his shaft alongside mine. Whether he means to I'm not sure, but it awakens my soul all the same. I gasp, stealing air from across the curving plane of his shoulder.

I take hold of the hem of his hoodie and he leans ahead, working with me to slide it off. My lips leave his skin for mere seconds, but it's too long. I travel back to his adam's apple and when my hand rests on his exposed side, his throat works under my lips. He's freezing, and the skin beneath my palm is rough.

"Can I keep going?"

"Y-yes. I'll tell you if it's too much."

"Promise?"

He releases a breath and laugh intermingled as one. Gods, how I wish I could see him, but this is more than I deserve as it is. I hum in contentment, tongue tracing along his collar bone. I find divots and caverns in his body, unable to tell just how they connect in the darkness. It feels different than the skin underneath my palm.

I caress his stomach, soft and full, and he trembles. His hands slide up and down my shoulders, nails grazing. "Arlo, please."

I chuckle, pressing kisses into the soft hair along his belly. "Please, hm? You're awfully polite. What do you need, darling?"

"*Arlo*," Thatch whines, rocking up into my chest. *Fuck.* "We still have *pants* on."

"That *is* a problem," I agree, then lazily swipe my tongue across one nipple while my fingers meet the other. Thatch gasps, fingers diving into my hair. "You like that?" I ask, and he moans in response when I do it again. I play for another moment, then explore downwards once more.

Thatch flinches when I lay an open mouthed kiss on his right hip, over a particularly tight and rippled patch of skin. I lay another kiss there, softer this time and allowing him a chance to tell me to stop. He doesn't, so I tug at the hem of his pants with my teeth and fingers, earning a sweet moan as the fabric slides further down.

"Please." Thatch manages to effectively knock the wind out of me with one, simple word. He plays with my hair, nails scratching against my scalp.

"Please ... what, love?" I kiss skin as it's exposed, studying his body in the darkness the only way I can. But then, a soft light stops me in my tracks, and a soft moan of pleasure escapes me.

A soulmark the size of my palm stretches across his left hip, glowing a soft orange.

The sight ignites the witch's heart in my chest and magick pumps through me with an ungodly force, intoxicating me. I trace the edges of it, processing a hundred different emotions as I face the definitive proof of what I already knew.

"You're mine." I murmur, then ever so gently, like I might erase the evidence by touching it, I press my lips to the center of the mark.

"And you're mine, Arlo." Thatch chokes on his words and I leave his hip in favor of his lips, kissing him through contagious tears.

"Hey, hey. I'm *here*. Don't worry about tomorrow, not right now. Okay? Stay here with me, stay in this moment," I whisper to myself just as much as him. He nods quickly, forehead pressed against mine. "We can get dressed, but don't—"

Thatch silences me with a punishing kiss, shoving me back with a hand to my chest, and a renewed fire to his glistening eyes. "*Love* me, Arlo."

Before I can say anything else, his hands and lips work down my body in a quicker fashion than I did his, but he savors me all the same. Biting and tasting and *needing*. He works on my jeans and I kick them off while he takes care of his own pants.

Instead of hovering over him, I lay against the headboard and pull him into my lap, offering him control. His thighs tickle my sides and my bare dick slides against his, drawing a gasp from both of us. Thatch wraps his arms around my neck and blankets my body with his. He hides his face in my shoulder despite the darkness and begins to grind against me.

"Oh, Thatch." I groan, reaching between us. I take us both in hand, the slight warmth leaking from us is just enough to wet the friction between us.

"My stars," Thatch whimpers, his nails dig into my neck and shoulder. His pace quickens, and I work us both in the same fashion. "You'll be my undoing."

"I plan on it." I grit out, feet planted on the mattress as I grind into him needily. "Kiss me, love."

Thatch unburies from my shoulder, diving in with less hesitation than he's ever had. His tongue parts my lips and sweeps against mine, smooth and hot. Just as our teeth meet, he rears back, out of breath and hips stilling. My hand pulls away immediately, but he says, "Arlo, I want to keep going."

I chuckle, settling for running my hands up and down his back as I listen. "Then why are you stopping?"

He sighs, an audible eye roll if I've ever heard one. "I *mean*, I don't want to finish like this. I want to ... you *know*."

His voice rises an octave, and I nip at his bottom lip, chuckling at his bashfulness. "Be inside me? Or do you want to be fucked? I'm fine with either love, you decide."

Thatch sputters, thighs tightening around me. "You are beyond crass."

"I think you like it, though. Don't you?" I ask, reaching down to take him in hand. He moans, forehead knocking against mine. I work him slowly, and when he doesn't answer, I pause my movements. "Tell me, I want you to ask for what you want."

"I want you inside me, Arlo, please. I need to know what you feel like, how you taste, what it sounds like when you come undone. I need it all, I'll beg if I have to. You have me at your mercy," Thatch confesses a breath width away from my lips, swallowing my resounding moan.

"My Gods, Thatcher. You put me to shame. Come here." I take him by the back of the neck, pulling him closer to me, but it's not enough. When he takes my cock in hand, my desperate kisses stutter. When he slides me against his entrance, I lose my mind.

We shift so he's on his back and I'm on my stomach between his legs, which he spreads for me without hesitation. I take his slender cock into my mouth and he moans, thrusting against my tongue without thought.

"Arlo, *oh*, you feel so good." His hips slowly work and his hands settle on either side of my face, fingers entwining with my hair. "*Oh*, stop me if it's too much."

I position myself better and open my throat to him, allowing him to lazily fuck my mouth with rolling, slow movements. I caress his balls which tighten when my fingers brush against them, then explore further down and massage his hole. He works faster, whining for me to keep going.

I release his shaft with an obscene, wet noise, then slick my fingers and go back to what I was doing. I slide one into him, moaning around his cock when his heat tightens around me. Thatch gasps, hands flying to my hair and the bedspread, clutching both desperately.

I lift my head again, leaving his shaft to press a wet kiss to his hip. I grind against the bed, the pleasure-pain arcs down my spine, spreading throughout my body like wildfire. "Relax, love. Let me see you touch yourself, show me what you like."

Thatch sighs, fingers loosening in my hair by a shade. I trace my tongue over another scar, waiting until he takes hold of himself. When he does, I massage just inside the ring of muscle and allow him to set the pace. He ruts into his fist slowly and with meaning, rolling his hips in such a sensual way it's like nothing I've ever seen. I've never had slow, intentional sex before, but watching Thatch as he loves himself in luxurious, long motions, is fucking beautiful.

I didn't know it could be like this.

I lift up and wrap my free arm around his waist, trapping his thigh between my legs. After aligning our bodies, I slip another finger inside him and shamelessly grind against his leg. Thatch's hips and hand stutters when my pace increases and I find his sweet spot, stroking against it with a fervent need.

"Arlo, wait, I'm going to—"

"Yes, come for me Thatch, don't hold back." I murmur onto his stomach, nuzzling into the sticky happy trail just above his cock.

"Good fuck," Thatch moans, snaking an arm around my neck and holding me tight to his stomach. His other hand strokes up and down his flushed cock once, twice, then a third stilted time. He releases and I stick out my tongue, catching some of the mess that spills. I thrust against his side, groaning at the taste of him.

"Let me have you," he says, pushing me back onto the bed. He straddles my waist and covers my body with his own, smearing his mess onto my stomach. Thatch kisses me with a new, confident tenderness, reaching around to align us.

"Ready?" He asks without breaking our kiss, and I laugh into his mouth.

"I'm ready, Thatcher Gaillot."

We both gasp and I find purchase in the softness of his cheeks, spreading him further. "Oh, love." I pant onto his lips, thrusting into him using the same slow, easy movements that Thatch seems to like. "You feel so good, darling. Made for me, isn't that what you said?"

After a few moments of working myself inside him slowly, I find myself buried deep inside my person. We are one and the same, there is only us.

Thatch whispers, "Yes, and you're made for me, my *leva*."

The endearment warms my heart, pumping love into every molecule of my being. He leans back, riding me with purpose that defies my slow efforts. "Oh, fuck, don't stop, that's so good." I groan, unable to hold back. I plant my feet and match his pace with firm hands encasing his hips.

Thatch cries out, one hand reaching back to take hold of my knee while the other grips the headboard behind me. "Make me yours, *please*."

"You don't have to beg, I'm already yours, now and always, Thatch, no matter where we are, no matter what happens." Magick rolls through my body in a wave, ready to be released. The vibrations along my skin return, startling a moan out of Thatch.

Am I seriously a *vibrator* right now?

I'm forced to file that away for *later* when Thatch's energy opens to mine like it did when we kissed for the first time. I can *breathe* again.

Over-energized magick pours into Thatch's being like an endless receptacle needing to be filled. Even in the darkness I can see the difference in his eyes, a brightness that wasn't there before. The ache I'm left with when Thatch isn't near me disappears entirely, replaced by ... something freeing, *endless*.

I don't pass out this time when my energy joins with his. Instead, I orgasm with an intensity I've never experienced before, the euphoria something I've never come close to achieving through bad habits, sex, or any other means. I shoot up to sitting and wrap my arms around Thatch, burying my face into his chest while I release inside him for what feels like an eternity.

He cries and holds me closer to him, breathing heavily into my hair.

Rain pounding upon the roof is the only noise that accompanies our breathing, neither of us ready to speak or move. Because when we do, the world will resume turning and reality will sweep away all that we've done tonight.

But for now, Thatch runs his fingers through my hair and I soften inside him, tracing my fingers up and down his spine.

We're both a mess, but when I lay us down and snuggle behind Thatch, he doesn't complain.

In fact, he entangles with me every way he can, pulling my arm around his waist and hooking his legs with mine. He falls asleep before me with a smile on his face. I wait a few minutes after his breathing evens out, then kiss the back of his neck and leave a promise there.

"I won't forget you again."

Friday

Not Yet

Thatch

Thunder rocks the house, startling me awake. A strong arm tightens around me, holding me close to a warm chest. Strangled daylight illuminates the bedroom and my impossible predicament. Arlo's fingers running up and down my thigh slung over his stomach, my drooling face nestled into his neck and hair.

We're naked, and he can see me now. The blankets are pooled around our waists, and I can't bear to look at myself or peek up and see where he's looking. My eyes burn. Of course he's seen my body, he was awake first. Will he still want to love me like the way he did last night after this?

"Morning." Arlo murmurs one word so raw and deep it works me up immediately, but my mind is *not* on the same page as my body.

"Mm, is that what time it is?" I hide my nose under his ear, unable to come to terms with the pity that must be written all over his face.

He chuckles, continuing his feather light caress of my thigh, rising dangerously higher every other stroke. "*Well*, if you want to be technical, it's almost noon."

I groan at the thought of being a person today, of having to leave this bed and Arlo's arms. If this is my last day, then I want to spend it like this. We should've spent them *all* like this.

Arlo kisses the top of my head, gently laying me back on the mattress. He stares into my eyes with a mischievous grin. "I hope you know time has no meaning today. I'm not going to work, and neither are you."

"Oh, that's ... is that *okay*?" I finally say, unable to form a coherent thought because his eyes are gold and green and *beautiful*. Relief washes over my frayed nerves and I temporarily forget my worries.

Arlo brushes his lips against mine ever so gently, then nudges my nose with his. "Of course it is. Shower?"

"It's a tub." I arch into him, curling my fingers into his hair. I bury my nose into the hollow of his throat, clinging to him. He strokes my back, tracing over the road map of my body. His palm rests over a patch of burned skin stretching over my hip, thankfully the fire didn't take my soulmark.

And before I can protest, he scoops me up and into his arms, dragging us both out of bed. "Arlo!" I squeal, flailing against his chest.

He laughs, the sound rumbles against my side with an intensity that spikes my heart rate. Arlo kisses my forehead, unable to keep his lips off me for more than a minute. "Lead the way, dear."

I flush with heat and nod to the door at the far side of the room, wrapping my arms around his neck. "It's right there, silly."

Arlo nods, all business. I laugh a little as he dramatically knocks the door open with his hip. He sets me on the edge of a claw-foot tub that's going to be a squeeze for the both of us. The bathroom is decent size, well kept and simple. Modest. Rain pummels the skylights overhead and I close my eyes, listening to the sound.

"We can go back to sleep after this, if you want. Food would be nice, though." Arlo remarks softly, and I open my eyes, finding him leaning on the sink across me, studying me with a fondness that coats his handsome features. He chews on his bottom lip, showing that rare vulnerability that only I seem to coax out of him. "I have questions, Thatcher."

I nod slowly, fighting the urge to look away. I owe him this much. "I'll tell you what I can. I ... I assume you remember me?"

"I have fragments of you there when Leon and I ..." Arlo shakes his head, jaw ticking. He steps forward and turns on the faucet, guarding me from the cold water until it warms up. He searches the room and I can't bring myself to tell him where the soap is because this is *it*.

A chance to face my life head on for what it is. I may not be able to tell him everything, but I'll tell him what I can, to his *face*, because he deserves that. Not me *'ghosting'* him or whatever Silas called it.

I gather the shred of courage that Arlo seems to bring out of me, because if he can convince me to jump out of a hundred story building on a rickety flying board, then I can do this.

"We've only met twice," I blurt out, startling Arlo as he pours the soap under the running water, causing him to drop the bottle into the tub. I reach forward at the same time he does, our foreheads collide violently.

"Oh fuck! I'm so sorry, are you alright?" I groan, hands flying to my temple. Arlo barks out a laugh and I blink at him. "What? What's so funny?"

Arlo kisses me swiftly, giving me the slightest hint of a smile against my lips. "You, swearing. It's cute."

My shoulders relax and I laugh despite myself. "*Stop*, I'm being serious. Did I hurt you?"

He shuts off the water and gestures for me to sit in the tub, so I do. He steps in behind me and wraps his arms around my shoulders. Water sloshes onto the floor and he kisses the back of my neck. "No, you didn't hurt me."

I almost say, 'not yet,' but I don't.

His palms run up and down my arms, not trying to extricate my twisted up hands buried under the water in my lap. I clear my throat. "You didn't say anything."

"I'm waiting for you to tell me, love. All I know is there are holes in my memory, and Caspian remembers you in the time I'm missing. He remembers you bringing me home after Leon hurt me. Hell, he's convinced you're the one who fried us both. All I know is that since the first time I've met you ..." He shifts behind me, and I can picture the frown on his face.

"I know that you feel like home. I know that you were a stranger who did not feel like a stranger. I know that you are my soulmate and that you are telling the truth, that you *can't* stay. I *think* that you want to stay, or I hope that you do."

"Of course I do." A ragged breath escapes my chest. I lift my hands from the water and cross his arms over my chest, gripping his forearms with all my might.

"I've never belonged anywhere, because I can't. I have a ... *job* to do, it's my calling, what I was *made* for. I do what I have to in one place, then I'm pulled to the next. I don't choose where I go or when. I'm allowed short bursts of free time, which is a relative construct in itself, time is. Could be a week in one world, ten years in another. But when I'm able to, I come here. The time I was allowed to stay used to be longer, but They ... they don't like it, I think. What I've been doing."

"They?"

I nod. "My ... *bosses*."

Arlo bends down and kisses my shoulder, my gouging scars.

I wait for questions I cannot answer. I wait for anger. I wait for him to ask about my body. I know he's seen the damage, *felt* it. Last night he kissed all of my body, worshiped it, even. My desire sparks as he continues to pepper my shoulders, neck and the top of my head with delicate kisses, humming softly as he does.

"I don't heal, magickally," I say, barely pushing the words out. "And I've lived a long time."

"You don't have to explain them, not if you don't want to." Arlo murmurs behind my ear. "But I will always be ready to listen."

"How are you so calm right now?" I breathe out, trembling. "How are you just *listening* and not asking and demanding and, and—"

He turns me in his arms and I straddle his waist, echoing how we were joined last night. Water splashes onto the floor and I hold my breath as he stares into my eyes, cupping my jaw with both his enormous hands.

"Because you need me to be. Because I'm going to do whatever it takes to keep you here. Because I believe in you, and me. I listen to you because no one else has, but I always will."

"Fuck, Arlo." I bite out through tears and try to look away. "You can't fight this."

He gently shakes me, forcing me to look him in the eyes, to face this. "Then I will love you with everything I have, right here, right now, and I will be here when you return." Arlo promises, like it's a given. I close my eyes, and he shakes me again until I open them. "I will *not* forget you again. I promise."

"You can't promise that," I cry, staring deep into twin pools of simmering gold. "You've forgotten me once. Everyone does. It's ... a side effect. It's something I've been *fine* with until I met you."

He smiles, wet and breaking and *brilliant*. "I'm pretty great, aren't I?"

I splash at him, and he laughs, pulling my face to his. I laugh onto his lips. He wipes my cheeks with his thumbs, and his tongue slides past mine. I move with him in an attempt to deepen the kiss, but he leans back.

Arlo brushes a curl out of my eye, breath quickening. "Tell me how we first met."

I take a firm hold of his shoulders. "Oh, Arlo. I don't know. I've written it down, perhaps it would be better if you read it."

He rocks his hips, *completely* manipulating me when he whispers, "Please?" into my ear. His hands envelope my hips, thumbs massaging deep into my skin.

"Fine." I blow out a long breath before I begin. "When I come here, I always return to this island. The last time I came, I had gathered my things and was heading into Levena. I'm always excited, it had been so long since the last time I came, but something was different this time."

"Sap," Arlo whispers, fingers tracing from my hip, up my spine, and back down again.

I knock my head against his. "I'm *serious*. I could feel that someone in this world was looking for me, well, the *idea* of me. People like me don't have attachments, let alone a *soulmate*. But it was ... this unknown pull I couldn't deny, one I didn't *want* to deny for once in my life."

"What do you mean?" Arlo pulls back, resting a palm over my heart. He stares into my eyes, waiting patiently and seemingly unbothered by the battleground beneath his hand. He makes me forget that I'm utterly naked for long stretches, and then it hits me.

I swallow, looking up to the skylight centered above us. "When it's ... *time to go,* there's a ... tugging in my chest, like They're dragging me to the next place. But it's not like that with you. I don't feel right until we're together, and when we are, it's like ... like I'm in your orbit, unable to get closer or farther away. Always from the outside looking in."

"I feel like that too, with you. You make me feel better." Arlo admits before pressing a kiss to my shoulder. My eyes flutter shut and a shaky breath leaves me. He gently cups my elbow and kisses down my arm, dangerously close to the slash lines. "Keep going, tell the story."

I nod, fighting the urge to hide, pull away. What good would it do now?

I clear my throat and open my eyes. He's staring at me with such love in his eyes, such *love*. Is it really all for me?

"You were sitting on the river's edge, talking to a family of water nymphs. Just talking, like it was the most normal thing in the world and they weren't fabled bloodthirsty beasts."

He grins against my wrist, wet lashes glittering as he looks up to me. "Because they're not."

I chuckle. "Well *I* know that, but most people don't."

Arlo scoffs, clearly displeased. "I'm not most people."

"Are you going to let me finish?"

"Yes, darling." Arlo murmurs, then traces his tongue over the light blue veins of my wrist. My ears burn and I lay my head on his chest, watching him memorize my palm and fingers with his lips.

"You noticed me right away, gave me that same look you did in the Market," I whisper, swiping my hand back and forth across his firm pectoral.

He peers down at me, forgetting my hand for a moment. "Look?"

"Like you saw me. Like I existed. As a person whose general purpose involves no real existence, it ... it was a profound moment in my life, those days by the river. I offered you my hand, and you pulled me down beside you, demanding to know everything about me.

"We sat there together for hours with the nymphs, and we met every day after that, at the same place, for two weeks. When I asked you why not the castle, you got quiet, so I let it go. I wish now that I had pushed harder, but ... I was selfish. I didn't want you to be angry with me. You held none of the disdain for me then that you did this time around."

My attempt to tease falls flat. Arlo brings my hand to rest on his shoulder, then wraps his arms around me and rests his chin on my head. He breathes heavily, heart pounding beneath my ear. I hope that he'll remember the time we shared, but something is different about Arlo. He's not like Dusan, or Caspian.

"I don't remember any of it, Thatch."

I inhale sharply like I've been punched in the gut. I expected it, but hearing him say it aloud is heart wrenching. "I know ... I'm sorry, Arlo. I don't mean to do it. It happens to everyone."

"But Dusan remembers you," Arlo counters, almost defiant. "And Caspian remembered."

"Dusan *forgets* me, she remembers me after I return and remind her, but without physical proof as a constant reminder ... this time, I didn't think she would. I don't know why she can recall me better than others, we've been trying to figure it out for ages. I would be willing to bet Caspian doesn't remember everything, just fuzzy details, like a bad dream. That's all I am to people."

"Not to me," Arlo says, softer this time. "And don't you say not yet."

I curl tighter into his chest. "And what is your plan then? Do you have one?"

He chuckles. "*Not yet,* but I have a *qieren*, *shedim*, fae, elf, human, and two witches at the very least who are willing to help. You have friends, you know. They won't forget you either. I won't let them."

"Smartass." I mutter, tearing apart his statement. "Does that mean you met Silas?"

Arlo groans. "Yeah, I did."

"*And*?"

"And he was all mysterious and not at all helpful, a complete smartass. I'm not sure what you want me to do with that."

I laugh. "The mystery part isn't his fault. He's trying to ... *solve* me, and found things he wasn't meant to, things that don't matter now. But the smartass is definitely all him, like another witch I know. I want you to guide him, like you're doing with Felix. He doesn't have anyone, Arlo. Thitwhistle made me promise to keep him under the table so he has a job."

He shifts uncomfortably underneath me. "Why don't we get dressed and you can tell me more over lunch?"

I agree, having long ago lost the feeling in my legs. "We might want to wash ourselves though, before getting out. That was the point, right?"

Arlo laughs.

We manage to keep our hands off each other long enough to wash, dress our bottom halves, and make it into the kitchen. I avoid my reflection and stand behind Arlo, my hands deep in his pants pockets. I rest my head between his shoulder blades as he cooks us breakfast for lunch. Thankfully, there's food left over from the ... *anomalies,* that I haven't told Arlo about and don't plan to. I have to fulfill my duty and help them save whoever needs saving.

Then it will be the next person.

The next world.

The next century, decade, new age.

Honestly, I'm past bargaining. I've gone through the stages, and I want today to be perfect. One way or another, Arlo Rook will be waking up alone, whether he believes it or not. I am what I am, and I cannot change that.

"What're you thinking about?" Arlo asks, a hand resting on my forearm as he flips an egg, crisping it to perfection.

"I want to show you something down by the beach after, if that's alright." I press a kiss to his flexing shoulder, and he hums. He reminds me of a cat, purring and humming whenever he's happy.

"Only if *I* can show you a thing or two at the beach." He murmurs, plating our food.

My kiss transforms into a small nip. "My goodness, have you always had these filthy thoughts about me? If so, you're incredibly well versed in restraint."

"Indeed I am," he says, then turns in my arms and grips my hips. "Do you want honesty?"

I stand on my tip-toes and kiss him with intent. He follows my slow and steady pace, a hand sliding through my freshly washed curls. I smile at him after leaning back. "Of course."

"Let me tell *you* how we first met." He lifts me up, hands under my thighs, then sets me on the counter beside our steaming plates. I hold on tight to his shoulders, grinning like a kid as he starts talking, all bravado.

"Here I was, minding my own business and looking for *oranges* out of all things. I already had my own shopping done, you see. I wouldn't have even *gone* to that end of the street if Kitt didn't hound me to bring oranges for Misfit night, don't ask me why, some new recipe she wanted to try."

I can't wipe the smile off my face. One of his hands flies through the air, the other blankets my soulmark, the glowing skin peeks out from the hem of my low slung sweatpants. His own mark is shining just as bright as mine is.

"Bosko was riding upon my head like he usually does, he says it's the best vantage point but honestly? I think he likes the smell of my hair. Anyway, he screeches at me to 'watch out!' but it's too late and next thing I know, I'm holding onto this *man*.

"He's unlike anyone I've ever met before, beautiful and rough around the edges with these eyes, *oh*, his eyes are like the first summer day a babe ever experiences. And he's looking at me like I'm someone, you know? Like in the sea of people around us, only I matter to him."

"I know." I nod, sniffling. He smiles despite the silent tears tracking down his cheeks. I reach up and cup his face, he leans into my touch and covers my hand with own.

"I haven't even told you the best part." Arlo laughs quietly, closing his eyes.

"What's the best part?" I ask in a stage whisper, unable to look away at his completely open face as he confesses to me.

"I watched the stars explode in his eyes. He had never seen fireworks before, can you imagine that? I saw the stars explode in his eyes and a part of myself that I shut down for *years* tore out of me with a fierceness that scares me to this very moment. I was scared, so *terrified* of it that I told that man 'no thanks' because who wants to get their heart broken again?

"But then, *then,* I couldn't stop thinking about him, and I had these thoughts I haven't had in years. What would it be like to kiss him, hold him, love him? We kept running into each other, *literally*, and who am I to evade what's meant to be?" His eyes flutter open, and he stares right into my very soul. "Who are we to turn away from what we're made for? No matter how much it hurts."

I answer him the only way I know how, because words are not enough.

They will never be enough.

I wrap myself around him and dive into his parted lips. He closes the distance and hoists me into his arms. My nails drive into his back and he moans into me, exhaling magick and lust. "Sorry." I murmur, but he shakes his head.

"You can't hurt me, but you can try."

Something is different about the way we touch each other now. Last night was reverence and memorization and love. But this, *this* is different.

I don't think of myself as a particularly violent person, despite the many creatures I've slain and battles I've fought. But when I tear from Arlo's lips and bury my face into his shoulder, I bite him without thought, needing to meet his challenge.

Before shame can heat me, Arlo purrs, hands digging into my ass and hair. He carries me to the dining room table, laying me out upon it. He stands between my spread legs and stares down at me with pupils blown, tongue washing over his bottom lip. "Fuck, Thatch. Is that what you like? Tell me, love."

A hand rests on my stomach, smoothing through the ginger hair there and following it up to my chest. I breathlessly watch him study me like I'm beautiful, like none of the destruction marring my body matters to him. His gaze flicks to mine and he raises a brow, waiting for my answer.

"I–I don't know. To be honest, I'm probably the inexperienced one here. Sex wasn't … I have too many feelings, and not enough time to do anything about them."

His fingers travel away from my tattoo, sliding up my neck, then to my lips. Arlo's thumb brushes over my bottom lip, skin rough and pressure feather-light. "Well, tell me anything I do that you like, and that you don't like, okay? *Especially* what you don't like."

"Okay," I whisper against his thumb, then capture it in my mouth.

He chuckles darkly, grinding against my erection straining through my pants. I moan around him, rocking my hips in time to his. His free arm hooks around my knee, pulling me closer as he moves against me. Arlo's thumb slips free from my mouth and his hand slides down to the small of my back, aligning us further. I arch forward and he groans, the outline of his hard cock presses into mine.

"I could come just like this." He grits out, bending down to mouth at my neck.

"I want to feel you against me, lose the pants and we can keep going."

"Your wish is my command," Arlo teases, making quick work of my pants and his. My *command*. I've never commanded anyone, not even myself.

We entangle once more, and he slicks his hand with spit, then takes hold of himself and works up *and* down with finesse. I whimper when he stops, and he gives me that evil smile. "You like watching me?"

I bite my lip, then nod. "You're breathtaking, my *leva*."

Arlo softens, losing some of that mischievousness but not all. He kisses me, then guides my hand to my own cock. I'm on display for him, laying out naked on my dining room table in the middle of the day, under full light. He's not looking at my damage though. He's licking his lips and watching me slowly thrust into my fist with that same awestruck expression I caught a glimpse of last night when I did this.

I kiss him, and he kisses me, and we don't stop.

No more words are spoken. We lean on the other and work ourselves in tandem, grinding and pressing and clinging as we do. His heavy breath washes over my neck and trace amounts of slick warmth meet my hand. I release myself and take hold of a thick cheek, rutting against him as I do so.

Arlo shudders and holds me like he did before, a hand under my back and knee. I hold onto his shoulder as we thrust against the other, sweaty and sticky and *real*.

"Thatch," Arlo whispers my name and spills between us, hips stuttering. I follow closely behind, vision whiting out and electricity arcing down my spine in glorious waves. We pant on the other's shoulder, slowly releasing our death grip hold into something more like a soft embrace.

"Arlo?"

"Yes, love?"

"I think our food's gotten cold."

Arlo laughs like there's no tomorrow. "That's fine Thatch, just fine."

Where's The Justice

Arlo

A waning sun, cloudless afternoon sky, and Bosko flying overhead reflects onto the river's surface. Thatch and I stand side by side in the chilly water, bare toes digging into the silt and seagrass covered bottom. I hold his hand, and he smiles to himself, watching Bosko. He's been quiet and unnervingly at peace. While I want to believe he hasn't given up, I know that look, intimately.

He's enjoying his last day on earth.

I shift my gaze back out to the water. The breeze tosses my loose and wild hair about my face, and I inhale, filling my lungs with the brisk air. "I tried to kill myself over a year ago."

Thatch's fingers nearly break mine. "What?" He whimpers, attention whipping to me. I swallow something hard and avoid his gaze. I don't know why, but I expected that he already knew. This just got a lot harder.

I lift a shoulder, goosebumps spread across my forearms and beneath my rolled up sleeves. "It was around this time of year, closer to summer than we are now though. Everyone was starting their lives, I had won the good fight. I spent most of my life fighting Leon, hating him and the movement he created, and ... missing who he was, who he could have been."

I shake my head, pulling Thatch closer to me. He wraps his arms around my stomach, and I avoid his eyes. I need to feel his body against mine. "I don't regret killing who Leon became, but once he was gone there was just ... nothing. I felt like my purpose was fulfilled. It took a few years, but ... they didn't need me anymore. Caspian got married, filled out papers to adopt. Kitt had Lindsey, and I was in the background."

Bosko lands upon a branch overhanging our hidden part of the world. I nod up to him, giving my old friend a sad smile. "Bosko decided he wasn't done with me yet. He found Kitt, and she ... that's what I regretted for the longest time, until I met you. Not that I tried, but what it did to my friends. No one should have to find their best friend in bed, heart—" I inhale sharply, veering away from details. "Not like that."

"Arlo," Thatch chokes on a sob, and I blink out of memories, holding him even closer to me.

"Hey, it's alright." I wipe away the tears from his cheeks, then press a kiss to his forehead. I exhale relief, the sensation of his skin on mine is peace inducing.

"I apologize," Thatch whispers, gripping handfuls of my sweater. He stares up at me, blinking away tears that don't stop coming. "Caspian's right. If I had been there—"

"No," I say firmly, surprising him. I take his chin between my thumb and finger, making sure he's paying attention.

"The choices I made were mine and mine alone. Whether it's because of the fucked chemicals in my brain that I ignored or the lack of self-worth I had, or maybe a little bit of both, I spiraled, and it wasn't for a lack of support. I just didn't know how to live. I still don't, but I'm getting better. I've asked for help and everything. Where I was *going* with this, is that I know when it feels like the end. But I can promise you, there's always another road. *Don't* give up yet."

"Thank you for telling me." Thatch burrows his face into my chest and huffs out a breath, then pulls back again, like he needed a moment to recharge. He searches my face for something and I stare right back, brushing curls from his face. "Come here," he finally says, taking me by the hand.

I follow him, unable to do anything else.

He leads me to a jutting tower of bedrock emanating so much ancient energy it electrifies my bodily wards when we stand near it. When I asked him about it earlier, he said 'not yet.' Must be he's ready now.

Thatch takes my hand and presses it to the stone, laying his over top of mine. I sigh as cool energy permeates my palm and rushes up my arm, a pleasant sensation that I didn't expect. A spark connects the stone, Thatch and me.

"If all else fails, I promise to do everything it takes to return to you, Arlo. And when I do, this is where I will be. I always have, and always will. This rock and I, we're old friends of a sort. Perpetual and everlasting."

"And I promise to be here waiting." I entangle my fingers with his, meeting his tired eyes. He looks so much better than yesterday, but there's a dullness to him that I cannot deny, like a fading photograph. "Always."

While Thatch is in the bathroom, I check my phone.

I scroll through the texts in the group chat from Elochian, Quentin, Doc, Gowan, hell even Silas wrote me back too. Everyone but Caspian and Kitt have responded with their theories regarding Thatch and how to trap a maybe-probably immortal being. I've scratched binding sigils into the trim throughout the house when Thatch wasn't looking and hidden charm satchels near the doorways, but both are halfhearted attempts at binding a being you don't have a name for.

Silas isn't surprised the book is missing.

Silas: i've forgotten the name too, we're back at square one. i found it at random, but now that we're looking for it, it's gone. like the more you look for something, the harder it is to find, and when you stop looking is when you find it. we have to stop looking

Doc: We need to solve the induced amnesia before anything else.

Loch: It's more than amnesia. Who took the book? Where did Kitt's article go? Who is erasing Thatch?

Quen: Who are the bosses, you mean.

Flowers (Gowan): How's Thatch?

That question stops me short. Instead of answering anyone else, I answer her.

Me: I don't know.

I put my phone away and rest a hand behind my head, staring out the window. Thatch pads into the room a couple minutes later, clean and wearing a different pair of pants. He smiles shyly at me, hurrying into bed so fast his curls bounce. Thatch nestles into my side, throwing an arm over my stomach and a leg over my thigh. I cover us both with the comforter, then kiss the top of his head and hold him close to me. I trace the harsh scars lining the inside of the arm slung across my stomach. Thatch's heart quickens against my ribs.

I have theories regarding those scars. I desperately want to point to each injury on his body and demand 'who did this to you' like an alphahole caveman, but I don't. I know what it's like to spill your story before you're ready.

I open my lips to ask how he's doing, but he speaks first.

"Those aren't from me. I never tried to do ... *that*. It's impossible for me to. I told you before that I can't heal, magickally." Thatch whispers, hiding half his face under the covers.

"Yes, you did." I murmur, caressing the shell of his ear. He relaxes into me the slightest bit.

"Long ago, I met a man pushing the laws of morality and science at the expense of children said to have died at birth and others who would never be missed. In all my years, I had never come across an enemy I couldn't best. But he knew what I was, because he *had* someone like me, and he knew how to nullify me. I thought I was the last for so long, it was ... I couldn't believe it. I didn't have to be alone anymore, all I had to do was outsmart *one* human. It wasn't an assignment, but I did what I thought was best, at the time."

"You traded places with them," I whisper, heart racing in time to Thatch's.

He nods against me, the arm around my stomach tightens. "Yes. I thought they would send help, or at the very least I would be a fresh body and could figure out how to kill him from the inside. I couldn't leave my brethren there or allow that man to live, I knew that much. But, no one came."

Thatch gingerly sits up, allowing the blankets to fall around his waist. He bites his cheek, pointing to one of the many tri-spiral marks carved into his body. "This was his mark. One for each year."

I swallow something heavy. There are four on his front alone. His fingers travel to a four inch surgical scar on his forearm, one that's a mirror to the scar on his other arm. Wordlessly, he continues to point out precise, medical grade scars that are comparatively fresher than the obvious battle wounds and burns lying beneath. These are neat and some have small pinpricks from stitches. After a moment, I put the horrifying pieces together.

Incisions over his abdomen. Slashes over the ligaments in his wrists, there's even scars over his kidneys. I press my hand to the raised scar stretching up and down his sternum. Did they take out his heart? His lungs?

Thatch's eyes grow hazy and I quickly take his hand, startling him. He smiles at me, but there's no feeling in it.

"He tested the limits of my pain, which are endless. He dissected and put me back together while I was awake. Not because drugs don't work, you've seen that they do, but that would've *tainted* the data. He pushed and pushed and *pushed*, but my body didn't shut down, no matter what he took out of me and *eventually* put back in, because even my organs won't die. I didn't ..."

Thatch absently rubs at his heart. "I was ... insane, for a lack of a better word, at the time. I watched my heart beat on the table beside me and I didn't understand it. How was this my life? If I truly didn't need a heart, why give me a body at all? How could the An–" Thatch scowls, tongue tied. He tries again, brow furrowed. "How could They watch me suffer?"

Magick thrums beneath my skin violently and I take a deep breath. When I release it, Thatch shudders and his eyes flutter shut. I open my mouth to apologize, but a soft smile tugs at his lips. I take his hand and kiss his palm, murmuring softly so I don't lose my shit. "How did you do it?"

His eyes blink open slowly. "Do what?"

"Kill him."

His pupils dilate, revealing more to the side of Thatch shadowed in vigilante mystery. The reaction passes and he looks away, cheeks flushing. "I assure you it wasn't grand."

"Oh?" I ask, gently pushing him back onto the bed. "Do tell."

Thatch covers his face and I nudge his hands apart with my nose, then kiss his eyelids, cheekbones, mouth. Thatch's glare melts but his blush doesn't fade. "It's exactly what you're thinking. I seduced him out of his protective charms and into a coffin, neck broken." He lets out a hollow laugh, rolling his eyes.

"Oof, where's the justice?"

Thatch shakes his head. "I was tired of blood."

"Fair enough," I say, then press my lips to his. "What happened to the other—"

"Retired, for lack of a better word, by the only ones who can." Thatch mutters, looking away. "Can we go back to cuddling? I think we've ticked off the depressing stories box for today."

I wrap my arms around Thatch and roll us so he's on top of me. He squeaks and I chuckle, running my hands up and down his back. "I've got you, Thatch."

We lay together for hours, touching and talking and laughing. He traces over my tattoos, trying and failing to hide his broad smile when I tell him the blue sun is for him. When he comes to the dragon, I swipe my finger over it. The ink flares to vibrant life and the dragon flies up my forearm, orbiting the immobile planet. Thatch giggles, petting the dragon which basks in his attention.

I follow the lines of his tattoo, smiling at the golden thread connecting two hands laid in black ink. "I made this the year after I won."

Thatch chuckles. "I fell in love with it immediately. It's us, you know?"

I answer him with a deep, endless kiss.

We eventually rest in comfortable silence, Thatch leans against the headboard with my head in his lap. He alternates between playing with my locket and hair. Night curtains the world outside our little room, but neither of us acknowledge it. I can't stop thinking about one particular scene, one I desperately want to paint. Thatch walking out of that monster's den.

"Do you know how badass you are?" I mutter onto his happy trail while he braids my hair, fingers sliding through the curls in such a way that must be magickal, because my eyes grow heavier by the minute.

He laughs a little. "Yeah?"

"Mhm. You didn't need magick or asshole superiors or anyone else. You saved your fucking *self*, Thatcher, and all those people who suffered by his hand. Standing alone, it shouldn't have gone that way, but the fact of the matter is you're still standing and *mostly* sane. Not to mention in bed with my fine ass."

Thatch really laughs then, so hard he's reduced to hysteria induced snorting that induces giggling in me, too. Eventually, he manages, "There's nowhere else I'd rather be."

I sigh, enjoying his fingers resuming their work in my hair. "Thatcher Gaillot, I love you."

Thatch releases my hair and takes me by the chin, tilting my head back to look at him. He stares at me with a fierceness that promises everything will be alright, one way or another.

Thatch Phantom, Thatcher Gaillot, no ... *Just* Thatch says, "And I love you, Arlo Rook."

Thatch

I kneel beside the bed, watching Arlo sleep.

He's sprawled out on his stomach, naked and only partially covered by the blankets.

I fight the urge to trace my fingers along his spine one last time.

The monstrous clock chimes eleven and my chest tightens with an altogether new pull, one that used to thrill me.

With much less of a heart than I had before, I stand and leave the room, softly shutting the door after one last glance at my person.

Silent tears fall as I descend the stairs. I thrust my chin out, unwilling to cower before my fate any longer. *Who are we to evade what we're made for?*

I walk into Funguy Park as Just Thatch. Black high tops, jeans, and a button up with my favorite suspenders, white sleeves rolled up. I'm sure there's circles under my eyes and my hair is a wreck, but this is the me the winner is getting.

I briefly wonder who won, what they will wish for, but it doesn't really matter. I hoped for Arlo to win, to find out what the clues *really* meant and what I was trying to tell him, but maybe over time he and the others can patch together the truth, if they find any. Nevertheless, I'm sure whoever solved it deserves the wish all the same.

I travel along the dirt path winding through the park I enjoy most in Levena. Neon umbrella mushrooms rival the tall metal lamp posts keeping me company, my favorite. Other types of fungi populate the densely packed area and the only way through the park are on these 'manicured' paths.

I come to a stop at one of the cleared, mossy rest areas reserved for picnic tables, benches and in this particular area, a little library. The winner stares me down, clearly kept waiting for far longer than they care to be.

I smile, completely sincere. "Hello, Caspian."

He lifts his chin, allowing the moons to illuminate half his scowl. "Hello, Scarlet. It's about time we have a chat, don't you think?"

Saturday

BREAKING NEWS

Arlo

I stretch out in bed, joints popping under the slivers of dawn filtering through our bedroom windows. I reach out and before my fingers brush his cool, empty pillow, I know.

He's not in the house.

Through a haze of panic and swiftly clearing grogginess, I pull my pants on and barrel down the stairs, forgoing shoes and a shirt. I throw the front door open and run like my life depends on it because it *does*. I have to tell him goodbye. He can't be gone yet, he *can't*. We *just* ....

I slide down the knoll hiding the shoreline shrouded in fog. I take off running once I find my feet again, toes digging into pebbles and decaying seagrass washed onto the beach. The bedrock pillar stands watch over the river.

Alone.

I crash into it, searching the rough surface like I can find Thatch in the cracks. The sediment, shells and fossilized memories of ancient sea creatures burn my palms, like the tower's baked in the sun all day. But the sun has only just risen, not reaching the beach at this early hour.

I fall against the pillar, arms wrapping around it as far as I can reach. Tears and rock shred my cheek to pieces, but I don't care. I meld every part of my body to the stone best I can, not giving a shit that the low tide plagues my nostrils and jagged sediment scrapes my face. In the pulsating edges of my mind, Bosko's mourning cry haunts the beach and woodland beyond, confirming what my witch's heart already knows.

Thatcher Gaillot is no longer in this world.

He's a Phantom.

I spend the day out there, reluctantly separating from the ancient bedrock inch by inch, and shivering endlessly. I watch the river come to life under the guise of a new day, wondering who constructed time. It's supposed to be a new day when the moons give way to the sun, but I feel like time has stopped despite the fact the sun moves over me with little care.

The world turns, whether I want it to or not.

I don't need to vent my magick today, it's grieving the lack of Thatch's magnetic pull and hiding deep within me. I briefly debate leaving the beach in search of clothes, but I decide to wait a little while longer.

Just in case.

I told Thatch I would be fine, that if I failed (which I *did*) that I would wait for him, no matter how long it took. I stand by that, but I should have asked more questions. *Prepared* for this. Instead, I argued with him and made love to him. How long will it be now?

Will it be longer than the eighty years he was gone for last time?

He said it didn't always used to be that way.

I need to talk to Dusan, before she forgets.

I stand abruptly, blood rushing to my toes so fast that I have to brace myself on the stone.

Elochian's right, we need to solve the amnesia problem first. I haven't forgotten a thing, and I won't. I *won't*. I need to write. I need charms to *bind* what I write so no external forces fuck with me. I need to find out who the 'bosses' are, and fight for Thatch to come home.

I take a step away from the pillar, then another. I push out a breath and open my clenched hands, then look over my shoulder.

Nothing but the river.

I keep walking.

I make it to the cottage without having another breakdown, but the thrown open door revealing an empty home prevents me from entering. Being alone is a heavy thought, but the idea of dealing with everyone's pity is bone crushing. Life doesn't just stop though, does it?

And Thatch was their friend too. He burrowed into their lives one at a time, leaving a Thatcher sized imprint on their hearts.

I step inside the house, half expecting him to jump out from behind the door.

He doesn't.

I run upstairs, afraid of my own shadow. My shoulders ease once I step inside the bedroom. It still *smells* like him in here, like he only just stepped out. Did he leave the moment I fell asleep?

Did he lay me with for a while, watching me sleep?

Or did he fall asleep and was pulled away, kicking and screaming?

I don't sit, because if I do, I fear I might not get back up again. I finish dressing in yesterday's clothes and pocket my phone. I don't look at it, not yet. I walk around the bedroom and straighten it up, taking a moment to bury my face in Thatch's pillow and leave tears there. I went from not crying in years to crying multiple times in the last few days. Out of joy and despair.

When I replace his pillow, my fingers brush against something cool and my heart *stops*.

My compass pendant, the edges of the locket popped open. I take it and gently open it as one would a book, finding a shallow compartment inside the circular piece. Energy sparks around my fingers and the air stinks of ozone. I find a piece of parchment folded in half, enclosed with an azure wax seal with only one detail. '*T*'

Fuck me.

I break the seal with shaking fingers and carefully unfold the letter.

My Dearest Arlo,

It's time for you to keep your promises. I expect you to be waiting for me when I return, because I *will*. You've instilled a fire in my heart that I have not possessed in years, and it will carry me home. There are a few things I've kept from you, and it's time I come clean.

Firstly, Thitwhistle's is now yours based on the stipulations that you keep it just the way it is, name and all. The cottage is also yours to do with as you wish, not as a caretaker but a property owner, perhaps a home for Wayward Witches? I like the sound of that.

Your accounts are flush, call it an investment for any and all future Hedge Witch Extraordinaire activities. Yes, yes, I can hear you calling me a 'sugar daddy' from here, oh dear, I hope that's the right term.

I'm sorry you didn't win the Game, but I have a feeling you have better things coming your way. I regret that it's the last one, but it's time to shed my skin, so to speak.

You are my heart, dear Arlo. I would live for another ten thousand years just to meet you again, and I am counting down the moments until you are in my arms once more. I hope you will be thinking of me as often as I will be thinking of you, and know that I will be crafting all my wildest fantasies for you to exploit when I return.

I know you believe otherwise, but if by chance you happen to forget me and this letter turns to little more than empty paper, I will remember for the both of us.

Be my Rook, my solid foundation in between worlds that I can always return to. I love you, my *leva*.

Yours, and yours alone,

Just Thatch

The shaking in my hands subsides after my third read through, but only to a subtle trembling. I fold the letter with as much care as possible, then go to tuck into my jacket pocket. Only, I'm not wearing it. I haven't had it in days, the last time I saw it was the night of our date, Thatch was wearing it. The thought of a small part of me accompanying Thatch on his journey threatens to fracture what composure I've mustered.

I tuck the letter into my pants pocket and slip my necklace back on, expecting a false sensation of Thatch's arms around me, but I receive nothing except a cold press to my sternum. I'm in the living room, when did I get here? I bury my hands into my hair, unable to reconcile with the fact that this place is mine now, *and* Thitwhistle's.

Why?

Only one way to find out.

I take out my phone and unlock the screen, illuminating 5% battery and *hundreds* of notifications. Fuck, I don't have my charger. I wasn't exactly thinking about packing for an overnight stay when I came, I wanted to find Thatch. My breath catches and I force it out, then open the group text to find the messages I received shortly after I put my phone away last night.

Flowers: He's probably scared. Take good care of him, Arlo.
Doc: Call us in the morning, we'll get this figured out.
Quen: If you need anything, just call.
Kitty: Tell Thatch I said don't get eaten. (11:53 PM)

I blink at that, unsure what the fuck she's talking about.

Caspian: I'm sorry, but you'll thank me for it. (2:22 AM)

My stomach drops to my feet. What did he do?

A series of phone calls beginning at 7:00 AM are next. I scroll through the names of nearly everyone I know, finding multiple calls from each of the Misfits except for Caspian and Kitt. A shiver runs down my spine and pieces start to click together in a way I don't like. They've both been acting odd.

Silas didn't call me, but he texted me. The only one to do so this morning, everyone else resorted to calling only. That's never good.

Silas: we'll figure it out. read this, then come find me at the cafe. (9:31 AM)

My finger rests over the link for a hesitant moment, then I remember the last time I let information slip through my fingers.

BREAKING NEWS

The infamous 'Game' put on by the Scarlet Illusionist was solved a day early by local resident Caspian Daermarrel. What Mr. Daermarrel has claimed as his prize and how he solved the Game is unclear, given he is refusing interviews at this time. While Mr. Daermarrel did not need the last piece of artwork to solve the Game, the painting known as 'Phantom' has been making headlines as the last and most obvious clue to the game maker's identity, especially since the artist is unknown. Some people are theorizing the artist is the game maker themselves.

The identity of the infamous Scarlet Illusionist is none other than Thatch Phantom. Philanthropist, an expert in multiple fields, and CEO of several businesses throughout Levena, not to mention the world. Mr. Phantom has long been a figure shrouded in mystery and only a part time resident of Levena, but it's safe to say the identity reveal was a shock to all, including to those who knew him. Mr. Phantom is unavailable for interview at this time, sources say he fled the city.

Stay tuned for exclusive updates throughout the day, including what the residents think of Mr. Phantom's farewell letter stating this will be the *last* Game.

What. The. Fuck.

Thatch's words from the letter rip and tear, shredding me into raw pieces. *I'm sorry you didn't win the Game, but I have a feeling you have better things coming your way. I regret that it's the last one, but it's time to shed my skin, so to speak.*

I laugh hysterically, commencing my second breakdown of the day.

I knock on the door of Garren Castle and am promptly let in by Felix. He blinks up at me and tilts his beanie covered head. "Why are you knocking?" He asks, ushering me in.

I shrug, doing as I'm told. "Don't know. How're you doing?"

Felix lifts a shoulder, giving me a taste of my own medicine. "Alright. It's quiet around here without you or Kleo." He says it with no malice, but the words make my heart ache all the same. I ruffle his hair and give him a weak smile. "I know, kid. I have to talk to the Headmaster, but maybe we can talk after. Would that be alright?"

Felix nods, smiling quietly. "I'll be in the Kitchen."

We part ways, and I travel through eerily quiet halls. It's late evening, there should be kids running around after dinner. I try not to think much of it, focusing only on my destination. I knock on Dusan's office door without hesitation.

"Come in, Arlo."

I inhale deeply, then do just that.

Dusan sits in the high backed chair behind her desk, legs twisted beneath her and upturned palms resting on her knees. She opens her eyes when I stand before her desk. I stare down at the person I've trusted most in this world. I had planned hundreds of ways to make her feel an ounce of the betrayal I have, but the fury dies on my tongue.

Instead, I whisper, "Why didn't you tell me?"

Dusan simply says, "because it was not my story to tell, Arlo."

"It was part of *mine*." I grind out. "I brought him here and you said nothing. You didn't tell me we had met before, or that he was *mine*, or that he's the Illusionist!"

So much for extinguished anger.

Dusan shakes her head, dropping her gaze to her left palm. "That was just as much a surprise to me as it was to you. As far as your memory, would you have believed me? Would it have made a difference? You fell in love again regardless."

"Of *course* it would have," I say, bracing my hands on her desk. "I could've ...."

Dusan's piercing eyes flash to mine. "We need to find out what he is, Arlo, and what's trapping him. There was nothing you could have done, not now. I don't know how to help him, and I've been trying since I met him. Given the ... *amnesia*, may have had a hand in slowing down my efforts."

I shake my head slowly and close my eyes, willing myself to calm down. "How long do we have?"

"What do you mean?" She asks, and I open my eyes. Dusan tilts her head at me.

"Until he ... fades." I grimace at the idea of it. His scratches are fresh in my back and my lips tingle with the imprint of his.

"You haven't talked to Caspian, have you?"

I fluster at that, having to immediately straighten. "No, but we *will* have words. Why he thought–"

"You will do no such thing." Dusan snaps, standing from her chair. "You will *listen*, and he will tell you why he did what he did. Out of all us, he's the one who figured out who put on the Game, all for *you*. Do you understand me, Arlo? You will *listen* to him."

The child deep inside me cowers. I don't let it show on the outside, but I bow my head. "Yes. You're right. It's just ... I can't believe I didn't *see* it. How the hell did Thatch do it? We were together most of the day, even when the alerts came in!"

A tiny smile breaks through her stoicism. "You were preoccupied with the real thing. You gave that man more life in a week than he's ever experienced. I'm quite sure you changed him, for better, of course."

I can't deny how I soften at that. "I would hope so. He changed me."

Hurry Up And Wait

Arlo

I stand outside the yellow house. Tobias opens the door, rushing me into a tight hug. His wings are out and Daisy bounces in circles around our feet.

I hug him back.

He trembles in my arms. "I had no idea, Arlo. If I had known I would've told you, you know this right?"

I squeeze my friend tighter, hooking my chin over his shoulder. Feathers tickle my face. "I know." We pull away and I peer around him to the open door revealing an empty landing. "He in there?"

Tobias nods, scrubbing at his eyes. "It's been a long day, but at least he's not drinking. He had me dump everything this morning." Tobias looks to the house, then back to me. "If you don't want to see him, Arlo, I understand, but he's ... so lost, Arlo."

I shake my head. "No, I need to. Thanks for everything, Tobias. We'll figure it out."

Tobias nods wearily and leads me inside, then heads upstairs where a childish babble waits for him. I take a deep breath, then walk down the hall and into the open kitchen.

Caspian sits at the dining room table in his chair, back to me and shoulders hunched.

I take a seat opposite him, coming face to face with his trimmed and tired features.

His notebook, neatly organized piles of papers, and photocopies are laid out between us. Cas lazily twirls a pen in his fingers, pinched gaze trained on me. He waits, and I say nothing.

Finally, he sets the pen down beside his notebook, straightens it, then leans back in his wheelchair with a guarded expression. "Why aren't you saying anything?" Cas' voice is rough, but his eyes are clear.

I lift a shoulder, then remove my hat and set it on the table. "I'm giving you the benefit of the doubt. I'm sure there are reasons why you, and Kitt, I'm presuming, withheld the knowledge that Thatch was the Illusionist. I'm not sure what else you know about him, but I'm sure it is infinitely more than I do."

Caspian chuckles, shaking his head. His shoulders relax a fraction. "Why can't I figure out if you're passively aggressively threatening me, fucking with me, or are completely serious?"

I nod to the papers. "Let's find out."

Caspian pinches the bridge of his nose, sighing. "Alright." He leans forward immediately, struck with a burst of energy as pent up words fall out of him.

"When I first started having the dreams, they were just colors. Flashes of red and orange followed by blue. Then, I started to dream about the day Thatch brought you home from getting your ass kicked by Leon, the same day the first painting was found. It wasn't … it wasn't always the same, or clear, but him bringing you home, all fucked up, that was crystal."

I want to ask when he decided that Thatch wasn't the enemy, but I keep my mouth shut.

"I kept thinking that Loch's painting reminded me of Thatch's hair, but I chalked it up to being pissed off at him 90% of the time. Lots of people have red hair, right?"

Caspian lays out a copy of the first painting and I study it, remembering what Elochian said. It hits me then, the night at the bar. Thatch and Elochian shook hands and Loch had asked him, *"Do I know you?"*

Thatch's face fell when he said that.

Elochian was right all along, he saw the Illusionist, but Thatch's ... *curse*, blurred the memory.

"And he kept saying these weird things that were completely out of era, and not by just a few years, either. Thitswhistle was dodgy when I asked about Thatch, and he's never like that, so I asked a few people at the museum about him, and the hospital. They knew *who* he was, but ask them what he looked like, and *no* one could accurately describe him."

I rub my face, irritation rising. "Fucking Gods, you were *investigating* him. If you were so concerned, why didn't you tell me? If you *truly* thought I was in danger, why didn't you *say* anything?"

Caspian looks away from me. "You were stupid happy, and nobody else said a word. I thought *Kitt* would've remembered him, she was there too that day, but she didn't say anything. So I started to think maybe *I* was crazy. Then I saw his chest and I *knew* he was not who he said he was."

"His chest?" I ask, struggling to keep up.

Caspian nods, setting an article before me, titled; *Leviathan and the Malefactor*.

I take it immediately, glancing between him and the paper. "I thought I had lost it. Must be this is where Kitt comes in?"

Caspian flushes and he scratches at his hair. "The day at Kitt's, he had taken his shirt off and ... well, he's ...."

"Yeah, I know," I say softly, cheeks burning.

"*Right*. Well, he went back the next morning and got the tattoo, right? Well, Kitt started asking me all about the Leviathan, sent me that article and asked me what I thought about the supposed villain of the story, the Malefactor. I told her I thought it was just another version of the myth, but she said it was *true*, swore upon it. Then she asked me if I *really* read it, because I missed–"

"Oh my Gods ..." I breathe, tracing over the caption beneath a work of art. An illustration of a great Leviathan rearing from the ocean beside a coastal city, facing off a singular man with bright copper hair that sticks out from the rest of the vibrant painting.

I keep reading, finding that the story goes on to say that the Leviathan ate the man, the Malefactor, and he *cut* his way out, defeating the monster without cause. He had murdered a great beast, a God of the Sea, for seemingly no reason.

I laugh. "That's not—"

"He told Kitt the story *himself*, Arlo. A story that time warped to cast him as the villain." Caspian warns, cutting me off. "The marks across his shoulders? That's what they're from."

I shift in my seat as Kitt's parting words to Thatch settle in. '*Don't get eaten.*' I set the paper down gingerly, tapping it with a finger. "What does this prove?"

"That he's a lot older than a few hundred years, Arlo. Try over two thousand, and that's just when the story dates back to. So, when Kitt saw the clue regarding the temple, I thought, 'what better place to check out ancient races than there,' right?

So while she was looking for the painting, I studied the lower levels. I was *supposed* to be her lookout—"

"Ten thousand," I whisper, catching Cas' attention. "He told me if he had to wait another ten thousand years to find me, he would. That would mean he's been here since ... the beginning of everything, wouldn't it?"

Caspian mutters something involving the words disgustingly sweet, then clears his throat. "Well, that goes along with what I found."

I lean forward. "And what did you find?"

"Nothing," he says, opening his hands.

"*Nothing*?" I raise a brow, echoing him.

"There's a missing link, like someone abducted all the religious texts and marred the faces of an ancient race that came *after* the Gods and *before* everyone else. Four thousand years go by from the supposed 'creation' of our world by the 'Allmother' with nothing concrete to show for it, *until*—"

Caspian pulls out a few pieces of paper filled with notes. "These scriptures from the early Atlanteans which talk about someone watching over them."

I stand abruptly. "The Watchers. The *book*, the book Silas found, it was called *Watchers and Where Are They Now?*"

He nods, watching me pace the room. "They describe them as guardians of a sort that passed on knowledge, the gift of writing and reading, protection, but at a great cost."

"What was the cost?"

"Free will," Caspian says softly. "I imagine the amnesia is a side effect of such consequences, or one of them."

"A side effect," I repeat, the same words that Thatch used. I nod, rubbing my chin as I mull over everything he's said. Things *I* should have figured out.

"That doesn't explain how you and Kitt knew he was the Illusionist," I say finally.

"She didn't know all that, Arlo. Only that Thatch needed help. It was the broadcast, that's what made it all make sense, to me, later on," he says, meeting my eyes cautiously.

"*I cannot tell you who I am. What I am. Why I'm really here.* I didn't know for sure, I didn't have proof then, but it just … I don't know, I could *hear* him saying those words in all the ways he wasn't telling the truth, like *cannot* was underlined. He said he hadn't been back in eighty years, and the broadcast said something similar. I was trying to figure it all out … solve it for you."

"I'm a fucking idiot." I groan into my hands.

"You're not an idiot, you're in love," Caspian says, surprising me. I look up and find a lopsided grin. I give a halfhearted smile back, and he rolls his eyes. "After you and Kitt found the painting of the river, that was it for me. It was *that* day, preserved into art. I was going to make my guess and if I was wrong, then I was paranoid and wrong."

"So why did you choose Saturday morning?"

He shifts uncomfortably in his chair. "If I failed, I wanted you to have as much time with him as you could. Even if I didn't like it, it was very obvious that you weren't going to listen to me. I didn't know if once I solved the Game he would disappear or how it worked, but I wanted to be safe."

"Hence your bitchiness the last few times I saw you."

"*Listen*, you're supposed to be the smart one. I'm not cut out for this shit." Cas scoffs, gesturing to the papers we've been going through one by one.

I shrug. "Looks to me you did just fine."

I stand at the end of the table and pick up the photocopies of the last two paintings, ones I haven't seen yet. A digital piece of a castle against a night sky with a very obvious constellation, the phoenix. Thatch's worldly death and rebirth.

A charcoal piece of a person standing beside the cottage on the island, embracing a ghost in the twilight. A Phantom.

"He left me all the clues," I whisper, thumb hovering over the couple. "Why didn't I know?"

"If you don't like my love answer, then the practical idea is it may have to do with the consequences of being a Watcher, more than anything," Caspian says offhandedly.

That makes me feel a little better, but there's no way to be sure. "I had a book on Watchers, I lost it. Or it was stolen. If I had read it when Silas gave it to me maybe I would've figured it out. Thatch told me what he could, which makes more sense now than it ever could've before. Maybe it was like Silas said, the harder I tried to figure out Thatch, the farther away the answers got."

"Time for would've, should've, could've is over, Lolo. And we have the book, by the way. Well, Silas does, it appeared in Thitwhistle's this morning. You have your work cut out for you there."

I blink at him. "What? How?"

Caspian's ears turn red and he looks away from me. "We won't have any more interference. It's all up to Thatch now. The fact my notes haven't vanished and we can *say* things like Watchers just proves that it worked ... I think. It's only been a day, but I *really* think that it worked, Lo."

"What worked?" I cross the room and plop into my chair, staring at him intently. I wait for him to explain, and he shifts in his seat.

"My wish," he says, flustered. "I asked for Thatch's free will to be returned to him."

I lean back, chest hit with a ton of bricks.

Caspian goes on in a whirlwind, hard facade cracking. "I didn't know whether to ask for that or knowledge or for a curse to be broken, but considering we don't know the facts, I thought that was the safest bet. If a person has free will, then they can *choose* not to be forgotten, right?"

I try to breathe, but it won't happen. The Game was Thatch's doing, he couldn't possibly break the ... *curse* with his own magick when someone *else* asked, could he?

Cas wheels around the table and takes my hands in his. "Arlo, *please* tell me I did the right thing. I'm so sorry for keeping all this from you, it started out because I was mad, then I was scared, and you were just so *happy,* and I started to doubt myself.

"I just wanted you to be *happy*, Arlo. And Thatch ... he deserves to have a life, with you. I know now that he was never the bad guy. He's a *person*, he doesn't deserve to spend forever alone and not ever being able to make a choice for himself. He's *your* person."

I take a shuddering inhale. My *person*.

"All we can do now is hurry up and wait, but ... " I grip his fingers tight, watching my tears fall onto our joined hands. "If he *could* stay, why didn't he?"

"He said he would try to come back, that he had to leave but he would *try*. He told me to tell you that ... he loves you, and to wait for him." Caspian murmurs, then straightens abruptly. "No. Fuck waiting. We have work to do, history books to rewrite. We need to get Thatch's story straight, and others like him. Even if he doesn't ... you know. Besides, I hear you own a few select pieces of property now. What're you going to do with all that?"

I knock my forehead into his. "I have a few ideas."

A Few Weeks Later

A closed sign rests on the front window of Thitwhistle's, but it's far from empty. The Misfits sprawl out on the couches surrounding a lit hearth, drinking coffee and eating mocha scones. Silas sits by himself at a nearby table, tapping its surface as he listens to violins and dubstep.

Marlena and Zeke waddle through the place, tugging at curtain pulls and chewing on things they shouldn't. Caspian and Tobias chase after them and resume conversation, only to be pulled away again when their children begin terrorizing something else.

When they scramble underneath Silas' table and startle him, his head tucks into his left shoulder and he *'hmms,'* then blows out a ball of icy blue energy similar to how one would blow a bubble. He gently taps it and it floats down, into the reach of the kids. They eagerly swat at it and giggle when it fluidly changes shape in their hands at random.

"He's really good." Felix murmurs, watching Silas with an intensity he reserves only for the chaos witch. Silas intrigues him, from his clothes to his magick and how he blends in seamlessly to wherever he is. Problem is, anytime Silas talks to Felix, the kid locks up. It could be one of two things, and I'm *really* hoping it's not the first one.

I'm just glad I helped Silas start the process of emancipation, keeping it in the family is *not* in the cards here.

"So are you, Little Witch." I gently squeeze Felix's shoulder from our place behind the counter, earning a smile from him. "Alright, let's get this show on the road, shall we?"

Bells chime, ringing in Elochian's arrival. He stands just inside the door, shaking wet flakes off his wings. Quentin sits up a little bit straighter from his spot on the couch but doesn't break conversation with Iris and Gowan. Kitt meets my eye and gives me a knowing wink while she twirls Lindsey's hair around her finger. I missed Kitt's proposal during halftime at Lindsey's championship, but playing best man and Kitt's personal wedding planner has made up for my accidental transgression.

"Sorry I'm late," Loch says, hanging his overcoat on a potted tree with gnarled, jutting branches. "I didn't miss anything—"

At the swift finger over my lips, Loch nods and beelines for the empty seat beside Quentin. Ever since Quentin moved into the apartment upstairs, Elochian spends almost every morning here and suspiciously only before Q goes to work. While the two are only friends, the three of us have been working closely regarding Leon's latest bullshit, and it's like I'm not even there when the two get to talking.

"Alright, are you ready?" I ask, then place a white box in Felix's waiting arms after he nods.

"What is this even for anyway? Who eats cake if it's not for a birthday?" Felix scoffs, asking several very good questions in a patchy voice. He's come into himself more and more, and I hope this is the right thing to do. I feel like it is, truly.

I laugh, following behind him as he leads the way to the hearth. Tobias and Lindsey clear off the coffee table, making room for the generously sized white box. Felix glances at Silas as the chaos witch stands and inches closer, then he looks up to me. I clap my hands together, facing all my friends and their easy smiles with a heavily thumping heart.

"First off, I want to say thank you all for coming to Misfit Night. I also want to say that regardless of certain events, I wouldn't be here and who I am today without all of you. Kitt and Caspian especially, but only because you two terrorized me for the longest."

Laughter gently bubbles around me, and I reel in my anxiousness. Caspian takes my hand and squeezes gently, giving me a wide smile. I nod once, pushing out a shaky breath.

"After some consideration and a *lot* of paperwork, I've decided to expand the cottage and turn it into a home for young witches. I'm *not* taking the university job, and I'll be only working one day a week at the studio so I can focus my efforts on the cottage and here. I know it sounds mental and the opposite of what I've always said I wanted ... but I was chasing what's considered normal, and this is what I want. To help witches, others like us." I nod to Tobias, Silas, and finally, Felix.

He beams up at me, proud and brilliant.

"That's wonderful, Arlo," Quentin says, followed by Lindsey and the others. Gowan already knew because I discussed lowering my hours with her, but she congratulates me all the same.

"Gotta admit, never saw you as a professor." Cas grunts out past a cocky smile. "I'm proud of you, Lolo."

"You're gonna help a lot of people, Arlo," Bias says, reaching from his spot on the couch to take my hand.

I smile at both of them. "I'm hoping to. I ... I'd like to do what I do for Loch too, eventually. Here or at the cottage. Art therapy, you know?"

"Here we go with emotions, is it time for cake?" Loch asks, a corner of his thin lips turned up slightly. He winks at me and I breathe deeply one more time, catching Kitt's eye. She nods, her tiny smile wet and beautiful.

"Yeah, sure, of course. Felix, if you would."

Everyone leans in conspicuously and Felix stares at us all like we've gone mad. He raises a brow at me and I shrug. "We're hungry, get to it, Little Witch."

Felix rolls his eyes, then opens the lid on the box. He looks down and *freezes*, knuckles blanching as he grips the white cardboard. His chest rises and falls in rapid succession as he stares at a finely decorated cake made by Silas himself.

Felix's head jolts up, only having eyes for me.

"*Really*?" He whispers, as if uttering one word may shatter the truth.

I nod, welcoming the tears that slide down my face relentlessly. I kneel and open my arms to him, echoing the words cast in scripted icing. "Welcome to the family, Felix Rook. Welcome home."

Years

Pass

War

Begins

Friends

Fall

In

Love

Miss

You

Rest In Peace

In Remembrance of Thatcher Levena Gaillot, founder of what is formerly known as Min Isle and will henceforth be known as Levena in honor of the man who endlessly put others first.

Savior of over 300 Min residents during the Fire of 38' which burned Min Isle to the ground.

While others fell in the flames, he perpetually put himself in danger time and time again, not stopping until he brought everyone to the river, to safety, until he succumbed to his injuries and was taken by the flames.

He was a friend to all those he met, endlessly loyal and an instrumental figure in what Levena has become today.

Thank you for watching over us from wherever you are now, for your continued protection from beyond the grave. We will strive to live like you did and never forget your kindness.

Rest in Peace Thatch

THE RADICKAL MAGICKAL GAZETTE
TRUTH AND TRAGEDY
January 14th

Thanks to the work of Arlo Rook and his team comprised of witches, scholars, and friends at Scarlet University, the truth regarding a world once hidden to us has come to light. During the past few months since Caspian Daemarrel won 'The Game', the pair have been working tirelessly to reveal who Thatch Phantom really was and what his motives were.

While some claim that Mr. Phantom was no more than an imposter, Mr. Rook has found conclusive evidence to prove not only Mr. Phantom's involvement, but also the fact that if it were not for Thatch, Levena would not be what it is today, and for that matter, the world.

According to their work, Mr. Rook and Mr. Daemarrel believe there has been a chunk of history stolen from our timeline. Not just Levena's history, but all of the Nether Isles for that matter. Shortly after the creation tales of the Atlanteans, any new stories, glyphs, or evidence of the time between then and a few thousand years later is non-existent. This basis for modern technology as we know it, along with our writing and language system, is simply not there. Until now, that is.

Documents, tomes and artifacts once thought to be lost to thieves and time have also begun to make appearances in the most bizarre of places, spurring a new, unintentional round of the Game. Mr. Rook denied having any knowledge as to who or what is bringing these objects back, but he stands by his word that history is righting itself, one way or another. Kitt Meissa, Director of the recently renamed Gaillot Museum and a member of Mr. Rook's team, has stated that she agrees with Mr. Rook. According to her, even the stories we do have are gravely misshapen by time and miscommunication, such as the Tale of the Leviathan, a true occurrence in time once thought to be a myth.

Mr. Rook has also suggested that Thatch Phantom's true identity was consistently lost to those who knew him, a curse of sorts placed by the very beings that spun the universe into motion. The same beings that have been hiding our history, along with Thatch Phantom's purpose.

Yes, the Gods.

Mr. Rook believes that Levena used to be a village called Min Isle. According to him, most of the population there were families of the acolytes who served at the Temple of Min, a place dedicated to the original Primordial Gods that gave birth to the Children Gods that many worship today. How Min Isle became Levena has been a mystery to the research team, but like many other things as of late, has been solved by something that simply wasn't *there* before, and now it is. A gravestone that has been restored upon its discovery declares the resting place of a Thatcher Levena Gaillot, the founder of Min Isle. The gravestone indicates that the town was rebuilt in his honor, after Thatcher died of his injuries in a fire.

While there is speculation on *how* a thousands year old gravestone has not succumbed to time, and if Thatch Phantom is truly Thatcher Gaillot, (making him the oldest living being to date) the mayor of Levena has taken it upon themselves to meet with Mr. Rook and his team in regards to properly rewriting history. Mr. Rook believes that Mr. Phantom is, for lack of a better term, a type of being called a Watcher that allowed him to survive the fire. Mr. Rook credits Mr. Daemarrel entirely, but the pair insist that they have only uncovered the surface of Thatch, and history.

What they have found suggests this;

Watchers are the missing link between early civilization, and us.

Watchers provided knowledge, wealth in some cases, safety and protection.

Watchers are thought to be controlled by the Children Gods who have until now, wanted the knowledge of Watchers and how they impacted the world to be kept secret.

Watchers are powerful, inter-dimensional beings that can affect the world around them with ease.

Watchers have altered the course of our evolution as a society, as a culture, working as the Gods' instruments to determine fate.

Watchers are without free will, and for better or worse, we are at their (or the Gods, for that matter) mercy.

Watchers are solitary beings, and Mr. Rook has insisted that he believes Thatch Phantom is the last known Watcher alive. His whereabouts are unknown, but Mr. Rook firmly believes that Mr. Phantom has only left, not died.

While there are those who say his work is ridiculous, there are others who lean to the opposite extreme. The recent Anti Witch Organization rallies have been boosted by a new group that calls themselves Normals For Justice. Normals for Justice are humans and magickal beings who claim they are different from the AWO, in the sense they don't want *just* witches detained and removed from the city. They say those who hold a certain threshold for power, such as Watchers (who they claim to have knowledge of more Watchers than just one, but won't divulge further details), Draconians, and Celestials, are a danger to society and an unequal force that is applying pressure to the impoverished North End. While the AWO is outwardly aggressive, the NOJ insists on a peaceful resolution including but not limited to forced eviction.

I will say this. If we forget history, we are doomed to repeat it. The impact of a discriminatory and violent encounter known as The Taking is not that much different from what we are seeing today and we cannot suffer such a horror twice. It is up to us, the common people, your neighbors, family and friends, to band together and find the truth, protect it and those who may come to harm in light of it. Let us allow the truth to bind us together, not drive us apart. If such beings as Watchers do exist, we cannot expect such a person to hold our hand and show us how to love and trust each other properly.

Only we can do that.

Until next time,

-Finnegan Wroughtfern

Hello

Thatch

Dead leaves catch a gust of wind, drifting over the pebble beach I land upon with an otherworldly grace that is unfamiliar to me. Time has softened my clumsy edges and removing the leash on my free will has done wonders for my coordination. I sink my high tops into the wet stones beneath my feet and inhale deeply, absorbing the smell of a distant wood stove and the last remnants of this harvest's pollen.

I can't bring myself to turn around and take in how the island has changed. Standing here, looking out over the river, it's almost like I never left. The mountains in the distance cut through the sunset and fluffed clouds which leak amber and gold onto the island. It's colder, perhaps closer to Yule than the Harvest.

I tighten the worn leather jacket around myself and bury my nose in the collar that's threadbare at best, searching for the faint remnants of a man I used to know. At the last moment,

I snagged his jacket from my stash before leaving all that time ago, needing to bring physical *proof* of my person.

My heart races at the thought. Over the years it's been a pleasant daydream, something to keep me going, but something I never thought I'd *actually* achieve. Despite all the promises from Caspian and the others, I thought for sure something would keep me from coming home. Keep me from Arlo.

But now I'm here, and within seconds of landing the most important question is answered. He's *alive*. I sense his gentle magnetism reaching out for my spirit, which begs more questions to come forth, ones I can't bear to explore the answers to.

Does he remember me?

How long has it been?

Did he truly wait for me?

Can he feel *me*, too?

With a heavy sigh, I exhale and turn away from the river. I'm pleased to find new saplings tucked into the woodland surrounding the beach are the only distinct differences from last time. It's indeed not the same season, the trees have fully shed their rainbow of leaves which crumple underfoot. The ground is damp and frosty, like it'd rained the night before, and the decaying tree resting over my trapdoor is slick with a layer of thin ice.

I roll the timeless dead wood back like I've done so many times before. I call forth the trapdoor hidden beneath the sod and woodland debris, barely touching upon my newfound magick to do so. The routine procedure settles my nerves a little bit, and I drop down into an expansive, reinforced dugout. I snap my fingers, bringing forth an orb of soft blue light to illuminate the space.

I stagger backwards, heart stricken. The rudimentary book-shelves lining the wood braced dirt walls around me are stripped of their contents. Coat trees once full of my favorite hoodies are empty. Memorabilia I've collected over the years, ancient tomes, modern knick knacks, once neatly folded piles of clothes, the painting Arlo made for me, my phone.

All of it, it's *all* gone.

I regain control of my limbs and lunge forward, frantically sweeping my hands over the shelves, branches of coat racks, dusty squares on the wall where paintings once rested, going in circles around the room until I'm forced to a halt by an unfamiliar, single item.

A puzzle box rests in the center of a top shelf and I reach for it hesitantly. I don't sense any malicious energy in here, rather a crowd of energies that have melded together over time. There wasn't just one person in here, but several, and not just once. In all my years, I've *never* been stolen from, not like this.

I cradle the small box in my hands, surprised when I find no energy signature there, either. I turn it over, looking for details or markings to denote the craftsman, but there's nothing. I experiment by disassembling the removable pieces along the edges of the box.

After a few minutes, I realize this won't be solved easily and settle down cross legged on the floor, blessedly distracted. I turn, flip and reassemble pieces for who knows how long, but eventually crack it. The lid pops open, stealing my breath. I set the box in my lap and trace my fingers alongside the lid, then gently open it.

A piece of paper folded ten different ways to Sunday waits for me on a pillow of crushed copper velvet, and I chuckle. A puzzle inside a puzzle. I work the folds open for a long time, eventually unfurling it properly into a frontal silhouette of a house with a chimney. Windows, trim and flower boxes come to life, rising from the paper and detailing the piece in three dimensions. Two words cut into the paper before my eyes, like someone's taking invisible scissors to form the letters, gently moving the paper in my fingers.

'Welcome Back'

I climb out of the hole like a spooked fox. I tuck the puzzle box under my arm and run to where I last left the cottage, heart pounding out of my chest with too much hope. I climb the small knoll separating the beach from the rest of the island, unable to catch a glimpse of the cottage through the trees. Now that I'm ducking and weaving through the undergrowth and woodland instead of looking from afar, I can see now that time has wrought knots into fattened trunks and ancient sentinels have fallen.

Approaching voices stop me in my tracks, infringing upon my memory.

For reasons I don't care to admit, I hide behind a tree and listen.

A strained and distorted masculine tone meets my ears first. "You're too worried about the end result. You have to *feel* the magick as it works through you. It's—"

A young man bellows out a laugh. "A process, yeah, yeah. Hate to tell you, but *no one* wants to think of magick as a process."

"Breathing is a process, isn't it?" A rustling sounds, and silence quickly follows. I peek around the trunk to find two men about twenty feet away, melding as one against a tree with passion. Tan hands dive into long, white hair, and pale fingers stroke cropped golden brunette. Sweet nothings are murmured between the pair and my heart aches.

Something wet and sniffling presses against my hand braced on the tree. I won't lie, I *absolutely* scream and fall onto my face, scraping my hands onto gnarled roots in attempts to catch myself. I jerk my head up in time to see the two figures retreating at a dead run. One glances over his shoulder and locks eyes with me.

Felix.

Grown up, scruffed and rough around the edges, but undoubtedly Felix.

He laughs as he runs away from me, followed by a golden canine and a silver cat.

With a groan, I roll over onto my back and stare up at the canopy shrouded sky. That was definitely him, and Silas, I think, unless there's someone else Felix's age with stark white hair. If he remembers me, surely he wouldn't have run away. And if he *doesn't* remember me, then Caspian's wish failed. He was laughing like a kid who got caught with candy, not like he saw an old friend. I *think* we were friends, anyway.

I sit up.

That was *Felix*. He's only a young man.

I shoot up to standing.

I couldn't have been gone that long, then.

I can't give up hope, not yet.

I brush myself off and frown at the wet, grassy stains in the knees of my jeans. I rake out the leaves from my hair, then start towards the cottage at a barely controlled walk this time. I approach the break in the trees and happiness overcomes my heart. I step into the grassy clearing, one hand sliding into my pocket as I marvel at what Arlo's done with the place.

The original cottage has changed in the most subtle of compounding ways, which when combined provides an entirely new home than what I left behind.

There's a fresh coat of paint, deep purple trim complements the gray stone. Flower boxes hang from new, tall windows that have plum shutters. A flagstone paved path meets the front, now double, doors and the cottage is surrounded by a wrap-around porch laden with hammocks, bowl chairs and benches.

A similar looking house sits on the opposite side, two stories high, and a few outbuildings lay beside it. Birds fly in and out of one with wide, screenless windows. Young witches congregate on the porch of the main house, in the clean cut front yard, or dangle from trees. There must be more in the lawnless garden out back too, but the exotic plants and pergola hide whoever is gathered out there, chatting and laughing. Smoke curls from a chimney attached to the side of the cottage and from somewhere in the backyard. I open the puzzle box and take out the piece of paper, comparing the paper house to the one before me.

They're the same.

I take another step closer and a few heads turn in my direction. I wave awkwardly at the closest group of witches, a bunch of pre-teens sprawled out in the lawn and playing a card game. One stands, a *shedim* with a checkered shirt and platform shoes, crimson leather wings tucked behind their back. The young demon cocks their shaved head at me, more at ease with a stranger than their wildly curious friends are.

"Um, hello," I say, widening several pairs of eyes.

The *shedim* smiles at me, red tail swishing back and forth behind them, then nods once. "Looking for Arlo?"

I can't help the smile that overtakes my face. "I am, in fact. Is he home?"

They tilt their head as if listening. "Why don't we meet him out back?"

"That would be excellent." I nod, tucking the box under my arm. I extend my hand to her small one and she shakes mine firmly, like an adult would. "I'm Thatch, and you are?"

"Marlena," she says, releasing my hand. "Just Thatch?"

"Yeah, Just Thatch." I agree, chuckling. We walk side by side, and I glance at her a few times, wondering if she's Tobias and Caspian's Marlena.

"I am," Marlena says, grinning sideways at me. "Sorry, you're being very loud in there, and I'm not really able to shut it off yet." She taps the side of her head. "Not she, by the way."

My mouth drops. "You're a Teleth!"

Marlena nods. "Sure am. There's a lot of us now, witches that is. Arlo's been busy, trying to keep us all safe. Things have gone to hell over the past few years."

I prepare a volley of questions but words die upon my tongue when we round the corner of the house. The voice that's kept me company for an eternity echoes throughout the clearing and breaks my heart.

Arlo comes around the other end of the house just as we do and he *stops*. A human I belatedly recognize as Quentin is tucked under his arm, and both their laughter dies upon seeing me. A fire pit, seating area filled with people I can't pay attention to right now, and a thick garden separates us.

Arlo and I stare at each other and my heart falters at his vacant expression. Quentin gives nothing away either, his handsomely wrinkled face pinching in confusion. My heart twists uncomfortably. This was a mistake.

Marlena gives me a gentle nudge. "Go on."

"I...."

Arlo makes the decision for me, weaving his way to us with quick hellos thrown to others along the way. I only have eyes for him, unable to comprehend who he's talking to. He's dressed in a rainbow duster, jeans, combat boots and a new knitted hat. A mottled black and white owl takes off from his shoulder. His hair is longer than before, highlighted with silver and hanging in curled waves from beneath his azure hat. Thick, dark hair lines his jaw, precisely trimmed and accentuating his perpetually handsome face.

And then he's there, standing before me, hands in his pockets. His irises flash neon green at the same time his soulmark brightens to vibrant life. My eyes *burn* at the sight. He scans my face with an indecipherable expression. Upturned lines have slightly creased his eyes and the corners of his lips. He's aged beautifully and I can't help but wonder what I would age like, if I could.

I'm sure I look the same as I always have.

We stare at each other for what feels like forever, and not enough.

"Do I know you?" Arlo Rook asks, and my whole world *shatters*.

Despite the pounding in my ears, I extend a trembling hand and introduce myself to my soulmate for the third time. "I'm Thatcher Gaillot," I say, hating how choked out it sounds.

He forgoes my hand and embraces me fiercely. I stand there in shock, unsure what to do. Arlo shakes against me and after a full five seconds, I start to register what happened. I push him back and when I find wet eyes and a *stupid* fucking grin, I slap Arlo with everything I've got.

Then I kiss him with everything I don't.

And he kisses me.

I don't let go.

Not when the cheers start and meld with hollers.

Not when Arlo's hands explore my body dangerously.

"I can't believe you." I murmur, lips a breath width away from his.

"Did you really think I could ever forget you?" He replies, brushing his nose against mine. "Welcome home, Thatcher. Did you like my puzzles?"

I laugh breathily, pressing my forehead on his. "I assume you're the villain who took my things?"

"Without a doubt. This place is just as much yours as it is mine, your possessions belong here, not in a hole in the ground. Come inside and see, we can catch up the others later." Arlo takes me by the hand and leads me through a world of color, sounds and people that are nothing but a blur to me.

I'm home.

Acknowledgments

First off, I want to thank Henni Eklund (@gagakumadraws on IG) for all her hard work on the illustrations inside the book and always having an open ear, especially regarding these characters we've both come to love so much. Also, thank you for allowing me to include Ren in this story.

Luna Daye is an incredible author who I've been lucky to call my friend since I began this journey.

I'm so grateful to have met them both, along with all the other indie authors and artists I've become friends with.

Huge thanks to Bear Pettigrew for crafting the cover and putting such wondrous detail into it. Hours and hours of their sanity and time have gone into this piece, and I will forever treasure it. I've always admired their work and am beyond thankful to have worked with them.

To Kait, who listened to me talk endlessly about cheesemakers and a villain named Bob. Shroom and Pus are characters of their design.

To my Husband, for loving me through it all. For being my rock in the storm. For listening to me talk about fictional characters and magical lands and offering your advice whenever I asked for it. For accepting me, and for being my person.

And last, but not least, thank you, fellow reader. I hope you enjoyed this story, and welcome to the Misfits.

About the Author

A queer fantasy punk author with young witch vibes, endless coffee stains, and a craving for adventure. Aelina's work is heavily influenced by their love of the outdoors and a need for more inclusive fiction. Aelina also writes under the pen name Noah Hawthorne.

Visit https://aelinaisaacs.com for information on their other books, playlists and more.

@neshamapublishing on Instagram and Tiktok

@neshamapub on Twitter

Also By Aelina

What happened during the years Arlo and Thatch were apart?

Find out in Quentin and Elochian's story, Matsdotter and Adrastus, which releases in December of 2023. M&A focuses on the building of Witch House, war with enemies old and new, and more witches we didn't get to meet in Phantom and Rook. Thatch's mystery will also be further explained in the next book.

When Witches Sing is a Yuletide novella that takes place two days after Thatch returns, and includes connected short stories from the perspectives of Felix and Silas, along with new characters Calen and Lysander, during the time he was gone.

Take me to Iverbourne is a dark steampunk fantasy series, and The Eternal Machine is the first book Aelina wrote.

Ingram Content Group UK Ltd.
Milton Keynes UK
UKHW041354210723
425561UK00004B/172